Under the Sugar Sun

Under the Sugar Sun

To Shannon:
Happy reading!
Jennifer Hallock

Jennifer Hallock

Book design by Stephen Wallace

Cover photograph used under license from Shutterstock.com

Maps of the Philippine Islands and the Visayan Islands used
with permission from http://d-maps.com/carte.php?num_
car=15358&lang=en

Printed in the United States of America

First Printing, October 2015

ISBN-10: 1517785707
ISBN-13: 978-1517785703

Little Brick Books
PO Box 498
Weare, NH 03281

www.LittleBrickBooks.com

For Stephen, the ideas man.

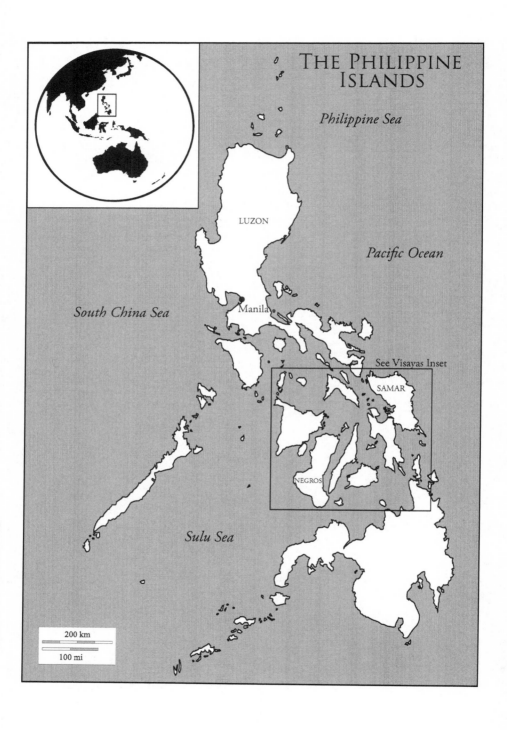

THE PHILIPPINE ISLANDS

Philippine Sea

LUZON

Pacific Ocean

South China Sea

Manila

See Visayas Inset

SAMAR

NEGROS

Sulu Sea

200 km
100 mi

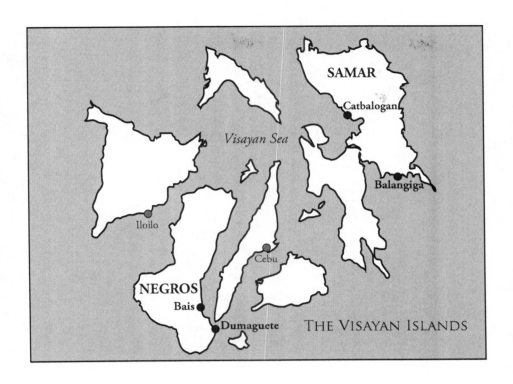

THE VISAYAN ISLANDS

SAMAR

Catbalogan

Balangiga

Visayan Sea

Iloilo

Cebu

NEGROS

Bais

Dumaguete

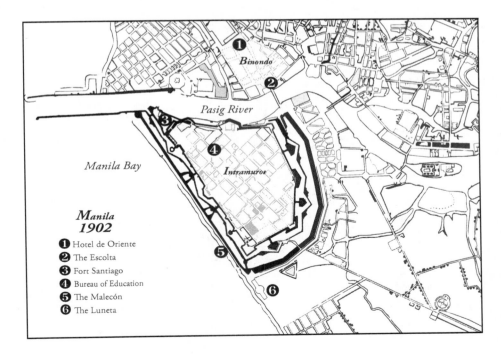

Binondo

Pasig River

Manila Bay

Intramuros

Manila
1902

❶ Hotel de Oriente
❷ The Escolta
❸ Fort Santiago
❹ Bureau of Education
❺ The Malecón
❻ The Luneta

The primary reason for the rapid introduction, on a large scale, of the American public school system in the Philippines was the conviction of the military leaders that no measure would so quickly promote the pacification of the islands.

Census of the Philippine Islands, 1903

The primary reason for the rapid introduction, on a large scale, of the American public school system in the Philippines was the conviction of the military leaders that no measure would so quickly promote the pacification of the islands.

Census of the Philippine Islands, 1903

Part I: September 1902

Manila, Philippines
August 1, 1902

Dearest Georgina,

I regret not being able to welcome you in person, but I cannot stay another day in this filthy city. Every week feels like a year when under siege by cholera. If I were a more suspicious person, I would say the rebels are deliberately undermining American sanitation efforts, without a care that it is their own natives who are the most susceptible. The fools scatter like cockroaches from the inspectors, hide their sick from detention, and steal their dead before cremation—spreading infection at every turn.

Always be on your guard here. Though many women dispense with the custom of wearing gloves in the tropical heat, you must not risk direct contact as the Filipino sweats the cholera germ right out of his pores. Chance nothing but the Hotel de Oriente's water and, as soon as you are able, arrange passage out of the cordon to Dumaguete. From there it is a short trip to Bais, where we will establish our new school.

I remain,
Your ever devoted,
Archibald

PS — I found no trace of your brother while in Manila, but perhaps you will have more luck at Fort Santiago than I did.

CHAPTER ONE

First Encounter

Georgie was not lucky—never had been—but even she could not believe her poor timing. The growing fire was only a few streets away. In this city made almost entirely of wood, the buildings separating her from the fire were a mere appetizer when compared to the towering three-story Hotel de Oriente, where she was now standing. If the Oriente burned down, it would kill scores of Americans who chose this very hotel to protect them from the dangers of the city. None of this was part of Georgie's plan: she had come to the Philippines to start a new life, not end the one she had.

She blew out the candles, pinched the wicks between her fingers to be safe, and fled the room. She ran down two flights of polished wood stairs, almost flattening a bell-hopper in the empty lobby as she charged the door. Where were the other guests, and why was no one evacuating the hotel?

Once in the street, Georgie took a moment to get her bearings. She'd had a clear view from above, but now the eastern horizon of the plaza was blocked by the La Insular cigar factory. The dull light of petroleum lamps did not help much either. She ran toward the open square in front of Binondo Church to get a better look and then followed the glow of flames down a dirt road. She had just arrived in this city, but she could still guess that tall, redheaded white women should not race through the streets of Manila at night.

She wound her way down to the canal where the fire was digesting rows of native houseboats. Families stood on shore and watched helplessly as their homes burned. Women comforted children and men cradled prize roosters as houseboat after houseboat disappeared into the flame. A dozen Filipino firemen in khaki uniforms and British-style pith helmets stood idly, their shiny engine from Sta. Cruz Fire Brigade Station No. 2 sitting unused, too far from the water line to do any good. Judging by the men resting casually against the cool iron, no one had lit the pump's boiler yet.

Georgie had read that the natives here were natural fatalists—a long-suffering, impassive people—but this was just ridiculous. She approached the firemen.

"Put water there," she demanded, pointing to boats that had so far escaped the flames. If doused heavily enough they might only smoke a bit. She struggled to remember the word for water she had learned earlier that day. "Tabog, tabog," she said.

The men looked at her blankly. She tried again, working out the mnemonic device in her head: the Philippines were islands too big in the sea...too big...tubig.

"Tubig," she said, pointing. "Tubig, tubig."

They shrugged but kept staring at her, more interested in the novelty of a hysterical Americana than in the fire. Looking for help elsewhere, Georgie slipped around the front of the engine to find two men arguing loudly in English.

"I've warned you before not to interfere with the quarantine, señor. I'll not explain myself again, especially to the likes of you."

The speaker, a squat American policeman, had comically bushy eyebrows that did not match his humorless tone. No doubt he had been interrupted from his evening revelry to carry out this duty, and he planned to finish the job quickly and get back to the saloon. Georgie had grown up around men of his stripe, their ruddy noses betraying a greater exposure to alcohol than sun.

She did not have a good view of the man the policeman was speaking to, but she heard the fellow give a short cluck before responding. "There's nothing in your law to prevent me from standing here, and I'll do it all night if I have to." His British accent amplified his condescension.

"You're interfering with a direct order of the Bureau of Health," said the policeman, "and that could cost you five thousand dollars—gold, mind you—and ten years in Bilibid."

"You can't be serious."

"That's the law—need I translate it into goo-goo for you?"

Sensing she was missing something, Georgie edged forward to get a better look at the Brit and discovered that he was not a Brit at all. His angular face bragged of Spanish blood, but the blackness of his hair and eyes revealed a more complicated ancestry. She had heard about these mixed-blood Filipinos, many of them wealthy and powerful, but she had not expected to meet one shirtless on the shore of the canal.

"I read law in London," the Mestizo said. "I need no lectures on the King's English from a blooming Yank."

Proud words from a naked man. Well, not naked exactly, but the black silk pajama bottoms—Chinese-style, embroidered with white stitching—did not hide much. He was the tallest man in the crowd by half a head, and his powerful torso betrayed some familiarity with labor, yet he spoke to the policeman with the studied patience of a man used to commanding those around him.

"Put out this inferno," he continued. "If you don't, there'll be nothing left to disinfect. The entire city will burn."

"That's hardly likely. We're protected by water." The American waved his fat hand toward the walled-in core of Manila and the bay settlements beyond, the places where the colonial regime was headquartered and most foreigners lived. The wide Pasig River in between would buffer the elite from the "sanitation" of this canal.

A tall flame bit noisily into the woven roof of a houseboat, devouring the dry grass in seconds. Georgie followed the Mestizo's gaze from the grass to the bamboo-pile pier, nipa huts, and market stalls. Wood, wood, and more wood—it was all bona fide fire fuel straight up the street to the Oriente, the hotel that contained all her possessions in this hemisphere.

The Mestizo turned back to the policeman and tilted his head toward this path of destruction. "I'm sure you've considered every possibility," he said acidly.

"I don't have to listen to this." The American stalked away, still eyeing his adversary, and nearly collided with Georgie. In something close to relief, he directed his frustration at her, a new and easier target. "Miss, this is no place for a woman. What are you doing here?"

Georgie wondered the same thing—though her concern had little to do with her gender and more to do with the fact that, in the thirty hours she had spent in Manila so far, she had been temporarily abandoned by her fiancé, maybe permanently abandoned by her missing brother, and now threatened by a fire that her own countrymen would not even bother to put out. That last part bothered her the most right now.

"Why aren't the wagons being used?" she asked. "You have enough equipment to douse the flames."

"The fire's a necessary precaution, I assure you," the policeman said.

Georgie frowned. "A precaution?"

"I have orders from the Commissioner to sweep this district—"

A loud crack interrupted him as another boat frame split under the strain of falling debris.

"You set this blaze?" she asked, still not sure she was getting it right.

The policeman looked quickly at the fire and then back at her. "We did what we had to do. After we burn out the spirilla in this nest, the entire area can be disinfected with carbolic acid and lime."

Georgie knew from experience that fire was a risky ally. She had grown up near the tenements of South Boston, twelve acres of which burnt down in the Roxbury Conflagration. "Isn't that a rough way to go about it?"

Her skepticism exasperated the policeman. Clearly, he had not anticipated this challenge from a fellow American.

"Rough?" he cried. "People should be thanking us for our help. For months we've been distributing distilled water all over the city for free. We've built new encampments and staffed them with doctors and nurses to treat the stricken. We've even reimbursed people for the loss of their filthy, worthless shacks. Are these efforts appreciated? Instead, savages like him"—he crooked his thumb at the Mestizo—"stir up trouble, talking of tyranny."

The dark-eyed man in question did not respond, but crossed his arms across his bare chest. When he caught her looking at him, she turned away, embarrassed by the impropriety: his in dress and hers in curiosity.

"And what's the natives' answer to the cholera?" the policeman continued. "Candles? A few prayers? Carting some wooden saints around?"

Georgie thought he had a point, albeit one badly made. It took no more than an hour in the city to realize that Manila had no sewage system, making it ripe for plague. Nowhere that she had wandered today had been out of olfactory range of the Pasig River, its estuaries, or the Spanish moat. Using the same water for drink and toilet did not make for a pleasant bouquet, never mind good health. That thought gave her some sympathy for the beleaguered Insular official. This morning's *Manila Times* had reported that cholera deaths were down to a quarter of their July high, so something must be working.

"Maybe he's right," she said hopefully to the angry man. "They're killing the germs, after all."

The Mestizo ran a large hand through his short hair and sighed. "His plan would've been better if he hadn't chased off the infected people who used to live here, spreading the disease farther. That's not just stupid, it's bad policy. Do you know what the people will say tomorrow? 'The Americans are burning the poor out of their homes to make room for new mansions.'"

"That's absurd!" she said.

The policeman did not deny it, though. "These brownies are like children, always looking to blame someone else. I can't control what they think, nor would I deign to try."

The Mestizo clenched his fists at his side, unconsciously tugging at the silk pajamas. Georgie wished he would not do that, especially since it was clear he was not wearing anything underneath. She turned away to watch the flames.

A piece of fiery thatch floated through the air near her head. A fresh gust of wind blew it up and over the street toward a cluster of neighboring homes whose occupants were still in the process of pulling out their belongings. The fireball rose and fell, dancing through the dark sky in slow motion, until it landed on the grass roof of one of the huts, igniting in seconds.

Everyone, including the firemen, rushed to warn those inside, but somehow Georgie got there first. She climbed the ladder into the hut and found a small boy holding a baby. He looked at Georgie with wide eyes as if she, not the fire, was the monster devouring his home. She inched forward, hoping her exaggerated smile would bridge the language gulf. She motioned him forward, her hand outstretched, palm up, fingers beckoning—but to no avail. The boy backed farther into the bamboo wall, acting like he had never seen such a gesture before.

Georgie looked up and saw that the whole roof was in flames. How had the fire grown so quickly? "Please!" she shouted, even though she knew her English was worthless. "You have to climb down with me." She waved her arms furiously, only adding to the boy's terror. She couldn't will herself to crawl more deeply into the hut, though. That would be suicide.

"*Ven acá,*" a deep voice said. She turned to see the Mestizo behind her on the ladder. "*Dito.*" He motioned with this hand, too, but his palm faced down, brushing his fingers under like a broom. It seemed a dismissive gesture to Georgie, but the boy responded right away and crawled toward them.

The man handed the baby to Georgie before scooping up the boy. "Now go!"

The Mestizo swung back on the ladder to let Georgie down first. Just then the fire surged out of the hut, raking the big man's back. Grunting in pain, he shoved everyone the rest of the way down and pushed them all to the ground. He fell last on top of the human pile, providing cover as the platform of the house gave way in a single explosion. The flames reached out to claw at them one last time before retreating. The Mestizo pulled Georgie and the boy onto their feet and dragged them farther from the burning hut, just to be safe.

After a few moments Georgie started to breathe again, devouring air in large gulps. She could feel the heavy sobs of the boy wedged into her side, but she did not have a free hand to comfort him. The baby, on the other hand, made not a sound. Georgie looked down at the little one, wondering what kind of life the infant had led so far if tonight's episode was not even worthy of a good bawl.

A single beat of peace passed before a throng of excited Filipinos descended on them. A young woman swooped down to grab the two children, leaving Georgie alone in the Mestizo's arms. He continued to hold her close, brushing the ash and dirt off her ruined white shirtwaist. It was a useless attempt, but she didn't stop him.

"Are you all right?" he asked. He was still sweating—a musky, sweet scent that distracted her from the smoke. When she looked up at his face, she noticed details she had missed before: the dimple in his chin, prominent among his dark stubble; his full bottom lip, swollen a little from an accidental elbow in the face by the boy; and his low, dark eyebrows that framed his strong, straight nose. He was handsome but unrefined—too urbane to be a blackguard but too unruly to be a gentleman.

"Are you okay?" he asked again, shaking her lightly. "Can you hear me?"

She was embarrassed to be caught staring. "Yes," she answered. "I'm sorry. I'm fine."

"Not hurt?"

"No, I'm okay now. I've just…I've never felt so useless. The boy couldn't understand me."

The Mestizo shrugged. "Believe me, had you spoken his language, he would have been more scared."

Georgie laughed, surprised at her ease. "I don't know how your heart isn't racing."

The man paused, his smile not softening the look in his eyes. "Who says it isn't?"

So he might be a bit of a blackguard after all, she thought.

Georgie noticed that the natives had stopped watching the fire and instead were watching her. She glanced over to the American policeman. The man did not need to speak to communicate the extent of his disgust. No self-respecting American woman would allow herself to be held this way by a half-naked Filipino. Upper-crust accent, Spanish features, and English law degree notwithstanding, he was still a "brownie."

Georgie tried to loosen the Mestizo's grip by twisting away. When that didn't work she gently nudged him with her elbow, but he didn't take that hint either. A seed of panic bloomed in her stomach. If they did not separate, there was liable to be more trouble for them both. She planted both palms on his chest and pressed lightly, but no one on the outside could see her resistance. All they saw was a suggestive caress.

The policeman's eyes darkened. A small man like him—diminutive in both stature and intelligence—would no doubt resort to the power of his office to reestablish authority. Dash it, he had said as much even before the Mestizo had gotten his hands on a white woman.

Georgie summoned her strength and shoved the Mestizo away, hard. His heel caught on a rock and he fell, grimacing as he landed flat on his injured back.

A few bystanders laughed. Some would have laughed at anyone's misfortune, but others relished the embarrassment of a proud man. Not surprisingly, the policeman's guffaw was the loudest.

The Mestizo's cheeks flushed red, but fury trumped pride. He got up immediately, rising in a single fluid motion while glaring at Georgie. She wanted to say something to defuse the situation—to explain, apologize, something—but the moment passed before she got up the courage. The man pivoted on his heel and walked away, not bothering to brush the gravel from his burned, torn flesh.

Georgie sighed in regret. Her first full day in Manila had not been a success by any measure. Unfortunately, it was too late to turn around now.

CHAPTER TWO

Javier Visits Escolta

J avier's back felt like it was still on fire, and when it didn't burn, it
itched. It had taken his *muchacho* well into the morning to remove
the rocks and sand from his charred skin, and after that Javier had
tried to sleep but failed. He did not have time to go see a doctor, so he
tucked slices of aloe under the bandages. What he really wanted was a
draught to anesthetize him from the entire American occupation, but
Botica Boie sold no such prescription.

Look at them, he thought. *Yankis* marred his view of Calle Escolta,
Manila's High Street. Soldiers' drunken catcalls echoed off the staid
church walls. To be seasoned at this hour—and so far from the brothels of Sampaloc—was a feat only an American could pull off. Though
Governor Taft had banned saloons on Escolta in order to protect respectable women, there were still more chemists' advertisements for
beer than for medicine.

The street itself was designed to make the colonial shoppers feel at
home, right down to the imported cobblestones. And the illusion was
effective—that is, until a carabao lumbered by, hogging half the street
with its wide horns and heavy load. The architecture was a similar
patchwork of foreign and native elements: stone foundations topped
by light wood structures, an elegant yet practical design in earthquake

country. Huge sliding panels opened up to the breeze, their rectangular frames checkered with iridescent *capiz* shells that let in light but wouldn't shatter at every tremor. It was a mongrel style, and it suited Javier.

He belonged here, not the Americans. That thought gave him the determination to stand his ground and force the oncoming soldiers to swerve around him, rather than the other way around. Besides, at a little more than six feet, Javier was hard to ignore. He had a strong frame, one that came from overseeing a thousand acres on horseback, while his Spanish features and London-tailored suit gave him the appearance of civilization.

Some Americans trusted Javier because they assumed that as an *ilustrado*, a member of the European-educated elite, he had a vested interest in peace and stability, but the truth was that he hated being at their mercy. The longer the foreigners stayed, the more laws they changed and the more precarious his position. Their meddling had cost him dearly these past three years. If sugar did not fetch at least five silver dollars per picul next season, there would be no more fine clothes for Javier—not even to replace the bloodstained shirt he now wore.

He turned right onto Calle Rosario and walked into one of a dozen seemingly identical Chinese hardware stores that lined the street. It was cramped and dusty, but more money flowed in and out of this nondescript storefront than Malacañang Palace. From here Lim Ching-Ong—known to Javier by his baptismal name Guillermo Cuayzon—bought and sold half of the sugar and hemp grown in the islands. Being indebted to this man was a rite of passage for any *hacendero*, but Javier's obligations were particularly heavy: Guillermo held a note on two hundred acres of Hacienda Altarejos and could end up owning the whole thing if Javier was not careful.

A tangle of Chinese voices erupted in the backroom, but Guillermo sat, serene as always, drinking tea and reading three newspapers at once—two Spanish and one Chinese. He did not trust anyone else to analyze the markets for him. It was a shrewd trait in a man's broker, and a worrisome one in a man's banker.

"Javito, it's been too long," Guillermo said in Spanish, slowly rising from his seat. Guillermo was tall and had a smile that compressed his whole face into large crinkles that made him resemble a Shar-Pei. The job must have been taking its toll, though: he had aged ten years in as many months, had lost at least a stone, and had dark circles shadowing his eyes.

Guillermo took a hesitant step forward but lost his balance.

"Memo, be careful," Javier cautioned, crossing the room in two quick strides. He grabbed his friend's arm and helped the man back into the chair.

The strain of bending ripped open the scabs on Javier's back. It hurt terribly, but his expression betrayed no pain. As he righted himself, an aloe leaf shaving slipped through the bandage and down to the small of his back, leaving his wound without any salve. He would deal with it later: his body's ailments must take a back seat to those of his hacienda.

"Thank you," Guillermo said in a voice barely stronger than a whisper. "Go sit. I'll be fine."

Javier was not sure of that, but he did as he was told and walked back around the desk. Most likely it was cholera, not stress, that had aged his friend so quickly. The Chinese community had fared better than most in this epidemic—they boiled their water for tea and never shared chopsticks—but they were not immune. Poor laborers from southern China had brought the disease to the Philippines in the first place, and Guillermo smuggled more than his share of coolies. He was a victim of his own success.

Unfortunately, a man of his stature could not stay home, no matter how sick. The day Guillermo's chair sat empty would be the day he lost control over a trading empire that spanned the entire South China Sea. Javier had met some of the other Cuayzons, and he thought it fair to say they would sell their own children for the chance to unseat their cousin. Rumor had it that in the Fukien dialect, the Cuayzon name meant "grandson of a whore." For most of the men in the family, it seemed apt.

Guillermo, on the other hand, was a tough negotiator yet a fair man—a combination that made him more vulnerable than ever right now. How long could integrity alone shield him from unscrupulous rivals, especially men of his own circle who knew his weaknesses? And what would that vulnerability mean for Javier's business? The *hacendero*'s ability to navigate this current bear market depended on Guillermo's good will—and his capital.

"Tell me how your mother is doing," Guillermo said. "She's a lovely woman."

Since the Chinaman rarely traveled, he had probably never actually met Lourdes de Altarejos. Asking about her was a kindness and a part of the game.

"Stubborn, as usual," Javier said. That, at least, was honest. A weak-willed woman could not have coped with burying three out of four infant children. She had raised Javier with no regrets for what might have been, and anything good within his character she alone had put there. "She asked me to invite you and your family to Bais for Holy Week." Guillermo might as well come see his collateral.

"Ah, a kind invitation, though I swore I'd never go back to those parts again."

Guillermo's warehouse in Iloilo had been a casualty of the old Southeast Asian dictum: "When times get tough, blame the Chinese." The revolution against the Spanish had been a time for score-settling, and moneylenders were easy targets.

Javier nodded sympathetically. "How are your children adjusting to Manila?"

The merchant's face brightened just enough. "Everyone is well, thank you. Our son started his studies at the Ateneo this past April."

"Ha, those old Jesuits still around, then?" The previous year the Americans had barred the parochial college from receiving municipal funds, creating a financial crisis for the school and a hell of a lot of gossip in town.

"Yes, though I am confused about this 'separation of Church and State,'" Guillermo said. "I say that if the brothers run a good school, all the more reason for the government to support it."

Javier could not bring himself to badmouth the one thing he liked about the new administration. Finally someone had the bollocks to challenge the friars' monopoly on education. Most Filipinos would not dare do so—they had always been more obedient to the Church than the Crown. Chinese mestizos were similarly devoted, although at home they still tended their ancestral altars, just in case.

"So your boy's all grown up?" Javier asked, changing the subject. "That certainly makes me feel old. I remember trying to teach him how to play *sungka*, but he kept hiding the stones in the spittoon."

Guillermo laughed. "He was crafty."

"And precocious. He almost beat me."

"Not as precocious as some boys I have known. Do you remember the day your father first brought you to my office in Iloilo?"

How could Javier forget? Every time they saw each other Guillermo brought it up. The man found it amusing to remind him that he was once young, hot-tempered, and more than a little rude.

"My bad manners that day helped get me shipped off to the *colegio militar* in Spain." His antics—including being expelled from school in Cebu—had made the decision rather easy for his father. "Maybe it wasn't a bad thing, though. Back then my *yaya* did just about everything for me but wipe my backside."

"I'm sure she did that too. But then you were what…sixteen? Maybe you found other 'helpful' women in Madrid?"

Actually, the Spanish women were nowhere near as adventurous as those in Paris, but he had learned the value of discretion since then, so he did not share this observation. "I ended up spending most of my time in London at King's College." And those had been the best years of his life.

"Yes, that's right, getting those fancy degrees. Your father was very proud of the connections you made for us in the London market. I wish you could do the same in Washington."

"I barely have time to travel to Manila to see you, let alone America," he said. Actually, they both knew it was not time but funding that curtailed Javier's travels, and that was why he was here now. "So make this journey worth my while, eh?"

Guillermo shrugged, but Javier knew the man's nonchalance was an act. The future of Philippine exports meant as much to him as they did to any farmer.

"Don't hold your breath for the free trade legislation to pass," the merchant cautioned. "The American sugar lobby is too powerful. They've invested in huge plantations in Hawaii, and they have no interest in more competition."

Javier leaned forward, hiding his clenched fists under the desk. "I don't understand. We're either a colony or we're not. The *Yankis* don't let us trade with the rest of the world, and now they shut us out of their home market, as well? Some 'Open Door.'"

History had taught Javier to be a skeptic. In the last four years, everything that could go wrong had gone wrong. Sugar planters in Negros had sided with the Americans in the hope of keeping the peace, but their workers ran off into the hills to join the *insurrectos*. No labor, no harvest. The Americans punished the rebels by burning rice stores and closing the ports, but such draconian tactics ended up hurting men like Javier most of all. In the end, not only had a quarter of his crop rotted in the ground, but there had been no way to ship the harvested cane off the island. By the time the ports opened again, a freak rinderpest epidemic had killed most of the carabao. Replacing his herd put Javier so far in hock that he had been forced to put up a fifth of his land as collateral. And those were just his problems from last season.

"We're lucky that Taft was able to hold onto his twenty-five percent tariff cut," Guillermo offered a little too optimistically.

Javier took a deep breath. Many schoolmasters had tried to teach him restraint with their rods, but to little effect. "If I wanted propaganda, Memo, I'd read one of those poxy American newspapers. Tell me something useful."

Guillermo's eyes sharpened a bit, signaling that it was finally time to talk real business. "What is it you're looking for this time?"

"Men, cash, contracts...I need it all. But most of all, I need time. I'm not going to lose my father's land, I can tell you that right bloody now."

Guillermo sat back in the chair and looked carefully at Javier. Sick or not, the merchant still had a gaze that could humble most mortals. It was the same look that Javier's father had used on his adversaries—and occasionally his son. This time Javier swore that he would not buckle. Lázaro Altarejos, that old bastard, would have finally been proud of him.

Guillermo waved his fingers at a runner and gave a quick order in Chinese. An unopened bottle of Oloroso appeared on the table. "Have a drink, Don Javier. It's going to be a long afternoon."

CHAPTER THREE

Fort Santiago

Georgina looked up at Fort Santiago, the stone embodiment of Spanish paranoia that capped the fortress city of old Manila. A bas-relief of Saint James the Moor-Slayer stood guard over the gate. Not the most observant Catholic, Georgie liked the thought of Iberian explorers braving the long, lonely journey across the Pacific only to find themselves back where they started—fighting Muslims. Judging by the number of churches they left behind, conversion had been a spiritual test they had met with gusto.

The Filipinos may have bowed before the Spanish Conquest in 1565, but by 1896 they no longer feared the conquistador. Revolution raged in the Philippine heartland until the Crown negotiated a truce with Emilio Aguinaldo, the emerging leader of the Filipino *insurrectos*. Aguinaldo was either very shrewd or very pliable: in exchange for $800,000 in Mexican silver—half up front, deposited to his personal account—he agreed to exile in Hong Kong. If the Spanish believed that would rid them of the pesky rebel forever, though, the joke was on them. In May of 1898, in breach of his truce with the Crown, Aguinaldo returned to Manila on board an American warship.

At first it seemed the Americans and Filipinos would work well together against their common enemy, but less than a month after reassembling his forces, Aguinaldo declared full Philippine independence. President McKinley was not amused. He had been developing plans for a Far Eastern colony, plans he was willing to back up with force. The Filipinos were no match for the 5,000-man American "army of liberation," which turned into a 70,000-man army of occupation, but they fought back anyway. The Philippine-American War had begun.

Georgie had viewed all these events through the only source she trusted: letters from her brother Benji. At first he had been optimistic: the Army's early engagements had been quick and effective. Even after the Filipinos switched to petty guerrilla tactics, the Americans still outmaneuvered them. They captured Aguinaldo and pressed him into taking an oath of allegiance to the United States. Benji thought the rest of the Filipino people would follow suit, the islands would quiet down, and the people—whom he had described as poor but generous—would enjoy great prosperity as America's Asiatic entrepôt.

Benji had even talked of opening a Manila branch of Shay's, their family's tailoring business, to cater to the growing American population in the city. That bit had been a surprise considering that he had not wanted any part of the trade back home, but she took it as evidence of how much he liked Manila. He had complained of the constant drilling in camp, of course, but in his spare time he had begun learning a little of the local language, Tagalog. When his unit served as honor guard at the installation of Governor Taft on July 4, 1901, Benji had found the ceremony itself tiresome but exulted in the glamour of the assignment. All his letters had been hopeful—until he got to Samar. After a few short notes from that island, he stopped writing altogether. His last letter was dated September 3, 1901, almost a month before the massacre. Since then no one, not even Uncle Sam, seemed to know where he had disappeared to. Georgie had come to Fort Santiago to find him.

Georgie looked at the American soldier who stood beside St. James's gate, wondering how many times Benji had performed that same duty. The private wore the same blue wool campaign shirt that her brother had been issued on enlistment, perfectly comfortable in New England but hardly suited to the tropics. Her eyes rose to his collar. The badge there had two crossed rifles with regiment and company designations: 27th Infantry, Company A.

"Miss, may I ask your business here?" The soldier's felt campaign hat did a poor job of shading his face from the late morning sun, and Georgie could already tell that he would pay for it this evening.

"I'm a Thomasite," she answered. In a way, she and this soldier were comrades, since bringing American teachers over to set up a public school system had been the Army's idea. It was benevolent assimilation at its best. Georgie was not a charter member: she had arrived in Manila on the transport *Sheridan*, a full year after her fiancé Archie and his compatriots arrived on the *Thomas*. But the distinction did not seem to matter to the Filipinos, who had christened all American teachers Thomasites—a pseudo-order of educational missionaries.

The soldier shook his head. "You're in the wrong place then. The Bureau of Education's no longer under Army control. It's in city hall. Tell your driver you want the Ayuntamiento building. He'll know."

She knew this already because she had been to the Ayuntamiento building—also known simply as the Palace—to check in. But she let him continue his directions, touched by his clear explanation of how to negotiate a hack. She was not much of a flirt, but she gave the soldier her most winsome smile and hoped that she did not look as silly as she felt. "It sounds like you've been in Manila a long time," she said.

His eyes flicked away before returning to hers. "I've mostly served in Mindanao." The way he said it, she could tell his story was not an entirely happy one.

Strangely, though, that gave her hope. She changed her manner from that of coquette to confidante. She moved closer and lowered her voice. "Actually, I'll tell you why I'm really here. My brother disappeared in Balangiga, or some time after…I don't know."

The soldier whistled in surprise at her mention of the battle. By the skeptical squint of his eyes, she could tell that he did not give Benji good odds. "You're thinking to find an answer inside?" he asked.

"No one else has much to tell me."

"Normally, civilians can't enter the camp without good reason," he began, looking around the empty street. It was almost noon, a time when most people stayed out of the sun unless they had urgent business—or direct orders. That meant fewer witnesses. Like any good co-conspirator, she stayed quiet while he judged the risk. "But I'm about to rotate off duty, anyway. If anyone asks who let you in—"

"I won't be able to remember a thing," she said quickly. "All you men in uniform look the same."

"I hope not, miss." He gave her a bittersweet smile. "And good luck finding your brother, one way or another."

Georgie did not like the sound of that last bit, but she nodded and walked through the gate. Though the fort was not all that large, she quickly got lost inside. The coastal artillery station was designed to defend, not inform, which was probably why there was no map posted in the courtyard. She looked around for soldiers affiliated with Benji's 9th Infantry Regiment, but all she saw were badges of the 27th, the 31st, and the 36th. Eventually she was directed to a junior clerk whose haggard appearance cast some doubt upon his value. He was short, fair-haired, and wore round wire-rimmed glasses that had been bent and unbent so many times that they sat crookedly on his nose.

"Excuse me, sir," Georgie said sweetly, trying to wrest the corporal's attention from the stack of papers in front of him. "I was hoping you could help me."

"I don't see how," he answered without looking up. "Unless you want to know our current stock of rubber ponchos, and I can't tell you that for a few minutes yet."

Georgie guessed that she would not be able to duplicate the rapport she had built with the guard at the gate, so she kept it simple. "I need your help. I'm trying to find my brother, and I think he might still be here in the islands. He served in Samar with the 9th."

The soldier looked up, startled. "You a word-slinger, ma'am? Or one of those socialists? We'd prefer not to kick up any new dust now that the general's court martial is over."

"I don't know what you're talking about," she lied.

He looked suspicious, as well he should have. Everyone knew what happened to the officers who had tried to avenge the dead. "Where'd you say you're from again?" the clerk asked.

"I'm not from the Anti-Imperialist League or anything. Really, I'm just a teacher."

Still he hedged. "And you came all this way to pick up your brother? My sister wouldn't cross the street for me, even if my unit did make the papers."

A smart woman, his sister, but Georgie did not dare say that aloud. She needed a new approach. She pulled a heavy envelope from her bag, untied the string, and dumped out clippings from the *Daily Globe* and the *Evening Transcript*. A few slid off the edge and floated to the floor. She picked them up and placed all the pages together in a line:

> Disaster in Samar. American Troops Surprised at Balangiga. Forty Officers and Men Killed by Insurgents. Company C 9th Attacked While at Breakfast.

> Death List. Names of Those Lost at Balangiga, Samar. Five of the Number Went from Boston to Philippines. Thirty-Five Killed and Died of Wounds. Eight Missing.

> Nine Boston Men. Seven of Them Were Enlisted Men, and It Is Feared They Were All Among the Lost at Balangiga.

> Wounded at Balangiga: Boston Loses One More.

It had been the worst American defeat since Little Big Horn. But while George Armstrong Custer was a stranger on a Budweiser poster, Benji was her big brother, her champion, and, once upon a time, her protector. She was here to return the favor.

"I understand you're upset," the corporal said quietly after glancing at the headlines. "But some soldiers don't write home that often, certainly not about actual battle. Consider yourself lucky your brother's alive."

"That's the point. I don't know that he is."

"He should be in here one way or another." He put his finger on the article with the list. "Name and rank?"

If it were that easy, she thought, she would not have bothered crossing the Pacific. "Sergeant Benjamin Potter."

"I see a Ben Cutter," the clerk said. "That's probably him." He sounded sure, as if the Army made such mistakes all the time. Maybe they did. He would know.

Georgie pulled another article to compare side by side. "Half the names are spelled differently from one day to another," she explained. "Cutter one day, then Carter, then Palmer. And here all of the Boston soldiers are described as dead. All of them! My mother and I bought every paper, every edition, for a month, trying to find a new official list that made any sense. And you know what the Army told us? Nothing! No telegram, no letter, nothing." She was not normally one to create a scene, but she had come a long way for the truth, and she was going to get it.

The corporal remained unruffled. "They don't send cables to the families of the enlisted. It would cost 30 bucks each, maybe more, listing each man's full regimental assignment."

"I suppose if he'd been an officer, he'd be worth the money." She knew her sarcasm was counterproductive, especially when directed at this poor corporal, but she couldn't help it.

"It's not like that," he said, but his tone seemed to indicate it was rather like that. "Officers have code names, which shortens the cable to a buck fifty. That's a big difference. Anyway, if you didn't get a death notification by mail, he's probably alive."

Probably was not good enough. "Then why didn't he come home?" Georgie asked, hearing the desperation in her own voice. "The rest of

Company C returned to the States in June. My mother wrote to him at Madison Barracks and got no answer. The Army didn't even send a forwarding address."

"Maybe he stuck around here, though I can't imagine why. This climate weakens a man in time." The clerk eyed her breezy white frock with envy. From what she could tell, only the officers in the Army were issued cotton uniforms. She felt bad about the corporal's discomfort but not bad enough to ease up on her questions.

"Do you have a list of which men were aboard the ship home?"

He sighed. "There were dozens of transports—"

"It was the *Hancock*," she said quickly. She found another clipping in her envelope, "Coming Ashore of Ninth," and laid it out beside the others. "It arrived in June, so it must have left sometime in May. I've just done that trip. It only takes a month."

The corporal did not state the obvious: he had made the trip too. He looked like he was starting to question whether she should be here asking such irksome questions, which could mean the end of her investigation. It was too late to play cute, Georgie thought, but basic courtesy might help. "Please?"

The clerk pushed himself up off the stool very slowly, moving like an old man with gout. "Just a minute," he said, hobbling slowly to the door.

Georgie had heard that dengue fever caused excruciating bone and joint pain like that. Few died, but they wished for death. She wanted to be compassionate, but giving up her quest for the sake of one clerk's convenience was not an option.

She waited alone, pretending to be at ease, as if she hung out at Army Division Headquarters all the time. Ten minutes passed, and she began to wonder if the clerk had collapsed somewhere en route. Who put a man back to work in such condition? Finally, he returned holding a thick ledger, and with great effort she refrained from snatching it out of his hands.

They found the right date and manifest, and spent several more minutes reading through the hundreds of names. No Benjamin Potter went home with Company C. Or Company A. Or Company D. Or E, F, G, H, K, L, or M. She tried to remember as many of the survivors' names as possible so that she could contact them later.

The corporal looked up at her. "He didn't go anywhere on that ship." He closed the book and pushed it aside, wordlessly closing the case.

"Earlier you said he might have stayed here?"

"He would've needed a job. We don't discharge soldiers in the islands without proof of employment."

"He wrote to me about opening up shop here in Manila," she suggested.

"On a sergeant's take? Not likely."

"Who might have hired him?"

The clerk sighed, a clear sign that his patience was wearing thin. "There's a few jobs in the civil government—the Constabulary, Scouts, city police, fire department. Have you tried any of them yet?"

Georgie was not eager to talk to any more American policemen, but she pulled a pencil and small pad out of her bag and began taking notes anyway. "Tell me about the Constabulary."

"They're not so different from the Army Scouts: native soldiers, commanded by American officers. They're tied to a specific district, like a sheriff's jurisdiction. They do a lot of the cleanup work in the islands now. Your brother could've become an inspector with them. Even an NCO can manage a bunch of goo-goos."

She looked at the corporal and the Filipino staff behind him. Apparently he knew this from experience. "Do you have the names of these inspectors?"

The soldier moved again, his reluctance obvious in each step. He walked to a shelf in a corner of the room and brought down a group of small booklets bound together with string. He dumped them in front of her, leaving her alone to sort through the pile of incomprehensible records.

A while later, she reached the last page no more enlightened than when she started. No name was even close. "What else are soldiers qualified to do?"

The clerk made a few more notations on his own papers before answering, as if to point out that soldiers were qualified to count rubber ponchos if only silly American ladies would leave them alone. "There's the Benguet Road project up in the northern mountains, where the 48th Infantry is," he said. "If your brother's got any experience at construction, he could be there with Major Kennon."

She could not discount it, but it sounded too dismal a job for Benji. He was strong but easily distracted.

"And I guess there's always the business district in Binondo," the corporal suggested. "It's outside the walls and across the river. If he did set up shop for himself in Manila, he'd be there. But you best be careful, ma'am, 'cause you can't trust these pickaninnies at all. If you stick to Escolta Street—in the daytime only, mind—and don't wander around too much by yourself, you should be fine. Stay away from the cross-streets; those are the haunt of John Chinaman."

Georgie didn't explain that her hotel was in Chinatown and that she had recently taken to running around alone at night. She could imagine the clerk would not approve, and with good reason. She had learned her lesson.

She thanked the corporal and started to leave. Happy to finally be done with her, he waved her off with a brush of his hand. She hurriedly made her way back to the gate and looked for her friend the sentry for whose kindness she had a new appreciation, but the watch had changed.

Georgie caught a *calesa*, a two-wheeled hack, which took her along the embankment of the Pasig River, lifeblood and latrine to two hundred thousand people. Her undersized, malnourished horse was not fast, but at least he smelled better than the river.

Tears welled in her eyes, tears that had nothing to do with the dusty road or the rank river. All she knew was that she had failed. Her search could not be over already. There had to be someone else to ask, some other Insular official to appeal to. This was the Army, after all, the same one that had brought Benji here to Asia instead of to the tidy little war he had been promised in Cuba. How could the generals hope to win a war if they misplaced their men so easily?

Indignation slipped into depression. Georgie had paid a heavy price to come out here, but she had believed that finding her brother would make it worth it. That had been an article of faith for her, as strong as the Apostles' Creed. Now, though, realizing that she might not find him at all...

No, she thought. Georgie wiped her wet cheeks with a firm hand, promising herself that she would not cry here. She was enough of a side-show curiosity as it was; she did not need to add any further attractions to the bill.

She rested back against the cramped seat and commanded herself to appreciate the colorful clutter of the city. Warehouses lined the shore, each with a bold standard painted on the roof: Singer sewing machines, Mayon Coffee, the Perfumería Moderna. Everyone seemed to be out at once, rushing between the shops or selling their wares on the street. Girls in pretty patterned skirts and fresh white blouses sat in front of their fruit carts. This was Benji's type of place, Georgie thought. He could definitely be here.

"Calle Escolta," the driver said, coming to a stop at the intersection. Georgie resisted the urge to jump out and run down the street, calling her brother's name at the top of her lungs. One step at a time, she reminded herself. Forward. Just keep moving forward. She descended from the carriage, picked a store at random, and opened the door.

CHAPTER FOUR

Tough Markets

Javier had long ago loosened his tie, and now he took it off entirely. He had been sitting in Guillermo's office for two hours, trying to get the help he needed to put his sugar plantation back on track. He needed money, and he trusted Chinese credit more than American. Other *hacenderos* had been undermined by the bankruptcy of Russell and Sturgis, the Boston commercial firm that had once given easy advances on machinery throughout the islands. When that well had dried up, it took a sizeable chunk of sugar production with it. What did the Americans care? They would leave soon enough, and whatever damage they did to local industry would be forgotten. The Chinese, though, were here to stay. They had been here long before any Europeans, and it was they—not the Spanish—who had built the economy. Unfortunately, none of this made Guillermo Cuayzon any easier to bargain with.

The accounts of Hacienda Altarejos were spread across the table. Javier did not want to put any more liens on his land, but he was quickly running out of collateral. He supposed that the merchant could demand his firstborn, but it was unlikely there would be one at this point. An heir required a wife. One long shot at a time, Javier thought.

Guillermo took a long drink of his tea. "I can give you the cash, *amigo*, just as I did for your father's mill and for your new carabao. You only need ask."

Javier refrained from raising his eyebrows at the "only." If it were "only" that simple, he would not have to endure this financial disembowelment of his hacienda.

The merchant continued: "But what is the point if you have no one to sell to? The American tariffs have priced you out of all your old markets."

Javier remained silent, waiting to hear what the man would say next. He had to be building to something.

"You should bring your crop to Manila this year," Guillermo concluded. "I can sell it here."

Javier looked at him curiously and asked, "Why change now?" Iloilo had always been the center of Philippine cane sales because it was so close to Negros, the most productive sugar island in Asia. It also sold higher quality sugar, not the dross that the northerners made. "My family has been shipping to your agent in Iloilo since you were that agent, Memo, maybe before. My father always said that no self-respecting Negrense would lower himself to begging at the Manila market."

"Then it is a good thing I'm asking you, not him." Guillermo opened his palms to the air as if to show that there was nothing up his sleeves. "Javito, you know that your father would not have fared well in the upheaval of these past few years. He was…a man of his conveniences."

That was a nice way of putting it, Javier thought. "Why should I be any different?"

"Because you see the need for change, especially now. Your muscovado sugar used to be the best in Asia, but until you get one of the new centrifugal mills—"

Javier laughed at the very idea. Building a sugar central was well beyond him, and every other Philippine producer too. No banker in his right mind would lend Javier that kind of money, not even Guill-ermo. "So my product is no longer up to Iloilo's standards?"

"Now you do sound like Lázaro," the merchant said, shaking his head. "Iloilo 'standards' are not the issue. Your customers are. Until the Americans loosen the reins and until you can build a central, we have only one solid market: China. And the Chinese buy their sugar in Manila."

Javier sat back and considered the idea. Tariffs into China were absurdly low, courtesy of the Western powers, and there was no one better to control both sides of that trade than the Cuayzon family. But did Javier want to be even more deeply dependent on one syndicate? As opposed to his other options—probably. Guillermo's thirty-year history with Altarejos patriarchs made him less likely to seize the ha-cienda on a whim—maybe. So, if the man wanted to run the game out of Hong Kong, Jolo, or even Timbuktu, Javier had no choice but to consider it.

Still, it would not pay to agree too easily. Javier would need some incentives. "It's an interesting proposition, but I have to consider the expense."

The man smiled. "Don't you trust me?"

"As much as I trust anyone."

"So suspicious, my friend." Guillermo feigned insult, but it was shallow.

"It's business, Memo. You know that, just like you know that Ma-nila's three times as far," Javier said, fresh from the trip. "I already pay too much for transportation—over six percent of my costs. And I've not shipped to Manila before. I don't know the rates for the lighters or the bribes. Then there's the American port expansion and the new breakwater. Construction is always a hassle."

Guillermo shifted in his chair. He had held up remarkably well throughout their long meeting, but now Javier could see signs of strain. The merchant's gray skin was growing paler by the minute. His right hand trembled, causing him to spill a little tea on his shirt. His voice was still strong, however, when he made his declaration: "If this is just about business, then let me say this in business terms: you either sell in Manila or you do not sell at all."

Javier wondered how his life had come to this. As if the tariffs, drought, and cattle plague had not been tests enough of his mettle, now he had to battle tradition. At least in one thing Guillermo had been right: his father would not have survived the twentieth century. Javier just hoped his father's plantation would.

Ultimately, Javier did have faith in Guillermo's ability to make money—for both of them. And if it turned out his own broker was working against him, then no decision of Javier's would make a difference anyway. "It's worth a try," he agreed in surrender. "But I'm going to need more cash."

Actually, he was going to need a lot more cash. By the end of his stay in the city, he would be lucky to own even half the hacienda outright. It would still be days before they would come to a final settlement, but he knew it was inevitable.

"As you wish," the merchant said. "You'll not be sorry. And I'll have people look into the transportation for you. I'll even have them measure it. Three times as far you say? Maybe you'd care to wager?" Guillermo grinned, his face flattening out in big horizontal creases. He loved to vex Javier, almost as much as he loved to gamble.

Javier rose. "Look it up, Memo, but this time you'll lose. Anyway, I've got to find Allegra before she spends a whole season's income on a new dress." He knew that his cousin would not really do such a thing. Well, probably not. Allegra shared his commitment to keeping the hacienda intact. In fact the crazy girl wanted to be his next overseer, and she pestered him about it constantly. Javier would never let that happen, of course. He knew that unruly men would not listen to such a tiny scrap of a thing, no matter how tenacious. She needed a husband, God help the man, not an occupation. Javier would be relieved when Allegra finished her degree and came home.

Guillermo nodded. "I'm sure she loves it when you're in town."

"She's better at charming salesmen into extending credit than I am. Maybe I should have brought her with me."

"I think you've done just fine on your own, Javito. Lázaro would be proud."

Javier was not sure his father's pride was worth the bowing and scraping he found himself doing these days. There was a time when Javier had sworn off trying to please that adulterer. In the end, though, the man had left to Javier—and Javier alone—the family's land. And the wistful, obedient little boy inside him—the boy who believed in love and loyalty—would not let that go without a fight.

CHAPTER FIVE

Singson's Shop

"It is beautiful, yes? From Brussels, the best lace on the Continent. Hard to find after the war. Americans make good beer but bad fashion."

Georgie would not know. She didn't drink beer. Fortunately, though, the young Filipina in front of her didn't actually require a response. Señorita Allegra was perfectly happy to keep the conversation going all on her own, just as she had done for the past half hour. They had met by chance at a dry goods store, and Georgie had not been able to shake the woman since. Allegra could not believe that any American would walk the Escolta without shopping, so Georgie now found herself unfolding a delicate slip of lace, pretending to consider it despite its prohibitive price. Even though Georgie was supposed to be getting married soon, she did not feel sentimental enough about the occasion to plunge into debt over it. This treasure was not for her.

Allegra kept talking. "I have to sew my flowers on dresses now, though Hermana Teresa will jump off the Puente de España before she believes it. Yesterday she says I will fail domestic labors class. Fail! So I say it is okay—one day I will hire her as my *costurera*. Do you hear nuns curse before? Very quiet, but they do."

No doubt nuns cursed around this young woman a lot, Georgie thought. Allegra looked demure but was really quite untamed. Black, roguish eyes set off her fair, delicate skin. Her pink lips were small but curvy, as exaggerated as the outlandish words that came from them. Even her clothes were deceptive: her blouse looked a touch worn but was finely embroidered. Of course, Allegra had probably not sewn a stitch of it. Despite her boasts, she did not seem to have the requisite patience.

In contrast, Georgie felt more rigid and plain than ever, an uncouth giant in her high-necked white cotton dress. Being around elegant women usually made her uncomfortable. She remembered the pair of Radcliffe girls on the steamer from San Francisco, each with perfectly combed blond tresses unruffled by the salty wind—as if even Poseidon himself would not dare disturb a single strand. It had been the same at Wellesley, a lonely place for a scholarship girl from Lower Roxbury. Though Georgie would soon join the upper crust as Archie Blaxton's wife, she wondered if she was doomed to feel this same unease all her days. Her own children might end up a mystery to her.

Still, Allegra was different than those others—lovely, certainly, but an earthly spirit too. An ally. Right now Georgie needed one of those. She had taken a break from her search to enjoy the woman's company for a few more minutes.

"The lace would be perfect for a bride," Georgie offered. "Maybe you?"

The Filipina smiled wistfully. "No, I do not marry yet, but maybe when I do the lace will be here. Señor Singson, you will not sell it, no?"

Mr. Singson's English was not as good as Allegra's, and it took him a moment to think through his response. Earlier, when Allegra had needed him to understand something quickly, she spoke in the local language, Tagalog. Then Singson turned to the young man behind him and told him in Chinese to get the requested item. Everything would be so much simpler when everyone spoke English, Georgie thought

"You marry soon, señorita," Mr. Singson finally said. "I sell to you." He had probably intended his statements as questions, but he did not raise his inflection so it sounded like he had inside knowledge of Allegra's love life.

The women were alone with the clerks in a cramped "storage" room in the rear of the shop, where more merchandise was displayed than in the retail store up front. Apparently this was a common practice since nothing sold in the back room was taxed. Sticking close to Allegra along Calle Rosario had been enlightening.

The Filipina sighed. "Before a wedding, Señor Singson, I must find a husband my cousin likes. For how long I have rested in your store, probably he thinks I marry you...ooh, here he is—Javier!"

Georgie turned to the door. Her first thought was that even she could not be this unlucky.

The Mestizo was wearing clothes now, thank goodness, but no threads could possibly cover up his most distinctive characteristic: his ego. His finely tailored suit only exaggerated that conceit, despite the open collar and tie dangling from his pocket. His dishevelment might have made him look tired had he not been quite so angry. His eyes, dark as molasses, were unforgiving. Georgie was too substantial a woman to be easily intimidated, but she still took a small step back.

Georgie waited for the man to exact verbal revenge for the damage she had done to his pride—and his back—the previous night. She regretted that this scene would no doubt ruin the companionship she had developed with Allegra.

The Mestizo—Javier—walked toward his cousin, forcing the young woman to bear the brunt of his displeasure first. "What are you doing here, *primita*?"

"Oh, Javito, do not treat me like a girl," Allegra said dismissively. "Everything good is selling in the back. You know this. It is where we shop."

He responded in Spanish, speaking too fast for Georgie's rudimentary skills, but the focus of their argument seemed to be the expensive lace now in Mr. Singson's hands. Allegra did not appear at all chastened; in fact she laughed. Once again Georgie pitied the nuns at the *colegio*.

"You are rude to my new friend," Allegra declared. "But I will make introductions, as is proper. Please meet Miss Georgina Potter. Miss Potter, this is my cousin, Javier Altarejos." She leaned toward Georgie and whispered: "He is not as bad as he looks."

Georgie was not so sure about that. His scowl seemed rather genuine. "Mr. Altarejos," she acknowledged quietly, staying flush against the counter to avoid his wrath.

The expected tongue-lashing never came. Amazingly, the man's expression softened, and he dipped his head in a slight nod. His voice was stiff and formal. "Pleased to meet you, Miss Potter."

"Señorita Potter is the new teacher for Bais," Allegra explained, pronouncing the town's name in two distinct syllables: Bah-ees. Her tone was especially enthusiastic, as if trying to force her companions to like one another through sheer willpower. "Of all towns in the Philippines, they send her to us!"

On that cue, Javier advanced, brushing Georgie's shoulder as he turned in the tight quarters. She thought the jostle was deliberate but was not sure.

"Will you be working with the Stinnetts at their new Protestant institute?" he asked.

Georgie shook her head, guessing that he did not really care where she worked. Good manners proved nothing.

"Señorita Potter will help me advance my English when I come home," Allegra said cheerfully.

"'Improve' your English," the man corrected, talking to his cousin but still watching Georgie.

"*Sí, claro*, improve my English. Only she is more nice than you." Allegra pouted the last few words—but insincerely, as if she were playing a part in a script.

The man looked over at his cousin and smiled, showing a family resemblance at last. "No one could be nicer than me, *nena*," he said.

Allegra laughed. "Of course. You are full of charm. I have to beat the ladies with a stick."

"Beat them 'back' with a stick. Yes, I'm sure you do." He returned his gaze to Georgie, his fierce concentration now softened a little by humor. "How long do you Americans plan to stay?" he asked.

Was she responsible for the entire administration? "My commitment is for two years, long enough to establish the central school."

"Why do you think anyone in Bais needs to learn English?"

She eyed him critically. "You ask that, yet you speak it fluently." Actually, he spoke the language precisely, like an apprentice wielding a tool with skill but not ease.

"But what use do farmers have for your lessons?"

Georgie was only a few generations removed from poor Irish tenants and took this personally. She supposed that working the land was beneath this man. "Don't you think everyone should be offered an education?"

"I am curious why you Americans think you should be the ones to provide it."

Because you Spanish already had your chance and failed, Georgie wanted to say. But as an ambassador of sorts, she tried to be diplomatic. "We bring simplicity. So far today I've heard four or five languages spoken, but I'm not sure anyone understood anybody else. All this confusion, it blocks progress."

Javier thought for a moment, or at least pretended to. She could not read him well enough to know the difference. "At least you could choose a language that's native to these islands."

"But your cousin told me that your family's first language is Spanish!" Georgie exclaimed. Had this man no shame?

Javier raised his chin. "Actually, I grew up bilingual, learned three more languages in school, and another while traveling. It's only Americans who can't seem to manage more than one."

Georgie could feel heat rising in her cheeks, and she cursed the fair complexion that betrayed her reaction. She did not know why she had expected this posh to understand her mission when he barely understood the needs of his own country. "What other option do we have? Most peasants know only a few words of Spanish—the friars were more interested in lining their cassocks than teaching."

"Ah, the friars," he said, chuckling. "Americans love to ridicule the friars—so do we, for that matter—but it's because of their failure that Tagalog and the other languages of the islands still exist. Unlike in Mexico, our heritage has survived into the new century."

"What a bunch of pop! Preserving your culture? Look at you. What does someone like you have in common with the average Filipino?"

"You think I'm the hypocrite?" Javier leaned closer. "I thought the fire would have made more of an impression on you, Miss Potter. I couldn't have come up with a better example of your government's sham rule if I'd tried. In the name of 'sanitation,' you Americans scattered thousands of the sick throughout the city—just like how in the name of 'democracy,' you've brought us a foreign governor backed up by a foreign military. And if your policeman friend from last night heard me say any of this to you, he would throw me in jail without a second thought, all in the name of 'liberty,' of course."

Prison might do this man some good, Georgie thought. No doubt he saw democracy as a threat to his privileged position. She knew all about his type.

"What you're talking about are just temporary measures," she said calmly, gathering her wits. "When peace is restored to the islands, a true Filipino government will be created. That's the whole point."

He tilted his head back a little, looking down at her even more severely. "So that's why you're here: to indoctrinate our next generation? I suppose that when you're done with the children of Bais, they'll all be flag-saluting 'Yankee Doodle Dandies.'"

"Any education is better than none!" she shouted. She would have been embarrassed by her outburst if she were not so angry. Those who opposed the new administration were either ladrones or robber barons, and she knew which of the two was standing in front of her.

"Any education, as long as it's English, right? Do you even know what language you'll be extinguishing in Bais?" he asked.

"Extinguishing? That's a little extreme." Georgie crossed her arms in front of her chest, hoping he would not pick up on her dodge. The only local language she had heard of was Tagalog, and based on the smugness of his tone, the answer could not be that easy.

He tilted his head. "You don't know, do you?"

Drat, she thought. Proving this man wrong would have been so satisfying. She fantasized about flattening him with her mastery of all things Philippines, turning on a heel, and striding out of the store in haughty righteousness.

Instead she was stuck in this stifling little room with him, unable to concentrate on anything other than her discomfort. She stuck a finger inside her collar to pull the fabric away from her neck. A rush of air cooled her skin, sliding down to her bosom.

She could not stall any longer. "No, I don't know," she admitted quietly.

"*Hay sus*, even the friars learned the languages." Javier's words were sharper than his tone, though. He seemed a little distracted by her collar tugging.

The intensity of his gaze made her snappish. "Languages like...?" She held out her palm, waiting for the answer.

He drew his eyes back up to hers. "Visayan. Specifically, the Cebuano dialect."

"So you'd rather that we taught in Cebuano?"

He snorted. "Hardly. The western half of Negros speaks Ilonggo."

"Ha! You can't choose a language for one island, let alone all of them!" She stood up straighter, pleased with her parry. "Meanwhile, English has become the commercial language for all of Asia." The man's confused logic had just handed her the win.

Or it should have. Javier did not seem as impressed as she.

"You may be full of zeal now," he said, "but how long before the costs of this little expedition force you to abandon it, just like everyone before you? I've seen your kind before. The worst thing you can do is raise the people's expectations and then dash them."

Georgie puffed up her chest proudly. "The Spanish may have been fickle, but we Americans finish what we start."

The smug bastard actually laughed at her. "We'll see. Maybe I'll ask my bookkeeper to run the odds on you still having your job in six months."

"How dare you, you arrogant—"

"*Silencio!*" cried Allegra, ending her silence. The feminine pitch of her voice did not soften its iron will.

Admittedly, Georgie had almost forgotten Allegra was in the room. The well-timed interruption was humbling.

Now that the young Filipina had everyone's attention, she softened her manner with a sweet smile. "I am sure I will see Señorita Potter in six months, with a job already."

"With a job 'still,'" her cousin suggested.

"No lessons, Javito," Allegra said firmly. "Not ever, if you teach like so. You learned manners in Europe? You forget them. No, for sure there will be one student for Señorita Potter!"

"At least one, I am sure." Javier looked down at Georgie's face, amusement crinkling the edges of his eyes. He seemed almost happy, strange for a man who had lost the argument.

Allegra was not finished with him yet. "Maybe she will teach you polite conversation."

"Actually," he said with a laugh, "I'm certain that's something to which Miss Potter and I are equally ill-suited."

Georgie shook her head. "There's a difference between being expressive and being ungallant, Mr. Altarejos."

"Ah, a distinction that is lost on me. I'm afraid I don't have the time to learn how to say nothing in as many words as possible."

Was that what this had been? It felt far more elemental. "I should let you return to your business."

To her relief, Javier agreed. He straightened up and took a step back. Georgie offered him a handshake in the well-drilled American manner, but when he took her hand he surprised her by bringing it to his lips and kissing it lightly. "Until we meet again, Miss Potter."

Georgie was not sure if this was a promise or a threat.

Part II: October 1902

...The Philippines is the only place in Asia where the mixed race are considered superior to purebred natives. It is a fiction perpetuated by the half-breeds themselves, who are more to blame for the impoverishment of their countrymen than even the friars. These parasites did not oppose Spanish rule because of any idealistic objection to foreign authority—how could they, when they live their own lives in perpetual imitation of an Iberian? I have met mestizos who, having spoken Spanish from the cradle, know less of the Tagalog language than I do. The sole Malay trait they have not effaced is tropical indolence. The only reason they troubled themselves to organize a revolution was because Spanish rule was the one restraint holding their greed in check.

The amigos we have raised into office may have made an oath of allegiance to our union, but they would just as easily salute the Kaiser's flag if it filled their pockets. All in all, it makes for a lonely life, and I am lucky to have been in Manila this first year where at least there is a growing American community. I expect to be reassigned to a remote barrio this summer, as the Bureau has been swamped with requests for new schools in every corner of the islands. I have no expectation of encountering any society worth the name out there.

Georgina, I know that our acquaintance in Boston was brief, and when I left for Manila I had no intention of continuing our attachment. My mother's concerns about a match between our families are well known to you, so I need not mention them again. Still, no one sends more letters or asks more questions about my experiences here than you. I know that you are anxious about the safe return of your brother, but maybe it is more than sisterly devotion that has prompted your correspondence? I have begun to consider whether it would suit both of us for you to join me here. Superintendent Atkinson is a fellow Harvard man, and he has confided in me that they are currently offering a pass examination to several hundred Catholic teachers in order to mollify Church supporters both here and at home. I believe, and hope you will agree, that the great advantage of my prospects outshines the inconveniences of two years in the wilderness. Dearest Georgie, would you join me in the Philippines and become my wife?

> *Hoping to hear your acceptance soon,*
> *Yours ever truly,*
> *Archibald Blaxton, Jr.*

CHAPTER SIX

Hotel de Oriente

Javier strolled through the Plaza Calderón de la Barca, a square most noted for the Moorish Revival masterpieces of Spanish architect Juan José Huervas y Arizmendi. The high lattice archways and sculpted moldings of one of these, the La Insular tobacco company building, looked more fit for a sheikh's palace than a cigar factory.

Javier walked into the similarly ornate Hotel de Oriente, headed for its spacious restaurant, and looked around for his luncheon partner. While he waited for the man to show, Javier chose a table under a giant *punkah*, but the fan did not do much to cool him because the servant boy operating it tugged more at his uniform than on the rope. Javier could empathize: the starch of his own shirt was doing terrible things to the mending flesh on his back. Unfortunately, physical discomfort was the least of his problems.

His predicament seemed almost Biblical: protecting his patrimony in the middle of war, tyranny, and plague. Sometimes at night he lay paralyzed in the sheer bloody terror of the whole project. The rest of the time he stayed focused on each isolated task, one after another, until he could push the panic away.

Javier could not finish paying his machinist for the latest adjustments to his sugar mill, so he had arranged a meeting to work out terms for extended credit. At this meeting, though, he would be required to feed the machinist a high-priced meal that would only delay repayment even further. Business was full of silly games like this. Had he taken the cheaper option, maybe invited the man down the street to eat Cantonese rice noodles, it would have proven to everyone how bad his finances really were. Javier was maintaining appearances by using one chit to pay off another, keeping no one waiting for too long. When he got stuck, he turned to Guillermo. He was relieved that at least one merchant in Manila was discreet.

Javier looked at the lunch menu. "Lunch" was a rather onomatopoetic word for the way these Americans ate, shoving food in their mouths like it was a time trial for the Olympic Games. Certainly, the insipid cuisine at the Oriente did not deserve such relish. What was Chicken à la Colorado anyway? Maybe it was boiled, like the ham and ox tongue. The days of British management, when they served the best curry in town, had long since passed. Javier read down the list to item seventeen, preserved peaches—a travesty in this land of fresh, sweet mangoes. He dropped the menu in disgust.

His eyes kept wandering around the room, watching the women. There were a few in the growing crowd, but none stood out. More precisely, none had distracting red hair. He knew that he would be better off forgetting that impossible American. She was too self-righteous, too sure of her pedagogical mission, and just too American. He had not forgotten how appalled she was that first night when he had touched her. He had saved her life, and still she had shoved him away like he was infected with rinderpest. On the other hand, her reaction in the back room at Singson's had been a little different—there she had been annoyed, yes, but not repulsed. And he had enjoyed their verbal jousting. She was wrong about everything, of course, but he liked her conviction, even if misguided.

Before he got too carried away, Javier reminded himself that this was not London or Paris. White women in Manila did not throw themselves at wealthy half-breed Spaniards solely for the novelty of it. Coming home had been hell on his love life, but Miss Potter was not the answer. Nor were any local beauties, like the ones Allegra had suggested introducing him to at the Luneta. One thing Hacienda Altarejos did not need was a precious blossom who knew only how to spend money in the shops of Escolta. If he ever did marry, he needed someone with enough backbone, common sense, and frugality to take over from his mother, Doña Lourdes.

Impatient to be done with this errand, Javier scanned the room again for his tardy machinist. He drank deeply from his iced tea, a luxury of the American sanitation regime and its Insular Ice and Cold Storage Plant. The plant's two working boilers had easily run local vendors out of business, though while the city was engulfed by cholera, that was not such a bad thing. Javier liked to think that he did not oppose progress, just unnecessary change.

A quiet, but insistent argument behind him interrupted this thought.

"Ma'am, can you tell me anything about what the man looked like?"

"He...he was wearing a loose white shirt and dark pants," the woman whispered. She was trying not to be heard, which of course made everyone around her all the more interested in listening. "He carried a bundle of laundry on his shoulder, tied up in a cloth and balanced on some sort of stick."

"That could be any Chinaman of a thousand, ma'am. Anything else?" Javier could hear a slight undertone of annoyance in the voice of what had to be a hotel employee.

"Oh, I can't tell any of their ages—they either look young enough for the nursery or old enough for the grave, nowhere in between." The flat, breathy whisper was unremarkable, but the accent was clearly American. Never had Javier met a nation of people so unfit for travel abroad.

"Any other features you noticed?" the hotel man asked.

"Black hair, black eyes...how should I know?" The woman gave up her vain attempt at discretion, and a shiver ran down Javier's sore back as her argumentative tone started to sound familiar. "I didn't speak with him long," she said. "I thought that since he was here in the lobby of the hotel, he was an employee. Oh...all my clothes...what am I going to do?"

Javier peered over his shoulder only to confirm his suspicion. The woman was apparently inescapable. She was giving the assistant manager a hell of a time too.

"How did this 'laundryman' expect to be paid?" the employee asked.

Miss Potter's eyes flickered down in embarrassment. She had paid up front, no doubt. Her clothing and her money were gone forever—unless she could find her mystery man among the sea of Chinese faces in Chinatown. Since she had not mentioned an identifying eye patch or wooden leg, Javier figured the odds were slim.

Miss Potter's sigh meant that she knew it too.

Javier reached up and touched his cheek, not sure why he had imagined her breath against his skin. If he were smarter, he would leave her alone; she was already turning him into a prize sap.

Miss Potter shook her head at the hotel man. "I suppose I should put this down as my first lesson in Asiatic travel: 'Don't trust a man in pajamas to give you back your pants.' I must admit, though, I'd have preferred the knowledge at a more reasonable price."

The woman did say the damnedest things, Javier thought as he laughed. The noise gave him away, not that he had been hiding anywhere but in plain sight. Miss Potter's gaze moved to his table, and her eyes widened as she took in her audience.

Accepting the inevitable, Javier stood and walked up to her.

"I'm Javier Altarejos," he first explained to the hotel man, who was relieved to have any excuse for an interruption.

"Yes, of course, Don Javier. You're staying with us again?"

Javier shook his head regretfully. He preferred the flexibility of a hotel, but it was cheaper to rent a flat for his longer stays in the city. "No, I'm here for luncheon, but maybe I can be of help. Miss Potter, it's a pleasure to see you again."

"It's certainly a surprise, Don Javier," she forced out.

He was pleased that she adopted the honorific "don," following the manager's lead. She paid attention to small things, and he liked that—no matter how little he cared for the title, or how little he deserved it.

"May I be of assistance?" he asked her.

"I don't see how, unless you happen to own a corrupt Chinese laundry."

He shook his head, deliberately not smiling again lest she think it was at her expense. "I'm afraid that your garments have probably been sold—after being washed."

"Of course," she said under her breath. "At least they're clean for somebody."

"But we could take a *calesa* ride and see if you recognize anyone," Javier offered. It was a ridiculous plan, and he did not have the time to be doing it. Nevertheless, he said it before he could stop himself.

"Thank you, but you have your food to eat. If you just point me in the right direction, I'll take a walk by myself."

He gave the *Americana* a significant look, hoping to discourage her from compounding her mistake. "I wouldn't recommend investigating the depths of Chinatown on your own."

He could see her warring with herself. How much did she want the clothes?

"My stuff isn't fancy," she said, "but it's all I've got."

"Miss Potter, I promise to be on my best behavior." That was not much of a guarantee, but she did not know that.

She looked him in the eyes, probably weighing the enemy in front of her against the one who had taken her clothes. Javier read the answer on her face probably even before she admitted it to herself.

CHAPTER SEVEN

Friends

"After you," Javier said, gesturing toward the door of the hotel. He paused to write down a quick message for when his machinist finally turned up. The Scot would not mind waiting as long as he could drink a bit of whiskey on Javier's tab. Javier looked longingly back at his own iced tea before turning to leave.

The *Americana* was already on the street trying to hail a cab when he joined her outside. "I'll hire someone for the day," he offered. "It's easier than getting a hack every time you need one. This way."

"Wait a second," she said, stepping out of his shadow. "I don't understand. Why would you abandon your luncheon on my behalf?"

Javier was not surprised by her directness. "Why wouldn't I?"

"It's not like we're friends."

"It's precisely because we are friends."

She folded her arms across her chest. "Acquaintances at best."

"You're friends with my cousin."

"Whom I've only met once."

"Well, you and I have met twice. That must count for something."

"Neither time really went so well," she said.

Javier had had more fun with every meeting, actually, but he was not going to say so. Miss Potter was not in a trusting mood.

"Okay, maybe we need a truce," he said. "Or, better yet, a fresh start." He offered her his hand like he would a man, the gesture she had tried once before. "Hello, I'm Javier Altarejos y Romero, sugar planter."

She hesitated, looking at him a long time, before shaking his hand. "Georgina Maeve Potter, schoolteacher."

He thought it sporting that she compensated for the lack of an *apellido materno* with her full given name. He was not sure if she was trying to mimic Spanish customs or undermine them.

"You're really a farmer?" she asked, letting go of his hand.

"Yes, we grow *caña morada* in Bais. Didn't Allegra tell you that?"

Georgina shook her head. "She told me how difficult Hermanas Teresa and Elenteria were making her life. We also speculated on why her teachers college would still bother with classes on flower arranging when geography would prove more useful."

He laughed. "That sounds like my cousin." Allegra had a keen mind, but Javier rarely saw her use it for respectable ends. "It never ceases to amaze me that she's training to be a teacher," he said. "She's been such a horrible student most of her life."

Georgina smiled. "I did get that impression, actually."

"She's too smart for most of the poor nuns who teach her and too shrewd to be properly disciplined." Mischief ran in the Romero family line, though he had tried to put those days behind him.

"Maybe she's not the problem. The corporal punishment she described is not only barbaric, it's counterproductive."

Javier was the last person to argue with that, but would the Americans really prove any different? Maybe this one would. "You and Allegra have much in common," he said. "I just hope that the rest of us survive the friendship." He gestured in the direction of the hotel stables. "Shall we get going?"

It took an extra minute to negotiate a rate for the day because the first driver took one look at Javier's white companion and doubled the usual fare. The second did the same. The third man looked at the line of eager drivers behind him and must have recognized that a day's work at the official rate was better than no work at an exorbitant one. He pulled his pony and carriage up to a clear bit of sidewalk for his new passengers to climb in.

Tucked together on the small bench of the *calesa*, Javier and Georgina searched the streets of eastern Binondo and into the district of Tondo for the "missing" laundryman. They passed by the northern side of Divisoria market, the giant emporium that straddled several city blocks. Escolta may have been where the wealthy shopped, foreigners included, but Divisoria was for everyone else. Javier knew that if Georgina's clothes were being resold, they would end up in some stall there. Unfortunately, the market had to be explored by foot, and he would not subject her to being stared at like a circus freak. The dark tunnel-like entrances must not have looked that inviting to Georgina, either, because she did not ask where they went.

Javier probably should have felt bad about his lie of omission, but it would have been a futile errand in any case. Even if they found the garments, he knew that proving her ownership would be impossible. As they continued along in the carriage—Georgina scrutinizing every poor fellow they passed—he knew that he was wasting their time looking for a single thief in a city full of them. They had made a full circuit around Binondo and were heading back to the hotel when they got stopped in traffic. Javier leaned forward and stood as best he could without hitting his head against the sunshade of the open-air *calesa*. He saw dozens of men clogging the road with wheelbarrows.

"What's going on?" Georgina asked.

"It's pay day," Javier said with a shrug. He motioned for her to get up and crouch beside him. "Don't worry, I've got you."

She rested one hand against the back of the driver's seat and the other on Javier's elbow. Because of the shaky balance of the *calesa*, even at a standstill, she held tight.

"What's in those things? It looks like—"

"Silver coins." Wedging his right shoulder against the side of the carriage to keep his balance, he used his freed hand to take a single coin out of his pocket. "You've probably noticed how heavy a Mexican dollar is. It's hard to carry around a lot at a time, so—"

Just then the *calesa* began moving, throwing them both off balance and back into the seat. Javier pulled Georgina onto his lap, and his already sore back took the brunt of the impact for them both. It hurt but was worth it, especially when the woman lingered a few seconds.

"Are you okay?" he asked.

Georgina did not answer right away; she slid off his leg and inched to the other end of the bench. "Paper bills would solve that problem," she said.

"What?"

"The problem of the coins, you know, being heavy."

"Ah, yes." He paused to pick up the dollar from the floor of the cab. It took a few seconds, but eventually he formulated a reasonable response. "People don't trust a paper currency when they are uncertain about the government that issues it. Instead we buy on credit and settle up at the end of the month. This," he said, waving his hands around, "is pay day."

"Stores collect cash in wheelbarrows?" As they neared the plaza, the noise on the street grew louder. Georgina leaned in to be heard and he did the same, drawing their heads together like conspirators. She was so close that when she spoke, it was directly into his ear. "My family would have never sent me out into the street with an open cart of coins. I'd have been robbed...or worse."

"Your family ran a business?" Javier had never considered what these Americans did before arriving in the islands. He did not think of them at all, not until they were his problem.

"It was my grandfather's tailor shop," Georgina explained. "And he would have never extended credit to anyone. Not in our part of Boston, at least."

Her people were tailors. Suddenly the answer to her problem seemed so simple.

Javier got the *cochero*'s attention and told him to turn off before Calle Rosario. The man was probably happy to avoid the crush up ahead, which is why he did not wait for his passengers to brace themselves as he drove the horse into an empty side street.

Javier put his arm around Georgina's shoulder to steady her and then did not let go. "Sorry," he said, not sure whether he was apologizing for the jolt or the liberty he was taking.

"I'm fine." She blushed as she straightened up, but she did not pull away from him this time. He decided that meant he had only apologized for the jolt.

"Riding with you is an adventure," she said.

He was having fun himself, and he smiled. He was pleased to have a plan now, to have found a discreet answer to a discrete problem. If only the rest of his worries were so easily answered.

CHAPTER EIGHT

Two Seamstresses

It took only a few minutes to arrive at the center of Calle San Fernando, the street where the storekeepers from Escolta and Rosario bought their piña, silk, and lace. The driver pulled over on Javier's command.

"Why are we stopping here?"

Javier hopped out of the cab. "This woman is an old friend of the family," he explained as he helped Georgina down after him. "She used to be our seamstress in Bais until her children moved to the city. That's when we set her up here. I would have taken you to La Puerta del Sol or Paris-Manila, but this will be better—and cheaper—than a store."

"We're giving up on the laundryman?"

Javier nodded. "Adventure requires flexibility. Think of your lost clothes as unintentional charity."

Georgina looked a little uneasy about giving up on her search, but she let Javier lead her into the small shop. The room was barely larger than the sewing machine it contained. He introduced her to Nina and sent them both out to find appropriate fabrics. All it cost him was an unbearably smug look from Nina. The old gossip had even winked at him.

Javier knew that the women would be awhile, so he excused himself and made the short trip back to the Oriente to check if his machinist had finally appeared. When he finally returned to Nina's an hour later, Georgina's booming voice spilled into the street. She was trying not to shout, but failing.

"I don't understand—we bought all that fabric, discussed designs, took measurements…and you can't tell me how much it will cost?"

Javier knew that Nina only spoke Cebuano, Tagalog, and some Spanish. No English at all. How they had "discussed" anything was a mystery to him.

"Chit? Bill? *Factura?*" the *Americana* continued. "Write down the numbers? Do you understand?" He heard her sigh and then mutter, "Oh, what am I going to do?"

Javier decided it was time to intervene, mostly because he imagined Nina was more confused than Georgina. He stepped into view of the open door but did not enter the crowded room. "Miss Potter, is there a problem?"

Georgina had never seemed so happy to see him—which, of course, was not saying much. "Yes, Don Javier—"

"Please, just call me Javier." A dignified señorita would never be so familiar and drop the title, but he hoped she would not know that.

"Javier," she said, "thank you for coming back. I'm trying to pay, or just put down some earnest money on all these clothes she's making, but I can't get her to give me a price."

Without a word, the older woman handed Javier a meticulously itemized invoice.

Georgina looked betrayed. "You understood all along," she accused the seamstress.

Javier looked over the order. Georgina had bought a decent amount of fabric, all in a medium price range that probably meant it was sturdy and utilitarian. It was what he expected from a girl who grew up in the trade.

Nina verified his hunch, speaking to him in Cebuano. "I think if I let her use my machine, she would sew the dresses herself. She must have spent a lot of time with her family's *costurera*."

Javier did not correct the woman's assumption that every American was rich enough for servants. "Did she get enough dresses?" he asked.

"Some dresses, some blouses and skirts. She drew me the styles, but Don Javier, I've never made anything like them. First, she refuses both satin brocade and piña, insisting upon plain cotton. To put such a lovely woman in that—"

"You did as she asked, though."

"Of course, but such a waste!"

He laughed. He saw that Georgina was struggling to understand the conversation, but since the woman had not even known that the Cebuano language existed two days ago, she had little chance of understanding what was being said.

"And the designs," Javier asked Nina. "Can you make what she asked?"

"I tried to show her how to wear the *pañuelo*, but she just wanted this floppy bow." The *costurera* pointed down to the drawing on her table. "The shirt is so mannish, with a stiff collar and buttons down the front. I've never seen such a thing!"

"It's the American style. They do things differently."

"Well, it's a shame, if you ask me. Look at that hair! If I could've gotten her to choose something with a bit more color—"

"I thank you for following her wishes," Javier said, ending the complaints decisively. He understood Nina's confusion, but the seamstress could not be allowed to question Georgina's tastes. Such was always the delicate balance with domestic staff. "I need this to be a fast order."

"Of course, it will be my only thought!"

By now, Nina surely assumed Georgina was his betrothed. Why else would he be so interested in her wardrobe?

So when Javier then handed Georgina the chit, the *costurera's* eyes grew wide in disbelief. He knew that any way he handled the payment, one of the two women in front of him was not going to be happy—and the *Americana* was far more stubborn. "Nina was holding the invoice for me," he explained to Georgina.

"Thank you," she said, accepting the paper without hesitation.

He actually wanted to pay. That was the strange part. "But if you would allow me—"

"No, Javier," she cut him off. "Anything else would be, ah, inappropriate."

He could have insisted, but he understood pride. Georgina paid for the raw fabric and gave a small advance for the sewing. Javier explained that the clothes would be delivered to her hotel, and she could pay the remainder at her leisure.

She smiled. "Should I find myself a wheelbarrow, then?"

"That's a good idea," he said with a short laugh.

Georgina extended her hand to the flustered Nina, and the woman took it in a dainty pinch of thumb and fingers. The *costurera* looked embarrassed by the attention, but also pleased.

The Americana then held her hand out to Javier. "I am not sure I deserve all the kindness that you have shown me today," she said, "but thank you."

He pulled her hand to his lips. The last time he had done this, he had been mocking her. This time he was sincere.

Georgina spoke through what was clearly nervousness. "I'm actually looking forward to a calm evening at the hotel. It's funny—I haven't begun to teach yet, and already I need a break."

Javier tried to keep his voice casual as he lowered her hand. "We're not going back to the hotel."

"We're not?"

"No."

"Why not?"

Javier looked Georgina square in the eyes, still holding her hand. "You'll see."

CHAPTER NINE

Luneta

Touring the Luneta alone with Georgina would be far too forward, so Javier suggested that they invite Allegra to join them. It was a convenient improvisation. The *calesa* pulled up at the front entrance of the Colegio de Santa Rosa, a massive three story building that occupied an entire block in Intramuros. Javier's father had given money to help rebuild the school after the 1882 earthquake, and while he claimed the donation was in honor of his wife, a graduate, Javier suspected the gift was more calculated than generous. His father had likely foreseen the need to "encourage" a school to admit his orphaned niece, a hellcat even in baby's napkins.

While at the *colegio*, Allegra had proven that even a nun's patience has its limits. Since taking over her guardianship, Javier had received countless letters about her conduct: his cousin refused to observe silence at meals, faked illnesses to get out of classes, and had a scandalous habit of bathing nude—thankfully, alone. What really gave the sisters apoplexy, though, were Allegra's secret excursions to play *sipa*. No matter how many times they confiscated her footbag, she could be found bouncing one off her bare heel the next day. When Javier declared that this was not a very ladylike pastime, she boasted that she could do over a hundred hits nonstop, and would he care to see?

Given how relieved the nuns usually were to hand Allegra over, Javier was surprised by their reluctance today. On Wednesday afternoons, he was reminded, the students had lessons in sewing and housework, subjects his cousin already had made a habit of missing. He tried to get the directress to release the girl when classes were over but was told that Allegra could not possibly skip the evening benediction and rosary, let alone study hours or nighttime prayers—the last being especially important for a young woman in so much need of spiritual direction. He pressed his case, but no matter how effective he was negotiating with Chinese merchants, he got nowhere with the Daughters of Charity. He was about to comment on the inappropriateness of the order's name when Georgina saved him.

"I respect the discipline and commitment that you require of your students, sister," she said without a hint of insincerity in her voice. "As the English tutor for the señorita, I understand the troubles you've had with her, and I apologize for our unconventional, last-minute visit. It's just that this may be my last chance to review with my pupil before I take a posting in the provinces."

The nun looked skeptical. She had been a member of a Catholic mission in Hong Kong and knew English too well to be duped by a fast-talking American. "Allegra has a tutor? This is news to me, Miss—"

"Georgina Potter."

"And where will you be heading, Miss Potter?"

There was a moment of hesitation, and Javier prayed she didn't say Bais or even Dumaguete, nowhere near where he and Allegra lived. *Hay sus*, the school had addressed enough correspondence there.

"Basey, Samar." Georgina said it casually, like she told barefaced lies to nuns every day of her life. She pronounced Basey the wrong way—or, more precisely, the American way, with a nasally vowel sound—but that did not lessen its impact.

"Oh my," the sister said, pulling in her breath. The troubles in Samar would elicit sympathy for anyone headed that way, especially an American who might not return. For a moment Javier felt bad about misleading this servant of God, but then remembered the permanent white marks on Allegra's hands.

"Well, Godspeed child," the nun said to Georgina, giving her shoulders a sincere squeeze. "Of course we can make an exception." She rushed off to find Allegra.

"You know I'm going to hell for this," Georgina confessed in the near-empty hall.

"Maybe," Javier admitted. He would be happy to show her the way. "I'm wondering, though, how you've heard of Basey?" He mispronounced the town's name for her benefit.

"My brother's final letters were posted from there."

Brother? Javier wanted to know more, but if her brother was dead—and it sounded like he was—now was not the time to ask.

The news of Allegra's liberation traveled quickly to the third floor. He heard his cousin charge down the hallway. Someone admonished her in a furious whisper from the top of the stairs, resulting in Allegra's quick, if disingenuous, contrition. The sound of Allegra's steps grew heavier and faster before she finally burst into the foyer and hugged Georgina as if they had parted years before. He could tell the *Americana* was not used to such unconditional enthusiasm.

Eager to be free of the sisters' control, Allegra begged to accompany them to the promenade at the Luneta, as Javier expected. The park was one of the few places that sheltered young maidens could socialize in public. Even the Daughters of Charity made an occasional appearance there, though Javier was probably a more forgiving chaperone.

Happy to oblige any whim that would prolong what felt more and more like a holiday, Javier led the women out the school's gates before the nuns had a chance to change their minds.

The Luneta's coastal park spread south from the city walls of Intramuros to Manila Bay. There they joined hundreds of Manileños who were enjoying the centerpiece of their day. Wealthy doñas, notoriously late risers, would bathe and dress just in time to catch the evening breeze that cooled the bay and blew away the mosquitos. Once there, they would catch up on the latest *tsismis*, gossip passed from *calesa* to *calesa* like a tattler's telegraph. Then they would be off to eat and dance at a friend's house, returning home shortly before dawn to sleep through another morning. Meanwhile, their servants ran their households, farms, and shops.

Javier's carriage got in line with the others circling in comfort, leaving the poor to walk the shoreline. Calling the Luneta a park was a bit generous, considering the utter lack of trees or foliage. The only decorations were incandescent gas lanterns circling the perimeter, sort of like candles on a vast birthday cake. In the center, on the wooden grandstand, played the newly formed Filipino Constabulary Band. They had only been practicing together a few weeks, but they were not half bad.

"Hey, that's 'Hot Time in the Old Town,'" Georgina exclaimed. "How'd they learn American music?"

"The 'Hototay' we call it," Allegra said. She sat between Javier and Georgina, but she was too tiny to be much of a barrier. "The song is everywhere, even funerals. Filipinos think it is your national anthem."

Georgina laughed. "Maybe it should become yours."

"You suggest we adopt the drinking song of an occupying army?" Even before Javier finished the question, he regretted asking it. *Hay sus*, why couldn't he keep his mouth shut?

Allegra gave him a dirty look and rebuked him in quick Spanish. "Don't forget that Tiyo Lázaro welcomed the *Americanos* as soon as they arrived in Negros," she said. His cousin had adopted a Boston schoolteacher as her new best friend, and she would not forgive Javier if he soured their day together.

"I'm sorry," Javier said, looking over Allegra to address Georgina in English. "I've been suitably reprimanded for my bad manners."

"I thought that was your natural charm."

"*Verdaderamente*," Allegra said, waving her hand. "I try to help, but he is not a good student."

"That's not true," he objected, but the women shared a look that said it was. Still, he had to defend himself. "Don't listen to my cousin, *Maestra.*"

Georgina gave him a queer look. "Did you just call me...mistress?"

Did she think he would insult her so? Yes, he supposed that was what she thought. "Maestra is an honorable term for teacher. You'll hear it more in these islands than your own name."

He had barely recovered his footing in this conversation before he was silenced by the six o'clock *Angelus* bells which rang from every church in the city. The horses stopped, the men removed their hats, and all heads bowed to chant three Hail Marys.

Allegra, the fastest prayer-reciter in the Philippines, broke the peace first. "Georgie, now I am thinking about your...short name."

"Nickname," Javier supplied.

His cousin ignored him. "It is the name of a boy, yes?"

The *Americana* showed more indulgence of Allegra's lack of tact than Javier's. She even looked a little wistful when she answered. "It was my brother's way of being affectionate, I guess, and I just got used to it."

Allegra nodded thoughtfully. "A Filipino brother may do the same, but would use 'Ina.' We like the end of names more."

Georgina rejected the suggestion with a shake of her head. "'Ina' sounds like some exotic beauty: confident, poised—"

"How would you describe 'Georgie' then?" Javier had to know.

She shrugged. "A tomboy. You know, gawky...uh, a little clumsy, I suppose."

This woman was none of those things. She was tall, yes, and not in a thin, bending reed sort of way. Javier appreciated her strength— though if he said as much, she would probably storm out of the carriage. If he said nothing, though, she would assume that he agreed with her own humble assessment. It was a delicate jam. Georgina must have assumed the worst because she quickly changed the subject.

"What would happen if we turned the carriage around and circled in the other direction?"

Javier laughed. "You are a rebel, Maestra."

"No, really," she urged on. "This whole orderly migration—I just can't reconcile it with the chaos of the rest of the city."

"That's why the Spanish liked it," he answered. "Only the archbishop and governor-generals' carriages were allowed to pass against the line. That way you had no excuse but to recognize and salute them as they passed."

"You could get in trouble for forgetting?"

"Absolutely. The *Peninsulares* believed it important to punish people for small sins lest they attempt any larger ones. It's not an uncommon assumption among occupiers."

Georgina's mouth started to open in protest, but Allegra beat her to the draw. "Javier, no more of that. You are boring us. Right, Georgie?"

He watched the *maestra* try to steer between her desire to be truthful and her reluctance to hurt Allegra's feelings. "I suppose I'm not very genteel," she said, "for I do sometimes like to discuss such things."

Discuss? She meant argue, Javier thought. This one redhead would take on all challengers to the Insular regime, and he respected her conviction, even if he distrusted the government she defended.

Allegra, no paragon of protocol herself, nodded. "I like things not for proper ladies, but politics is not one. Oh! I see friends by the stage. I leave you to discuss what you will."

"No, wait—" Georgina began.

But Allegra had already hopped out. Javier was suspicious of her quick departure, not because she was heading to the bandstand to speak to young men without a chaperone—though he should have been worried about that—but because he had the feeling he was being set up. If so, he was impressed. His cousin read him well.

Javier had been alone with Georgina already today, but then she had been distracted by her own problems and had not really noticed their close quarters. Now, sitting so close in the small seat, she had to recognize her fate.

Fate? He was a little surprised to find himself thinking in such terms. In the years since returning home, Javier had kept his attention fixed on the earth, not the clouds. Today, though, he wondered if survival was enough. As a boy he had dreamed of his own family; and as an only child, he had dreamed that family to be a large one: a loving wife, lots of children, aunts, uncles, and grandparents—everyone living together at the hacienda. It would be disorderly, loud, and sometimes difficult. It would be home.

But what if his wife spoke only rudimentary Spanish and came under the wrong flag? Would that be any less his dream?

He was pretty sure that this was the craziest idea he'd had all week.

CHAPTER TEN

Malecón

What was she doing, Georgie wondered? For Heaven's sake, she was engaged. Archibald Blaxton would certainly not approve of her riding around a gaslit park, unchaperoned, with a Filipino half-breed. She tried to remind herself that there was no one here to spy on her. Ha! No one but every blessed American in the Insular Government.

She was being careless, but the line between careless and carefree seemed blurry. She reassured herself that all would be fine if she kept conversation to polite topics—the safer, the better. "There are a few friars here," she said, pointing to a man in a long white frock who was talking to a wealthy mestizo couple. "You said the people hated them."

"That may have been a bit simplistic," Javier admitted. "Filipinos can be more loyal to God than to each other. That, plus a little fear, usually helps them forgive the friars' excesses."

"Excesses? I've heard that some have…families."

He chuckled at the genteel euphemism. "You mean they have lovers. Yes, they do. Sometimes the padres keep their beauties right in the *convento*. Men can have quite greedy appetites, no matter their faith."

Predictably, little pin-pricks of sweat dotted Georgie's reddening cheeks and forehead. Had she been raised properly, this conversation might have totally done her in. Instead, she felt a little flushed, and she covered that reaction with anger. "How...how can people stand for it?" she stammered. "Who cares for the innocent children of these unions?"

"You tell me."

"Huh?"

Javier tilted his head in Allegra's direction. It took a moment for Georgie to put together the pieces. "She's—"

"Probably the daughter of a friar."

"Probably?"

Javier held out his hands as if weighing guilt in the air. "My aunt never made a public accusation, of course. And my grandparents managed to marry their daughter off to a respectable, if not terribly intelligent, man. Unfortunately, even he could add. My aunt named the baby Allegra, hoping her husband would believe the child a miracle of rapid gestation. As you might imagine, their marriage was not a happy one."

"And then what happened?" She whispered the question.

"Allegra's mother was beautiful and mercurial—family traits, it seems. Only a few months after she gave birth, she ran off with a young Spanish captain. No one's heard from her since. Allegra came to live with us when I was away at school in Cebu, which meant that I was the last to know. I came home for Holy Week and there was a little baby girl in a basket in my parents' bedroom. I thought she was my new sister, and I suppose I still think of her that way."

Georgie glanced over her shoulder at the young woman in question. "Does she know?"

He nodded. "It probably explains some of her difficulties at Santa Rosa. She's a born skeptic."

"I thought she had inherited her obstinacy."

Javier smiled. "It could be that too."

Georgie stared at him, more curious about this man than she wanted to admit. He distrusted outsiders, but he could be just as critical of his own countrymen too. Was there anything he held dear?

"Do you go to mass?" It was a question that only a Catholic would ask, but for the first time in years she did not feel the need to mask her roots.

"I suppose."

"Is that a yes or a no?" Georgie's mother had always insisted there was only one right answer.

"That's a yes, but only when Mamá and my chaplain talk me into it."

"Chaplain?" Not parish priest?

He shrugged. "The man I employ for the chapel-at-ease on my land."

"You have your own church? Your own curate? Why do I feel like we're going in circles?" She waved at the parade of carriages but meant it figuratively.

His cocky smile held only mischief. "I can fix that."

"Wait, what are you doing?"

Before she could intervene, he ordered the driver to turn the *calesa* away from the crowd. Georgie was happy to escape the immediate attention she had been attracting as a mestizo's companion, but trotting off with him would probably not do much to discourage anyone's tongue from wagging. She briefly wondered if she could make a clean jump out of the carriage. Allegra had made it look easy—though at the time their horse had been moving slower than an ox in heavy traffic. Georgie shrank back into her seat, not anxious to risk injury at this clip. Buffalo Bill's Wild West Show would not be hiring her anytime soon.

Javier was annoyingly relaxed. He stretched out on his side of the bench, with his right ankle draped over his left knee, effectively trapping her with one expensive shoe. Even though a fashionable derby shaded his eyes, she could still see them glow with amusement. "What do you do for fun, Maestra?" he asked over the wind.

"I don't race horses, that's for sure," she said as they picked up speed.

"First time to the Malecón, then? The beachfront isn't much fun without a good wager. Shall we find one?"

Was he kidding? Georgie looked at the horse in front of her and wondered how he could pull their carriage at all, let alone race. Manila had larger cockroaches than horses. "This may all be derring-do to the men, but I imagine the animals just hope to survive."

Javier had more faith in their steed. "He may not be the best example of horseflesh, but his nature and temperament are well suited to his environment. I have great sympathy for mixed lines."

"Is this the type of horse you ride, then?"

He paused, and the telltale silence gave him away before he admitted the truth. "Actually, Nico was line-bred off two Andalusians from Jerez de la Frontera, Spain. I suppose that makes me a—"

"A fraud. Yes, definitely."

Javier laughed as if the impulse was a surprise. "I was going to say 'man of good taste.' Still, you shouldn't write off our friend here, you know." He nodded toward the animal. "He has spirit."

Georgie was ready to concede—no proof necessary—but Javier had already leaned in to talk to the driver. It took only a few words to inspire the man's imagination. They launched off in search of an opponent, an easy task since several others had come to the palm-lined Malecón for the same thrill. They pulled even with another scrubby horse and carriage.

"You know," Javier said, "I've seen many of these races before but have never tried it myself."

She turned to him. "Why start now?"

Had she expressed her fear more forcefully, he might have called it off. Maybe not, though: bravado is hard to moderate. And, anyway, it was too late. The charge had begun.

The two vehicles ate up the open road. Georgie did not consider herself a coward, but she was torn between fearing for the horses' safety and for her own. Maybe sensing that, Javier put his arm around her shoulders, pulling her closer to his side. It was too cozy by half, but it steadied her enough to make the frenetic motion bearable.

The two nags kept changing the lead. One would break out in a small burst of speed, and then slow in recovery while the other made his move. They had at least a mile to go until the "finish" at Fort Santiago, and it seemed that Georgie's original prediction was on the mark: the sole surviving animal would win. It was less a race than a gladiatorial bout. Unfortunately, their own horse showed signs of exhaustion first, probably because he pulled an extra passenger. His movements became choppy. His head drifted to the side, and he kept jerking it forward, again and again, as if the motion could create the winning momentum.

With every spasm of the horse's head, the carriage jolted. Soon, the frame on Georgie's side started shaking. The roof above them was supported by three thin pieces of bamboo, and she watched one pull out of its fastener. The front corner of fabric flapped wildly in the wind, pulling hard at the other two rods. Even more worrisome was the squeak of the wooden wheel to her left. If that splintered, the whole apparatus would collapse, probably pulling the two men and the horse right on top of her. The sound of hooves, wind, and screaming jockeys drowned out Georgie's increasingly frantic warnings.

Or so she thought.

Javier tapped the driver's shoulder. Hard. When the man didn't respond, he grabbed the fellow's arm and shouted. The driver argued back, probably insisting his animal could still win. Javier glanced over at Georgie briefly and added something in Spanish about "the lady." He signaled again, this time his face quite stern. Javier's scowl was, no doubt, the most effective weapon he had.

Georgie was grateful. They were finally slowing down. "The carriage is falling apart," she tried to explain when she could finally be heard over the din.

"I know," Javier said in quick English, peering over her lap to the wheel beneath. "We'll make it, don't worry. But I blamed quitting on you, so act like you might swoon."

Georgie fanned herself wildly with her hand and threw back her head. Was that right? She had never before tried to feign fragility—it was not a safe thing to do in South Boston.

Javier watched her for a second, an unreadable expression on his face. Then he laughed—at her this time, not with her. "Wow, you do that badly."

She gave him a little swat on the arm. "What a terrible thing to say."

One eyebrow rose. "I don't think so. I dislike weak women."

"Then why put on a charade for the driver?"

Javier glanced up at the disappointed Filipino. "So he and his horse wouldn't lose face. Honor matters even for a Manila cabbie, so I thought a little play-acting from you would be an easy solution. Now I'm not so sure."

Georgie did not like her competency questioned, even in such a ridiculous arena. "I had no idea that theater was required. How convincing does this have to be?"

He looked at her intently. "Very."

She slumped back in the seat, trying again to look helpless.

"Ridiculous," Javier murmured under his breath as he reached out to her. Before she could react, he pulled her close, tucking her right shoulder under his arm and pressing her solidly against his chest. He gently brushed her cheek with his fingertips, the way one might soothe a skittish child. Up until that moment, Georgie had only pretended to faint; now she actually felt light-headed.

"Are you okay, *cariño*?" His words played to the driver, but they felt genuine enough to her.

She looked up. This close, she could see honey-colored circles in his brown irises. They looked like rings on a tree. Did she see in them the same fire she felt, or was this a part of the show?

Gently Javier tilted her chin up, his lips now inches away. No one had ever tried to kiss her, not even Archie—his amorous attentions had all been by pen. She thought about resisting, but that was all it was, a thought. Javier's breath was clean. Only the smallest bite of scotch lingered from lunch. Given her past, Georgie had never believed alcohol could be an aphrodisiac, but on this man the crisp scent was provocative. He smelled of confidence and power, yet his lips looked surprisingly soft—

"Good race!" Their rival, gay in victory, smiled over at them from only a few feet away.

Spell broken, Georgie flew out of Javier's arms, throwing herself back against the seat so hard that she banged a rib or two. "Ow," she exclaimed, pretending clumsiness was the reason for her mortification.

Javier's left arm dropped to the small of Georgie's back, adding a firm cushion between her and the hard bench. He rubbed away the soreness, spreading the heat of his large hand down her spine. It was not proper, not at all. He turned away from her to speak with their rival, probably to complain that the silly woman in his carriage was the reason for their last minute capitulation.

The champion led them to fresh water for the horses and collected his gentleman's dollar for winning the race. Georgie did not speak a word the entire time. As they all returned to the Luneta, she tried to put the near-kiss out of her mind. Nothing had really happened, so there was no point dwelling on it.

In the park, the parade of carriages had stopped, and all the men—both Filipino and American—had removed their hats again. When Georgie heard the crisp notes of the Constabulary Band playing the "Star Spangled Banner," she knew that Fate was not finished with her.

Javier looked at her, a bit of suspicion tainting his gaze, even though she had no control over the music program. Refusing to be intimidated, she stared back. She had not put her foot down on the horse racing, but that did not mean she was wishy-washy about everything.

She was just as patriotic as the next American. Whatever had just happened between them would not change that.

Javier reached up and tipped off his derby. He leaned forward and whispered in her ear, his breath dancing against her flesh. "It's a pretty song, but it's not mine. Just like it's not my flag."

"You don't want it to be yours?"

He pulled his arm from behind her back and looked at her silently. He gripped his hat tightly in both hands and brushed sand spray off the brim. Finally he spoke, his voice mild but certain. "No," he said, "I don't."

CHAPTER ELEVEN

Skating the Floors

Georgie spent the next week exclusively in the company of Americans, not just for her own sanity but also for the sake of her search. No one knew anything about her brother Benji. Most of them did not want to say it, but they thought him dead. It had been Samar, after all, and everyone knew that Samar was the charnel-house of the islands. But everyone had to be wrong. If Benji had died, surely the Army would have informed their mother, just like the corporal had said.

Not one to leave such a thing to chance, each morning Georgie prayed. She brushed off an adulthood of lukewarm faith, got on her knees, and pleaded. "Please, God, let him be alive," she whispered. "I'll do anything." No living soul heard these words, but they still helped her ward off the melancholia—until, on her last day in Manila, Georgie lost steam entirely.

She may not have gotten dressed at all had she not needed to go downstairs to meet Nina and pay for her clothes. Later, she forced herself to take a brief walk through the plaza outside, grateful for the unseasonal break in the heat. The wind blew down from the San Mateo mountains and funneled in between the buildings. It ripped through her kinky auburn curls, picking up entire locks and tossing them in front of her eyes. She twisted her hair into a thick rope down her back in an effort to tame it, but she knew it would be a tangled mess again by dinner.

Who was she trying to impress, anyway? Certainly not Javier Altarejos. That fragile amity was over. After their awkwardness during the "Star Spangled Banner," things had only gotten worse. Georgie had spotted her least favorite policeman—the one from the fire, on the other side of the bandstand—but she had not told Javier. Why? She still wasn't sure. Maybe it was because she hadn't trusted the Filipino not to call the policeman's attention to the prize in his carriage. Without hat or parasol, and with no way to stop the steady rotation of *calesas* by the stage, Georgie would have been bared to her compatriot's scorn. She had tried to sink anonymously into her seat, but the hard wooden bench would not yield to her shame.

When Georgie had then asked Javier to return her to her hotel, he had looked surprised. "Really?" he said. "You don't want to circle again?"

"That's all right, I'm—"

"Embarrassed to be seen with me by our policeman friend?"

She should have known better. Despite all his other flaws, Javier had never given her reason to think him stupid. After that, Georgie had not been able to look him in the eye. They picked up Allegra in silence; and, not surprisingly, the young woman had been forced to carry the conversation the whole way home. She could not have helped but notice the tension, but she ignored it. Later, as she hugged Georgie goodbye in front of the Oriente, Allegra had whispered, "Ignore half of what he says."

Georgie had smiled, but she knew the truth: Javier was not a man who could be easily limited to any one of his halves: half-Spanish and half-Malay; half-Catholic and half-heathen; or half-civilized and half-wild.

Besides, it wasn't like she could change her mind now. Her job, her ability to stay in the country, and even her search for her brother were all tied together in a single commitment to Archie. At the time, it had seemed a very practical, very sensible plan.

"Love gets worn down, Georgie, like all the most beautiful fabrics," dressmaker Margaret Potter had warned her daughter. "Velvet is a friend for a season, but wool sticks around for a reason."

It was a lesson that Georgie's mother had learned from experience. Overcome by passion, young Maggie had married John Potter, a Protestant, in her church rectory parlor. The ceremony was attended only by immediate family and a reluctant Catholic priest. But Maggie and John's love had not worn well and, by the time Georgie was a girl, even their friendship was in tatters.

Georgie would not repeat her mother's mistake: she would marry with her head and not her heart—and within her own society. In this new American colony, religion was far less a barrier than color. Blazes! Even to reject Javier's attention meant that she had to acknowledge it. This was no time to become distracted. She had done plenty to jeopardize her position already and, in order to move forward, she needed to cut him off entirely. She even ignored the letter he left for her at the front desk. This was not a gracious thing to do, but it was for the best. He would get over it. He had probably even seen it coming.

Standing now in the little park in front of her hotel, Georgie felt more confident than ever of her plan. If anyone could help in the search for Benji, it would be Archie. By now, he had to have connections everywhere. He was too much of a Beacon Hill Blaxton not to be pulling a few strings. Most importantly he had money: ample funds, properly used, could turn over any stone, even an entire island. Once they were married, she would persuade him to put these resources to use finding his brother-in-law. Archie was only her wool, not her velvet, but he was still the finest merino variety.

Feeling lighter than she had in days, Georgie virtually skipped back to her hotel and up the stairs to her room. When she reached the second floor hallway she paused. She spied two Filipinos hovering by a guest room door. They were each dressed in loose peasant pantaloons, not stiff white hotel uniforms—a suspicious detail that she would not have noticed before her laundry debacle. She stayed hidden behind the giant fern at the bend in the hall, expecting the men to pull out a lock pick, a crowbar, or some other instrument of vice.

Instead, the two men covered each of their feet and hands with a small burlap bag, tugging tight at the drawstrings around their wrists and ankles. They eased down to all fours, like puppies still unable to keep their balance on oversized paws. Then they pushed off their hindquarters, sliding from one end of the passageway to the other, smiling and laughing as they shimmied. Georgie noticed a reddish layer of wax on the floor and the faint smell of kerosene. Each pass with the rags buffed a little more of the substance off the hardwood floor, leaving behind a beautiful dark shine.

Occasionally, the men bumped into each other—a game, Georgie realized. The smaller man changed his position, turning face up and walking like a crab. It gave his kicks just enough accuracy to sweep his compatriot off his feet. The bigger man lost his purchase on the smooth floor and fell on his face.

It looked fun. Georgie remembered wrestling with Benji in the tiny sitting room that their mother reserved for fancy company. Since they never had any fancy company, it was the least used and least cluttered room of the house and therefore the obvious choice as the siblings' secret place of Bedlam when no one else was home. To this day, only she and Benji knew about the hopscotch squares they had drawn beneath the big sofa. The memory of the childhood joy was fresh enough to make Georgie laugh out loud.

Surprised at the laughter, both men scrambled to their feet—not an easy or graceful maneuver when wearing burlap socks. After several tumbles they stood, dipping their heads in shame at being caught in their fun by a guest of the hotel, and a woman no less.

"Ma'am," the larger one said, dipping his head, as demure as a girl at her first cotillion. Georgie felt guilty for suspecting the worst of the two men. Men? They were hardly more than boys.

She reached out to one and pantomimed a request for the burlap gloves. He submissively slipped his off and gave them to her. Georgie pulled off her shoes and tied the sacks to her feet. When the laborers realized what she was doing, they protested in their language, but she returned the bogus look of ignorance she had received so many times this past week.

She cautiously moved one foot forward. It slipped easily but had enough traction for her to stay upright. She pulled the other foot in behind her, making sure to keep her balance high and over her hips. She skated all the way down the hall. Her mother would not approve. She kept skating anyway.

The boys hooted and cackled like children, and she joined in. She knew that they should not be making so much noise, but the joy of youth was intoxicating, whether it be in Manila or Lower Roxbury. No nearer to finding Benji, she felt as close to him as she had been in years.

She must have covered every board a dozen times. In fact, she was enjoying herself so much that she did not notice when her new friends grew silent. She turned to take a long lunge down the esplanade and ran straight into the chest of a tall white man in a well-pressed shirt. He grabbed Georgie's arm to keep her from falling backwards down the steps. "Be careful, Miss—"

"Potter," she supplied between heavy breaths.

The man released her, letting her move safely away from the stairs. "I'm Mr. North, the manager. I can see that you have been enjoying your stay."

Georgie nodded, too embarrassed to speak.

"Good, good. I was wondering if I could, uh, borrow back my employees so that they may finish their work before the rest of our guests awake from siesta."

"Oh…yes…certainly," she sputtered. "Of course."

Georgie forced herself to straighten up then, determined to act like the schoolteacher that she was now, not the naughty child she had once been. It worked a little, at least until her foot slipped out from under her, sending her tumbling again.

Georgie reached out to the closest solid object to break her fall—the large fern plant. She pulled the rim of the pot down to the floor with her, cracking it and spilling soil all over the clean, freshly polished wood. The plant covered her in a mess of vibrant green foliage.

Georgie was surprised by North's reaction—a booming laugh that echoed all the way down the hall. Had he wanted to wake the whole hotel, he could not have found a better way. Georgie teetered between shame and outrage but was not about to show either. "Mr. North, I would appreciate a little more decorum," she said in her best schoolmarm voice. Of course, she commanded little authority from under her leafy camouflage on the floor.

The manager raised his eyebrows and kept laughing. "Decorous is not exactly the best description of your position," he said. The man was kind enough to pull the fern off of her and help her to her feet, though with the burlap socks it took two tries. Georgie brushed the dirt off her skirt while the hotel employees busied themselves anchoring the plant to its proper upright position.

"If you don't mind, Miss Potter, but the fabric on your feet—"

"Oh, yes, I'm sorry!" She had to raise her skirt up to her knees to untie the sacks and take them off. She handed Mr. North the burlap, picked up her belongings, and walked to room 22, trying to infuse as much dignity into her gait as possible. The men behind her were quietly respectful—at least until she closed her door.

Georgie lay down on the bed and sank her face into the dense cotton pillow, trying to ignore the guffaws outside. She could not afford to get into any more trouble once she became Mrs. Archibald Blaxton. It was time to grow up.

CHAPTER TWELVE

Homecoming

Javier was not worried when no one was waiting on shore in Dumaguete to greet him. He preferred to come and go unannounced, and sometimes liked to surprise his employees with his unpredictability. Rarely did he catch anyone misbehaving, but he thought it a good deterrent. The best management practice, though, was simply to stick around—and yet, knowing that, he had lingered in Manila for days after his business had been completed.

He normally disliked Manila. It was crowded, disease-ridden, and expensive—and those were not its worst points. It was also full of pompous clergymen, tyrannical administrators, and their panting Filipino retainers. In the past Javier had always been anxious to leave, taking the first available steamer out. This time he had taken the seventh. He felt like a fool each time he had traded in his ticket for a later departure, just as he felt like a fool each day he had arrived at the Hotel de Oriente to find his letter of apology unopened. It sat there in Georgina's box, taunting him.

Had he imagined the attraction between them? After all, it had been a long time since Javier had dabbled at romance. His last liaison had been with a rich widow in Paris who had indulged his youthful carnality whenever the mood suited her. As a patroness of starving artists—some talented, most not—her choice of a dark, serious man from Asia as her next lover had been unexceptional. Their affair had not yet settled into the sated, comfortable phase when he was summoned home. Maybe if he had taken another woman to his bed since then he would not feel so off balance now.

He tried to pinpoint what it was about the Potter woman that intrigued him. She had the same confidence he found alluring in European women, but hers came with a fierce, unapologetic streak that he thought must be authentically American.

Javier berated himself for his misplaced priorities and promised to refocus his attention on practical matters, like finance and agronomy. This past week had been a good start. He spent it in Cebu, working with a broker to hire enough migrant laborers to get the season started. When the contracts were finally drawn up, Javier caught the next steamer home to Negros.

After the porters unloaded his luggage onto the beach, Javier hired a *calesa*. He offered more than the normal Bais fare, directing the driver to first drop him off at the hacienda's southeastern boundary before continuing on to deliver his bags to the house. Javier cut through his fields on foot. There was no better way to find out how work had progressed in his absence than to view the land for himself at ground level.

Many hours later, when he finished his journey down the brick drive, he finally started to relax. Coming home always had that effect on him. Though he had been packed away for boarding school when he hit puberty, and though he had stayed away for most of the next sixteen years, nothing could break the connection he felt to the hacienda. Some men might resent not having a choice of occupation, but Javier had never considered any other life than this. His biggest worry, in fact, had been that his father would judge him unfit and give the land away to some bastard begotten off a mistress in Cebu or Iloilo. All of his father's by-blows were well vested, no doubt, but the don had left the hacienda to Javier alone. That meant something.

Javier was obsessed with the land and the sugar it spawned. Sugar was such a greedy crop, drinking the lifeblood of the soil like the *aswang* demons that peasants feared. It was a constant challenge to heal the earth after harvest, and Javier had tried all the local methods, including carabao manure, copra cake, bagasse ash, and even bat guano. The best results came when he alternated the sugar with mung beans, but that was done at great cost, since legumes were not a lucrative crop. The American answer was commercial fertilizers, and some of his competitors had begun dousing their soil with ammoniated super-phosphates. Given the expense, though, Javier thought it just another way the big *Yanki* import houses were enfettering the local farmer. Even if the fertilizers were truly chemical miracles, Javier could not afford them.

As he walked up the drive, the *hacendero* looked at his house and silently promised not to do anything to endanger it. He ducked through the pedestrian *postigo* cut into the arched wooden *puerta mayor* and stepped into his home's main entryway. The stone base of the house served as a storeroom for everything that made the hacienda hum: carriages, rice, tools, chickens, and—of course—sugar. In the middle of this above-ground cellar, on a wooden platform just high enough to avoid flooding during the rainy season, sat Javier's overseer, Geno Canda, hard at work at his desk.

Geno looked up at Javier and did not hide the relief on his face. "I'm glad I didn't pay for a dead man's bags," he said, nodding toward the delivered luggage.

Javier wiped the sweat off his forehead and neck with a handkerchief. It had been a hot walk. "I'm glad the driver didn't steal them."

His manager pointed out where the bags had been opened and reclosed clumsily. "I don't think he would have gotten much. Better to collect the other half of the fare."

It was a sad day when a *calesa* driver found your personal belongings unfit to fence. Javier sat down and handed over the new loan documents from his jacket pocket.

Geno looked up at him in confusion. "Another *pacto de retro*, Don Javier? Two hundred acres, that's—"

"Too much, I know, but we need the men, and they will insist on being paid an advance, as always. We have no choice."

Geno still stared at the contract. "Leaving the land fallow might be better than losing it entirely."

Javier sat back and shook his head. "Believe me, if we leave it fallow, we will definitely lose it. I can't pay my bills if I have nothing to sell."

"But trusting the Chinese? I heard the Jordanas are making friends with the Americans."

"They've seen how well the Larenas have done, so I'm not surprised." Javier thought the tactic both unpalatable and shortsighted. Getting to know a few Insular judges could forestall seizures of his land, but it would not keep his creditors at bay forever. "No, let's just grow sugar and stay out of politics."

"It's a game, señor. You just have to know how to play it."

Javier raised his eyebrows. "I've never been any good at *sipsip*."

Geno laughed. "No, we're probably better off if you don't talk to anyone outside the hacienda at all." The overseer enjoyed enough seniority that he did not worry about his boss taking offense.

Besides, Javier thought, it was true enough. "If I could send you off to the *bailes* and receptions in my stead, I'd be happy to, *amigo mío*."

The older man laughed, his wide nostrils flaring. "With all those lovely señoritas? I'm surprised you'd be willing to risk Adelita's wrath." Geno's wife was not to be underestimated; with one good, swift kick the stalwart mother of eleven could probably ensure that Javier remained childless forever. Still, despite her gruff demeanor, the woman had been a dependable ally since Javier returned home to take over, probably because having him around made his mother happy. Women on this land tended to stick together.

"And how is she?" Javier asked. Geno beamed proudly. Javier knew what that meant. "Number twelve?"

"You wouldn't understand," the overseer said, waving his hand. "You're as celibate as a priest. This is why a man takes a wife."

Javier rolled his eyes. "Don't start. You sound like my mother. Speaking of whom..."

Geno leaned back in his chair. "She's waiting for you upstairs, Don Javier. Counting the silver."

That was not a good sign. Javier had not hid the state of their finances very well if Lourdes was already preparing to sell off family heirlooms. He ascended one side of the double staircase and rounded the first landing. When he reached the foyer, two men shuffled past him with a small but heavy-looking trunk stretched between their shoulders. They respectfully dipped their heads as he passed, lowering their gaze so far that Javier worried they would miss the start of the stairs and fall down on their polite arses. The "princess" steps had been fashioned deliberately shallow to allow for the modest ascent of a young lady in her skirts. Javier had stumbled down them many times, both as a child and an adult, and he never failed to swear up a storm as he did. Sometimes he wanted to take an axe to them, and he might have done that long ago if they were not such a rich Narra wood.

Javier moved into the dining room, finding his mother at work directing a few servant girls in their folding of a gold-threaded tablecloth. He spoke before she saw him. "I see you've not hocked your bridal trousseau yet, so maybe we're not as far gone as I thought."

"Javier!" his mother exclaimed. Lourdes Romero y Fuginato de Altarejos rushed over and hugged her son enthusiastically. Even if he was a foot taller, he always felt like a little boy in her arms.

"*Hola, Mamá. ¿Cómo estás?*" When she looked up at him from this close, he worried that she would strain her neck.

"I thought maybe you'd run away on me," she said in Spanish before backing out of his embrace and dismissing the maids.

"I tried, but no one would take me. They've heard that I have made my mother so poor she's selling the used linens."

She shooed away his exaggeration with her hand. "Well, I haven't gotten down to the linens yet, but half of the silver is gone."

That was worse than he had feared. "Gone?"

His mother sat down again to organize the forks she had been counting. She was not one to stop working for very long. It was the least Iberian thing about the well-bred mestiza. "Benita ran off with that new *muchacho*, Carlos. And because he couldn't afford what her father demanded as dower, a few of our spoons went missing."

Javier rubbed his temple. Benita the washerwoman also owed them two months' worth of salary advances, and he doubted they would recover that now either. "Do you know where they went?"

"I informed the *Guardia Civil*—"

"Mamá, they're called the 'constabulary' now." The new name did sound particularly harsh when juxtaposed against the elegant lilt of Spanish.

"—but I don't expect to hear back. All the two of them have to do is flee to the mountains for a few months, and everyone will forget about them, just like Peping. I could have asked Geno to send another of the *muchachos* after them, but it seems like a shame to throw good men after bad. Besides, we wouldn't recover much, even if we found them."

Every dollar mattered, but he could see her point. It was not worth the risk. "What are you doing with the rest of the silver?" he asked.

"What can I do with it now but sell it? The Yucos will give me a decent price in town—less than Manila, of course, but sending it to Allegra would cost us the difference. It was only a few settings from my mother, hardly worth worrying about. We still have the Romero silver and the whole Altarejos collection left to you by Tiya Agustina. Your wife won't know a thing is missing."

"Mamá—"

"Of course, that's if there ever is a wife. I don't suppose Allegra introduced you to her friend María Josefina Urrutia?"

Javier had no doubt that if Allegra had meant to "accidentally" introduce him to this María Josefina, she would have managed to. More likely, his cousin had changed her mind when their paths crossed with the red-haired *maestra*. Javier wondered how long that news would take to reach his mother. He certainly had no plans to mention it.

"It must have slipped her mind," he said.

"Or you slipped from her noose?" his mother asked.

Javier smiled. "That too."

Lourdes was not amused. "It's well past time you married, *hijo mío*."

"We can't afford it," he said. He regretted the words the instant they came out of his mouth. He did not want to worry his mother any further, nor did he did want to make it seem like marriage was something that he was being unjustly denied.

"What about the money I'll make from this silver?" Lourdes asked, as concerned as he had feared.

"Use it to hire new staff for the house. I spent more than I planned in Manila and Cebu."

"Then I'll sell the Romero silver."

His mother, bless her heart, was unstoppable. Javier held up his hand. "No, please, don't sell anything more right now, okay? If I need you to auction off the pantry, I'll let you know." He had no attachment to any of these things, but it would look bad if word leaked out. "If I knew any of Papá's other assets, I could mortgage those instead."

"Javito—"

"We don't know about everything he owned in Cebu, Panay, or even Luzon. He could have left you with more."

"He thought this would be enough," she said, gesturing at the house and the land surrounding it. "It certainly paid your way through Europe."

It was the same argument he had with his mother every time. Javier had never demanded more for himself, and he had more than made up for his school expenses with the business he generated for his father in London and Paris. In fact, he had stayed in Europe because his father had asked him to. But she would not admit to his father being anything less than generous in how he had divided his estate.

"He should have seen what was coming. The market had already collapsed by the time he died. He couldn't have sat down and written a better will?"

"Don't be greedy."

He was stumped. "I don't understand you, I guess," he said, shaking his head.

"No, the person you don't understand is your father."

It was true. Javier never had. Their relationship had been one based on expectations, and—too often—disappointment. The latter judgment had gone both ways. "Mamá, I don't want you to lose the one part of him you had to yourself."

"I know what Lázaro and I shared," she said. "I'll always have that."

What could he say to that? Lourdes's faith in her husband may have been undeserved, but it had kept her going through difficult times. There was a line of small headstones in the chapel's cemetery that made it hard to fight with the woman about the importance of family.

Javier bent down and brushed a quick kiss across her forehead. "We'll make it through the season, I promise. It's got to get better."

They both knew his pledge was useless. Javier could not rally the troubled Filipino sugar industry on his own. But he made the promise, and the look he gave her warned her not to challenge it. Not today, at least.

Javier wanted to retire for a siesta before facing the work in front of him, but he had no time. He left his mother and took the shallow steps, four at a time, back down to his overseer's office. He needed Geno to review the most recent accounts to see who else had run out on their debts. Hopefully he would not need to sell the Romero silver after all.

CHAPTER THIRTEEN

S.S. *Elcano*

Georgie peered over the railing of the S.S. *Elcano*, the Compañía Marítima steamer carrying her to Dumaguete, and watched the waves bubble against the hull. She wondered which was filthier, the boat or the passengers? The previous evening she had watched her fellow travelers "clean" the serving spoon by licking it thoroughly before putting it back in the jar of guava jelly. She would dine on crackers and bananas for the remainder of the trip.

At least the rusty heap was moving. For two days they had sat quarantined in Manila Bay under the yellow cholera flag, a standard precaution to identify any ill passengers. Apparently some were sick, because the ship was remanded to Mariveles Station where it had to undergo another five-day quarantine. While the patients were taken to hospital to be treated, authorities disinfected all the remaining passengers' clothing and luggage.

As a Thomasite, Georgie was supposed to uphold and even preach Major Carter's sanitation regime, but at what cost? Her belongings now reeked of formaldehyde. Besides, she just wanted to get to Bais and get on with the business of the wedding. That was not exactly a romantic sentiment, but she had not seen Archie in over a year so it was hard to be sentimental. She even struggled to remember what he looked like. Details eluded her, like the shape of his jaw or the set of his eyes. Georgie reminded herself that he had a fine face, for it had always pleased her enough when they were together. In fact, it was precisely the anonymity of his pale blue eyes and washed-out blond hair that guaranteed the purity of his Boston Brahmin lineage, or at least that is what her friends at college had told her.

Sometimes the only thing she could recall was the sound of Archie's voice—not the best memory since his voice was rather nasally, especially when pontificating about progress, education, and empire. He was not the kind of man to whisper tender words of affection, even between the waltz and two-step at Harvard's Senior Spread. She had thought their connection severed until he began writing her letters from the Philippines, letters that made him sound like a sad little boy far from home. Evidently, he had become lonely enough to propose to this granddaughter of an Irish tailor. For a Blaxton, that was awfully lonely. Soon after, he had sent for her, much like he might have ordered a gramophone from Sears and Roebuck, and—poof!—within a few months she was in Manila. In his correspondence, Archie had made no small point of how fortunate she was to receive her position, given her "limited qualifications." Whether he had been speaking of her credentials as a teacher or as his wife, she did not know. Probably both.

She could not blame him for his skepticism. Her people, the O'Sheas, had raised themselves up to respectability only in the last few generations, and their shop still skirted the edge of the working class slums. Georgie grew up above a neat storefront that read: "D. P. Shay & Sons: Breeches makers, ladies' costume & habit makers." The Anglicized name had not fooled anyone, but it made it easier for the suburbanites south of Dudley Street to venture inside.

Of course, Archie had never been down to see her home. He probably had not seen much of Boston outside of Beacon Hill or Cambridge. Even that was a bit too broadening for his mother, Elspeth Blaxton, who felt that Harvard was becoming too plebeian under its president, Mr. Eliot. She blamed Archie's professors—"Socialists, all of them"—for the disappointing turn in her son's career. As if to illustrate the point, Archie had turned down an offer to teach at Mr. Peabody's school in Groton and instead applied with the Army—"the Army of all things!"—to traverse the undoubtedly-misnamed Pacific Ocean in order to teach English to a bunch of "brown heathens."

"Mummy, they're not heathens," Archie had protested at the one luncheon to which Georgie had been invited. "Almost all Filipinos are Christian."

"Papists," Elspeth replied, grimacing as if she tasted something rancid.

Georgie, a grateful recipient of a scholarship from the Boston Academy of the Sacred Heart, shifted in her seat and said nothing.

Archie patted her hand under the table and smiled, sure that she was just as amused as he with their subterfuge. Mrs. Blaxton didn't know of Georgie's Irish roots, only that she was pursuing her degree at Wellesley, a college that good Catholic girls were known to avoid. Even this pedigree did not endear her much to Elspeth, though, since the matron thought it "rather middle-class" to concern oneself with an "unnecessary" academic distinction like a degree, especially in something as "occupational" as teaching: "A lady's education should emphasize the arts, and it should never get in the way of one's dancing, music, or charitable works."

Georgie remembered that rebuke well. And if one's own family was a charitable work? That did not bear consideration.

At the time, of course, Georgie simply agreed with all that her hostess said. All outward politeness, she lowered her eyes to examine the intricate grapevine design on the Tiffany silverware. Her inner Robin Hood was calculating how many Haskins Street tenement families she could feed on the proceeds of one stolen spoon when Archie touched the tip of his finger to Georgie's salad fork, assuming that her attention to the silver meant she was unsure of which utensil to use. Oh, how she had wanted to throw that fork, with its beautiful raspberry motif and poppy-shaped tines, right at him. Her teachers, the sisters of the Society of the Sacred Heart, had regularly hosted foreign monarchs, distinguished ambassadors, and Papal legates—all in the midst of their instruction on Virgil, Homer, plane geometry, and chemistry. Georgie may have had a hard time paying the tuition, but her etiquette was as good as anyone's.

She was so composed, in fact, that she did not react when Mrs. Blaxton called the serving girl a "silly little bridget" in front of the whole lunch party. Georgie's Irish grandmother had actually been a Bridget, both in true name and domestic occupation, but pointing that out would only have prompted Elspeth to count the silver. This little bridget knew how to hold her tongue. Georgie was still proud of her restraint a year and a half later. Now she stood on the deck of the foul *Elcano*, smiling like a fool, because the one thing she already loved about the Philippines was that it was thousands of miles away from her future mother-in-law.

The *Elcano* neared the shoreline of Dumaguete, where a few buildings—barely even a town—sat at the foot of an imposing mountain. Georgie focused on the beach where people had gathered to meet the steamer. Would Archie show up? Or would he leave a note as he had done in Manila? Georgie scanned the crowd once, found nothing, and then brought her eyes back around for another pass.

She noticed an old man with a cane pushing away from his companion to get a better look over the heads of the crowd. When Georgie realized how tall he was—and that his hair was not white, but pale blond—she knew it was Archie. She had been hoping for a spiritual recognition, something that felt right in her core as she caught his eye. She must have momentarily forgotten that she did not believe in such nonsense.

The surf kicked up, preventing the crew from loading passengers onto the *bancas* that would ferry them to dry land. The *Elcano* danced back and forth in the tide, too far away from Archie to talk to him but too close to avoid staring. She had so many questions that she did not know where to start. Why the cane? He was definitely thinner—too thin for a former Harvard oarsman. In fairness, she probably appeared a little disheveled herself. She used her sleeve to wipe away the perspiration on her chin, an unladylike gesture that had already become habit.

The sea finally calmed enough to allow loading of the *bancas*, and the Filipino passengers cleared a path for her to reach the steps first. It was odd how naturally it happened: their deferral and her acceptance. The most dangerous part of colonialism was just how easy it was to get used to. Her small boat fought against the waves, dragging out the otherwise short ride. When it reached the beach, two boys splashed out and pulled the whole thing high onto the sand.

Archie stood at the farthest edge of the crowd, far enough away that Georgie had to hike through the thick sand to meet him. She was surprised to find that he was not alone. A petite Filipina stood protectively at his side, and for a split second Georgie wondered if the woman had been hired by Elspeth Blaxton to protect her precious son against fortune-hunting Irish bridgets. Then another possibility crossed Georgie's mind, one that she liked even less: what if Georgie were not the only fortune hunter interested in Archibald Blaxton? Even after only three weeks in this country, she had heard all about the local women. They were generally both beautiful and poor—a provocative pairing for most American men, whether buck privates or commissioners.

Archie spoke first. "I can't believe you're finally here." He leaned down to kiss his fiancée, but the Filipina's ruthless grip on his forearm prevented him from doing anything more than grazing Georgie's cheek.

"You're so thin," she said, unable to stop herself. He was pale, too, as if he had spent the last year in the Antarctic.

"Oh, Georgie, I'm fine," Archie said with a genuine smile. "Getting better, right, Rosa?"

The slight, pretty woman beamed. She had long hair, the top puffed out like a dark crown over her sweet, round face. She had delicate features with a pouty bottom lip and tiny chin. She was attractive, no doubt about that, but it was the devotion in her eyes that posed the biggest threat.

"This is Rosa Ramos, my nurse," Archie said.

Rosa did not speak, but she offered her hand, obviously familiar with American customs. Her thin fingers felt firm yet fragile in Georgie's large grip.

"Nurse?"

Archie nodded. "I had some sort of ague, probably malaria. I'm sure it was that stop in Cebu where I caught it, but I've recovered swiftly with Rosa's help. I'm sorry that I didn't tell you about it sooner, but I couldn't exactly rush off in the middle of her regimen."

"Wha—"

"Rest, saltwater, and brandy," Archie said, anticipating her question. "The island remedy."

"Well, that mix could either cure you or kill you," Georgie said.

"I think the brandy is the most important part, but don't tell the Stinnetts."

"Who?" she asked, feeling like she was still at sea. Maybe it was her head that was spinning.

"An American couple in town. You'll see. They're putting you up for a few days before we head out to Bais. Nice people, if a little narrow. When I first got sick, Daniel and Mary convinced me to stay here. Better care and all that. They even hired Rosa to look after me."

"I'm thankful to them," Georgie managed to say. "Have you seen an actual doctor, though? I mean, are you sure it's just a fever? It's not...cholera, is it?"

"Georgie!" Archie backed away, alarmed. He looked around before announcing: "We don't have cholera here in Dumaguete."

Anyone who read the papers knew otherwise. "But—"

"Well, maybe up in Bacolod, sure, but not on our half of Negros," he insisted.

"But—"

"Believe me, I'd know. A few pals and I got work as cholera policemen during the June vacation." He shook his head at the memory. "God, that was a miserable month. I must have stood in the doorway of two hundred contaminated houses, and if I didn't get sick then, I'm hardly going to now."

He was sick, though—was that too obvious to point out?

Frustrated, Georgie changed the subject. "Well, I'm glad you're here to greet me. I'm afraid I don't have the slightest clue how to get to Bais."

"I couldn't let you arrive alone," he said earnestly, despite having done exactly that last month in Manila. "And I'm feeling much better, ready to get started. With Rosa's assistance, we should be able to open our school next month."

"She's coming to Bais?"

Archie nodded a little too enthusiastically. "She's from there, lucky for us. We'll need all the help we can get. You're going to find that the best thing about these islands is the people. They're so quick to take direction."

Was that a compliment, Georgie wondered? She smiled at Rosa, pretending it was, just to salvage some manners.

Pleased, Archie kept on. "And through Rosa, I've rented us an empty shop that we can convert into a couple of classrooms. Of course, who knows what shape it's in now."

"What about the old Spanish school?" Even if the former masters had given up easily on their education "expedition," as Don Javier had called it, there was bound to be some infrastructure left.

Her fiancé dismissed the suggestion immediately. "Most of them were run by the Church, which we can't depend on for obvious reasons."

Yes, obvious reasons, Georgie thought: like the fact that the Church would never let them inside the door. She had heard that priests were warning parishioners away from the American schools, which they believed were really Protestant missions in disguise.

"How far away is Bais from here?" All Georgie wanted right now was to lie down on a bed that did not smell of mildew and urine. She would not miss the *Elcano*.

"About twenty-five miles north," he said. "It's a much smaller town, so don't expect much."

Of course not. She was learning to lower her expectations daily. She wiped her hand across her eyes, not sure if she was exhausted from the trip behind her or from thinking about what lay ahead.

Archie was quick to pick up on her body language. "We'll let you get some rest, don't worry. Daniel and Mary can't wait to meet you, and it'll be nice to eat recognizable food before we head out into the *bundoks*."

"Boondocks?"

"Mountains. The hinterlands."

"Okay," Georgie said, trying to be optimistic. "It sounds lovely."

And yet Archie hesitated. He had something else to say, it seemed, but needed to work up the nerve. If Georgie had been any less tired, she would have encouraged him on with a kind word. Right now, though, she let him struggle.

"I...I hope you don't mind if, well, I was thinking that we might want to, ah, postpone the wedding a bit, you know, just until I regain my strength?"

She managed to feel relieved and rejected at the same time. "If that's what you want. I suppose there's plenty of time."

Archie hurried to reassure her. "I just want to be feeling my best. You understand, right?"

She did. The problem was that Rosa looked ebullient, and this fact—more than the postponement itself—unsettled Georgie. The Filipina also seemed to understand more English than she let on.

"Come on," Archie coaxed. "I'm sure you want to freshen up. Let's go." He leaned heavily on his cane as he started up the beach, each step a slog. Rosa followed him but kept a step behind, her head down.

Georgie did not move. She turned to the sea and tried to imagine Boston over that eastern horizon. Her old life seemed so far away, and her new one felt like it was still in quarantine.

CHAPTER FOURTEEN

Colonial Society

Georgie worried that her baggage might not make the half-mile trip up the beach. Her trunk had been thrown on top of a bulging pile of feed sacks, crates, wooden chairs, and other what not, all of which was tied down to a pitiful cart with three measly ropes. Fortunately, the carabao pulling the cart plodded along too slowly to knock loose any of the cargo. Not even the whip of the young rider could entice the beast to move any faster. She envied the animal its dispassion.

Georgie followed behind the motley group. She entertained herself by studying Rosa's footprints. The woman's pinky toe jutted out perpendicularly, clawing deep into the sand. It was a wonder that small feet like hers could make such huge prints—probably a product of life unbound by shoes. The woman did not slow for either hot sand or jagged rocks. In fact, her soles looked so calloused that she could have stepped right into a cow chip and not noticed.

Fifteen minutes later, they all arrived at a large house facing the shore. Out front, two boys in white uniforms kneeled in the dirt, pulling half-heartedly at some weeds. One of them, a skinny child with wavy hair parted stylishly off-center, called out: "*Halo*, Maestro!"

Archie raised his cane only a few inches in the air, but the eager boy read this as hearty greeting and scrambled for the front door. He hesitated briefly there, torn between the excitement of announcing new visitors and the need to clean off his clothes. Manners won out, and he spared a moment to furiously brush off his knees before dashing inside.

Rosa led them to the same door but then stepped aside to let the Americans enter alone. In contrast to their ease on the beach, Archie and his nurse parted like strangers.

Georgie followed her fiancé into the welcoming chaos of the house. Singing gave way to a clatter of young voices ricocheting off stone walls. They followed the noise to a makeshift classroom, where a middle-aged man led a confused chorus of Filipino boys and American matrons.

"Good afternoon, everyone," Archie called out above the fray. He motioned Georgie inside the room, where there were about a dozen or so boys all dressed like the gardener, save the dusty knees. The boys stared open-mouthed at Georgie. She was probably the first person they had ever seen with red hair.

Archie began the introductions. "Georgina, this is Daniel Stinnett, president of the Brinsmade Institute."

Stinnett wore the "uniform" of the American male in the Philippines, a white suit in sturdy cotton duck. Archie wore the same, but his jacket and pants fit badly due to the weight he had lost. Stinnett's was tailored better, but he, too, looked rather thin. Most everything else about the man was unremarkable. He had medium brown hair, longer on the top than the sides and parted neatly in the center. In addition to his thin, wire-rimmed spectacles, he wore a look so serious that it aged him ten years.

Georgie smiled and shook the man's cold hand. It was a strange thing to notice—but, really, who was cold in the Philippines?

"It's a pleasure to have you here," he said. "Archibald has told us so much about you. This is my wife, Mary."

He motioned to the much younger woman at his side. Mary was not nearly as tall as Daniel, but she seemed larger. She was not fat, just frontier solid. Her dark brown hair was pulled back into an improvised bun, but the many tight curls at the front fought against confinement. Mary had a round face with a pert nose, all instantly likable. As she gave Georgie a genuine Midwestern hug, the two older women standing behind her tut-tutted their disapproval at such familiarity. One even harrumphed.

"Oh, where are my manners?" Mary apologized, pulling away from Georgie just as quickly as she had approached. She kept her hands in front of her, wringing them tightly as she introduced the old maids as the McAffry sisters. "And this is Georgina Potter—soon to be Georgina Blaxton. Isn't that wonderful?"

The sisters pursed their lips so tightly that their mouths actually turned white. Apparently, they did not think Georgie's marriage was all that wonderful. She wondered if they objected to the individuals involved or to the institution itself.

"The McAffries are esteemed Presbyterian missionaries," Mary explained. The two women certainly personified every dour preconception of that occupation, Georgie thought. Neither sister spoke, leaving Mary to do all the welcoming while they judged her at the task, as they no doubt judged her at everything. Daniel reached over and stilled his wife's twisting hands.

Eventually Mary spoke again, her spirit a little more subdued. "You must be exhausted from the trip, Miss Potter. Let me show you upstairs and help you get settled." Georgie nodded and eagerly followed Mrs. Stinnett out of the room, liberated from the close quarters inspection.

"Will you join us for our service at four?" Mary asked as they walked. "Daniel will be delivering the sermon."

Georgie had almost forgotten this was Sunday, though it did explain the choir practice. Archie had likely hidden her Catholic past from his Protestant missionary friends, so she could not think of an excuse not attend. "Yes, that would be nice," she lied.

"Oh good," Mary exclaimed. "It's always nice to have another soprano in the choir."

She had to sing now? How quickly could she develop a convincing case of laryngitis?

Mary led her upstairs, past the students' quarters and into a tiny room squeezed tight with three beds. Georgie looked at the one designated for her, right in between the McAffry sisters. The injustice was frustrating: the Guardians of Good Christian Chastity would mind her every move while Archie was free to return to his private house with his beautiful Filipina nurse. But then Georgie reminded herself that just because Rosa was smitten did not mean that Archie thought of the woman as anything more than a servant. If there was anything she could count on, it was Blaxton prejudice.

When Mary left, Georgie sat blissfully alone on the rattan bed. She did not plan to sleep, just change clothes and wash her face. The combination of wind, salt water, and sand had left her skin feeling like cracked paint. She made the mistake of lying down after her toilette, though, and the next thing she knew one of the McAffries was shaking her awake—which one did not matter since the women's frowns were identical. It was going to be a long evening with the good pilgrims of Dumaguete. On the upside, she had slept through the Sunday service.

Georgie joined the group outside as they ambled along the promenade lined with newly-planted trees, a little Luneta of their own in the Visayas. There was even a Filipino band, a rough brass quartet playing their hearts out. Archie set the pace with his cane but no one seemed in a hurry. Without the horses, men, and buildings to hem them in, the afternoon sun did not seem nearly as oppressive as it had in Manila. She thought she might adjust to provincial life rather well.

Daniel called her over to show her the pride of Dumaguete, the old brick belfry next to the Catholic church. "It's the oldest in the province," he bragged. "They built it so they could sound an alarm in case of pirate attacks."

"Pirates? Really?" Life had become a strange mixture of *Robinson Crusoe* and *Alice in Wonderland*.

"More like slavers, I guess."

"That's reassuring," she said with a laugh. Daniel looked at her oddly, like he had never heard sarcasm before. "I mean, tell me about them," Georgie corrected herself.

"Well, before the local population grew big enough to defend itself, tribes from the southern islands would come here to steal laborers for their fields. The name of this town, in fact, comes from the marauders who would swoop down upon the island and *dagit*, or snatch up, the people."

"I hope those days are over," she said. She would rather be a wage slave in a Massachusetts textile mill than a real slave to a Moro pirate.

The missionary continued his lecture on the history of the islands, from the Muslim rajas to the Spanish conquistadors. "The only good thing about the Catholics," he concluded, "is that they are still slaughtering the Mohammedeans down south."

Georgie was not sure whom he discredited the most with such remarks: Muslims, Catholics, or himself. But she nodded and smiled, slowly steering herself away from the men's conversation. Unfortunately, that left her with one of the McAffries—Georgie still could not tell which—and the old woman spent the whole walk ranting about a former Tennessee volunteer who had dared to open a saloon in town. It was filled with soldiers at all hours, she said, and on payday it could take in as much as four hundred Mexican dollars in a night. The Tennessee veteran sounded like a savvy businessman, but the teetotaler missionary was quick to attribute his luck to the darker arts. Georgie thought the natives of Dumaguete were getting a surprisingly representative sampling of America from these two extremes: wet soldiers and dry church ladies.

Later that evening at dinner, the cook erred by boasting that her brother had killed the centerpiece turkey by pouring brandy down its throat. Death-by-applejack sounded pretty good to Georgie, but the Stinnetts and McAffries gasped in shock. One of the spinsters was so upset that she almost left the table, but Daniel cajoled her to stay and defended his wife's reputation as a respectable Presbyterian home-maker. Mary herself looked like she wanted to sink into the floor-boards.

Daniel ordered the bird removed and thrown away, a decision that Georgie's stomach protested audibly. Nine days on a steamer had left her hungry enough to eat a flock of turkeys, pickled or not. More-over, the loss of the poultry left only one piece of milkfish on the table for the meat course. While it was mouth-wateringly garnished with silver onions and bits of ginger root, Georgie's polite-sized portion was not filling. Instead she had to stuff her stomach with a heaping portion of overly firm potatoes. She envied the cook who had most likely sent the turkey home to her own family, all the while marveling at the crazy Yankees she worked for.

"How are your relations with the townspeople?" Georgie asked.

"At first, they weren't so good," Mary admitted. "The Catholics tried to prevent boys from enrolling, and one friar even threatened to excommunicate all our students. We thought things would get better when they gave Santa Catalina over to a Filipino, but—"

"I don't know who's worse," Daniel interjected, "Spanish friars or Filipino padres. Father Gallofin had the audacity to come talk to me about my putting our troublemakers on the *bingcong* squad, as if mak-ing boys clean the yard is cruel. When I think of the crimes of that priest's predecessors..."

"There's nothing wrong with a little wholesome labor," Georgie chimed in, happy to agree with her hosts on at least that point. "It's not like you whipped them."

Once she said it, she regretted her presumption. Just because the Bureau of Education did not believe in corporal punishment didn't mean all other Americans agreed. Archie, the one person at the table who should have been supportive, shook his head at her.

Mary took pity, though, and tried to make light of it. "Well, not whip, of course. And Daniel is the worst at discipline, really. He usually feels so bad afterward that he treats the boys to a limeade. He's like a father to them, honestly." Georgie had experience with a father like that, but she kept her mouth shut.

"So, you're starting a public school in Bais?" asked the McAffry to her right.

"Yes, we are," Georgie said, happy to change the subject.

The old woman scowled. "I wouldn't get near those mountains if I were you. You know what's happening up there, don't you?" Georgie was afraid to ask, but the spinster needed no prodding. "Witchcraft," she whispered. "I've even heard of human sacrifice under Papa Isio—"

Daniel cut in, annoyed. "Please don't worry, Miss Potter. Pope Isio is far to the north, almost to Bacolod. Besides, the Larenas insist everything's under control."

"Who are the Larenas?" Georgie asked.

"They're the first family of Negros," Daniel said smugly. "One brother is the mayor here in Dumaguete and the other is governor of the whole province. They're far more enlightened than most of the natives, drawing people out of the cockpits and friars' pews and into the twentieth century."

"Without their support, I just don't know what we would have done," Mary added. "You do have to be careful, especially in Bais, because some of the *hacenderos* only pay lip service to American authority."

Georgie drew her finger through the condensation on her chilled glass of ginger ale, a special treat made possible by the ice delivery on the *Elcano*. She held her tongue for at least another five count before saying, as casually as possible, "While I was in Manila, I met someone from Bais. His name was Altarejos."

"Don Javier?" Daniel asked.

"And his cousin, Allegra," she said quickly, sensing Archie's eyes on her. "Are they big landowners?"

Daniel nodded. "Some of the biggest. About a quarter of the economy of Bais is dependent on his sugar in some way or another."

A McAffry chimed in. "His sugar? Ha!"

"Now, now," Mary said, "That's not polite."

The missionary continued anyway, ignoring her host. Truth be told, it was difficult to figure out who was in charge in this house.

"I'll not be silenced on a matter of conscience. Those peasants work like slaves to harvest the sugar for Don Javier, just so he can hold their salary as 'repayment' of some trivial debt. The *hacenderos* prefer that, you know. They like hiring the men who drink and gamble, the men who have more wants than the moral and sober native, and who must work more days in the year in order to satisfy their desires. The poor sinners drink themselves into an early grave, but no doubt Don Javier looks forward to that, too, because every funeral expense means a drawer full of new chits to control the next generation. If anyone tries to run off, he is captured and returned—or left to die in the mountains."

Mary looked conflicted. "That's the system here. Even the Larenas have a hacienda."

The McAffry woman was not convinced. "How can you compare Governor Larena and his support for our blessed mission to that Altarejos woman? The doña practically lives in that chapel of hers. Every coin unjustly earned goes right in the padre's collection basket. What chance do we have of bringing these planters along if all their sweat and toil ends up in the coffers of the Vatican?"

"And the *hacenderos* are surprised when their evil deeds are returned upon them," the other McAffry added. "Like that man up in Escalante."

"Please," Daniel said, giving a sharp look around the table. "Let's not worry Miss Potter with gossip."

"You know it's true. Miguel Pastor was murdered by his own men! They blamed it on the cholera, but no one believes that. No matter how sudden or tragic his illness, a planter isn't buried in only his undershirt and socks."

"Enough!" Daniel was losing control of the dinner and he did not like it. Georgie wondered how many nights he had endured the sisters' company in the name of Presbyterian solidarity. Did they always try to scare the guests half to death?

And Georgie did fear for Don Javier's safety—and her own—in Bais. "Were the murderers ever caught?" she asked.

"Yes, don't worry," Daniel said, eager to put the matter to bed. "The judge will see that justice is done. He's a capable sort—an Illinois man."

"Things are changing," Mary said with false cheer. "And isn't that why we're all here? I for one would rather minister where I'm needed."

Georgie looked over at her frowning fiancé and wondered what he was thinking. The esteemed Archibald Blaxton was a Harvard man, for pity's sake: he liked his privilege and he liked his drink. She doubted he was wasting a second thought on the *hacenderos'* labor practices. Had the Blaxtons been born on Negros, she was sure they would be running the place like their own Congo Free State. Archie was more like Javier Altarejos than he was like Daniel Stinnett—but was that a recommendation or a warning? And could Javier really be the feudal tyrant the McAffries portrayed? At times he had been stiff, formal, even a bit abrasive; but she thought him better than a debt slaver. On what basis she pinned that ridiculously naive hope, she did not know. Maybe she just didn't want him to be killed in his pajamas and socks.

Archie caught her gaze, and though he had no way to peek into her head and see the direction of her thoughts, Georgie tried to put Javier out of her mind. Archie had a way of looking at her like she was beneath his regard, and she did not need to make things worse. Truthfully, what she really wanted to do was grab her fiancé by his prominent ears or his slightly bulbous nose and shake the disdain off his face.

None of this was the fresh start she had hoped for. Georgie was beginning to think that no one who married was happy. Maybe the McAffry sisters had it right. They could say whatever they wanted, without a care for whom they insulted. So what if neither had ever been kissed? Neither had Georgie. Maybe physical love was not necessary for happiness. Copulation was likely to be messy and embarrassing, anyway. She could stick to self-pleasure—a sin for sure, but not one that would rot her mind and soul, as the nuns at school had always threatened. And if she went to hell…well, then, she would go alone. Right now it sounded better than keeping company with these old stodgers for two years. It was going to be a long posting.

CHAPTER FIFTEEN

The Shooting

Javier watched the slashers at work on the far edge of his fields. They battled the heat and humidity as much as they did the ten-foot cane stalks. Javier forced his workers to take frequent breaks, not because he was a softhearted employer but so that he would not lose anyone to heat stroke. He barely had enough hands to get by as it was. Another couple of rogues had taken their advances and run, which—while expected in this business—could not continue. He needed to show his men that he was home and paying attention.

His thoughts were interrupted by a shout from behind. "Don Javier!"

Padre Andrés Gabiana drew closer so that he could address the *hacendero* more familiarly. "Javito, come quickly! The Tallo boy's been shot."

Though Javier did not know all his workers personally, Ramram Tallo had distinguished himself as a promising young cane slasher. He could not have been more than fifteen years old.

Nico, Javier's horse, felt the *hacendero*'s agitation at the news and stamped his front hoof. Javier placed his hand soothingly on the top of the stallion's muscular shoulder and tried to keep his voice calm. "Are the ladrones back?"

Andrés shook his head. "Apparently it was an accident—"

"How could it be an accident if there aren't supposed to be any guns on my property?" Except his own, of course.

The priest shifted uncomfortably, signaling more bad news. He held his hand over his eyes to shield them from the sun as he looked up to Javier's high perch. "Peping is back."

Hay sus, Javier thought, that was all he needed. José "Peping" Ramos had been enough trouble while still a paid member of the hacienda workforce; there was no telling what kind of trouble he could stir as an aimless drifter. "Who the hell let that man back on my land?"

Andrés looked sharply at the sugar baron, as if to remind his halfbrother that he was not a field hand and did not take orders. But Javier—as head of the Altarejos family and the man who had conferred the benefice of San Honorato de Amiens on Andrés in the first place—already knew this.

"Don't be so sure you know everything that goes on here," the priest warned.

"You think a padre does?"

Andrés shook his head slowly. "This time, no. Honestly, had I known a scourge like Peping was back, I would have told you right away."

Peping had once almost started a civil war on the hacienda. He had believed that his long history with Lázaro, the elder *hacendero*, meant that he had the right to ignore the new safety rules adopted by Lázaro's son, Javier. As a crew leader, Peping had instructed several dozen migrant workers to follow his example, costing them their jobs. By the time Javier had found out who was responsible for the mutiny, Peping's byzantine machinations had already sparked fights between the resident sharecroppers and the seasonal migrants—incompatible communities at the best of times—forcing Javier to call in the constabulary to keep the peace. The ultimate resolution was to "escort" Peping off the property and rehire some of the migrants, but Andrés had had to work hard to calm both factions before anyone returned to the fields. The priest had used his chapel more that month for political persuasion than religious salvation.

Javier knew that his brother would not willingly shelter Peping, no matter what the Gospel of Luke said about forgiveness, but that did not mean the scoundrel would not return on his own. Peping's family had chosen to remain on the hacienda without him: his wife Vicenta Ramos still worked as a maid in Javier's house, and his daughter Rosa helped in the kitchen when she was not needed at the mission hospital in Dumaguete. These women had patiently endured in the shadow of Peping's scandal for months, and now the wounds would be opened all over again because the deuced idiot was back for aid and comfort.

"I need to go find out what happened," Javier told Andrés. "Come with me, eh? The Tallo family will be glad to have you there when I ask them questions."

"Because everyone is afraid of you."

"*Sí.*" As it should be, he thought. He reached down and helped the padre onto Nico's back, and they rode together through the northeastern field.

"Javito, don't make the situation worse by putting the parents through an inquisition," Andrés said.

"Someone around here disobeyed my explicit instructions." The *hacendero* did not bother to turn his head or moderate his voice. "If the Tallos invited Peping back, then they've only got themselves to blame."

Andrés sighed. "That's a little harsh, especially since we don't know if Ramram will survive. How about offering some comfort?"

"Like 'leaving it in God's hands'?"

"That could be appropriate, yes."

"This is not God's hacienda, *hermano*, nor is it yours."

Even from behind, Javier could imagine Andrés's face darkening. "Believe me," the priest said, "I'm reminded of that every day."

Javier sighed, angry at himself more than at Andrés. Neither of them could change the past, so why did he bring it up? "I just meant that it's my call," he explained by way of an apology. "I'll let you take the lead, but if you start rambling on about 'God's mysteries,' I'm leaving."

"The Tallos might appreciate God's comfort, you know. They're the genuine article, never missing a mass. Not everyone is a cynic like you."

No, that much was true. Andrés clung to his idealism, even in the face of a disappointing reality. In fact, Javier believed Andrés to be the most virtuous man in Negros with or without a priest's collar.

"Thank God for the Tallos, then." He managed to make the words sound only mildly sarcastic.

Andrés clapped him on the shoulder, forgiving Javier too easily, as usual. "Absolutely."

When they arrived at the small nipa hut, two supervisors were already there asking questions of neighbors and witnesses. The priest dismounted easily and walked into the house to deliver his message of hope and resilience. Javier needed that speech as much as anyone.

As soon as the *hacendero* swung down off Nico's back, he released the reins to one of his supervisors and sent the other man off to the mission hospital to fetch a nurse. With her help, they could cart Ramram down to Dumaguete tonight, as long as the nurse did not think the trip would kill the boy. Unfortunately, the American doctor would not make a house call to Bais, no matter what the emergency. Javier had tried to convince him to open a clinic in town, even if for only one day a week, but the American had not been interested. Javier suspected that the good doctor believed people should come to him and not the other way around.

Javier braced himself to face the Tallo family. If they had brought Peping back, he would have to cut them all loose, a decision that no one would like.

He entered the hut. It had only two rooms, one of them really just a tiny loft that the unmarried daughters shared. Ramram was laid out on a mat in the middle of the main room, and a young girl sat and fanned insects off his face. Dried blood stained the bamboo floor.

Ramram's wound had already been cleaned and bandaged with an old shirt.

The local *babaylan,* or folk healer, chewed a mouthful of guava leaves to mix with coconut water for a poultice. In her betel-stained fingers she gripped a wrinkled piece of cigarette paper. The prayer written on the paper—an incoherent mixture of initials and pig Latin—would be pasted to the wound, binding in the herbs. Javier thought the woman no better than a charlatan, thriving off of the laborers' uneducated delusions, but he also knew that she was cheap and usually did no harm. The Tallos could have more easily commanded a typhoon strike in the middle of dry season than pay a real doctor's bill.

He could tell that the family did not know how to react to his presence. They easily sought solace from the padre, but they kept their emotions under wraps in front of the *hacendero.* The most humane thing he could do was quickly express his concern, ask his questions, and then retreat from the house. He would let Andrés handle the rest. Fortunately, Ramram's father seemed genuinely angry that Peping was back, suggesting that he had not abetted the scoundrel's return.

Satisfied, Javier prepared to leave, but a repellant mixture of dirt, mildew, and incense caught his nose, eliciting an abrupt and loud sneeze. Two strong fingers twisted the skin on his right arm—hard. "*Aray!*"

He turned to find Andrés standing by his side, satisfied that he had just warded off evil spirits with the well-timed pinch. One could not be too careful when sharing the air with the dying, or so the theory went. "I suppose you owe me now, eh?"

Javier glared at him, unamused. "You're a Catholic priest."

"So?"

"Shouldn't you be above such superstitions?"

"If it makes the others here feel better that I've pinched you, then I'll do it as many times as I need," he said, smiling.

"The boy's not beyond the reach of medicine, so let's not jump right to the magic, eh?"

Javier escaped into the golden sunlight of late afternoon before he could be the subject of any more nonsense. Egay, one of his supervisors, was watching over Javier's horse, guiding it to a new patch of rough grass.

"Where's Peping now?" Javier asked Egay.

"Long gone. Probably halfway up the mountain by now."

"How long was he on my property?"

The man did not want to answer that question, knowing the information would not be well received. "Probably a week."

Javier had been home the whole time. "How is this possible? Why didn't anyone tell me?"

Egay retreated into the shadow of the huge horse. "None of us knew," he insisted.

Since this kind of thing was exactly what Javier paid him to know, it was not an acceptable answer. Though his field supervisors were literate men—timekeepers and lieutenants, not physical workers—they were also native Negrense who lived side-by-side with the men in nipa huts only slightly grander than the rest. This meant that if men gathered after work to grouse about the *hacendero*, the supervisor would find out. If the women gossiped while doing the wash in the river, a supervisor's wife would hear about it. Something had to be a well-kept secret to avoid the notice of a man like Egay De Los Santos.

"If you find out which men were sheltering him, fire them." Javier hated to do this—more than he could say, really—but harboring a villain like Peping could not be tolerated. "How did Ramram get caught up in this?"

"Everyone says it's not his fault," Egay explained. "Peping wouldn't leave them alone. He had come to collect the commission he thought he deserved for getting them their jobs here. When Tallo refused to pay, Peping returned with a gun."

Andrés emerged from the hut just in time to hear this. "But they're cousins!" he exclaimed.

Javier turned to him and said quietly, "You minister to the flock, padre, and leave me to run the hacienda."

Andrés raised an eyebrow in response, quietly calling Javier on his bluff. An hacienda resembled an extended family as much as a business, and as such the workers needed two parents: one compassionate and one hard-boiled. Keeping these in balance was the secret to a productive estate. Javier had not been around to do that, and now he paid the price. It did not really matter that Peping had shown up after Javier returned from Manila; the mistake was that he had been away too long in the first place.

Javier turned back to Egay. "He has a point, though. Even for Peping, it's pretty heartless to shoot his cousin's boy."

"Seems that bit was a mistake. Peping was waving around the rifle a bit, acting like a big man, when he lost control of it. Fortunately, he was standing far enough away that the ball was spent by the time it hit Ramram."

Javier hoped so. That and the placement of the bullet would be the only things that might spare the boy. Chewed herbs and cryptic prayers were not going to the do the trick.

"I don't give a damn what Peping meant to do," Javier said. "No one brings a gun on my property but me. I want you to go to the constabulary and tell them everything. Let them see if they can catch the bastard."

"*Sí*," Egay said. He started to rush off, then turned. "If they catch him, they'll hang him."

"It's as much as he deserves." The only armed Filipinos nowadays were rebels, thieves, or police. Not everyone drew a distinction between the first two, but Javier did. He preferred men who fought for a cause—any cause—over bandits like Peping who refused to put in a hard day's work.

"The Tallos were talking in there," Andrés said, "And, well, they think Peping's become a *babaylan*."

That was not good news. Not all folk healers were gentle souls; some had leveraged their mystical reputations into messianism. If Peping had managed to ally himself with one of these apocalyptic movements up in the mountains, then he would be much harder to track down and kill. Even the Americans had not figured out a way to deal with them.

"He claims to be ordained by Papa Isio himself," Andrés added.

"Oh, come on, Drés. They don't really believe that, do they? This is Peping we're talking about."

"It would explain why someone here would take the risk to hide him," Egay said. "They're afraid."

"They should be afraid. If you find any other fanatics on my land, they can swing with Peping."

"Javier!" The priest did not have the stomach for the work of an *hacendero*, no matter how long he had ministered to one.

"Look, I don't care what twig-and-berry amulets they wear. Those men are criminals, and I don't want any on my land." He paused. "But I've got to say, worthless as the *babaylans* are, I'd be surprised if they'd waste their time with an undisciplined fool like Peping."

"And if you're wrong?"

Javier shrugged. If he was wrong, he would let the American Sixth Infantry take the troublemakers away. There had to be some benefit to suffering the soldiers' presence in Dumaguete.

"What are you going to do about Peping's family?" Andrés asked.

"They're better off without him. Whatever money Peping could have swindled from the Tallos family, do you think any of it would have gone to his wife or daughter?" Javier rubbed his hand down his face. Suddenly he was exhausted. "*Hay sus*, what a mess."

"Well, I'd better get to the chapel and offer a prayer for Ramram's recovery—on the house," Andrés said with the beginnings of a smile. When the Spanish friars ran the parish, they had charged for everything from prayers to burials. Their rates for the latter varied depending on whether the person wanted the priest to walk all the way to the gravesite, or just halfway. Fortunately, Andrés took his spiritual calling a bit more seriously. "What are you going to do, Javier?"

"What can I do? I can't afford to lose three cane slashers, even for a week, but it seems I've got no choice until Ramram recovers. Even I can't ask the rest of the family to work while their boy is unconscious, so I'll have to bring some of the new Cebu men over to this field. I can barely spare them, though."

"I'll let Señor Tallo know," the padre said, turning to reenter the hut.

Javier called out to him. "And tell him to keep his girls away when the Cebuanos are here, just in case."

Andrés hesitated, clearly uncomfortable. "If your hired men are dangerous—"

"No, they're probably fine." No doubt they were, but Javier had learned not to trust the pack mentality of men, especially on an island away from the civilizing influence of their own families. "Listen, Egay, can your wife look after the Tallo girls for a little while?"

"Of course," the supervisor answered quickly. "My daughters will take them along to the new American school."

Andrés grimaced. "Judging from the rags those girls were wearing, they'll be too ashamed to show up half-clothed."

Javier thought that was a simple thing to fix. "Tell them that I'll provide credit for the fabric, and Señora De Los Santos can help with the sewing." He looked to Egay, who again volunteered his wife's assistance with a nod. "They probably have a week or two yet before classes start."

"How do you know that?" Andrés asked.

Javier opened his mouth, and then closed it again. He did not know how to answer that question. He knew it because he listened to the gossip from town every day. That was how he also knew that the red-headed *maestra* had just arrived in Bais. "Apparently, I know what's going on everywhere but my own hacienda."

Javier dismissed both men to do their duty, leaving him alone to wonder what other surprises the season had in store. Each week brought a new test. Though he had passed them all so far, they still whittled down his margin for error. He could think of ways that he and his mother could economize at home, but keeping up a show of prosperity was important for business. If people knew how close he was to folding, they would not bother making good on any of their debts to him. That meant the holiday party his mother was organizing could not be cancelled, nor could he easily sell any of his properties in town.

At least he had some tenants. Apparently, one was the *maestra* herself. She was a temptation he did not need right now, but the arrangements had been made in his absence. Javier usually didn't believe in such things, but Fate did seem to be working awfully hard to throw this woman in his path. Fate was a real son of a bitch.

CHAPTER SIXTEEN

Home, Sweet Home

The Stinnetts meant well, but their constant scrutiny had turned Dumaguete into a seaside prison. By the time Georgie left for Bais, she had no expectations for her new home other than some needed privacy. What she found was so much more. The town was sandwiched between a green mountain ridge on the west and aquamarine bay on the east. It was the most verdant, tranquil place she had ever seen. It felt like the world had set aside one little corner of its beauty just for her.

Archie also felt proprietary about their new home, only for him this meant that he assumed that the whole town worked for him. Georgie watched as he directed two passers-by to move his trunk into the mansion he had rented on the town square. This architectural showpiece was built on a base of imported Chinese granite—an extravagant expense, even in this prosperous sugar land. By choosing this residence, Archibald showed he still had the expectations of a Blaxton, even if he had to adapt his tastes to local conditions.

Until the wedding, Georgie would have to bunk above the schoolhouse's classrooms. Archie showed her to the vacant storefront he had rented for this purpose. A worn sign hung over the doorway: *"Kapehan sang Bais.*" Geno, the property manager, explained that this building had been the old coffee shop.

Archie turned to Georgie and laughed. "What idiot would sell hot coffee in the Philippines? No wonder the place folded."

Geno looked like he was about to say something, but then remained silent.

Archie promptly left Georgie to clean the schoolroom on her own. Or maybe he assumed that was what Geno was for. Judging from the quality and cleanliness of the Filipino's shirt, though, Georgie doubted it. Fortunately, word of her arrival spread quickly and people came to look for work from the new, rich American. Georgie was beginning to understand that, despite having little coin to her name, she was still a "rich American" by local standards.

Geno turned away four boys who were young enough to go to the school themselves. A few other prospects turned tail and ran when they caught sight of who was conducting the interviews. Geno gave brief chase, energetically directing them back toward the fields from which they came. Eventually, Geno hired three older teens, all a little on the scrawny side, Georgie thought. She was puzzled by the manager's criteria, but she followed his advice—Archie would have argued simply to have the last word.

She led the *muchachos* upstairs to clean her apartment, which was in even worse shape than the old shop below. She opened the tall sliding windows to air it out, but she knew it would be impossible to erase years of neglect in one day. Then again, maybe it had only been a few weeks of neglect. Dust seemed an unreliable chronometer in the tropics.

The house did have its charms. The solid hardwood that framed the building and lined the floors was far more reassuring than the woven grass houses many Filipinos lived in. Even better, an interior washroom had been fit into an extension that overlooked the back door. It was an exclusive bathroom, if not a fully private one. Its floor was constructed of tied bamboo strips that would effectively drain the water but could also leave her visible to the casual pedestrian outside. She would have to time her baths for the dead of night.

More people showed up at the apartment looking for work, this time women hoping to be hired as cooks and maids. Unfortunately, Geno had not stayed long enough to help her interview these prospects, so she was on her own to bridge the language gap. In the end she chose a woman named Julieta who had brought a Spanish letter of reference. Georgie could not understand it, but only the elite would be fluent enough to write something of its length, which lent the maid an air of respectability. Even more important, the woman was willing to work for only twelve dollars Mexican a month; she did not even try to haggle up from Georgie's initial offer.

Julieta's first domestic task was to coordinate the cleaners, which she did with surprising authority. Within twenty minutes another *muchacho* arrived with a half dozen eggs and a sack of rice. When Georgie tried to pay for the goods, Julieta shook her head energetically and spoke in quick Cebuano, which Georgie understood about as well as slow Cebuano. Deliveries came and went several more times, including dry goods and tableware. Georgie tried to wave it all away, but either no one understood her or else they pretended not to. She had suspicions that it was the latter.

After cleaning up for the evening, Julieta went home. It was the first time since Manila that the *maestra* had been alone. Although most people had their maids live in the house, Georgie did not want someone around spying on her full-time, especially after her experience with the McAffries in Dumaguete. That rationale had made sense in the light of day, but now she wondered if she had miscalculated. Someone sleeping downstairs would be reassuring.

Georgie unpacked her trunk and pulled out the copies of *Harper's Weekly* she had stuffed in the bottom. An hour later she had covered her walls with Mears and Underwood cartoons. Though her decorating style was not going to win any awards from the William Morris estate, it would do in Bais. She had worn herself out and lay down for a short break. Before she knew it, the short break turned into a nap, which then turned into bedtime.

While drifting in the lovely bliss between consciousness and slumber, something cold and dry brushed her arm. And then it brushed her hand. She reflexively grabbed at the thing, only to feel a thick rope slither right out of her grip. Georgie awoke mid-leap.

Her first semi-conscious thought was that the Serpent had returned to earth to finish off all womankind. It took a few seconds for her brain to register the fact that this was not a dream. There really was a big snake at her feet.

The beast was huge, as thick as her arm and as long as the room. No doubt it could flex its jaw and swallow her whole. Georgie was a city girl: she had no experience evicting even a garter snake from her house, let alone a prehistoric monster like this one. One might think something this big would be slow, and that with all its twists and turns there would not be much forward motion. Not so—it raced along the wall toward her living room.

"Saints preserve us!" They were her grandmother's words, but they seemed appropriate for the situation. Invoking a little heavenly protection could not hurt.

Georgie looked around for a weapon. Jesus, Mary, and Joseph, she couldn't fight this thing—but neither could she sleep with a predator in the room. She carefully stepped down from the bed to grab a hammer but realized that the tool was not up to the task. Its small face would not do much to hurt this leviathan. She dropped it and padded out to the kitchen, raising her lamp to look for a knife. A machete would be preferable. She had seen the *muchacho* use one—a *bolo*, he had called it. Georgie searched the stacks of utensils, finally uncovering the native blade set aside in a soft cloth wrapper. She picked it up and swung it through the air a few times, getting a feel for its heft.

"Come on, you can do this." She repeated the encouragement out loud a few more times in the hope that some part would sink in. The snake was now leaving the bedroom and moving toward the large shutters in the main room. Instead of escaping through the wooden slats, it began climbing the walls. She could see the coroner's certificate now.

Cause of death: flying boa.

The snake turned and moved toward the bathroom. There was no way she was going to ever bathe again if the thing somehow disappeared in there; and needless to say, it was too hot to swear off good hygiene. She had to stop the beast, and stop it now. Without actually thinking how scared she was, she raised her arm and swung the knife.

The snake was so thick—and her hack so faint-hearted—that she could not cut all the way through its neck. Did snakes have necks? God, she didn't know.

She let go, leaving the blade sticking out of the snake's body a short way down from its head. It tried to slither a little, but the heavy kitchen tool restricted its movement. She must have also cut an important internal organ because there was a lot of blood. Up until that moment, she had not even known that snakes bled.

Georgie retreated like a coward. She couldn't finish the job. Never had she felt so ineffectual or so cruel. She wanted the poor thing dead, true, but not suffering. Fear, however, won out over compassion. She ran to her bedroom, turned an end table on its side, and made a barricade. She climbed onto her bed, hugged her knees to her chest, and cried.

It wasn't just the snake; it was everything. The islands had been against her from the start. Exhibit A was the cholera fire. She should have turned around and taken the first steamer home after that night. And then, when her clothes were stolen, how could she have seen it as anything other than a divine reproof? That had led to the situation with Don Javier—a man she was bound to see again in town, proving there was no escape from a curse.

And then there was Archie, of all people, complicating her life. She had not entered into their betrothal for love, but she had hoped for a pleasant companionship. Yet here it was, only the first week of their reunion, and already they both seemed to prefer other people's company. This stint in the Philippines was meant to be their honeymoon tour. No doubt their problems would only get worse when they had to return to the real world of Boston.

Finally, Georgie despaired of ever finding her brother. She had not expected the search to be easy, but she had hoped to at least have some information on Benji by now: an address, a sighting, a friend, or maybe even a Filipina sweetheart. Instead, she had little evidence that he had even stepped foot on Philippine soil.

All in all, she felt nothing like the intrepid adventurer she had conjured in her daydreams, and she wept in disappointment. She blamed herself one minute and everyone else the next. By the time Georgie exhausted her body's supply of tears, she was too tired to care anymore. She slept like the baby she was.

Shortly after sunrise she heard a noise downstairs. It sounded like someone was trying to open the back door, which was jammed from years of rain and sun warping its frame. When it finally gave way, Georgina could hear the light puffing and grunting of a small woman. Julieta had arrived. Thank God.

"Julieta, ven aquí! Pronto!"

"*Sí!*" Julieta answered, clearly alarmed. Her feet pounded up the stairs, stopping abruptly at the top. "*Susmaryosep!*"

Despite herself, Georgie smiled at the exclamation. It was reassuring that Catholics swore the same the world over.

The maid peered in at her boss. Georgie gave her a smile that was equal parts relief and embarrassment. Julieta crooked her finger, calling the great snake slayer from her safe perch to come examine her handy work. In the light of day, the dead snake was covered in a layer of ants so thick that it looked like it was shedding its final skin.

Julieta laughed at something—or, more likely, someone. The Filipina walked over to the window and shouted down to the street, calling up two of the *muchachos* from the day before. When they got upstairs they looked at Georgie with pity, as if being an ignorant American was some sort of unavoidable disease.

For her part, Georgie wondered if any of her newly-hired employees were ever going to clean up the snake. One of the older boys shouted out the window, and a diverse crowd of onlookers assembled outside the door, everyone from milkmaids to kerosene hawkers.

"Hey, I do need some gas," Georgie mentioned to Julieta.

Her maid, though, paid her no mind. A man with a large pole across his shoulders sauntered up to the door. On his pole hung three snakes—as big or bigger than the one she had killed the night before.

Georgie was glad to see the man. A snake catcher was just what they needed. Hers was already dead, but maybe he would clean it up for a few centavos. He might even be able to sell it for meat—if the ants had left enough behind. She did not care what he did, as long as he got it off her floor.

One of the *muchachos* descended the stairs, joined the snake-catcher, and pointed at one of the snakes. He looked up at Julieta for approval, but she shook her head. When he moved on to the snake on the right, she nodded. He pulled one end of the coiled boa away from the stick to show the snake's full size.

Julia turned to Georgie. "*Sí? Aquél?*"

"What about it?" Georgie asked meekly.

"*Culebra casera,*" Julieta explained. House snake.

"Are you kidding?" Georgie asked, even though she had not known Julieta to be a jokester. Humor required communication, whereas rudimentary conversations like this one were reserved for teaching basic survival skills—like why one invited a serpent into one's home.

Julieta pinched up her face and made a squeaking sound. "*Ratones,*" she said.

"Mice," Georgie translated.

The maid nodded. "*Para matar a los ratones.*"

"What if I'd rather have the mice?"

Julieta smiled passively, which Georgie already recognized as the woman's default expression when she did not understand her employer.

But Georgie had another idea. "What if I get a cat? *Gato?*" A good mouser could keep her company too.

The maid nodded enthusiastically, and the *maestra* thought maybe they were making progress. "*Sí, sí!*" Julieta said. "Snake eat *los gatos, también!*" The woman mimed taking a huge bite out of the air, and there went Georgie's hypothetical cat, down the gullet of a very real snake.

She had moved to a town where monsters were pets, and pets were breakfast. Welcome to Bais.

CHAPTER SEVENTEEN

Hospital

Nico was sweating, but Javier could tell the horse was happy. After being ignored for weeks, the animal relished the attention from his owner. While Javier had been gone in Manila, his stable boys had walked the gray stallion but no one had the courage to ride him. Even the townspeople of Bais who saw Nico every day backed away in fear as he trotted down the street. Nico accepted their deference with regal bearing. Few Spaniards had as big an ego as this horse.

Javier dismounted and tied the long reins to the base of a tree. He walked into the mission hospital and looked for a boy to bring out a bucket of water. Whether the child would get close enough to let Nico drink—well, that was another story.

The hospital was a surprisingly roomy building even though it was only one floor. It looked like someone had taken the top layer off a large house and plunked it down on the dirt. Javier had warned the Americans that they should raise the platform higher, but they had not listened. Not surprisingly, the hospital had flooded twice since opening.

Dr. John Hemmerlein sat at his desk at the far end of the building. The doctor was penning a memoir of his experience saving the lives and souls of misguided Filipino peasants in a backwater Visayan town. Javier knew this because a few of the nurses were daughters of his hacienda workers. When they returned home for fiestas, they made fun of the doctor's silly boasts, like how many Chinese he had baptized—only sixteen, though he expected to find a few more in the new year. The doctor was the type of Christian who preached humility but did not have the least idea how to practice it. It was a fault Javier found in many missionaries, though this one had managed to become a minor celebrity. His self-serving exploits were regularly reported back to an eager cub reporter in Manila and printed as news.

Hubris or not, the man was a talented doctor, and thankfully medical skill was all that was needed from him at the moment. As Javier approached Dr. Hemmerlein, he noticed Ramram sleeping soundly in a bed to his left. He took this as a good sign.

"Good afternoon, Doctor."

Dr. Hemmerlein had sunken eyes and a gaunt face, making him look more like a worn out country farmer than a youngish Chicago doctor. He parted his dark hair on the far left side and sported a thick mustache, yet neither affectation did much to distract from his enormous ears.

At Javier's greeting, the doctor looked up but did not bother to rise. "Good afternoon, Mr. Altarejos."

Some Americans adopted the titles "señor" and "don" as a nod to the Hispanicized culture they were joining. Some did not.

"Call me Javier," the *hacendero* volunteered. If he was going to bend to American custom, he might as well do it thoroughly, even though the doctor would not likely reciprocate. "I've come to see how Ramram—Ramiro—is doing."

The doctor looked over at the boy and frowned. "I've removed the bullet, but my biggest worry is infection. Ramiro is in God's hands now, I'm afraid."

The boy would have a better chance had he gotten into Hemmerlein's hands a little earlier, Javier thought. It had taken hours to get

Ramram to the hospital in Dumaguete, and in that time the rough, dirty cart had done its damage. "How bad is he?"

"He has a fever, which is the body's way of fighting off contamination. If he burns too hot it could kill him. That witch only made things worse by rubbing mud into his wounds."

Javier would normally be the last person to defend a *babaylan*—he was the one paying for Ramram to be seen by a real doctor, after all— but to hear the faith healer insulted injured some reflex of national pride. "I think she meant well, doctor."

"Peasants are gullible and used to obedience, which that woman uses to her advantage," Hemmerlein said. "The men told me she actually chewed the grasses in her own mouth before she inserted them in his body. Had she wanted to kill Ramiro, she couldn't have found a better way to do it. If I ever find her, I'll turn her in to the constabulary for attempted murder."

That seemed excessive. Guava leaves were a traditional antiseptic treatment in the islands. The *babaylan*'s methods may not have been tremendously effective, but they were probably better than nothing.

"She was the one who stopped the bleeding in the first place, Doctor."

"Of course, because what good would a dead patient be, you see? She patched him up just long enough to earn a few dollars."

Not nearly as much as I'm paying you, Javier thought. He held his tongue, though, because Ramram deserved better than having his doctor's honor insulted. A resentful man was not a clear-headed one. "Thankfully he's here now."

"And I'll need to keep him until the fever breaks. The next few days are the most crucial."

"Anything I can do for him?"

"You can send his family away," the doctor said without hesitation. He pointed to the boy's mother and grandmother sleeping on the floor next to the bed.

Javier could not imagine what problem they posed. "They're here to tend to him."

"That's what I have nurses for—skilled nurses who can't do their job as long as those two are in the way."

There was no way on earth that the Tallo women would leave an unconscious Ramram in the hands of an unsmiling white man in a flood-prone bungalow at the tail end of rainy season. For all his modern diagnoses, Dr. Hemmerlein was just as much of a quack to the Tallos as the *babaylan* was to him. Nevertheless, Javier said that he would speak to the women.

The doctor was not finished, though. "And we're running out of clean water more quickly than we can draw it from the well."

"I can hire you another *muchacho* to do that." That was another ten dollars a month on Javier's account. He was more than a little afraid to do his books.

Hemmerlein accepted the donation easily. Javier supposed that missionaries were used to living upon the fruit of their patrons' guilt. At least Presbyterian piety seemed consistent: men like the doctor lived within the means his church provided him, unlike most Spanish friars before him.

Javier thanked Hemmerlein and turned to the Tallos. It took a few minutes of coaxing in Cebuano to convince them to follow him out, but he assured them that they could return after the doctor left for home. The Filipina nurses would not protest. Satisfied, the two women walked to the tree line outside the hospital and settled in to wait out the American. Javier did not begrudge them their persistence; he would do the same for his child.

Javier untied Nico. The pesky horse had pinned the frightened boy to a coconut tree, apparently hoping for a nugget of raw sugar like the ones Javier kept in his pocket. Javier gave Nico a playful swat and a loving scratch, and then tossed the minder a small coin for his trouble. He led the horse back to the water bucket, and only gave the beast a muscovado lump after it had finished drinking.

Javier did more business in Dumaguete and then stayed the night to rest his horse. The next morning Nico was eager to stretch his legs in a good trot back to Bais. Once they hit the outskirts of town, though, Javier slowed and dismounted. He walked Nico along the edge of the square, avoiding the school but keeping an eye on it the whole time.

He did not see the red-haired teacher. He was not surprised: even though it was not the hottest time of day, most people stayed out of the sun if they could help it. While passing the market, though, he ran into Julieta, his former cook, whom he had assigned to keep a watchful eye over Georgina's household. She bowed her head in greeting, a formality that made him feel older than his years. "*Ma'ayong buntag,* Don Javier. *Kumusta po kayo?*"

"*Mabuti, salamat.*"

Formalities complete, Javier made the switch from Cebuano to Spanish. Julieta took great pride in her ability to speak the language of high-class mestizo kitchens. It was too bad that she was going to have to start over with English now.

"Where are you going this morning?" he asked.

"Back to the market, señor," she said, a bit sheepishly. She had probably bought chicken feet or pig's intestines that morning, thinking that she would make Georgina some Visayan comfort food. She would learn that Americans could be fussy about what part of the animal they ate.

"Is everything going well with Señorita Potter?" he asked.

The woman nodded, and Javier could swear he saw amusement flicker across her face. Whether she was laughing at Georgina or at his interest in Georgina, it did not matter. The last thing he wanted was for the *maestra* to become a focus of *tsismis.* "I hope you know that I trust your discretion, which is why I sent you."

Julieta nodded again, more seriously this time. "Of course, señor. I'll look after her as if she's my own sister." It would not have been a meaningful pledge from just anyone, but Julieta was close with all her siblings and supported many nieces and nephews on her salary.

"That reminds me, how much am I paying you?" he asked. The cook was silent. It was an unfair question, Javier realized. She would never presume to name her own salary. In fact, so far this week she had been working on faith. "I mean, how much is Miss Potter paying you?"

"Twelve dollars."

"That's all?" It was a third less than she used to earn at his own house, and she was worth far more. The only reason Julieta had stayed on at Hacienda Altarejos for so long was that she had family nearby. Otherwise, he might have lost her to a wealthy hemp supplier in Cebu or even a commissioner in Manila.

"Sí, señor."

"I'll pay you ten a month on top of that."

Julieta's eyes lit up at the two dollar raise she had just earned.

"But I need you to look after the *maestra*—protect her, do you understand? And watch those *muchachos* I sent over too. They're trustworthy enough to carry water and sweep the schoolroom, but I want them to stay out of the flat unless you're there."

"Of course," she replied. She was too polite to say that she knew such things already.

Maybe he was making too much of nothing. He did not want to be too transparent, especially to the help. "She's my responsibility as long as she's staying in my building."

Julieta nodded, playing along as if this was the only reason he could be interested in the affairs of a silly American teacher.

"How's the school coming along, then?" he asked.

Julieta thought a bit. "They seem pleased."

"They?"

"The other teacher, a man." She looked like she regretted bringing it up. "Very pale, like a ghost."

Javier did not know whether that was a compliment or not. Usually, in island terms, pale skin meant Spanish blood, wealth, or a combination of the two. On the other hand, Filipinos did not make supernatural comparisons either lightly or fondly. Javier tried to remember what his overseer Geno had told him about Mr. Blackstone—something about being a pompous idiot. It did not clear up matters much.

"When will they open classes?" he asked.

"In one more week. The beginning of November."

That was just in time to break for the holidays. No Filipino would have bothered trying to start a reasonable teaching schedule before January. Javier almost suggested as much but then decided not to interfere. "Did she ask who sent you?"

"She looked over my recommendation papers but didn't ask any more than that."

He had touched up his mother's reference letter—one written under great duress since Lourdes did not want to lose Julieta. Javier had sold his mother the same story about proper treatment of foreign guests on Altarejos property. He also embellished the signature on the reference, disguising it with enough flourishes to make it illegible.

Julieta smiled. "She'll be in the best of hands, Don Javier. Don't worry."

He worried, though—mostly about why he was inserting himself into such a game to begin with. If he could be content to simply watch from afar, that would be one thing. He knew, though, that it was only a matter of time before his will would break and he would emerge from the shadows.

Part III: November 1902

Dearest Georgina,

...The lads here are jealous of our recent news—those who have shown restraint and stayed true to their race, at least. Fear not for me, for I may kiss the tips of your pure fingers with unsullied lips. Others are fools, falling for dusky natives who shame them, then laugh behind their backs. What will happen when these men return to the trusting hearts who have waited so patiently? What ugly stories will follow them home? Manila papers, or even Manila attorneys, may drop a bombshell across the waters. What then?

When do you arrive?

Your own,
Archibald

CHAPTER EIGHTEEN

First Days

Maybe I'm letting the man get to me, Georgina thought. She looked down at her *Baldwin Primer*. Some of the first words the book taught were just as jingoistic as Don Javier had assumed. Until her arguments with him, she had not even considered the possibility that the textbooks might be inappropriate for Filipino students. But she could not defend what she saw on page fourteen: a full-page color illustration of the Star-Spangled Banner—"our flag," these children were instructed to think—and a bald eagle raising its wings to fly.

She called out over the flimsy barrier that split the room into separate boys' and girls' classes. "Archie, have you taken a look at the primers?"

Her fiancé was on the other side with the two Spanish-trained teachers, Juan and Salvi. Before the Americans arrived, these men had run what barely passed for a school; now they were reluctantly learning modern methods. Neither spoke good English, nor did Archie speak Spanish, so it was a difficult pairing. But since everyone expected a disproportionate number of boys to show up the first day, Georgie had encouraged the Filipinos to help Archie first. Besides, the two men had no interest in teaching girls, a fact they had made plain.

Archie strode around the wall, barely needing his cane to take his weight anymore. "What's the matter with the books? Are they damaged? Mildewed? I was worried about this dratted humidity—"

"No, they're in good shape," she said regretfully. "But do we really want to use them? I mean look at this."

He peered at the pages she held up. "What's the matter?"

"Don't you think it's a little strange to teach these children as if they're living in Iowa?" She turned the page. "Listen to this: 'I love the name of Washington. I love my country too. I love the flag, the dear old flag, of red and white and blue.'"

He shrugged. "What's wrong with that? It's a catchy poem."

"For an American."

Archie looked at her as if she had ingested too much smoke during her steamship travel. "George Washington is an important part of everybody's history. He's the defender of the world's best democracy."

Georgie did not argue with his claim, even though she had no right to vote in Archie's "best democracy." All she needed was to be pegged a suffragist; she would never hear the end of it. Instead, she flipped the pages randomly and found a more subtle offense. "Look at this." She held out page thirty to him.

Archie was unmoved. "An oak leaf. What possible problem could you have with that?"

"How many oak trees have you seen here?"

He rolled his eyes. "You're making too big a deal of this. The children know these are American textbooks, and they know what a leaf looks like. So what if they've never seen this particular tree? You're underestimating them."

"But—"

He turned away, no longer listening to her. "I've been in this country for a year making these decisions, Georgie, choosing these books. I've seen them all, and until we publish our own, this is the best we've got. If you're done wasting my time, I've got to keep an eye on the other two idiots here."

Georgie found it amazing that Archie could both defend and degrade Filipinos in the same conversation. She supposed it was a particular sort of talent. And it had not escaped her attention that he had lumped her in with the "idiots." She watched him leave and then dropped her head in her hands, suddenly very tired. The conversation had gone exactly how she had expected it would, and she now asked herself why she had even brought it up. Archie was right, after all: the students would make do. A flawed education was better than none at all.

In any case, taking on the Insular Government was not why she was here. She reached into her drawer and pulled out a blank sheet of paper. She had been writing the ranking constabulary inspector for every town mentioned in Benji's letters, hoping that her brother had been recruited into one of these units. She had heard nothing back yet, but it was early. She reminded herself that she had plenty of time—two years, unless the Bureau found cause to fire her. She would have to learn to keep her mouth shut and wait.

As she began another letter, her eye was drawn to movement along the base of the left wall. Before she even recognized the shape as a rat, she screamed. She should have been ashamed of her sniveling cowardice, but she couldn't help it. It had been a long week, and it was a big rat. Juan and Salvi ran into her room. Archie was either no longer at school or did not care what had frightened her.

"Maestra?" Juan, the taller man, was the first to speak, though both men held the same question in their eyes.

"*La rata!*" she exclaimed, pointing to the dirty brown rodent sniffing her floorboards. Juan saw the thing and charged after it, brandishing his ruler like he was challenging a dragon with a sword. The rat fled outside through the open doorway, but Georgie knew it was only a temporary reprieve: if it could get out that easily, it could also get back in. She thanked Juan anyway.

"*La maestra necesita una culebra casera—*"

"Unh-uh, no snakes." She had refused to replace the one she massacred last week, especially after Julieta picked out an even bigger boa as its successor. Judging by Juan and Salvi's open smiles, they had heard the story. What did she expect? Discretion? Privacy? Anonymity? She was beginning to realize that such things did not exist in Bais—at least not for her.

Suppressing his laughter, Salvi dug through a box in the corner of the room and brought out a bamboo contraption that looked like a tiny bow. He held it up. "*Pas-ong. Es una ratonera.*"

He pulled one side of it away from the bamboo tube, affixing it to a catch. Whether the trap was big enough for the monstrosity she had seen earlier, Georgie was not sure. Salvi set it down and used his ruler to put a small amount of pressure on the slide. It snapped closed, bouncing about a foot off the floor.

Salvi handed the disarmed trap to a wary Georgina. She toyed with it a bit, but she had a hard time pulling away the bamboo "bowstring." Maybe she did not have to catch the rat, she thought; she could just adopt it as the classroom mascot. That might be better than losing a finger to the *pas-ong*. Still, she could not refuse Salvi's help without insulting him, so she let him set the trap with bait from his lunch and hoped for the best.

Georgie had never lived surrounded by so much raw nature: snakes in her bedroom, ants in her tooth powder, little lizards climbing the walls, and cockroaches everywhere. She was no stranger to roaches, but the ones around here redefined the species. Then there were all the animals that people kept by choice, like the infernal roosters! Whoever said that the birds sounded off only at sunrise had obviously never lived with any. Between their cock-a-doodle-doo and the buzz-buzz-buzz of the mosquitos outside her white netting, every evening was a concert.

Later that night she lay awake a long time. Tomorrow would be the first day of classes. She had never taught before, and most of these little girls had never been in a school before, which meant that no one would know what they were doing. In the end, the pressure was on the *maestra*, of course. She had planned her lessons as best she could, but no one at Wellesley could have prepared her to teach the daughters of cane slashers living in grass-huts on a distant Pacific island. When she really thought about it, the whole enterprise was terrifying.

She tried to clear her mind by counting roosters outside, separating each one by the tone and volume of its call. By the time she decided there were seven, she was relaxed enough to doze.

Morning came too quickly. She did have one treat to look forward to, though: Spanish chocolate. Julieta had introduced her to this new indulgence. The maid dried and shelled fresh cacao beans at home, ground them together with roasted cashews, and then rolled the mixture into one-inch balls. Then, every morning, she used one of these balls in combination with hot milk, sugar, and egg whites to whip up a creamy concoction in the blue enameled *chocolatera*. For this delight, Georgie would even endure the interruptions of the grim-faced milk-maid who entered the house unannounced every dawn to refill the clay pot with fresh carabao milk.

Archie thought Georgie was crazy to eat local eggs and milk in the midst of an epidemic. When she reminded him that he was the one who insisted there was no cholera in Negros, he simply walked away.

It might be risky, but Georgie did not care. Bais seemed safe enough, though neighboring Dumaguete had officially diagnosed a few dozen cases. The Stinnetts were considering shutting down for the month, according to Mary's recent note. Archie would not consider postponing their own opening, but he told her not to touch the students, just in case.

Georgie let out a heavy breath. Focus on the chocolate, she told herself. Julieta was in the midst of the preparation ritual when something on the street drew her attention. "*Los estudiantes,*" Julieta said.

Georgie looked at her pocket watch. "It's too early for any children to show up. I've not had my breakfast yet."

The maid shrugged her shoulders and looked outside again, more interested in the children's presence than in Georgie's dietary needs. Georgie thought the contest a draw. Nevertheless, she rose from the table and walked downstairs to investigate.

Sure enough, she found four little girls waiting outside her door, all of them nervously adjusting their kerchiefs as if expecting a strict inspection. Had there been one, all four would have passed. The girls had been carefully scrubbed and groomed, each mop of shiny black hair tied back with string. Though Georgie had not been dazzled by the sanitary conditions of peasant houses in Bais, the personal cleanliness of their inhabitants was impeccable. Each girl wore a freshly pressed white blouse and dark skirt. Georgie had watched Julieta wrestle with the charcoal-filled iron on her own clothes, using a banana leaf to keep the shirtwaists from getting burned. She imagined peasant mothers all over Bais doing the same this morning, methodically cleaning the contraption with coconut oil between each use. It was a tremendous amount of effort just to send a poor girl off to school.

Georgie ushered the children in and opened the room's windows one by one, hoping the pink morning light would cheer the place up a little.

"Hello. My name is Miss Potter," she said, enunciating clearly. She held out her hand, knowing that it was never too early to illustrate proper American manners.

The girls hustled right over, each in turn taking Georgie's hand and pressing it to their own small forehead—an unexpected greeting, but easy to recognize as a gesture of respect. Once her hand was freed, Georgie pointed at her chest and repeated her introduction. "Miss Potter."

One of the girls, seemingly the eldest, said confidently, "Maestra Misspot-tehr."

"Oh, no, 'Miss' is not my name. Maestra Potter," Georgie corrected.

"Maestra Pot-tehr," they obediently mimicked. The littlest still said "Misspot-tehr," but the first one slapped her arm until she dutifully squeaked, "Maestra."

Georgie gestured for them to say their names. The eldest was Maria De Los Santos. She introduced her sister, Rosaria, a tiny thing who hid behind the others. The other two were Carmelita Tallo, an adorable girl with unfortunate pox marks on both cheeks, and Sisa, her sister, who was missing two front teeth and could barely pronounce her own name.

Georgie had to save these girls a few hours of sleep in future mornings. She pulled out her watch and pointed to the small hand. "Six. *Son las seis y cinco. Escuela…*school…*a las ocho.*" She pointed to the eight. "*A las ocho en punto.*"

Maria nodded but made no move to leave. Georgie did not know if she had been understood, but she knew that she was stuck with these girls for two more hours. She made a motion of bringing a spoon to her mouth. "Eat? *¿Queréis comer?*"

They did not seem sure whether Georgie was inviting them or interrogating them. Her Spanish was admittedly limited, but she was starting to believe that the children's was worse. Fortunately, a hovering Julieta translated in quick Cebuano.

Maria declined the offer with an emphatic shake of her head, but her eyes kept returning to the stairs where the smell of frying eggs wafted from the second floor. Georgie knew what it meant to be hungry but proud: the sisters of the Sacred Heart had fed her, clothed her, and educated her no matter how little tuition her family scrounged together each semester. It was her turn now. She motioned for the girls to follow her. She made it a command this time.

They all crowded around Georgie's small table upstairs. Its wooden legs sat in little cups of kerosene, the only effective defense against ants. Julieta cooked up more rice and eggs. For girls who had initially refused food, they ate faster than most people would find polite. At least they did not stare at her, so focused were they on filling their bellies. In contrast, they barely touched the water, probably because it tasted strange after boiling—not exactly metallic, but not what they pulled from their river either. There was no possible way for the *maestra* to explain the health benefits of her way. Like the drunken turkey at the Stinnetts, boiled water was proof of inscrutable American taste. Georgie made it up to them with hot chocolate—partly out of generosity, and partly so she could drink it guilt-free in front of them.

It was an expensive morning. If she had to feed her students every morning, she would need a raise. Fat chance of that.

Breakfast over, she led the girls downstairs and waited. Others trickled in randomly, seemingly unaware of any specific start time. Archie, however, was committed to his schedule, so he did not show up until shortly before eight, leaving Georgie to entertain both the boys and the girls for almost an hour. At least she got over her nerves by being too busy to think.

When it came time to introduce the readers to her own class, Georgie gestured for several of the oldest girls in the front row to pick up a pile from the trunk and hand them out. These girls were certainly strong enough for the task: they did not seem to miss many meals, a physical fact that set them apart from the other students. One was even pushing the boundaries of overweight, a rare sight in Bais.

Georgie turned to write on the blackboard while the books were being distributed, but when she turned back around a minute later, she noticed that all the girls had stayed seated—without books. Georgie called the girls' names again—Inday, Leklek, and Ising. Still they did not move.

Adopting her most confident *maestra* posture, Georgie walked over to the front row and gestured for the students to stand. The whole class stood. She gently pulled on Inday's hand, and the girl slowly, reluctantly came along. None of her friends followed her.

Georgie tried to explain, both with her hands and with clear words. "Books. Books for everyone," she said gesturing at the others.

Inday would not take any from the trunk. It was funny. Earlier that morning, the girl had seemed to be one of her most promising students; now, though, she seemed less capable of independent thought than the trunk Georgie wanted her to empty.

Georgie grabbed five books and shoved them at Inday. The girl stood frozen, arms at her side, and let the primers fall to the floor at her feet. Before Georgie could say anything, the two Tallo girls rushed over to help, falling to their knees to pick up the books. After a nod from Georgie, they pulled out a dozen more texts and handed one to each student. Puzzled, the *maestra* moved on with the lesson.

At the end of the school day, the situation she faced became much clearer. A *muchacho* arrived after classes to carry Inday's books home—or book, actually, since all she had was the single primer. The weight of the slim volume hardly required any assistance. Another servant, a nanny, took hold of the girl's hand and walked her the few hundred feet across the square. Leklek and Ising were escorted in the same manner, their entourages guiding them on remarkably short journeys down the street. In contrast, the De Los Santos and Tallo sisters shouldered their own burdens, making their way into the cane fields beyond town. Apparently, Georgie would have to confront arrogance as well as ignorance in her classroom.

When Georgie complained to the other teachers later that afternoon, Salvi just shrugged his shoulders, but Archie surprised her by agreeing with her. "I think we shouldn't allow *muchachos* to carry their books," he said. "It goes against the republican ideals we're here to instill. Our students should distinguish themselves on merit, not money."

It was an unlikely sentiment for a man who had been handed everything from birth. It softened her heart toward him a little; she certainly did not see any of his fellow Porcellian Club members teaching the poor children of Asia their ABCs.

And then he finished his thought: "Besides, I don't want that riff-raff hanging around the school. The last thing we need is to be swarming with *bolomen* and *ladrones*. It's bad enough I have to spend my whole day trying to teach monkeys to speak English."

Georgie thought she would like her fiancé better if she only heard half of what he said. She would try to work on that.

CHAPTER NINETEEN

Progress

J avier stayed away from the new school for as long as he could. He had holed himself up on the hacienda for the last few weeks, and he probably should have stayed there still. Instead, he found himself leaning on the door jam of the newly opened school, as yet unnoticed by any of the students. Three dozen girls, aged six to thirteen, were squeezed tightly into three rows. Two village dogs were taking advantage of the shade, each sprawled under a bench in untroubled slumber.

Boys' voices rang out from behind a temporary barrier, and Javier wondered how the girls could concentrate on their lessons with so much noise. He was not having any trouble focusing on their teacher, of course, but he had his own reasons.

He tried to view her through the eyes of her pupils. Certainly she was the tallest woman these girls had ever seen, though she was anything but gangly. She had no desk or chair to lean on, but she did not slouch or rest on a cocked hip. Her elegant frame could probably remain standing all day without complaint. Javier found himself testing the bounds of his otherwise dormant creativity by imagining those long, lovely limbs under his fingertips. A flush of blood ran to his cheeks and he scolded himself, worried the girls could sniff out his luridness.

Maestra Potter had divided the new blackboard into sections—reading, geography, spelling, illustration, phonics, and music—each labeled in precise chalk calligraphy. It was now music class, and she was singing a song in a clear, beautiful voice: "This is the way we wash our hands, so early in the morning."

The children joined in, copying her motion of rubbing her hands together. Americans, Javier thought, shaking his head. If nursery rhymes could combat cholera, he would have gladly sung his way through Manila. The problem was not insufficient bathing; Filipinos did that several times a day. The problem was what they bathed with. Javier imagined that bastard policeman singing to these girls about boiling water and draining cesspools. That would have been a more useful song, if a bit absurd.

Javier chuckled aloud to himself, an outburst that earned him thirty-six turned heads. The young eyes then quickly looked away from the powerful Altarejos. The thirty-seventh pair, the deep green eyes of their teacher, met his gaze without flinching.

She returned her attention to the students, but he could see that she was a little unnerved. "Okay, let's do that one more time, shall we? Where were we? Oh yes, 'This is the way we cook our rice.' Remember rice, girls? Rice?"

"*Bugas?*" said Maria De Los Santos. Javier felt a little twinge of pride, as the girl was his supervisor Egay's eldest daughter.

"Yes, Maria, that's right." Georgina pointed to where she had written the information clearly on the board. "*Bugas*: rice. We cook our rice." She made a motion like she was stirring a pot of porridge, which looked nothing like cooking rice, but the girls seemed to get it and copied her.

Javier did not dare leave the doorway. His guerrilla courtship was admittedly a bit heavy handed, but he had little experience with flirting. Long ago he had stopped smiling politely at the wives and daughters of his tenants. His overseer had hinted that even Javier's most sincere, well-intentioned grins were interpreted as lascivious by the peasants—a quality that attracted some and repelled others. Either way, it was better to be seen as aloof.

His seeming indifference also kept fellow *hacenderos'* daughters at bay. Fine young ladies could hardly turn around and approach him without invitation. From the few social gatherings Javier had attended since returning from abroad, he had determined that most girls educated in expensive convent schools were docile, mild-mannered, and devout. Why these were considered valuable qualities in a wife, he would never understand—just as he did not know why the nuns of Santa Rosa insisted on draining his cousin Allegra of her natural boisterousness. How did people expect the species to survive if they bred out its spirit?

His thoughts were interrupted by the commotion that marked the end of classes. The little girls quickly filed out of the classroom, careful not to brush against Javier in the doorway. Their teacher continued to ignore him, turning away to wipe the chalkboard with a damp cloth.

Javier rarely waited for invitations, so he spoke first. "Maestra Potter, it is a pleasure to see you again."

"Also you, Don Javier." She glanced in his direction but did not meet his eyes. She pretended to neaten the chalk tray.

He knew that her clipped greeting was intended as a dismissal, but the challenge did not deter him. In fact he liked it. When a man owned as much of a town as he did, no matter how tenuous that hold, few were willing to defy him to his face. Even his strong-willed mother had become too gentle and accommodating. Everyone had grown dull.

"You didn't respond to my letter," he said.

"I didn't receive anything."

It was a lie in spirit, if not in fact. She had not received his letter because she had refused to accept it. He knew as much from the desk clerk in Manila. "Allegra hoped that we would become friends."

"When your cousin returns home, I do hope you'll bring her by for a visit."

They both knew that would not be for another few months. He was running out of conversational openings, so he reverted to a topic that was sure to spark a reaction. He nodded to the corner where the United States's flag had been laid, folded neatly into a triangle. "Have the girls learned their Pledge of Allegiance yet?"

She sighed. "Did you come here to annoy me?"

Yes, he thought, if that was what it took to get her to notice him. "You'd better teach it soon if you expect to quiet the rowdy natives." The few Filipino nationalist leaders who had not yet sworn their oath were currently in detention in Guam. He could see from the angry flare of her nostrils that she was also aware of the policy. The flared nose—which was slim, feminine, and turned up just a bit—distracted him from his intentional provocation. The nose was perfect for her character: generally sweet, but prideful at the edges.

"You should ask yourself why the natives are so 'rowdy,'" she answered. "From what I understand, you *hacenderos* have spent the last hundred years wringing every last cent out of this land and its people. I'm trying to give the children a better chance than they've had up to now. At the very least, they might avoid becoming indebted to dubious landlords who are only a step above slave owners."

He had been called far worse in his life, and by much less beautiful creatures. "I don't oppose every aspect of your mission, you know."

She raised her eyebrows, but said nothing.

"Basic literacy and trade skills are useful," he continued. "But that's all that most of these children need."

"Who are you to decide such things for them?"

"I'm their employer. They need work, and I need workers. You can fill people's heads with stories of the great new life that education brings, but how many poets do you think these islands can support? This island needs cane farmers, Miss Potter. It needed them twenty years ago, and it certainly needs them this season. If you encourage everyone to think of themselves as better than that, they will soon be disappointed—and hungry."

"Ah," she said, stepping closer to him. "Because reading and writing won't make you a better farmer. That is your argument, right?"

"It makes you no longer want to be a farmer," Javier said softly. He regretted upsetting her but continued anyway. He felt like a bad puppy, acting out to attract her attention in any way possible. Now that he had it, he no longer cared much about the argument.

Georgina, on the other hand, was still on point. "But how else will new techniques spread? How will your planters learn to use new machinery?"

"The same way that knowledge has always been spread on a farm: someone shows you."

"Oops, lost a hand," she said dramatically, holding up one of her own. "Too bad I couldn't read the label on the machine."

The more frustrated she became, the more Javier smiled. It was probably not an endearing response, but he couldn't help it. "How do you expect to fulfill these new expectations you create?" he asked.

"Progress will take its natural course," the *maestra* said, shifting her weight uncomfortably.

He saw a shred of doubt. And she should have doubt, he thought. It was a terrible answer. "Progress is a much prettier thing when viewed from a distance," he said. "Change is not always pleasant to those who suffer through it."

Georgina seemed to think about that, but then rejected it. "If education has so little to do with farming, then why does a rich planter like you need to go to school at all, let alone one in Europe? Can't you manage your farm though sheer force of personality?"

"Unfortunately, no," Javier admitted. "Most people don't find my personality to be all that engaging."

"No-o."

"Besides, if the Spanish were good at anything, it was at creating paperwork. The Americans seem to be even better. Working land

is straightforward, but owning land these days is downright complicated."

"I'll be sure to let your sharecroppers know all the trouble you're
saving them."

He was about to issue her an invitation to the hacienda to do just
that when a blond man emerged from behind the classroom divider.
The man hobbled up to the *maestra* with the aid of a walking stick and
languidly rested his palm on the small of her back. Javier did not like
what the gesture represented.

"What's all the arguing about?" the man asked with an exaggerated casualness.

Georgina made a polite, but perfunctory introduction. "Archie,
this is Javier Altarejos, one of the local sugar growers. Don Javier, this
is my fiancé Archibald Blaxton. He teaches the boys' classes."

Javier focused on the word "fiancé." He reviewed it several times
in his head, making sure he had translated it correctly.

So this was the "Blackstone" that Geno had told him about. His
overseer had not mentioned anything about him—or anyone else, for
that matter—being Georgina's fiancé. Surely this waste of a man did
not think he could handle a woman like Georgina? Archie was tall—a
little taller than Javier—but his feeble frame looked like it barely belonged out of bed. Ill or not, Blaxton had made a mistake in leaving
Georgina unmarried as long as he had. If it had been Javier, he would
have lined up the padre before even making the offer. Months wasted
on planning a wedding could be better spent.

Blaxton looked at Javier's extended hand for a moment before
deigning to shake it. "So you're Altarejos, our landlord."

"Our landlord?" Georgina asked. She had turned to Archie with
the question, but Javier was the one who nodded.

Georgina then looked at Javier a bit strangely, almost hesitant.
"Did you know that we would use these rooms for our school when
you rented out the space?"

He nodded again. "I ordered the chalkboards brought in from Manila."

"You're...you're the donor who gave these to the school?" she asked, waving a hand at the large slates.

"You seem surprised," Javier said.

"After what you said about—"

"I simply pointed out a few assumptions you were making, beliefs that may not be so easily transplanted to our soil. But I meant it when I said that I support your endeavor. Making my building available is one way I can do that."

She squinted at him with suspicion. "I do notice that we pay rent," she said slowly.

The *maestro* drew a shocked breath at Georgina's lack of manners, but Javier could not help but be amused. "I have my own expenses to cover," he said. "However, if there are any other services I can provide, please let me know. I want you to get your money's worth."

Blaxton stiffened. His sallow skin, most likely still discolored from disease, gave his face a macabre glint when he smiled. He drew the *maestra* to his side with a rough yank on her shoulders.

Javier was not displeased with the man's reaction, but to save Georgina embarrassment, he reworded his offer. "I'd like to offer you both my help in expanding your work here, maybe obtaining materials with more local appeal?"

He waved his hand toward the board where "A is for Apple" introduced the alphabet. All three of them knew that none of these children had ever seen an apple.

"I think we've got everything," Blaxton replied tersely. "We don't need anything from you."

As dismissals went, it was a rude one, and Javier dodged it with a show of manners. "At least allow me to offer my congratulations. When is the wedding?" He needed to know how much time he had to work with.

"Next week," Blaxton declared.

Georgina struggled to turn and face her fiancé, but he pulled her even tighter against his side. Javier watched her squirm a bit, relieved that she did not seem comfortable in the man's embrace.

She lowered her voice, probably hoping that Javier would be polite enough not to listen. She was wrong. "I'd rather not discuss this now. I thought we'd decided—"

"We'd decided nothing," Blaxton cut in. "We can get married as soon as we want. It's not like we need permission."

Despite Javier's urge to protect the *maestra*, he was thrilled that her fiancé was so easily vexed. It would be easier to undermine him in Georgina's eyes if he lost his composure at the first challenge.

Javier wondered what this man wanted from her. He gave the impression of aristocratic birth—or as close as Americans could really come to such a thing—yet he was anxious to marry a commoner, the daughter of a seamstress? Though Javier was intrigued by the *maestra*'s blend of pluck and gumption, he doubted that Blaxton saw it as anything but vulgar.

Georgina pried herself loose and turned away from both men. She walked to the blackboard to escape them.

"Georgie," the American said, his tone insistent. "Don't walk away from me."

She did not stop. She picked up her rag and finished cleaning the slate. "I'm not talking about this right now," she said, more to the wall than to Blaxton.

Javier was feeling better and better about his prospects. The two seemed barely friends, let alone lovers.

Blaxton must have also sensed that he was losing ground, because he turned back to dismiss Javier. "If you'll excuse us, sir, I need to speak with Miss Potter alone." He stressed the "sir" with such hostility that it bordered on insult.

Javier ignored the man as he walked right up to the board. There, he took Georgina's free hand, and brought it to his lips. "Good afternoon, Maestra. I look forward to our next quarrel."

She stared at him in surprise, unsure how to answer.

Javier turned and left the school, relishing the heavy silence he left behind.

CHAPTER TWENTY

Dirty

"Archie, why would you discuss our personal business in front of Don Javier?" The *hacendero* had just left the room, and Georgie wondered how much of her anger was left over from her argument with him and how much was truly directed at her fiancé.

"So it's Javier now, is it?" Archie growled. "Did you hear what he said? As if you'd let his black hands touch you."

Georgie felt a small pang of guilt but pushed it aside. There was no way Archie could know about the Luneta, so she kept her tone calm, measured. "He said no such thing. Besides, he's almost as light as you are," she said, "and certainly as successful."

"He can grow all the sugar in the world and it still wouldn't make a difference."

"He's a gentleman, and you can't—"

"Gentleman?! That bastard exiled Rosa's father, forcing the man to abandon his wife and child. I can't even talk about it without wishing I'd hit him when I had the chance."

Georgie hardly trusted the word of Archie's nurse, but neither could she defend Javier. Most of the American community seemed to have good reason to dislike the *hacendero*—was that his fault or theirs?

"Let's not argue about him when we should be talking about the wedding," she said. "Were you serious about wanting to get married next week?"

"Yes. No. I don't know." Archie looked at her. "What do you think?"

"I think we shouldn't move our whole schedule ahead just because you're angry with Señor Altarejos." She was careful not to call the man Javier again.

"You're probably right." Archie sighed and moved closer, reaching out to pull Georgie into an embrace. "I'm sorry I got upset. I don't want anyone to come between us."

He dipped his head to kiss her, a slight brush of his lips against hers. She let him, partly out of curiosity, and partly because it was well overdue. She thought it a sweet gesture until it escalated into an aggressive full-mouth assault.

What was not tongue was teeth or spit, as if he wanted eat a piece of chocolate cake she had hidden in the back of her mouth. Then his hand moved easily to her breast, as if he had been there a thousand times before. In a final indignity, he bit her tongue.

"Archie, wait...ouch." Georgie pulled her mouth from his. One nice thing about having played basketball at Wellesley was that she understood defense: she wedged her shoulder into Archie and pushed him away. He gaped at her, surprised that she was not enraptured by his deft seduction. She wiped slobber off her mouth with the back of her hand. There was no classy way to do that.

"Let's talk over dinner tonight," she said, just happy that the impromptu tonsil exam was over.

"Where?" He looked skeptical. "Here?"

"Why not?"

"Who's going to cook? That Tagal you hired?"

"Julieta." And she was a Visayan, not a Tagalog.

"Who knows what germs that woman brings back from that filthy hut she sleeps in? I told you to confine her to your house."

He wanted to talk about germs? Georgie looked up, seeking strength from the Narra wood rafters. "I'm not going to confine anyone, Archie. She is not my slave, and she's not dirty."

"And you persist in eating native vegetables—"

That was true. It was too ridiculous—and unappetizing—to buy tinned corn when surrounded by fresh. "Julieta washes them in boiled water."

"—and local meat."

Georgie refused to apologize for any of this. "Canned chicken costs three times as much!"

"Then don't buy from that thief Tina Yuco anymore," he said. Archie had spent the last few days complaining about how little their salary bought in the local *sari-sari* stores—and since the Chinese owned most of these shops, he had come to believe it was a yellow conspiracy to retaliate for the regime's restrictive immigration policies. "I've contacted the Sixth Infantry in Dumaguete and arranged a deal for some of their surplus rations."

She laughed. "What are you trying to do, kill us? That 'embalmed meat' probably finished off more soldiers in Cuba than the Spanish."

"I'd chew American leather before I'd eat a porterhouse from the hands of your Filipina cook. Don't worry, though. Rosa can whip up something."

She did not point out the inconsistency of his position. What was the point?

Georgie considered her choices. Rosa would not poison her—not intentionally—but there were more subtle ways to exact revenge with food. On the other hand, insisting that Archie come upstairs to her apartment was a worse idea. She considered the second floor her own snake-free sanctuary, and right now she counted her fiancé among the reptile class. It would be easier to leave Archie's house at the end of the meal than kick him out of hers. God forbid he try to kiss her again—or worse.

"All right," she said. "Let me get cleaned up and I'll be over."

He scowled. "You bathe as much as the Filipinos do."

"You have to choose, Archie: either the Filipinos are too dirty or else they're too clean. You can't have it both ways."

"Isn't it obvious?" he asked, wrinkling his nose. "They're the kind of dirty you can't wash off, no matter how much soap you use."

Georgie could not think of a single thing to say to that.

CHAPTER TWENTY-ONE

Pedro Hijacks Dinner

D inner was served precisely at six, proving that Rosa took direction well. No "Spanish hours" for Archibald.

The *maestra* picked at the "embalmed" chicken but could not swallow it. She did eat the canned peaches—well, the ones that had not touched the gray meat on her plate. She did not blame the nurse for the poor quality of the food; she knew it had more to do with Archie's paranoia than Rosa's culinary ignorance. The only thing that was delicious about the meal was the irony of a Blaxton eating like an enlisted man. Elspeth would have had a fit.

Georgie was so caught up in that amusing image that she did not immediately pick up on the commotion coming from the kitchen. Archie did not react at all—he was doing what he was brought up to do: ignore the servants. What neither of them could ignore, though, was the loud crash from pots being thrown around. Since this whole house—including the cookware—would soon be her responsibility, Georgie got up to investigate. Archie reluctantly followed.

She stopped inside the door and saw a young, irate Filipino man waving around a bolo. He looked like an *insurrecto*—lean and fierce from jungle warfare. Acknowledging his new audience, he pointed back and forth between himself and Rosa, shouting *"Matrimonio!"*

Archie, despite having studied a few Romance languages at Harvard, did not understand. "What does he want?"

Rosa would not answer. The dirty pans she had chucked at the man lay scattered on the floor, and now she was out of ammunition. She tried to back out of the room without taking her eyes off the bolo but stumbled into Archie. He set his palms on her shoulders to steady her, a gesture that looked a little too natural. The intruder thought so, too, because he pointed his knife at the two of them and spat.

The spitting seemed to particularly anger Archie. "Listen, you long-haired reptile—"

"Stop it!" Her fiancé would get them all killed, Georgie thought. "Rosa, please, who is this man?"

"Pedro." It was almost a squeak.

"How do you know him?"

"I...he—"

Pedro cut her off with a long stream of Cebuano and Spanish. The little that Georgie could parse together did not suggest an auspicious beginning to her housekeeping with Archibald.

"*Su esposa?*" Georgie asked Pedro.

Pedro looked straight at Archie—who was still sheltering Rosa—and he ran his finger across his throat.

Georgie turned to her fiancé, who still seemed oblivious. "This man came here for you," she explained coldly. "I think he wants to know why you're sleeping with his wife."

Rosa gasped, confirming Georgie's translation.

Archie regained enough of his wits to try to salvage his honor. "I don't know who this beast is, but he's lying. My God, you can't think such a thing!"

Georgie considered the accusation for a moment. Getting to know her fiancé better this past month actually gave credence to his protests. It was hard to imagine Archie seducing a Filipina, no matter how beautiful. He was genuinely insulted, no doubt about that.

Someone had to deal with this madman, though, and Georgie's vote was to let Pedro's "wife" do the job. She grabbed Rosa and pulled her away from Archie. For a split second, Archie's fingers tightened on the woman's shoulder—to hold her as a shield or for solace, it was hard to tell. But he relented, and Georgie shoved Rosa forward, keeping one hand on the Filipina's back to block off further escape.

"Get him to put down the bolo," Georgie commanded.

Reluctantly, Rosa nodded. She cleared her throat a few times first, searching for any excuse to stall. Then she mumbled something about "*matrimonio pro tem,*" or "married for the time being." Lovers, in other words. She was telling Pedro that she owed him nothing.

The young man took a step forward, and the nurse grew frantic again. "*Pasagda-i ko,*" she warned him.

She turned to Georgie, her eyes pleading for help. "He not touch me now," she said in English. "No more!"

The *maestra* wondered when she had become judge and jury, but clearly she had. Rosa lifted her skirts just enough to expose her ankles and calves. She pointed at several large scars on her legs, and then did the same with her arms. The marks had the thin, neat impression of healed cuts—deep cuts, like those made with a knife.

Georgie looked over at the weapon Pedro still held in his hand, and she shivered. No matter how she felt about Rosa, she could not send her away with this man.

She had to figure out a way to scare Pedro off. "The *Insulares* will come. *Soldados!*"

Filipinos had been put to death for far less than waving a knife in the face of an American. And what good was the Insular bogeyman if she didn't let him out of the closet once in a while?

Although Pedro was the only one brandishing a weapon, he withdrew as Georgie advanced. Accepting now that his grand romantic—albeit homicidal—gesture to win back his woman had failed, the deflated young man skirted out the kitchen door and down the rear bamboo stairs. He disappeared quickly. Most likely, he would take off to the mountains and rejoin whichever band of brigands had sheltered him so far. If he got caught along the way, Georgie thought, all the better.

Meanwhile, Rosa had collapsed into a mess of tears on the floor. Archie reached down to her and patted her shoulder—tap, tap, tap. To most it would have seemed a clumsy consolation, but it was the tenderest gesture Georgie had ever seen from her fiancé. What should have been a relief—finding that the man was capable of sympathy—was tarnished by the truth: he had feelings for this woman. He probably fought them with every ounce of his snotty being, but they were there. Georgie was starting to feel a headache coming on.

Poor Rosa. Even if Archie were not already engaged, he would never marry her. If Mrs. Blaxton disapproved of a shopkeeper's daughter from Wellesley, the woman would absolutely lose her mind upon meeting a country nurse from Asia. She would pay fancy lawyers to annul the union and then outfit Rosa with a scullery uniform to work in one of the family's many kitchens. From Elspeth's perspective, that would be the only place Rosa belonged, if even there.

This had to be why Archie was so keen to marry an American—any American he could convince to make the trip. He needed a chaperone, not a wife. Georgie now realized that she probably was not the first he asked, either, just the first who had accepted. That probably put her at the bottom of a long list. Even though Archie had not met Rosa by the time he had proposed to Georgie, no doubt there had been another beautiful belle who had tempted him—maybe more than one. How many "bombshells" did he have in Manila?

She could hear Archie mumbling about the charges he would file against Pedro, that "mad heathen."

"Pedro no come back," Rosa assured him between sniffles. "*Tua siya sa bukid*. Maestro save me."

The *maestro* in question smiled proudly, and Georgie wanted to hit him. She was surprised to find that she cared more that Archie was stealing her credit than she cared that Rosa was trying to steal her man. And that was when Georgie knew the engagement was over, at least in her heart.

CHAPTER TWENTY-TWO

Puntas

Javier waited outside Georgina's classroom door like the fool he was. He should have been overseeing the planting of new cane. The migrant workers were even more untrustworthy than normal, and his managers could not watch over everyone at once. Javier had the best horse, the best seat, and the most to lose. He could not afford to set foot off the hacienda before Christmas—yet here he was, again.

This time the *maestra* noticed his presence right away. "Good afternoon, señor. If you'd like to sit down, I'm sure we can accommodate you. We seem to have quite a few free seats today."

Her false sweetness did not match the stern expression on her face. Nor was it a good sign that she refused to use his Christian name. The few girls at school today all sat in the front row and stared at him with big brown eyes. They could hear the bitterness in their teacher's voice and must be wondering what he had done to put it there.

"And maybe you would be so kind as to tell me where the rest of my pupils are?" The *maestra* folded her arms across her chest, giving her a strange resemblance to Friar Pedro Juliá in the midst of a particularly frustrating Moral Theology lesson. "They've been gone for days, and Ising has just kindly explained to me that I have you to thank."

Yes, he knew where they were. He had seen the Tallo girls yesterday, in fact, soaking cane tops.

"Maestra, you have to understand—"

She did not let him finish. "I'm trying to bring together these children as a town, as a nation—something you claim to want—but I can't do that if half of them can't come to school because they're being exploited. How am I supposed to give any of them a better life if you chain them to the fields?"

"Chain them?" Javier sputtered, genuinely shocked. "Is that what you think?"

Georgina turned back to the mute girls in the front row and declared, "Class is over. You may go home."

The chubby one looked up at the *maestra*. "School no more?"

She nodded, "Yes, Leklek, go home. None of the boys are here, anyway. Special fiesta day."

Georgina tried to shoo the girls off with her hands, but none of them moved, unsure if this was a test. Inday Benitez probably understood, but she was happy to stay and witness the coming storm. The girl was just like her mother: a gossip of the highest caliber.

Georgina was not to be ignored, though. "Ising, Inday, Leklek, Kikay, Mena, Cora, Ingga." Each time she drilled out a name, one more pair of eyes snapped to attention. "Home. Now."

They grudgingly left, whispering to each other and stealing glances at Javier as they squeezed through the doorway. Once they were gone, he missed their civilizing influence. Now he faced the downright hostile schoolmarm all on his lonesome.

"You're free to leave, too," Georgina said.

"If you think my hacienda is full of pathetic orphans in iron shackles, it's a wonder you haven't marched the Sixth Infantry right up to my door. I hear they're getting quite good at the water cure."

Georgina stiffened but kept her cool. "The Army's kept peace on this island, and that's to your benefit. Besides, I don't think you need shackles to bind these people–your coin is just as effective as chains."

"So now I'm to blame for offering a fair wage?"

She walked past Javier and sat down. It was probably the first time she had been off her feet all morning, and she let out an exhausted sigh. Her whole body slumped onto the bench, shoulders sagging. By the time she looked up at him again, she had lost her ire—and almost immediately he missed it. He felt better arguing with an angry woman than a despondent one.

"Those girls can't afford to miss school," she said.

"Exactly what do you think they did before you got here?"

She looked at his finely tailored clothes. "They made you rich, I would think."

If only that were true. "The girls' work isn't so hard, Georgina. I've got men for the heavy labor—slashing, digging, and so on—though barely enough of those. The women and children soak the cane seeds and lay them out to dry—easy work for good pay. A few more days and they'll be back in class, I promise."

He neglected to mention that the girls would be back doing the same thing the next month, and also the month after. Every working field was replanted as soon as it was harvested in order to maximize the land's yield.

"A week's loss here and there—no problem, right? And then it'll be Christmas."

"But the holidays make what they earn particularly important," Javier explained. "Families will be expected to spend a lot on *aguinaldos* during Christmas and *Tres Reyes*."

"I didn't know your wages were such a boon," she said with an overload of sarcasm. "How much do you pay?"

Two dollars per *lacsa* would not sound like anything to Georgina so he stuck to relative terms. "For most of these families, it'll almost double their monthly income. That's reason enough to excuse the girls from a few classes, isn't it?"

She sighed. "So everything you said about supporting this school, it was just a lot of hot air?"

Javier was not enjoying this fight as much as the others, nor was Georgina feigning her disappointment in him.

He needed her to understand. "Maestra, this entire island's economy runs on sugar. If I cannot plant my cane, I won't have anything to harvest next year. If that meant only I suffered, I'd escort those girls back to school myself. But without sugar, no one gets paid and no one eats. It's more pressure than you know, and I'm struggling enough this season."

Javier stopped himself before he admitted any more of his financial troubles. It was unlikely that she would believe him, anyway.

"The girls love school," he assured her. "Even a heartless wretch like me knows that. I'm sure they hate knowing that the others are getting all your attention this week, learning what they can't. It's not fair, I know, but they need to work, not just for their family but for the whole community."

Georgina had not met his eye for a while. Instead she was staring up at the American flag she had hung in the corner of the room. After an awkward silence, she turned back to him. "That may be, but I still think you should go, Don Javier."

At least they were back to first names. Encouraged, he pressed on. "Maybe we could take a walk around the hacienda together. You could see for yourself what's going on out there—"

"I can't. I'm supposed to be offering night classes, and I haven't even started preparing for those. Of course, the adults may not show up, either, being so busy doing your work for you."

That seemed unfair, but Javier let it pass. Georgina stood up and walked back to the chalkboard, dismissing him just as she had the girls.

"You know your way out," she said.

Of course he did—it was his building.

"Maestra—" he tried.

"Señor, please." She looked back at him, her green eyes especially dark in the shade. "Go, and don't come back."

"I don't understand why—"

She cut him off with a frustrated sigh. "Can't you see that we want different things? The more girls I save, the fewer you'll have to work your cane."

She spoke like an evangelist, out to rescue the Filipinos from their own way of life. Had he misjudged this woman, thinking she was different?

"I'm trying to help your cause," Javier said.

"That's what you want me to think, but I'm catching on. Buying a few chalkboards and benches—that's nothing to you, a drop in the bucket. It confuses us teachers and keeps the school under your thumb so we don't threaten your control too much. Meanwhile, you come by here to distract me...I mean, distract the girls."

He shook his head. "No, you were right the first time. I came here for you."

"You don't get it! I'm here for a purpose, and that doesn't include whatever games you're playing. This job means even more to me now that everything else is falling apart."

"What do you mean?" he asked softly. She was tempting him with half-revelations. "I care about you, about your life, Georgina. Please."

The last bit of anger drained out of her in one breath, and along with it all of her strength. What was left in front of Javier was a shell of the Mighty Maestra of Bais. He wanted to hold her in his arms, but he worried that if he took even one step toward her, she would break. For the first time, he wished that she had a damned desk to sit at, instead of having to hold herself ramrod straight against the blackboard. The fragile chalk tray was the only thing keeping her standing.

"Really, I'm fine," she said. "Just go, okay?" Her voice broke as she pleaded with him. She was on the verge of tears. "Please. Go."

Javier could have pressed harder—forced her to spit it out—but the school doors were wide open. If someone came by, or if she screamed? *Hay sus*, his problems would be multiplied. The town's mayor was enough of a rival that he would not hesitate to ruin Javier with an opportune scandal.

Javier wanted to tell Georgina that she was wrong about him, that they could be allies, even partners. But there was another voice in his head that said maybe this was for the best. What could he really offer her, anyway? She thought they were at cross-purposes, and maybe they were. The *maestra* was winning, and she did not even know it. Her mission and her country were slowly strangling his way of life. Javier nodded once and left.

CHAPTER TWENTY-THREE

Basketball

It was not doing Javier any good to sit at his desk re-tallying his accounts. He kept coming up with the same meager result. That morning he and his mother had gone over the preparations for the family's annual *Sinulog baile*. Lourdes had insisted that they invite the families of several young women from Cebu, and he had let her, despite his knowledge that such matchmaking would come to nothing. The woman Javier wanted had kicked him out of her classroom last week.

And, of course, there was the inconvenient issue of this particular woman being engaged to another man. He had heard talk of trouble between the two teachers. Javier did not want to see Georgina hurt, but neither could he pretend that this news was unwelcome. Vicenta Ramos had been bragging among the housemaids that Maestro Blaxton would surely marry her daughter instead of the *Americana*. Rosa did seem to spend too much of her time at the man's house, even though it was obvious that Blaxton no longer needed a full-time nurse.

Javier was surprised that Georgina would allow this liaison to continue. She was no fool, nor would she want to look like one. Of course, a lot of Filipinos assumed that she was being savvy–wealthy men were not expected to be faithful, the sacred sacrament of marriage notwithstanding. As such, the townspeople assumed that Georgina was overlooking Archie's indiscretions in favor of an opportune match. Everyone knew the *maestro* was rich. How could he not be? He was paying a hundred and fifty a month for the Larena house. Commissioners in Manila might fork over that much for a shore-side villa on Manila Bay, but in Bais such a sum was worse than banditry. Javier only charged twenty for the school itself, and presumably the Insular Government paid that, not the teachers.

Other gossips believed that Maestra Potter was so pure that she could not be sullied by Blaxton's baser desires, and so she was passing the task off to a local girl. This practice was also well understood. Many pretty young *queridas* throughout the islands fed their extended families off such arrangements; it was better than starving. Others supposed that the American's dabbling was the reason the marriage had not taken place yet, and that Georgina was holding out until he pledged his fidelity.

It did not matter that these theories contradicted one another. Javier doubted that the *maestra* realized just how much the inanities of her daily life fed the town's appetite for gossip. Foreigners—whether Spanish, American, or Chinese—never seemed to realize that they lived their lives on a stage. Servants even took a surprising amount of pride in having the most extravagant and wasteful employer around, and they gabbed about everything from the cost of quality rice to the price of the finest champagne. Nothing stayed a secret for long. Why should the *maestra*'s love life be any different? Javier had pressed the point of privacy with Julieta, but the rest of Bais was not so beholden.

Right now, fortunately, the people liked Georgina. Parents had decided that she was a good influence on their daughters, and female enrollment in the school was growing quickly. But the more important she became, the more the town felt that it owned her. Adoring little girls followed her around all day, innocently reporting her activities back to the hacienda post-haste.

He appreciated the steady reports, but he knew his information would be incomplete as long as he hid at home. He needed to return to town and brave her wrath. His presence would certainly spark more *tsismis*, but he welcomed having his name linked with hers.

Lost in thought, Javier turned the corner of the public market and found himself swarmed by little girls. Although it was still early in the morning, there were streaks of perspiration running down their faces. Normally, Filipinos avoided any unnecessary sun lest it darken their skin and betray them as a common *indio*. Even farmers covered themselves up in long sleeves and pants. These girls, though, were still young enough that they were willing to endure the heat and rays for the sake of a big leather ball.

One of the girls backed into Javier, spinning around in full pique until she saw whose feet she had stomped. Maria De Los Santos's eyes opened in shock. Javier smiled and stepped aside, gesturing for her to continue the game. He had not meant to walk into the middle of— well, whatever this was—but he could not have planned a better way to get Miss Potter's attention. And she could hardly yell at him in public. Or at least he hoped so.

Georgina rushed over to him, biting the inside of her cheek so that it puckered into a dimple. Her stride was long and graceful, though the tight grip of her hands on a book gave away her agitation. When she was close enough, he could read the cover: "Basketball Guide for Women."

Americans had the strangest pastimes. For example, he had heard that Blaxton was trying to push a bastardized form of cricket as an alternative to cock fighting. It was an amusing misread of Filipino culture: locals might learn to play the new sport—they might even like it—but not in place of either roosters or gambling.

The *maestra* reached out and grabbed Javier's arm. It was a surprisingly forward gesture, he thought, until he realized that she was trying to drag him off the pitch. He let her have her way, disappointed that she dropped her hand once she judged them safe from the action.

"It seems that your students have returned," he said.

Georgina nodded. "They came back yesterday, reading pretty well despite the week off. Someone seems to have tutored them at night, but Maria wouldn't say who."

"Well, her father Egay is literate."

"In English?"

"No, but he could sound out the words easily enough, I imagine."

The *maestra* seemed to evaluate the set of his mouth. "So you didn't help at all." It was a question, but she said it flatly, daring him to disagree.

He wanted the credit, for sure, but he did not want to seem too eager to have it. "Tell me about this game you've got going on here. I've never seen such a thing."

He motioned in front of him, where a large chalk rectangle was subdivided into three identical sections. Girls ran around, waving their arms at the teammate with the ball.

"The girls can't move out of their third of the court, but they can dribble and pass."

"Dribble?"

"It means to bounce the ball, up to three times. They have to keep it above the knees, though, so that others have a chance to steal it away. It makes the game more exciting." The *maestra* smiled, looking like she would rather play than teach the sport.

"But it's all to what purpose? I mean, what's the goal?"

"Well, they keep moving the ball around until someone's free enough to try for a basket."

Javier looked at the wicker tub suspended from a tall wooden cross. That contraption was new to the square. All in all, it seemed a good use for crosses, of which the Philippines had plenty.

"Good job," Georgina called out. "Ditas, don't walk with the ball!"

The little girl's attempt to "dribble" was awkward and mostly unsuccessful, but the *maestra* encouraged her to keep going.

"I assume you play this game yourself," Javier said, trying to draw her attention back to him.

"I was captain at Wellesley," she answered, still watching the girls. Her eyes glinted with the fire of competition. "Oh, good pass, Neneng!"

"So, this game-playing at school, it's an American thing?"

She nodded. "We believe in educating both the mind and body. I'm trying to teach these girls good life-long practices—robust health through physical activity."

The *hacendero* thought most of these girls already lived a pretty robust lifestyle. In fact, that had been the point of their earlier argument, which he had no intention of pointing out. The girls did seem engrossed in the game, though. Their play wasn't rough, but it was definitely intense. "I have to admit," he said, "I'm a little surprised they're taking to it so quickly."

"I'm not counting my chickens yet."

"What do you mean?"

Georgina pointed over to the shade of a tree where Javier saw the daughters of the more prosperous town merchants gathered: the Yuco girl, along with the daughters of the clans Benitez, Pacaña, Dizon, Ramon, and more. They were braiding each other's hair and chatting as if at a picnic.

The *maestra* gave a little laugh. "I made a mistake by making the game optional at first, and now I don't know how to get them involved. The two groups don't mix."

Javier understood the different worlds. Though he spent more time with workers these days, he had actually grown up more pampered than any of the cherubs under the tree. He could not have imagined himself, pudgy little prince that he had been, putting much effort into anything. He had not lifted a finger in his house until he left for boarding school. And he meant that—not a finger. What other boy would have gotten a skin rash from not rinsing off his soap? One who had never bathed himself before, that's who. Military school in Spain knocked the final bit of daftness out of him, forging a better man from limited material. He had hated it at first, but his father had been right: it had been the making of him.

For the *maestra* to try to replicate such conditions here in Bais was admirable but unrealistic, and he said so. "I don't see any of those girls getting sweaty if they don't have to."

Georgina snorted. "No, not for anything. I've even had to stop their servants from carrying their books to school."

"Did you really?" He laughed, imaging how that conversation had gone.

"If I were asking them to carry an encyclopedia, I'd understand. But the primer couldn't weigh more than a pound."

Javier, by now intimately familiar with the primer, knew that to be true. It was a good book, despite the American propaganda it contained, and the clever illustrations inside had even ignited a discussion about how the Americans could have such large horses but such small carabao. Strangely enough, Javier had enjoyed his turn at teaching.

Nevertheless, the small size of the book would not matter to the merchants' daughters under the tree. "Knowing the Benitez family," he said, "I imagine that Inday just hands it off to the *muchacho* once she's out of your sight."

Georgina turned to him, the sun illuminating her myrtle eyes. "Yes, I've caught them all doing that."

Javier chuckled, and was rewarded with a sheepish smile from the *maestra*. She knew that she was a stubborn woman.

"If they carried their own books," he explained, "people would assume they were too poor to afford servants. It would be a loss of face in front of the town."

"Then what about these girls?" she asked, motioning to the girls playing in front of them.

"Look at who they are: my tenants' daughters, many of them. They're used to carrying their own water pails and washing their own floors. The only reason their families let them come to school is because they can be spared, at least for the time being. I've replaced most of the sick carabao on my land, but if those die, too, everybody will need to pitch in for a while. The girls will take over the housework, and their mothers will help with light labor in the fields."

He could hear her objection before she voiced it. "Now, don't get mad at me again—it wouldn't be my decision, but theirs. I'm doing the best I can to keep them here with you." He watched the girls play for another minute or so. "I bet this game is the bright spot in their week, possibly their year."

"Then it's worth doing," Georgina said. She looked over at the mestizas in the shade. "I'll get those others involved somehow."

The woman had only been here a month, and already she wanted a revolution. It was a small revolution, but it would stir things up in Bais for sure. Javier hoped she would succeed. The next generation deserved better.

Part IV: December 1902

Dear Miss Potter,

Your letter of October 8th gives me the opportunity to right a wrong. Yes, your brother survived Balangiga. In fact, he organized our escape from that damnable town on a small flotilla of native barotos. As terrible as the attack in town was, that boat trip was worse, so far as actual suffering was concerned. To his credit, it was not until we stumbled up the beach at Basey that I realized the sarge was wounded in the thigh—not badly enough to be sent to Tacloban, but too ill to return to Balangiga to bury the dead and set fire to the town. I think he regretted missing that; making a desert out of our corner of Samar became a near obsession for many of us.

While the rest of our unit was sent to Calbayog, your brother was reassigned as an aide to Major Glenn of the Fifth Infantry. Do not trust what the papers have said of Glenn. Sure, the bureaucrats court-martialed him for going after those people proper with the water cure, but that just goes to show that, like a great many other cold-footed tin soldiers, our generals seem to have come to the Philippine Islands to see the country and not to fight. You could contact Glenn himself, but I would not be able to advise you where to find him. Only one member of Company C is still in the Philippines—Themistocles "Tommy" Qula, last I heard somewhere in Cebu.

Godspeed, Miss Potter. I pray you will find him.

Cpl. Arnold Irish

CHAPTER TWENTY-FOUR

Dignity of Labor

Georgie put on her plainest brown dress because she planned to get as dirty as everyone else today. If some had to work, then all would work. Tilling the soil together would unify the social and academic divisions in her school. The town girls—Inday, Ising, and Leklek—had a head start in the classroom because they could already read and write Spanish, but that knowledge would not help them today. The Bureau of Education called it "dignity of labor," but the *maestra* called it gardening.

She had the perfect plot picked out. The soil behind the school building was dense and moist. Much of it got strong sunlight—good for sweet potato, Chinese cabbage, and eggplant—but there were also some shady portions for tomatoes and beans. All these vegetables would give the children more variety in their diets. Georgie bought the seeds and told the girls to bring whatever shovels they had at home, using "S is for shovel" on page 32 of their primers to illustrate. Ising Yuco claimed to never have seen such a contraption.

Growing up in Boston, Georgie had always thought that only the rich had the space for greenery. This was not how Filipinos thought about it, obviously, but even the most spoiled of the girls would have to be proud once she saw their hard work literally flourish. Just before eight o'clock, Georgie turned her head to see a crowd of students gathering by the building. Her enthusiasm fizzled when she saw field hands standing beside them. Girding herself for battle, she stood up and brushed soil off her skirt.

"Maestra Potter!" Inday rushed up to her, followed closely by her muchacho. "We make garden now!"

All of Inday's clique came forward and offered their day laborers, eight men in all. One man held out a piece of paper, a note signed by Leklek, who was mysteriously absent: "Dear Teacher, Mary had a little lamb; Its fleece was white as snow; And everywhere that Mary went, the lamb was sure to go. He followed her to school one day. Please, Teacher, I no go to school this day." Georgie regretted teaching the girls that forsaken poem, because now they thought it was some sort of special incantation to use any time they were not getting their way.

Everyone stared at the *maestra*, awaiting her instructions. She, however, had no idea what to say to this demonstration of force. Inday took her silence as encouragement, and ordered her *muchacho* to relieve the teacher of her shovel.

Georgie gripped the tool close to her chest, forcing the man to back off. "No, I'm sorry, Inday. We are going to do the work ourselves."

Neither Inday nor her *muchacho* understood, so Georgie hid the shovel behind her back like she was concealing a jewel. "*Dili!*" she said emphatically, using the Cebuano for "no."

She felt bad for the poor *muchacho* in the middle of this no-win situation, so she flashed him a brief smile before turning to Inday and holding the shovel out to her. "Inday, you will plant. You, me, everyone," she said, drawing her hand in a large circle to indicate all the girls. "We will make the garden together."

Inday gave her a blank look, but Georgie was no longer fooled by the act. "If you wish to come to school," she warned, "you have to join. Everyone joins."

Georgie knew that the hacienda girls and others like them—the ones who felt it was their lot in life to work—would pitch in. But if she could not convince the town-dwellers to participate, Leklek's truancy would be the least of her problems. Although the garden would survive, it would still be a professional failure, and when the new Division Superintendent of Oriental Negros came to inspect the school, he would surely notice.

Georgie wanted to impress her boss in case she needed to request a transfer to another part of the islands, an idea that she had hatched after the drama in Archie's kitchen. She had decided to hold off on telling Archie about her change of heart until she could line up a new posting so that he would have less time to interfere with her plans. She might have to depart Bais humiliated and alone, but she would not leave the Philippines empty-handed: she would stay in this country as long as it took to find Benji.

Georgie looked at the girls in front of her and carefully met the eyes of each one. Seconds stretched into minutes. The *maestra* considered that she might have finally met a group of people more unbending than she.

The voice that broke the stalemate was deep, male, and lilted with a British accent: "They come to school so that they don't have to do manual labor. Why do I feel like we've had this conversation before?"

Georgie looked to her far right and saw Javier, unruffled in tailored pants and a clean white shirt. He smiled in that confusing way he did when they argued. In the morning sun, she noticed the slightest appearance of crow's feet around his eyes. He looked a little tired, but it did not make him any less imposing.

"Even the First Lady of the United States gardens," Georgie insisted.

"How interesting." He walked toward her, drawn in by the challenge. "And respected schoolteachers sometimes polish the floors of the Hotel de Oriente."

"What? How did you—"

"I have many friends, Maestra." He grinned. "Mr. North was quite entranced by you."

"He was amused, not entranced. And that's not the point." She rested her weight against the standing shovel, afraid to admit that she might be outmatched but unwilling to give up on her project. "Why are you doing this?" she whispered.

Javier closed the final bit of distance between them. "Why are you?"

"Because what's the point in teaching the farmers to read if you don't teach the readers to farm? Just doing one of the two changes nothing. I know you helped the hacienda girls with their lessons, and now I'm going to show the town girls that they can work with their hands. If you're serious about making a difference, help me here too."

"So, just for the sake of clarity, you're willing to admit that I was right all along? That when I borrow my girls back again next month for planting, you'll not complain?"

"What? No! This is different—"

"Really," he said, laughing. "How is it different?"

"Come on, this is hardly backbreaking labor—"

"Maestra, do you ever admit that you're wrong?"

"—just a morning's exercise, not a whole week out of classes."

"Apparently not," Javier said. He then slowly unbuttoned his cuffs and rolled up each sleeve—baring light golden arms to his rapt audience—before gently taking the shovel from Georgie. She stumbled a little as she lost its support, but she was too stunned to refuse.

"If it is good enough for Mrs. Roosevelt," he said, "I suppose it's good enough for the rest of us."

He stepped behind her into the large rectangle that she had marked with a neat line of stones. She turned, her gaze following him as if glamoured.

Javier placed the shovel in line with the stones, put his foot on the top of the blade, and pushed it deep. It slid into the soil. Georgie watched Javier reach down and grip the handle low, a position that gave him more control. He lifted the earth and placed it carefully to the side. When he raised his foot again to the top of the blade, the tight line of his trousers revealed a strong thigh and backside. Color rose to her cheeks. She felt a whole different kind of dirty watching him.

Soon Javier had a neat row of soil lined up. The looks on everyone's faces—from Inday's horror to Maria's wonderment—were enough to tell Georgie how much his display had shaken the foundations of their world. They would not have been more surprised if President Roosevelt himself washed their linens.

Javier drew the girls toward him with a beckoning gesture and held up a fist-sized rock he had uncovered with his shovel. Though he spoke in Cebuano, Georgie knew that he was explaining how the point of turning the soil was to loosen it for planting and to remove rocks, branches, and weeds. He crouched down and dug one hand into the dirt, bringing up a fistful. He squeezed the loam into a tight ball and then crumbled it up. The soil was perfect for their task.

When he finished talking, he encouraged the girls to grab their shovels and continue the work themselves. Amazingly, most of them did. Little Inday stood there stunned, but the others did not hesitate. Javier spaced the students out, and he got each row started with a first hard cut. After that, the earth was looser and easier to manage. The girls copied the *hacendero*, moving the excavated soil of one trench into the next row, creating a fully turned bed. Ising struggled at first, unaware of how much force she needed to drive the blade into the ground, but Ditas soon came over and helped her. The day was a success.

Javier walked up to Georgie with a smug look on his face. "You know, Maestra, this teaching doesn't seem to be such a hard job after all," he teased. "For the second time this month, I've gotten all your children working together on task. It makes me wonder why you needed so much training."

She gave him a sour look for the sport of it. "I suppose the Bureau should hire you to take over for me, then?"

He raised his hands in surrender. "Oh, no, Maestra. Ten minutes with thirty little girls is about all I'm equipped to handle."

"You don't like little girls?" He actually seemed to be very natural with children.

"They make me nervous," he confessed in a low tone. "Eventually, they grow up to be women."

Georgie smiled. "I can see how that would terrify you. Maybe you should stick around and help with the planting. That way you can prolong your exposure, maybe build up a resistance to our charms."

"I could never become immune, especially to you."

Georgie rolled her eyes. The man was incorrigible.

"Where did you learn how to do all this?" she asked. "It's not like you plant your own fields."

Now he was the one surprised. "I have to know how it's done."

"And it's similar to what we're doing here?"

"On a bigger scale. Besides, there's nothing the English love more than their gardens. The Baron de Rothschild would talk of little else, and his sister, Lady Alice, even had a species of violet named after her."

"Her gardener must have liked her a lot."

"I think he was hoping that she'd be so pleased with the naming thing that she'd finally stop interfering with his work," Javier said, chuckling.

"Did she?"

"Would you have?" he countered.

"Once I fix my mind upon something, I'm pretty attached to it," Georgie admitted.

He held her eyes for a minute, not saying anything. Even the lively chatter of the girls seemed miles away. Georgie could not quite hear what he finally mumbled, but it sounded like, "We'll see."

CHAPTER TWENTY-FIVE

Misa de Gallo

Whatever the meaning behind Don Javier's cryptic remark, he did not follow up on it. He had left the school that morning without announcing any plans to return. Over a week went by, and Georgie did not hear from him at all—which was just as well because she had enough man problems, starting with her fiancé.

Like most little girls, Georgie had once dreamed of the perfect wedding. It began with a beautiful dress made of ivory satin. It would have simple lines, be trimmed with lace, and finished with a spray of orange-blossoms on the bodice. Add a tulle veil or even a tiara, complete with a diamond or pearl sunburst. The bouquet would be made of white lilacs, tied with satin ribbon, and held by flawless kid gloves. She would arrive at her husband's house with a trousseau of furs, lace, fans, parasols, useful jewels, and lingerie. The ring on her finger would be a simple band of twenty-two carat gold, engraved with the initials of the happy couple.

It was a pretty story, but no one ever wrote about what happened after the money was spent, the honeymoon over, and the guests gone. The perfect wedding did not necessarily lead to the perfect marriage, and the delusion of happily ever after only brought crushing disappointment.

Her own parents, John and Maggie, had believed themselves in love. In the end, though, they had been too poor to escape their problems; their apartment too small to hide from one another; and their lives too desperate for forgiveness. Their children learned first-hand what "marital chastisement" meant in the hands of an intemperate husband.

As a result, Georgie learned to keep her goals practical, seeking peace of mind over passion. The security of the Blaxton name had seemed a promising start. Surely she was not the first woman to have considered her future in such a mercenary manner. The scene with Rosa, though, had shown her that even practicality had its limits. She would not marry Archibald Blaxton, but she did not see any reason to tell the "groom" this news before she had to. The status quo, as awkward as it was, seemed the least upsetting solution—and the less she spoke to Archie, the better. Unfortunately, keeping her mouth shut around him was a constant challenge.

For one thing, he thought himself better trained in pedagogy than she. Georgie doubted anyone could top Fraülein Wenckebach's lectures on the subject, but Archie had gone to Harvard, so how could she argue? She would have loved to point out that he had no idea how to actually manage children. His methods might work in the cerebral classrooms of Exeter Academy, but they had no relevance to a poor Filipino boy whose biggest concern was where to stash his live rooster during lessons. Juan and Salvi, trained in the authoritarian Spanish style, reinforced Archie's autocratic tendencies. The result was an uncomfortable restlessness on the boys' side of the barrier, broken occasionally by bouts of quiet fear.

Georgie's demeanor was less formal, a blending of common sense and the Fraülein's theoretical training. Most importantly, she had learned to grab the teaching moments when they came along, rather than plan every word in advance. Her willingness to improvise was serving her students well, though Archie would never admit it. She still remembered his long scowl the day a goat tried to climb into her classroom through an open window. She turned it into a lesson on simple verb tenses: The goat will climb. The goat is climbing. The goat climbed.

She should have used: Maestro will get angry. Maestro is shouting. Maestro walked out. At least most of his tantrum took place after the children had already left for the day. She had not argued back, but it took a tremendous amount of self-control not to do so, and the effort wore her out. She retired to her room that evening, declining yet another invitation to eat at his house.

Georgie had hoped to relax during the Christmas holiday, but in retrospect that was a bit unrealistic. After all, this was the season that combined the most gregarious of Filipino pastimes: faith, feasts, and fiestas.

The cacophony started on December 16th with the *novena* masses. A graduate of Sacred Heart—and Margaret Mollie O'Shea's daughter to boot—Georgie was well acquainted with the nine-day-long series of devotions that built up to Christmas. Apparently, though, no one in Boston had been doing it right. Instead of convening at a respectable evening hour, San Nicolás de Tolentino's bells began ringing at three in the morning. A full band marched down the street, playing Filipino and Western carols as loud as their instruments would allow. And if a body still had not woken up yet, Father Cirilo Ávila knocked on every door.

The first time that Georgie answered this untimely summons, she had thought that she was being warned to flee another fire. Loud bells in the middle of the night had usually spelt disaster in Lower Roxbury. But when she hauled the door open this time, she had found herself face to face with the small Filipino priest holding a gas lantern. "Maestra! Come to the church, yes?"

Half in shock and half asleep, Georgie did not answer right away. First, she wiped the crust from her eyes. Then she took a moment to remind herself that Father Ávila had been nothing but welcoming to her and Archie. He had even encouraged local children to attend their school—after he "exorcised" the building, of course. Archie threw a fit over that last bit, but Georgie convinced him to look the other way for the sake of establishing public trust. It paid off too—few Thomasites enjoyed such a good rapport with their curate. And, no doubt about it, the priest was the most powerful man in town. Even Don Javier did not carry his authority.

So, instead of questioning the sanity of the man on her doorstep at this ridiculous hour, Georgie maintained her composure. "Is everything okay, Father?"

"Yes! We are all blessed in the season."

"So what are you doing here?" Apparently her good manners were still a little fickle.

"Mass at four, Maestra, because the men go to fields at dawn. Come join us to give thanks for the season. *Malipayong Pasko!*" The priest was positively jovial, without a trace of guilt for interrupting her slumber. Before Georgie could accept the invitation, the padre had walked off to the next house. So much for sleep.

Georgie obediently attended mass not only that night, but each of the seven that followed—not that she would have been able to refuse. She wondered how Archie got away with not going, but no one stopped at his door. She was not sure whether it was a mark of respect or reproach.

She wrote her mother about the services, knowing Mama would be thrilled that Georgie attended mass at all, let alone every day. In fact, both mother and daughter could have been sitting in their respective pews—one in Boston and the other in Bais—at the same moment, sharing a prayer halfway around the world from one another. It was a reassuring thought.

By Christmas Eve, when there was just one more novena to go, Georgie woke early, listening the first toots of the band practicing in the field outside town. A knock came at her door. "Padre, I'm up," she shouted from bed. It was not quite a lie.

The knocking continued. Father Ávila usually gave her a few more minutes than this. The bells had not even begun ringing yet. "Padre, I know!"

Still the pounding continued, harder now. Georgie got up and threw on her robe, but she did not bother to light a lantern. There were already so many torches outside that she would be able to see the pesky priest just fine. She navigated the stairs carefully and opened the door.

"Father, I promise I'm—"

She stopped abruptly. Standing in front of her were the two little De Los Santos girls. Her first thought was that they believed school was in session today, which made no sense. "Maria, Rosaria, good morning." Morning was a generous description.

"*Malipayong Pasko*," the girls said in unison, without any real holiday cheer. They must have woken up well before two in order to walk this far from the hacienda. Rosaria held a dim coconut oil lamp that looked like it should not have lasted the whole trip to town.

Georgie opened her door wide to admit the girls. Maybe they could sleep on her floor until dawn. "Merry Christmas. No school today, remember?"

Maria shook her head as if to clear away the fog inside. "Maestra, the *Misa de Gallo* today."

The service of the rooster—that name seemed appropriate. Was the padre now sending children to do his work?

"You want to go to San Nicolás together?" she asked.

Maria shook her head again. "No, San Honorato," the girl managed to murmur. "Padre Andrés want Maestra."

Georgie did not know a priest named Andrés, but she doubted he would appreciate Maria's indecorous phrasing.

"Is this a different church? *Dili* San Nicolás?" She added the Cebuano hoping it would elicit a clearer answer. The downside of doing this was that Georgie would probably not understand the reply, which was more than a little embarrassing after two months in Bais.

Finally, the girl stopped shaking her head and nodded instead. "Yes, Maestra go San Honorato."

"Where is San Honorato? *Asa?*"

Directions at this hour were too much for Maria. She pointed in the general direction that she trudged from every day, revealing neither how far it was nor how long it would take them to get there. Georgie considered sending the girls away in the hope of getting another fifteen minutes of sleep before Father Ávila came knocking. Then she looked at little Rosaria, whose tiny fists were rubbing tired eyes. If the *maestra* refused, they would have to trudge back home empty-handed, two hours of sleep sacrificed for nothing. Georgie could not have that on her conscience.

"Come inside. Come," she beckoned. She shut the door and led them upstairs.

They rested on her bed while she dressed. After she washed up, she nudged Maria and Rosaria, both of whom popped up reflexively like jacks-in-the-box.

Georgie refilled their lamp with oil, and they set off together to the mysterious chapel. As they walked, Georgie realized that she was heading to Hacienda Altarejos for the first time. She wondered if Don Javier would be at the service, but then dismissed the idea. He did not seem like the kind of man who would sacrifice his own comfort for a pre-dawn mass.

Georgie had vague fears about the tragedies that could befall them on the dark road. She reminded herself that this was a trip that her students made twice a day, every day. They would be fine—as long as the girls could stay awake and lead the way. At school Maria's sharp tongue usually harangued her sister nonstop, but right now Georgie did not need to scold anyone into silence—sleepwalking had the same effect.

An hour later they safely stumbled into a cluster of chromatic light. Georgie wondered if she had fallen under some kind of enchantment. The building in front of her was like nothing she had ever seen.

It was painted a milky green, the hue of celadon china. The windows, including one in the shape of six-leafed daisy, were outlined in dark green and white. A carmine-colored dome capped the chapel with a budded cross. Surrounding the church were hundreds of colorful star-shaped lanterns hanging off white-blossomed frangipani trees. Georgie stood frozen in place, overwhelmed by the feeling that she had entered a secret village of wood sprites.

Maria pulled Georgie's hand insistently toward the door, and they stepped through the threshold into the bright nave. Almost everything inside was painted white—the foundation pillars, the walls, and even the arches. The only contrasting color was the dark brown wood of the pews, relic cabinets, and altar. There was no shortage of crosses topping the furniture, but the religious artifacts almost seemed like an afterthought. Household objects disrupted the sense of sanctity, like the clock hanging by the doorway of the priest's room. She wondered how often worshippers found themselves paying more attention to the passage of minutes than to the words of the priest. Good old Reverend Daly had been smart not to tempt Georgie with such a distraction when she was a child.

Maria dragged Georgie up to the clergyman, who was welcoming worshippers in the front of the nave. Like Don Javier, the tall priest could almost pass for Spanish, but a Spaniard would not have looked so comfortable in such a whimsical little church. This man acted like he owned the place. Had Georgie not known better, she would have thought she was in the receiving line at the padre's cotillion, not his mass. When it came time for her to step forward, Georgie felt uncharacteristically shy. Did women shake hands with priests in the Philippines? Not knowing what to do or say, she simply stood there with a silly grin on her face until he made the opening.

"Good evening and welcome to San Honorato," he said in English accented with the musical cadence of a Filipino. "You must be the *maestra Americana*. I have heard much about you," he said.

It was meant to be a pleasantry, but his comment gave her pause. Accounts of her could vary widely, depending on the priest's source. "It's nice to meet you, too, Father…?"

"Everyone here calls me Padre Andrés."

"I'm Georgina Potter," she said, though she suspected he probably already knew her name.

"Have you been to the dawn mass before?" he asked.

"You call this dawn?" It was still pitch black outside.

The padre had a friendly, resonant laugh. "I suppose we Filipinos enjoy proving that we're more stoic in our faith than our once-mighty masters."

Either that or they were a nation of masochists. Georgie knew that many Americans believed the Filipino to be lazy, but she could not imagine getting a full house at this hour in Roxbury—and that church was a lot easier for its parishioners to get to. "Father Ávila has been more frenetic than stoic, I'd say, especially when he knocks on my door."

The priest winced. "Padre Ávila takes his duties seriously. It was not meant as a test, though. Had he known you were not Catholic…"

She heard the implicit question in his words and did not blame him. Georgie was used to people assuming that all Americans, especially Thomasites, were anti-Catholic. It did not help that the first Manila superintendent had been an officer in the YMCA and delivered lay sermons at the Presbyterian Mission. The stories of Protestant conspiracy had grown from there.

Georgie could have avoided answering, as she usually did, but she was Catholic enough to know not to lie to a priest. "I was raised in the Church, Father. I can't say that I plan to attend mass at this hour as a regular practice, but I'm glad to be here now. This is a unique place."

"Yes, our little chapel is special. Right, Maria?"

Father Andrés smiled at the girl hiding behind Georgie's skirt. The child's sudden timidity was surprising, but she could be excused for being a little star-struck in front of the man who headlined the pulpit every Sunday.

The priest returned his attention to Georgie. "You know, Father Ávila and I teach religious classes during the week but cannot seem to find a room in town large enough for our growing numbers."

She realized his game now: he wanted her schoolroom, and by law he had a right to it for half an hour, three times a week. It was part of President Roosevelt's attempt to placate Catholic critics, both in the Philippines and America. She sized up Andrés with her schoolmarm eye. "You don't seem like the kind of man who's usually coy, Padre."

He laughed again, a short outburst that seemed to surprise even him. "My friends tell me I should be more diplomatic, so I am working on it."

"I prefer men who speak plainly," she said with conviction.

"Well, isn't that fortunate," he mumbled and glanced behind her.

Georgie turned briefly but saw no one there. "Yes, well, I'm sure we can give you some time in the schoolhouse, probably in the evenings." It would have to be after Archie left for the day.

"Thank you, Miss Potter. Father Ávila has had difficulty broaching the matter with your Mr. Blaxton."

Georgie could only imagine. "My colleague is not so friendly to Catholics, I'm afraid."

"He is your fiancé, as well, yes?"

That was the question of the hour. She was about to mumble something vague when she was saved by the brass band's final overture. Father Andrés excused himself, but kept his eyes on her as he retreated. The man was too observant by half.

Maria led Georgie to a hard wooden pew where her sister had already fallen asleep beside their parents. Maria woke Rosaria with a quick pinch to the upper arm. Up sprung the little urchin, and Maria pushed her over to make room for two more.

When Father Andrés began the mass, Georgie regretted not having carried her Latin studies further at school. Though she had listened to the rites all her life—even studied them with the nuns in high school—for the first time she sensed significance behind the words. Father Andrés did not drone the Latin like an Indian Veda hymn; he spoke with inflection as if telling a story. She felt the same way about the Cebuano sermon. She only picked up a word or two, but from the faces around her it was a stimulating enough lesson to keep the somnolent crowd from dozing off or watching the clock. The full band may have had something to do with that too. In her experience, the only musical instrument deemed appropriate at mass was an organ, but this little chapel boasted a complement of brass, drum, tambourine, triangle, and castanet players. Georgie would not have been surprised if the whole congregation had started dancing.

By the time the mass was over, she decided that had the Spanish priests been as worthy as Father Andrés, they would never have sown enough resentment to foment a revolution. Incompetence, more than any other vice, must have lost Spain its empire. America could not make the same mistake.

At the end of the service, Georgie followed the crowd toward the doors leading outside. As she filed down the aisle, she looked up and saw Javier Altarejos standing in the balcony reserved for the rich and mighty. From the lock of his gaze, she could tell that he had been watching her for a while. The unsuspecting field mouse had just walked straight into the path of a cobra—and the infernal snake was smiling.

CHAPTER TWENTY-SIX

San Honorato

J avier entered his chapel tentatively that morning, half expecting to be struck down by a God who found him undeserving. Maybe, if he was lucky, the great piety of his mother Lourdes would shield him from divine wrath. He planned to stay by her side as much as possible, just in case.

The path from their house had been lit by *parols*, Chinese-style paper lanterns shaped like the star of Bethlehem. The lights were meant as a symbolic offering of sanctuary along the road, a fact that amused Javier since he had a hard time imagining any *hacenderos* making space in their manors for an itinerant shepherd or his laboring wife.

Though not quite four in the morning, the church was full. Javier and his mother made their way up to the small rear balcony reserved for the benefactors of the chapel. After the proper prostrations, Lourdes sat beside her son in benevolent study of their tenant farmers. The box felt empty without Allegra and the entourage she always invited. Javier wished he could have afforded to bring her back for Christmas, but it would have been another unnecessary expense. In any case, he knew she would be home for good at the end of March, and that would be trouble enough.

Andrés looked up and caught Javier's gaze. The padre raised his eyebrows, as if to ask what would bring his skeptical half-brother to the early morning mass of the most faithful. Javier nodded in his mother's direction in answer. Only one day a year did Lourdes manage to drag her son to Church. His mother was trying hard to save Javier's soul—that, or get him married off to a girl who would take over the job. She was failing in both endeavors.

Andrés, on the other hand, claimed to have given up on Javier years ago. No doubt the padre could even pinpoint the very night: January 29, 1889. Javier remembered it well: it was back when they were rebellious teenagers sneaking out of their dormitory in Cebu, as they did whenever Friar de la Canal dozed off early. But instead of their normal nocturnal wanderings, a randy Javier led Andrés to a *mujer libre* in her closed coach, a sort of ambulatory brothel. In what may have been the greatest disappointment of his young life, Javier found himself short of coin.

In the midst of their clumsy negotiations with the greedy pimp, another man showed up with his *mujer*, claiming rights over the street corner and therefore the boys' business, such as it was. Any sane person would have known that it was only a matter of time before the fracas alerted someone to their absence, but adolescent boys are not examplars of sanity. Cocky in all senses of the word, sixteen-year-old Javier protested that one of the two women—it did not matter to him which one—owed him relief. In his defense, he had not had a frig in months—not since suffering the friar's birch on his bare backside, a perverse sanction against self-abuse.

The Guardia Civil did eventually show up, though they probably would have turned right around and left had the boys not lost their courage and run.

The gendarmes caught Andrés first. "Javito!" he screamed. There was a soft thud of flesh against flesh. Javier turned—still running—to see Andrés fall to the ground with his hands cradling his stomach.

What else could Javier do? He surrendered, earning himself a blow in the bellows by an over-enthusiastic policeman.

The Guardia Civil returned the two to the *colegio* where, not surprisingly, the friars identified Javier as the corrupting influence marring Andrés's otherwise perfect record. Lázaro Altarejos was called in from Bais to separate his boys. Deciding that his heir had a lot to learn about discipline and responsibility, the *hacendero* shipped Javier off to Spanish military school. At least his time in that sink of cruelty had only lasted two years; fourteen-year-old Andrés had paid an eternal penance: he was transferred into seminary classes and told that his destiny lay in the priesthood.

The two young men had not spoken again for eleven years. Pride had prevented Javier from offering his friend and half-brother a well-deserved apology. It was not until 1900, when Andrés's nationalist sympathies jeopardized his ordination, that Javier saw a chance to mend the breach. Andrés could not have picked a worse time to finally discover his inner rebel. Had he avoided controversy, he would have been appointed Dumaguete's first native rector. Instead, Javier had to practically beg the Bishop of Jaro to allow Andrés the "privilege" of preaching to illiterate cane slashers in the family's piteous hacienda chapel.

Sitting in that chapel now, Javier found the place charming, not piteous at all. Still, he might be tempted to cast Andrés out of it if the priest chatted up Georgina Potter too much. He probably was doing it just to drive Javier crazy. No doubt that was why Andrés had invited her here this morning, summoning her with his minions. Javier looked up at the vaulted ceiling and wondered why he let himself be tortured by a God he did not believe in.

Lourdes looked over at him, mistaking his expression for devotion. "So the spirit finally moves you, *hijo mío?*"

"Not exactly," Javier admitted. He was unwilling to hide his profane nature, even if it disappointed his mother. "I was, ah...noticing the *maestra Americana.*"

"Ah, yes," his mother said. "Allegra mentioned Miss Potter in one of her letters."

He glanced at his mother, wondering how much she knew. Allegra was not one to "mention" any subject casually, so it was probably a thorough introduction. Javier normally would have pressed for more information, but right now his attention was focused on the American. In the brilliant light of a thousand candles, Georgina's hair took on an almost unholy color of flame. She had tied it back in a loose braid that left her neck exposed above her casually draped shawl. He could not see her pale freckles at this distance, but he could imagine them sprinkled across her breastbone.

Javier watched Andrés talk to her. Though the padre did not deserve anyone's jealous eye, Javier's clenched fists betrayed him. Georgina's manner was blameless: she looked bashful, almost reverent. The problem was that she had no idea how beautiful she was. No doubt she could tempt even a priest to hang up his robe.

"Does this *maestra* mean anything to you, Javito?"

He shifted a little in his seat, uncomfortable with his mother's much too observant presence. He never could hide anything from the doña, so he did not to try to. He turned to face her.

Her eyes locked on his, Lourdes nodded once. "I see."

Javier looked back down to see Georgina sit with the De Los Santos family. All he could see was the back of her head, but it was enough.

"She normally attends San Nicolás," his mother continued. "Every day during novena, they say. I like that she is a good Catholic girl, but around you she should be careful. I know that look in your eye."

He resented that. Not once had he done anything to shame his mother, at least not since his return. These past few years he had practiced the same self-denial as Andrés—only in the name of sugar, not God. Of course, in Bais, God and sugar were almost the same thing.

"Mamá, I'm hardly a scoundrel."

"Oh, no, that's not it at all," she said with a quick laugh.

"Then what did you mean?"

"I said I recognized the look," she said, "but not because I've seen it on your face before."

"Then whose?" he asked.

She sat back in her seat and smiled. "Your father's. When he met me."

CHAPTER TWENTY-SEVEN

Bodbod

B y the time Javier escorted his mother out of the church at the end of mass, the rest of the hacienda was awake and sitting on God's doorstep. Lourdes quickly went to work directing the house servants to put out the breakfast she had brought for the poor. It was the doña's duty to make sure her tenants' stomachs were full during fiesta, especially on Christmas Eve.

The *muchachos* unloaded boxes of *pandesal*, hard-shelled rolls that were one of Spain's more popular transplants. The rolls had been hard to get during the war since the Philippines did not produce its own flour, but of course the *Yankis* now had an answer for that: they encouraged dependence on American wheat at the same time they protected their own market against Philippine sugar. If Javier let himself think about this hypocrisy for too long, he would become thoroughly unsociable.

He took a deep breath and tried to enjoy the beautiful dawn. He walked around the front of the chapel, looking over the vendors selling the traditional sweets of *Misa de Gallo*: hot chocolate, ginger tea, and rice flour pudding.

Eventually, he found his true prey. When Georgina first caught his eye in the chapel, she looked half ready to bolt. Fortunately, she had been too curious—or too foolish—to escape when she had the chance. Now she was inspecting a sugary treat displayed on an unfolded banana leaf.

Javier approached her, but she was too engrossed in her study of the food to notice. He positioned his chin behind the nape of her neck. "*Bodbod,*" he whispered.

Georgina spun so fast that she lost her balance. Javier steadied her before she could crash into the table and ruin the peddler's week of hard work. She recovered, though he suspected her heart was racing. She pulled her wrist from him before he could count the beats.

Javier handed some change to the vendor and took the sweet in question. "*Bodbod,*" he explained. "It's made of sticky rice and chocolate. Here. You'll like it."

She tore off a small piece and held it up for further inspection.

"Really," he said, trying not to laugh. He counted off the ingredients on his fingers. "Rice, coconut milk, sugar, salt, and chocolate. No tricks, I swear."

Georgina ate the tiniest morsel possible just to make sure that he wasn't fibbing—no dried fish or chicken feet included—and then she plucked off a respectable chunk. "Oh my, that's good," she declared. She took an even bigger bite.

When this woman decided on something, she pursued it zealously. "I'm glad you like it."

"It's fantastic! Why haven't I had it before?"

"Stirring glutinous rice is hard work, so I doubt your cook has volunteered herself for the task." In fact, he knew Julieta would not appreciate this broadening of her employer's palate. "Here, try it with this."

He turned to another vendor, who sliced off a meaty side of fresh mango and cut a crisscross pattern through the orange flesh. Javier used a piece of bamboo to scoop out a single cube and lifted it up to her mouth. Georgina hesitated, but her curiosity won out. She let the mango slip off the stick and into her mouth.

"Oh, wow," she exclaimed, eyes wide.

"So what brings you to our little corner of Bais, Maestra?" he asked.

She did not answer right away, probably because she was paying more attention to her food. "Well," she said between bites, "I was sort of kidnapped."

"What?"

"I sleepwalked here, I think, but I woke up in time for the service. I've never enjoyed mass more."

Javier tut-tutted. "Enjoying mass—now that's an interesting concept."

"You're just spoiled," she scolded. "Father Andrés is quite an asset, you know."

"Too good for us, but don't tell him that."

She shrugged, mouth full of rice and mango. After she swallowed, she said, "Even Jesus ministered to the moneylenders."

He chuckled at the comparison. The priest had integrity, but he was hardly a model of tranquility. "No, Andrés shouldn't be hidden away in a country chapel like a dirty secret, even if he is my family's dirty secret."

When Georgina looked confused, he explained more clearly. "He's my half-brother, my father's bastard."

"There is a resemblance. Your mother accepts—"

"Yes," he cut in, not sure he could explain it any better than that. "In fact, sometimes I think she likes Andrés better than me."

Georgina smiled. "I can see how that might happen."

"I bet the gossips have given you quite an earful about the evil Javier Altarejos."

"I've heard plenty," she said, still smiling. "Enough to know that confession must never get boring."

"Well, if I went, it wouldn't."

She laughed, and he enjoyed the sound.

"But that says more about me than Drés," he continued. "I'm happy that you recognize his talents, even if his superiors do not." Javier knew that he should let go of his disappointment. His brother certainly had.

"Why has he been overlooked?"

"He couldn't keep his mouth shut. The Spanish are surprisingly thin-skinned."

Georgina looked up from the food in her hand. "But the Spanish are gone."

"You'd think so," he said. Americans had no appreciation for the subtlety of the *Peninsulares*. Of course, that was because subtle was not how the United States ruled. The *Yankis* pointed their guns, planted their flags, set up their schools, and immediately set to work "civilizing" their "little brown brothers." It was demeaning but straightforward.

In contrast, the Spanish had been insidious, carrying more Bibles than guns. In most provinces, the friar had been the only colonial official around, which meant that he had played the roles of tax collector, registrar, military draft board, health inspector, and—whenever he could find the time—spiritual guide. Negros had effectively been a territory of the Augustinian Recollects, not the Crown. When the people revolted against Spain, much of their ire fell upon the religious orders. The Recollects ran for their lives, all the way to Manila, Hong Kong, or even Spain—and in their absence the bishop had no option but to hand the parishes over to native priests, a first in the Philippines. Dumaguete, Bais, and even his chapel at San Honorato: all were in the hands of Filipinos...for now.

"Now that things have calmed down, the friars will try to weasel their way back into all of Negros," he explained. "They've already landed up north. It's up to Governor Taft to decide if they can return to their parishes."

"Why not leave the native priests in place? Who needs the Spanish here at all?"

"Now you sound like Andrés," he said, meaning it as a compliment. Georgina had come a long way in two months, though maybe it was easier to criticize the Spanish specifically than to find fault in foreign occupiers in general. American priests would not be any better. He tried to explain: "It's like your social clubs—*indios* can sweep the floor and pour the wine for the members, but they can't be a member themselves. The friars say it's because the native clergy is inept, immoral, and ignorant."

Georgina turned to look at Father Andrés, who was speaking with a small crowd of peasants in the door of the chapel. "Have they met that man?"

"In fact, they trained him. But let's just say that he's not always been this genial. If he's lucky, he'll be able to stay on when the friars return."

"Because they'll see what good work he's done here?"

"No, because they won't care two straws about my hacienda. Or, at least, I hope they won't."

"I guess Father Andrés is lucky to have a brother like you."

Javier wished she had said that in front of Andrés, if for nothing else to give the man a good laugh. "Well," he drawled, "we used to get in a fair bit of trouble together as boys. I was a bit wild back then. As a companion, he was mostly willing." It was true enough, if a little vague.

Georgina smiled, taking his answer at face value. Clearly, she had no trouble believing Javier on the road to the deuce. She was not the only one.

"But these are stories best told over good food and drink," he said, nodding to her almost empty hand. "The real eating begins tonight after midnight mass. We call it *Noche Buena*. I would be honored if you would share this feast with my family."

He knew that his mother would be delighted to host the *maestra*—after she got over the shock that Javier had invited a woman to dine with them.

Georgina shook her head slowly, and Javier sensed genuine regret. "I'm sorry, but the Stinnetts have invited me back to Dumaguete. And I have to admit that I'd like some traditional American Christmas foods tonight." Even so, she finished the *bodbod* with relish.

"What would such a dinner include?" Javier hoped she would not say Chicken à la Colorado.

"In Boston, my mother would start with oyster soup because Blue Points were available all winter long. Then we'd eat roast goose, apple sauce, cream of lima beans, and plum pudding." She stopped and stared at his broad grin. "I know, I know, I'm not going to get any of those things tonight."

"Maybe the oysters, though they would be easier to find on the other side of the island. Goose is unlikely, but if you need waterfowl you can buy duck from the Chinese. I thought Americans always celebrated with turkey?" The Filipino papers loved to cover the strange fiesta habits of their new conquerors.

"I don't think the Stinnetts will be eating turkey for a while," Georgina said with a strange finality. "Anyway, it's more of a Thanksgiving tradition for many of us. I, for one, would welcome any change from pork—if you call what my cook feeds me pork. I've had to draw the line at blood stew." She wrinkled her nose.

Javier liked Julieta's *dinuguan*, but he could not defend the woman's cooking without admitting to knowing her. He did not pass up the opportunity to tease Georgina, though. "I never presumed you to be the squeamish sort, Maestra. In fact, I rather imagined you heading out to shoot the turkey yourself."

"Are you kidding? This city girl can't even trap a rat, let alone shoot dinner. I'll leave that job to the soldiers."

He frowned. He did not like the reminder of the American Sixth Infantry stationed next door, nor did he like to imagine those men seated at Georgina's dinner table.

"The Stinnetts say it's their tradition to celebrate together with the local commanders," she explained. "Many of the first teachers in the islands were from the Army."

Javier tried to let the whole feast-of-conquest scene he conjured in his head drop without a challenge, as much as it irked him. "Of course."

He reached for her hand, and she was too surprised to stop him. "Goodbye for now, Miss Potter. I hope you get your Christmas bird."

Javier did not let go of her hand after he kissed it, and Georgina didn't pull back either. Their fingers remained intertwined as they brushed against the side of his thigh. They stood together for a wonderfully long time, each waiting for the other to act. When he thought she was finally about to pull away, he let go. He bowed and left quietly, his fingers still warm from her touch.

CHAPTER TWENTY-EIGHT

Noche Buena

Despite what she had told Javier, Georgina was not looking forward to the American party in Dumaguete, but neither could she figure out an excuse to stay home. Everyone at the Stinnetts' would expect her and Archie to behave as a couple in love. Mary quickly confirmed this when Georgina arrived to help her set up for the party.

"Imagine how beautiful we can make this room look with just a little decoration," the woman practically sang, hanging ylang-ylang blossoms in strands from an actual pine.

"Where did you get the Christmas tree?" Georgie had not expected to see one out here, and she half expected the woman to admit to conjuring it with a special prayer. Mary had a way of taming even the most exotic setting.

"The governor had it brought in from Valencia, ten miles up the mountain. It's perfect, isn't it?"

Of course it was, Georgie thought. The Larenas had found it. Just like the Larenas had rented Archie that beautiful house that she was supposed to share with him once they were wed.

Mary waved her hands around the room. "Imagine what they could do for your wedding luncheon if you had it here!"

Georgie eyed the huge space. It would hold everyone she knew in Boston, let alone the Philippines. "Mary, I appreciate it, I really do, but—"

"You've chosen another location?"

"Well, no—"

"Please tell me you've at least chosen a date."

She could not answer that demand either.

"Look, Georgie, it's up to you, but I think people are starting to find it strange that you're not married yet."

"I'm not going to rush into marriage just to avoid embarrassment," she said flatly.

"Of course not, dear." Mary brushed back one of the unruly curls that escaped her bun. "But don't you want to get married?"

Georgie's shrug answered the question better than anything she could have said.

Mary stared at her a few moments, and then looked away. "Everyone's going to be here tonight," she said in a soothing voice. "I think this party will be great for you—a boost to your spirits. It'll help you think more clearly." She listed the American officials who would attend—in order of rank—and then the prominent Filipino families.

Georgie was too tired to be evasive, so she asked straight out: "The Altarejoses weren't invited?"

"Oh, I had to invite them, of course, but fortunately they declined. Don Javier is so anti-American. We've got nothing to say to each other."

Georgie had a hard time imagining Javier saying nothing.

The memory of their last meeting flashed through her mind. She should not have allowed him to hold her hand in public. Even worse, she had brushed her fingertips against his thigh. She had never thought of doing that with a man before. She was no ingénue; she just found most men resistible.

"There's another thing," Mary said, a little cautiously.

Georgie stiffened in anticipation. Sometimes being with this woman was like hanging around a disapproving parent. "Yes?"

"We're heard that you've allowed priests to hold services in the schoolhouse."

Word traveled fast—it had been less than a day. Georgie was not eager to hear Mary's opinion on the matter. "It's the law," Georgie said. "You know that. I'm sure the same is done here in Dumaguete."

"The priest has his own building to use; he knows better than to ask for more. No one understands why the Church has to steal away what little space you have."

"Steal away" was typical Mary hyperbole. Besides, any good teacher would have seen that a cavernous church was not a great place for academic instruction. The schoolhouse had the only blackboards in town. "Governor Taft said we should share, so I shared. That's all."

Mary would not let it go. "Even the Larenas disapprove of that law."

No doubt the Larenas agreed with the Stinnetts on everything. Georgie had nothing against them, but she was not going to get caught up in the opera of collaborator politics. She said nothing.

Mary looked at her carefully. "Are you sure you're not a little swayed by your own, ah, history with the Church?"

Georgie almost smiled. So Archie had told her. "Because I'm Catholic, you mean?"

The woman raised her hand to her mouth in a tiny gasp, as if Georgie had suddenly declared herself Chinese. "I mean your mother may have been—"

"I was raised Catholic, Mary. My whole life. I was baptized in the Church, confirmed in the Church, and graduated from a Catholic high school."

"Mr. Blaxton told us you weren't committed."

Georgie sighed, wondering how much longer she was going to let this go on. "Archie believes what he wants to believe. I don't make a big deal out of it."

"So the rumors are true, then."

"What rumors?"

Mary looked around, afraid to speak the crime out loud. "That you've been going to Church every day in Bais."

"Only the novenas, Mary. Bais isn't a big enough town to avoid it."

"Mr. Blaxton doesn't go."

Mr. Blaxton was used to making his own rules. "No, he doesn't."

"Sometimes you puzzle me, Georgie." Mary bit into her cheek, thinking hard. "Well, you need to spend more time around the rest of us Americans, that's all. It's no wonder you're unhappy—you don't have enough variety of companionship out there in Bais. But tonight your compatriots from the Dumaguete school will be here: Mr. Dakin, Mrs. Reed, Miss Berry, the Conants, and all the others. Won't that be fun for you to meet them?"

They had not exactly reached out to welcome Georgie to the neighborhood, nor help her set up her new school in Bais, but they were American. "Sure."

Mary looked around the big, empty room. "It will be so lovely tonight, don't you think?"

"Of course."

And it would be. The officers from the Sixth U.S. Infantry Regiment would get a real American Christmas, complete with a tree, presents, and servants clad in red and green sashes. The centerpiece of the festivities were the tiny bamboo boxes painted in wrapping paper patterns and piled high beneath the tree, each one filled with candy for the local children.

After Georgie finished dressing for the party in Mary's quarters, she walked downstairs, only to find that many guests had already arrived. She had not seen so many of her countrymen in one place since the transport from San Francisco. In the midst of well-dressed, well-educated colonials, Archibald Blaxton stood out proudly, looking right at home. His suit was the finest example of Boston tailoring, and this was a crowd who would appreciate such a thing. He was speaking with a short, paunchy major with thinning hair. The officer's khaki uniform was wrinkled and sweat-stained, and Georgie wondered if Archie chose his companion to highlight the satisfactory comparison he made.

She walked toward the two men. The major acknowledged her with a nod, but carried on with the conversation as if Georgie were not there. He had a shrill voice that seemed to match his lack of height.

"No, Mr. Blaxton, I have to say that I do not find Dumaguete barbaric enough. A bit more wildness would at least make it interesting. I think the worst thing we could do is civilize these people. Left alone they'd at least be a curiosity, of interest maybe to naturalists."

"You don't agree, then, that we should be teaching them English?" Archie asked.

"Heavens, no! So they can parrot back meaningless gibberish and think they're actually communicating? It seems that whenever one of these goo-goos can't make himself understood, he just speaks louder. If there's anything worse than a Filipino's English, it's the same stuff shouted at the top of his lungs."

Archie laughed heartily at the major's complaint, even though it struck at the very heart of the Thomasite mission. "I know what you mean. You should hear some of the wretched boys in my class. Frankly, I don't know how they even managed to learn their own language."

The major huffed. "I'm not sure it is a real language. Maybe it's a complicated joke they're playing on us, keeping our linguists busy scribing their words so that we have to make sense of them."

Archie nodded sympathetically. "How the Spanish managed to teach these people anything is a wonder to me."

"While impregnating all the young girls at the same time, eh?" The major winked.

"Well, you've got to have some fun."

"Quite right!" The major caught Georgina's disapproving eye and flushed.

Archie clasped Georgie's arm tightly as if he had just noticed her presence. "There you are."

Georgie avoided his eyes. "You're looking well."

"You should have come found me the instant you arrived in town," he whispered. "People expected us to arrive together."

She was not surprised that his first concern was over appearances. "We've barely spoken in weeks. Why pretend otherwise?"

He pulled her into a quiet corner of the room, away from the candles on the Christmas tree. Georgie wondered if she was the only one in town who saw the brutish side of the otherwise-charming Mr. Blaxton. He was one of those people who could afford gracious manners while at ease—but when the slightest challenge arose, he became selfish and grasping.

She tried to resist without making a scene. "Archie, I don't want to discuss this right now. I'm going to head back to Bais before it gets dark."

"And miss dinner? What will I tell people?"

"Honestly, I don't care."

His eyes lit like dry timber. "So it's true, then?"

"What are you talking about?"

"You're leaving me here to be with him."

"Who?"

"Altarejos. Rosa told me that you were at his church this morning and that people saw you holding his hand. I couldn't believe it, Georgie. I'm telling you, I swore up and down that such a thing was not possible—that you wouldn't lower yourself to that. But it is true, isn't it? You've made a fool of me."

Georgie was stunned by the turn in conversation, though she should have realized that even the slightest misstep would eventually reach Archie's ears.

"It's just a misunderstanding, Archie. Don Javier kissed my hand. It is their custom and was a politeness, that's all."

"How could you do this to me?"

She knew that she should walk away, but she could not resist a little honesty. "I wasn't thinking about you at all."

"Obviously. Just to refresh your memory, Georgie, I got you this job—"

"So I could find Benji!" she interrupted.

"And if you want to find him, you had better not jeopardize your position here while you are looking."

She looked at her fiancé for a second before responding. "The Bureau has no reason to dismiss me." She sounded more confident than she felt.

"Whom do you think they will believe?" He looked over at the major, already engrossed in conversation with Daniel Stinnett. "When they ask the local Army commanders for character references, whose side will they be on? You know that if you're fired before the end of your contract, the Bureau won't pay for your transportation home. And, if you leave me, neither will I."

Passage home cost several months' salary, and Archie knew she could not afford it on her own. She had arrived in Manila with nothing, and the state of her bankroll had not improved much with the Bureau's lack of punctuality in issuing her checks.

"Why are you doing this?" she asked. "Why would you force me into marrying you when you don't even like me?"

"Nonsense," he said. His expression gave away nothing.

"Why not marry Rosa?" she whispered. "At least your wife and mistress will be the same woman, and there's some sense in that."

His blue eyes did not blink. "I'd be careful about throwing stones, Georgie. I'm not the one people are talking about."

"Because your indiscretions are old news." Some demon coaxed her into provoking him, just as she used to do with her father. Let the crowd see the true Archibald Blaxton, she thought.

Surprisingly, though, Archie did not explode. In fact, he drew back, took a deep breath, and composed himself. She could not help but be impressed by this rare display of self-control.

"Listen," he started calmly. "Let's not be rash. You're having a bit of trouble adjusting out here, and maybe it's my fault for not showing you the way of things. We should spend more time together, like we did in Boston. We had fun, didn't we? We're out here together, after all. To return home unmarried after all this…well, no one would understand."

It was a surprising change in tone, but she was not fooled. Archie had gone against his family's wishes in coming to the Philippines, and again in proposing to Georgie. To admit that he had failed at either endeavor would be humiliating. Elspeth would insist on choosing his bride-to-be the next time around.

Georgie thought about her own options. Like it or not, she was trapped here just as much as he was. Her bonds were financial and his were societal, but they were both prisoners of Bais. It was funny that neither of them even pretended to talk of love. All the better, she thought.

She took a deep breath. "I'll think about it."

He loosened his hand but did not let go. He planned to stick it out—both the party and the marriage. Georgie, on the other hand, was sure she could not make it through the evening, let alone a lifetime. But she would let him believe whatever he wanted. For now.

Satisfied that he had made his point, Archie released her and moved on to other guests as if it were his party. After circulating politely for a few minutes, Georgie excused herself, pleading a touch of the "Bais Bellyache," and left the party for home.

CHAPTER TWENTY-NINE

Aguinaldo

I t was almost one in the morning on Christmas Day, and Javier
wondered if Georgina had made it back yet from Dumaguete. If
so, had she been silly enough to go to bed already? Surely someone
had told her about the *daigon*.

Javier was happy to see that he was right in time for the send-off.
The band was marching down the road and most of the town was
either already assembled on the street or lingering in their doorways,
fresh from the *Noche Buena* feasts. Most Filipinos spent the whole
year looking forward to this night. The young belle playing the Virgin
Mary had waited her full fifteen-year lifetime for it. She was queen of
the pageant.

Javier noticed a lamplight begin to glow in the second story of
the schoolhouse. It would only be a moment now. The downstairs
door opened and Georgina stepped out, a bewildered expression on
her face. She was wrapped in a thin cotton robe over a very modest
nightgown. He watched her in the pale light of the *parols* as she tried
to finger-comb her disheveled hair.

Smoothing over the expression on his face, Javier walked to her
and bowed. "*Buenas Pascuas*," he said.

"*Buenas Pascuas*," she responded, still trying to blink herself awake.

"I thought that you might not be prepared for this particular festivity, so with your permission I brought you some supplies."

"Supplies?"

He turned to his two footmen, both of whom had arms full of candy, cigarettes, cakes, and wine. "*Aguinaldos*. Gifts for the townspeople."

"And servants to carry them," she said.

Javier smiled, remembering her dismissal of the muchachos in the garden. "Although I am capable of carrying most bundles on my own, I hope that you'll allow me to keep some secrets from my people. The men haven't stopped asking me to join them in the fields, now that they know of my expertise with a spade."

"Am I causing you trouble, then?"

She had no idea. "Nothing I can't handle, Georgina." It was the first time he had used her given name to her face. Either she did not notice his familiarity or else she chose to let the liberty stand. No matter which it was, he was happy with his progress.

The men set down the boxes of treats in front of her. "So, what do I give away?" she asked. "And to whom?"

"We can wait here for the party to arrive, but I think you would find it more interesting to see the whole show."

"The show?"

Javier offered his arm, which she took without hesitation—another victory. They walked toward the sound of the brass band, and once she recognized the tune, she started laughing.

"You were right about 'Hot Time,'" she said. "I'm beginning to think it's the American anthem, as well."

He was happy and laughed too. "They're just getting started. I'm sure 'Just One Girl' or 'After the Ball' will be next."

"Not very good Christmas songs, are they?"

"I suppose not, but they don't need to be. They're just to get your attention."

He guided her to a house with a pronounced balcony, the perfect place to start the *daigon*. Mary, Joseph, and a chorus of shepherds and angels were already assembled. Mary was dressed in a blue and white gown, her "pregnant" belly stuffed full of pillows. The band fell silent as the holy couple sang a plea for shelter to the owners of the house. One did not have to know Visayan to understand the girl's predicament.

The owners of the house responded in turn, and Javier translated in a whisper. "They're saying that the house is already bursting with people."

Then Mary sang again. "She's promising them heavenly rewards," he explained. "I think a literal translation is that 'their names will be written in the book of the chosen few.'"

"It's beautiful," the *maestra* whispered. "What did the people in the house just say?"

"They've turned her down. They said their house is not for the poor."

"How awful."

He found Georgina's innocence endearing. No doubt she knew the story of the Nativity as well as he did—probably better, since she actually went to all the novenas—but her rapt expression made it seem like she was hearing the story for the first time.

They trailed the crowd to the next house, where Joseph begged for a place for his wife, "even in the kitchen," but was told that the mansion was "only for nobles." When Mary insisted, the doña threatened to let loose her dogs on them.

Georgina looked around, noticing that they were almost at the school building. "They won't sing to us, will they? More importantly, I don't have to sing back?" She looked truly alarmed.

"No, don't worry. They'll finish before that, at the 'stable'—by which I mean San Nicolás. The crowd and the band will amble on, though, begging for refreshments, so we should go prepare."

Georgina's eyes lit up. "Your *aguinaldos*!"

He laughed and squeezed her hand on his arm. "Exactly—including your favorite: chocolate." He waggled his eyebrows, earning a smile in return.

"Do I have time to change my clothes?"

"Maestra, they're practically upon us."

"But everyone's dressed in their Sunday finest. I've never seen so many new pairs of shoes worn at once—half those children are already rubbing blisters—and meanwhile here I am in my robe."

"You look beautiful, Georgina. No one will notice." The last bit was a lie, but he hoped it was outweighed by the absolute truth of the first part. "Here comes the sacristan, so get ready."

Javier put an old Alfonso XIII peso in her hand. "Give this to that first gentleman in the cassock." He nodded down the road to the fellow carrying a silver dish topped with a cross. The sacristan rang a bell as he approached each doorway, bowing down on one knee to receive a donation. He approached Georgina and did the same, waiting until she placed the peso on the dish.

Afterward, Georgina grinned shyly at Javier and thanked him. "I wouldn't have been prepared for any of this."

Mary, Joseph, the shepherds, and the angels peeled off to the church, but most everyone else made a point to first greet the *maestra* with a polite *"Buenas Pascuas."* Javier rewarded the children with chocolate, and gave wine or cigarettes to the adults. Her stoop became quite a popular spot.

Javier enjoyed watching the schoolgirls compete good-naturedly for Georgina's attention, each singing a carefully rehearsed song prepared for the season. Each girl would perform it uncountable times throughout the night in exchange for an *aguinaldo* from kinder or richer relations. Those who could not sing—rare though it was in the islands—danced or told spectacular stories. No matter what their brand of entertainment, all of them charmed the *maestra* equally, almost to the point of happy tears. The students may not have noticed, but Javier saw her wiping the corners of her eyes. When they were reluctantly dragged off to church by their parents, Georgina's girls waved goodbye as they made their way down the street.

"I'll miss this place," she said quietly. Javier was surprised at the premature nostalgia, given that she had another year left of her commitment to the school.

She turned to him and scolded him gently: "You know, I really should have sent you away hours ago."

"What did I do?"

She rubbed her forehead, exhaustion beginning to wear through her happiness. "You already got me into enough trouble this morning, and now I've let you do it again."

He had heard the *tsismis* about their handholding. Adelita, the wife of his overseer, had been first with the news, and anything that rang of romance moved quickly on the hacienda. Still, he played dumb. "What happened this morning?"

Judging from her narrowed eyes, she was not buying it. "Apparently people around here think we may have formed an attachment. People like my fiancé's nurse."

So Blaxton had heard, he thought. Good. He would have to thank Rosa later. "You should know that folks here gossip as sport. Most people know it's not the sworn truth."

"Not after the entire town paraded by my house before dawn and saw us handing out gifts together—with me in my robe."

The robe had been a nice touch. "It's only right that someone guide you through our local traditions. I'm your landlord and benefactor. People will simply assume that I want you to feel at home."

"Well, maybe," she said, thinking on it a second. "But you still have to leave now."

He tried not to look disappointed. "Of course, Maestra. It has been a pleasure, as always." He kissed her hand and dropped it quickly this time, giving her no reason to stay angry. At least, he hoped so.

CHAPTER THIRTY

Corporal Punishment

Georgina had given Julieta the week off, leaving the teacher to do her own shopping. Boxing Day was business as usual, especially at the market, and it was just the crush she had feared.

"Maestra! Maestra!"

Neneng and Ditas rushed to her, their hands full of food from sidewalk vendors. Her pupils' *aguinaldo* bounty would not last long if they spent at this rate.

Ditas offered Georgie a snail from a newspaper cone. Neneng demonstrated how to eat the mollusk snack, using a long thorn to pick the meat out of the shell. Unfortunately, the thing looked no more appetizing nude. When Ditas offered a few roasted peanuts from her bag as an alternative, Georgie eagerly took them.

"Maestra, where you go?" Neneng's question sounded impertinent to Georgie's ears, but Filipinos believed that showing interest in a person's immediate plans was polite. In school, Georgie had tried to supplant their directness with a simple "How are you," but the more intangible question had not yet caught on.

"I'm going shopping," Georgie said. "Where are you two going?"

"With you, Maestra. We help you," Ditas said.

If the girls could help bargain down a price or two, they would be worth their weight in Mexican silver. Georgie moved from stall to stall, purchasing the chicken and vegetables she wanted but attracting a larger juvenile entourage than she needed. There was a small rotating crowd of five or six surrounding her at all times, and they insisted on carrying her basket in turns.

Neneng tried to lead her to the side of the market where the fish was, but Georgie resisted. "No, Neneng, thank you. I don't need any today." She had eaten enough fish in the last three months to last a decade.

But Neneng had a different agenda. "Maestra go see mother."

The girl guided her to a stall that sold all sizes and varieties of fish, both dried and raw. Standing behind the assortment was a dark-skinned woman with the same wide mouth and kind eyes as her daughter. The woman rushed around the table, grabbed Georgie's hand, and held it to her own forehead—a child's greeting to an elder. From one adult to another, it was awkwardly excessive.

Since Mrs. Lamdagan could not speak English, Georgie overcompensated with broad smiles and lots of eye contact—both of which gave her a headache in short order. Fortunately, Neneng was an enthusiastic (if somewhat sloppy) translator: "Mother happy for see Maestra. Mother happy for school with me."

Georgie had gotten pretty good at deciphering her students' creative use of prepositions and phrasing. Most of the time she corrected them, but this situation did not call for a grammar lesson. "I'm so glad."

"Emilio no good."

Georgie did not teach the woman's son Emilio, though she saw him escort Neneng home every day. "He's not well? Sick?"

"Emilio bad. Make Maestro Juan very mad."

Juan rarely raised his voice within Georgie's earshot, but she knew that he spent many hours alone with the boys in the afternoons, drilling them in rote memorization. It was an old-fashioned method of instruction, but Archie let the man continue his Spanish ways.

"I'm sure Maestro Juan is not angry. Sometimes all teachers can get frustrated, especially with so many students."

Since "frustrated" was beyond Neneng's translating abilities, Georgie rephrased: "He is tired, you understand?" That was not exactly what she meant, either, but precision was something she had learned to live without in provincial communication.

Neneng nodded, but that did not mean she understood. "Mama say sorry for Emilio. Maestro do right," she explained. "Hit Emilio. Emilio be good now."

Georgie felt a prickling heat on the back of her neck. "Maestro Juan hit Emilio?"

"Many boys the same." Neneng held up her palms to demonstrate where Juan had hit her brother, most likely with a ruler or stick. "Maestro teach bad boys."

Where had Archie been during all this, Georgie wondered? "How many boys?" she asked.

Neneng understood this question—it was an exercise they had been doing a lot recently: how many books, how many mangoes, and so on. "Many, many bad boys. Mama very sorry for Emilio." Since Neneng could not yet count beyond ten in English, this vague answer was very discouraging.

Both mother and daughter shook their heads in the same pitiful way, eyes lowered in shame. Georgie realized that theirs was not a complaint or even a cry for leniency; it was an apology for the inconvenience of Emilio causing his own beating.

That probably should not have been a surprise. The Thomasites' aversion to corporal punishment had been met with as much skepticism as praise in the islands. There were many Filipinos in teacher training colleges who scoffed at the idea of trying to teach peasant children anything without "proper" discipline as motivation. Some Filipino parents felt the same way, especially those who had been schooled under the friars. One mother had been so concerned about the Americans' soft touch that she had offered to beat her daughter on

Georgie's behalf; the *maestra* needed only to send word when the girl deserved it.

Certainly, the last thing Georgie wanted was for poor Emilio to have his hide tanned both at school and at home, so she tried to assure the Lamdagans that the boy's misbehavior—if that's what it was—did not imply wickedness on his part. She wanted to give a sense of the chaos in the boys' class without making it seem like the children's fault. "Girls sit well," Georgie explained. "But boys have so much energy. So many of them."

Both Neneng and her mother smiled as if the half-hearted explanation cleared up everything. Not that they would challenge Georgie even if it had not; her status as a teacher set her above reproach in Bais. Mrs. Lamdagan further emphasized her appreciation by foisting all varieties of dried fish on Georgie, and politeness demanded that the teacher eat each one with theatrical appreciation. The fish was an offering to seal a bargain—only Georgie had no idea what that bargain was. She was learning that Filipinos could be so indirect in their requests that sometimes it did not seem like they had asked anything at all. She left the market with a lot of dried fish and even more questions.

The whole situation bothered Georgie for the rest of her vacation. Were children being punished for the inadequacies of their teachers? Why hadn't Archie put a stop to it?

She had planned to approach the question carefully, but subtlety lost out to fury when, on the first day back, she discovered Emilio and another boy behind the schoolhouse kneeling on piles of dry mung beans. Their pants were rolled up to their thighs so that the pebble-sized seeds dug deep into their knees. To make matters worse, the boys struggled to balance cups of water on their outstretched arms—tried and failed. Liquid sloshed over the brims from the furious shaking of their muscles, and tears streamed down their faces as they fought the pain. They could not wipe their eyes, though, without spilling more water.

This ordeal was not a quick correction from a strict teacher; this was premeditated cruelty. Georgie had heard of such barbarism in parish schools under the Spanish, but witnessing it in person—at her own American school—outraged her. She grabbed the cups and dumped the water on the ground behind her. The boys gasped in shock, ready to protest, but she silenced them with a hand to her lips. She helped them to their feet and supported their weight as they hobbled over to a bench by the side of the building. They sat and rubbed their kneecaps like arthritic old men.

Georgie marched into the classroom to find Archie reading an old Manila newspaper while his aides ate a light *merienda* meal. It seemed like just another afternoon at the office.

"Do you two like mung beans?" she shouted at Juan and Salvi. "Are they tasty? I've heard they're best when they've been softened under a young boy's knees for a few hours."

She doubted the two men understood her exactly, but her anger translated well. She stormed up to the table and slapped down her hand. "We do not...DO NOT...beat or humiliate children in this school. If you can't live with that, then you can find yourselves new jobs!"

"Just a minute, Georgie," Archie said, rising to his feet. "You don't have the authority to fire anyone. I am in charge of this school." To emphasize that point, he quickly dismissed Juan and Salvi. He could not let Georgie challenge him in front of his Filipino subordinates.

Georgie seethed until the two left. "I don't work for you, Archie. We're equals."

"You think so? Maybe that's a question for the new division superintendent to determine."

Georgie leaned back on Juan and Salvi's desk—the desk that should have been hers, but that Archie had given away to his assistants. "Maybe it is."

"Too bad for you they're bringing Montgomery in from Bacolod. He and I knew each other well on the *Thomas*."

Because Georgie had not come over with the first batch of teachers on that ship, she was not a part of the ruling clique. Archie, on the other hand, had cultivated influence everywhere. It was the nature of being a Blaxton.

"And my old boss in Manila is now the head of the Bureau," he continued, folding his arms over his chest and settling into the fight. "Do you really think he's going to listen to you over me?"

"Those men may be your friends," she countered, "but they're not blind. What happens when this fellow Montgomery arrives and sees the scars on the boys' hands and knees?"

"It's not my problem. I didn't punish those boys."

"But you didn't stop it, either!"

Archie shrugged. "Juan's real problem is that his expectations are too high. He actually wants these brownies to become scholars. The best we can hope for them is a good industrial education: teach them how to make furniture or some other trade. Practical work."

She was flummoxed: a Harvard man teaching carpentry?

"What was the point of coming out here, if that's what you think? Don't you see how much potential these children have?"

"Ah, such the doting schoolmistress," he taunted. "I suppose you're speaking from your vast professional experience?"

"I've been here long enough to know—"

"You're only here at all because I got you this job." Archie's lips pulled back from his teeth in a snarl. "Good thing the Bureau considers beauty a drawback in female teachers—all I had to do was mention your gawky height and homemade clothes, and it won them over immediately. Maybe you could get promoted to principal on freckles alone."

Georgie gasped. "If that's what you think, why would you want to marry me?"

"I thought that you could be a proper wife: loyal, appreciative..."

"If you wanted appreciative, you should have stayed home and raised a Saint Bernard." She blew out a breath in frustration. "God knows I can't figure out what you're doing here. You don't like me, you don't like the school. You don't even like the children. It's not like you need to work, so why are you wasting your time in the middle of nowhere?"

Archie straightened up. "It's a new century, Georgie. No man will get anywhere in national politics without foreign experience. This colony is the chance for me to make my mark."

"Where exactly do you see yourself in thirty years, the White House?"

She had meant it as an absurdity, but she saw the unmistakable flash of ambition in his eyes. Lordy, she wanted to laugh at the irony: Archie had been too much of a fop to join the Rough Riders when Colonels Roosevelt and Wood had come calling at Harvard Yard, and now that the fighting was over he was trying to find his own piece of the glory. In the retelling, this staid little town would become the very edge of civilization, and he would regale audiences with the tale of dodging a dangerous ladrone right in his very own kitchen!

Georgie realized something else too. Despite Archie's disdain for those below his station, her modest background fit into this plan perfectly: the seamstress's daughter who had raised herself up to become a respectable teacher, laboring side-by-side with her husband on the wild Asian frontier. She gave him added appeal with the Boston Irish and with working people everywhere. People would think it a love match, and who could resist such a heart-warming story? And to think, all this time she thought that she had been the one using him.

"Archie, let me assure you that you'll never be elected to anything, no matter how many Filipino boys you 'civilize' over here. No one likes you. And I've certainly never met a man more unfit to lead."

His eyes practically bulged out of his head. "What do you know—"

"You can't even manage the finances of a two-room schoolhouse! You think you can run a whole country?"

"Like I give a damn about this god-awful school or these dirty little pigmies," he shouted. "Let this place choke on its debt—and I'll be damned if I pay one fucking cent to your black lover, Altarejos."

"My lover?"

The protest died on her lips as her inner devil took over once again. His ridiculous allegation demanded the most outrageous response possible. "Don't worry about Javier," she said, cooing the man's name. "I'll make sure he's satisfied, with or without your money."

The shock on Archie's face was worth it. He was speechless, an unprecedented treat. When he found his voice again, he spoke quietly but with a dangerous growl. "Well, I'm glad that we haven't acted in haste. I wouldn't want to keep you from your savage. It's fortunate that I discovered your perversions now, before I risked my family's good name in marriage. Consider my offer rescinded, Miss Potter."

"Fine with me." And it was. It was more than fine, she thought. She had no idea how she would find Benji and get them both home, but that did not change the fact that getting thrown over by Archie was the best thing to happen to her in months.

Part V: January 1903

Dear Miss Potter,

...Ben went off with Glenn to the Fifth, but when I ran into your brother in Manila in March, he was trying to arrange an immediate discharge. Judging by his condition at that point, I doubt that he had trouble getting the Army to let him go. You might be able to find out more by writing Glenn. Would you believe that man is in custody in Manila yet again? It is a wonder any of us got out of Samar unscathed by either a bolo or a court-martial....

Respectfully,
Tommy Qula

CHAPTER THIRTY-ONE

New Year's Debts

Javier easily picked out Georgina's voice on the crowded street. She was standing on the stoop of the Yucos' sari-sari shop, asking the young stock boy why he was sweeping dirt *into* the store. The boy, probably freshly smuggled in from Amoy, could not have explained his people's beliefs to the American schoolteacher even if he did speak English. Some traditions do not make sense in any language. The Americans were having enough trouble understanding Filipino ways; they had to be really stumped by the Chinese.

Javier figured the *maestra*'s business in the store was much like everyone else's. She might have stopped by to say a friendly hello to her student Ising Yuco, of course, but her step seemed more purposeful than social.

He had not seen Georgina in two weeks. Not that he had taken her dismissal of him seriously, he had just been unable to get away from the hacienda. Now he planned to make up for that absence.

He followed her into the store. She stood at the counter, too focused on the receipts in her hands to notice him enter.

Javier ducked behind the dry goods aisle and waited. He knew this sari-sari and its owners well. Despite the Hispanicized nickname, Pepe Yuco was pure *sangley*, the local term for a merchant-traveler from China. Though the man had lived here for over a decade, he still spoke neither Spanish nor Visayan, leaving all Filipinos to deal with Tina, his Chinese mestiza wife—as they probably would have done anyway, given that women dominated the marketplace in the islands. Pepe let Tina run the store, and he gambled away their profits at Chinese roulette.

Javier quickly recognized Georgina's small scraps of paper as chits, either for herself or for the school. Half the town owed the Yucos money, and all of it was recorded on receipts exactly like these. Tina Yuco's unblinking eye was making sure the *maestra* did not accidentally "lose" any while counting them up. Georgina did not notice the woman's suspicion, or maybe she just pretended not to. She wrote each debt into her own ledger, and then returned the corresponding slip to Tina.

Javier was not the only person in the store watching this scene play out. No one seemed to have anything better to do than to follow the *maestra Americana* and observe her strange ways; after all, it was the lull in the calendar between New Year and *Sinulog* when most townspeople lay low in intra-holiday half-tempo.

He could at least guess why she was so concerned about the money she owed, and it was probably his fault. In one of his overseer's attempts to collect the rent from Blaxton, Geno had explained—at Javier's suggestion—that most people paid off their debts before the beginning of Chinese New Year, which was rapidly approaching. The settling of debts was meant to bring good luck all around. Georgina must have overheard the exchange and had taken up the burden on her own.

The custom applied to people of all stations. This year Javier would stretch the books so that he could pay all his local debts on schedule, a necessary sacrifice to hide the true extent of his obligations from the blood-sucking *aswang* he called neighbors. He would fully pay off the Yucos in Bais but not the Cuayzons in Manila. Fortunately, he had a few more months until he faced the nightmare of the latter.

Georgina tabulated the total and turned the book for Mrs. Yuco to see. Javier leaned on the shelf beside the imported flour and waited. He had known Tina most of his life, and he knew that she did not take chances with her sums. After a quick calculation of her own, Tina agreed to the number. The *maestra*'s math was impeccable; Javier had not doubted it for a second.

"Señora Yuco," Georgina began, "I'm sorry that I don't have more to pay you now. I still haven't received my November paycheck." She pulled a Mexican silver dollar out of her bag and showed it to Tina. "I can only pay in Mex."

That meant the real bargaining was about to begin. The Yucos fancied themselves a better breed of merchant than others in Bais, and followed the Manila custom of pricing their goods in gold American dollars. Because everyone paid in silver Mex, and since the value of silver had been falling since 1901, this policy allowed Tina to further impoverish her customers with an unfavorable exchange rate. Javier did not begrudge the woman her living, but it was a system that unfairly favored the savvy.

Javier stepped forward before Tina could claim one more innocent. "Good morning, Maestra," he said. He turned ever so slightly to Tina. "Señora."

"Don Javier," Georgina said weakly, less happy to see him than he would have liked. That was too bad, but he could not stand by and watch her lose on the transaction.

He spoke quickly to Tina in Cebuano. "What rate will you give for the Mex?"

She wrote a number on her pad and showed him. He turned to Georgina and explained. "She's offering thirty cents gold to the Mexican dollar."

The *maestra* leaned close to him and whispered, "That's not a good rate, is it?"

"It's about a fifth too low," he admitted, talking softly to the hairline at her right temple. "The official rate is thirty-eight and a half—

but it will probably drop soon, and we're awfully far from a real bank. Tina's very frugal," he warned. "She practically grew up in an auction house."

"I'm from merchant stock, too," the *Americana* assured him. "I might as well embrace that fact."

Georgina wrote a number on a sheet of paper and slid it over to Tina: forty. It was the right opening bid—enough above the legal rate to give her room to negotiate, but not so high as to be ridiculous or insulting. The two women began their duel; it was pencils to first blood.

The others in the store crowded behind Javier. The cockpits were closed today by order of the Commission, so this bidding war between two of the most prominent women in the community was the best entertainment around. Javier even saw a few hand signals offering odds on the outcome of the women's transaction. Two different men bet that the storekeeper would not pay above thirty-four; they were probably right, too, which explained why no one was taking up the challenge. The people of Bais loved Georgina, but they feared Tina Yuco.

Javier nodded to the impromptu bookmaker and accepted both wagers. It was an act of chivalry that he hoped the *maestra* would never discover.

Georgina stalled at the official rate just long enough to indicate her seriousness. Strained smiles marked the two adversaries as they measured each other's resolve with new bids. Javier lost track of the action, almost missing the quick flash of victory in Georgina's eyes when they settled on thirty-six cents gold—a better rate than even he would have earned.

Tina was quick to pick up the paper before anyone else saw it. Georgina took out a pile of coins from her bag and pushed them over to the storekeeper.

"*Salamat*," Tina said, cupping her hands possessively around the coins. She held out one Mex at a time and dropped it on the floor so that she could listen to the sound each one made—it was the best way of detecting a lead counterfeit. Satisfied, she picked up the coins and tucked them in a box under the counter.

Georgina wrote the newly negotiated value of the coins on a scrap of paper, folded it twice, and handed it to Tina. Tina's rare smile was the sole thank you for her discretion. Javier was the only other person to know the bargain struck—and although he had clearly won his bets, he pretended the opposite, quietly paying out two *pesetas* to the bookie.

Tina tore up a quarter of the receipts, but a sizable pile remained in front of Georgina. The *maestra* looked at the stack with regret.

"What's the matter?" Javier asked her.

"I just...I knew I didn't have enough money, but I had sort of hoped—"

"You made the effort and gained a friend as a result," he said. "You'll have plenty of time to settle the rest later."

"But what if I don't?"

"It's over a year until the next Chinese New Year," he said, smiling. "You are here for a two year posting, right?"

"I'm supposed to be."

That was not the answer he expected. He gently took a hold of Georgina's elbow and pulled her closer to whisper: "Are you going somewhere?"

She pulled away in frustration. "I don't know."

Javier did not press her—not here. He knew that she could leave, just not that it was a serious possibility—not until now.

Tina pushed her accounts book over for Georgina to verify and initial the new total.

Javier acted swiftly. He figured what the hell—if he was headed for insolvency, he might as well do it in style. He wrote the total of her remaining chits on a blank slip and signed it. Tina took Javier's new note and filed it away in a different book, the ledger that held his hacienda account. She pushed Georgina's chits his way—they were now Javier's to do with as he chose, and he chose to rip them in two. He stacked the halves together and tore them one more time, tossing the small pieces on the counter.

It felt good. The union of their debts was a semi-legal tie that bound Georgina to him, and he liked that. Although she could always walk away from what she owed him, she was far too principled for that. He smiled in satisfaction. "Well now, it's all settled, Maestra."

While she choked on her protest, he tipped his hat and walked out of the store. She may not like how he picked teams, but she would learn to play on his side. And when it came time to pay off the Yucos, maybe he could get her to negotiate a silver price under his name, too—their name, if she would have it.

CHAPTER THIRTY-TWO

Javier's Invitation

If Adela buys a gallon of milk and Rita buys three quarts, how many quarts have they both?

Georgina looked at the lonely question written on the board. She had planned to introduce American units of measure this morning, but there were no students in attendance. Adela and Rita—prosperous milkmaids though they might be—were counting their quarts at home.

Everyone seemed to be home for the *Sinulog* holiday—everyone but Don Javier. The big pest had just sauntered into the schoolhouse and perched himself on the edge of the new desk that had mysteriously appeared for Georgie last week. He sat on the thing like he owned it, which answered the mystery of where it had come from. She should have rejected the gift for its impertinence, but she was done with "shoulds."

"Greetings, Maestra," Javier said, his voice low and rich. "You seem to be on your own."

It was true. Despite the wide open door and windows, no one would dare enter as long as the mighty Altarejos was here. And anyway, Georgie's usual coterie of children had disappeared to the town market to spend their last Christmas coins.

"All these fiestas," she complained. "I don't know how people expect my girls to learn anything." She held out her fingers and counted off each offending holiday. "The novena, *Noche Buena*, *Niños Inocentes*, Rizal Day, New Year, *Tres Reyes*, and now *Sinulog*—a festival for the saint of a whole other island—"

"So?" The side of his mouth twitched.

"So you're just making days up now."

"Who is?"

"The whole town," she said, stretching her arms out to encompass the strange place she would never understand and never call home.

"Oh, we wouldn't do that."

Georgie thought they most certainly would. It was a general confederation against her—either that or a phantom of her own homesickness. She was not about to admit the latter, though, especially when this man had come to gloat. "Soon it will be Chinese New Year," she said, "and then Candlemas. Have I forgotten any?"

Javier was trying not to smile. Georgie did not know which he found funnier: her troubles or her thorough catalogue of them. "How about February twenty-second?"

She sighed. "Not another saint—"

"From what I've seen of you *Yankis*, exactly that: George Washington's birthday."

Of course, she thought, how could she forget? Apparently the conspiracy extended to her own government too. "Out of the last six weeks, I've only been able to teach two. My division superintendent could show up any day now, and I'll be back to page one of the primer."

To her relief, Javier did not make the easy crack about the American primer having only one page worth teaching. "I saw the De Los Santos girls carrying their books around the hacienda," he said. "You will be surprised how much all those girls will revise together. They'll catch up quickly."

She shrugged. "The super will find a way to fire me anyway. And then who knows how I'll get home—"

"Hey," he said, straightening up to reach out to her. But then he seemed to change his mind and gripped the edge of the desk instead. "Don't worry so much. Do you think yours is the only school affected?"

"I suppose not." She brushed some chalk off from her cuff. It was white dust on white cotton, hardly noticeable, but right now the sight of it bothered her. "I don't know how you people get anything done in this country."

"Remember that we're farmers, spread out over vast fields and mountains. Fiestas bring people together 'under the bells' of the Church. Not to mention, it's a nice break from work."

Georgie looked up at him and raised a brow. "And how much time are you giving your men to rest, Pharaoh?"

"*Touché*," Javier said, still smiling. "But I didn't come here to—"

"I know exactly what you came for."

He tilted his head, interested. "Really?"

Georgie held up a finger to quiet him, and amazingly it worked. Javier crossed his arms, leaned back against the desk, and waited.

She reached for the bottom right drawer and pulled, but it moved only a few inches before hitting Javier's calf. She peered up at him through stray locks of her own hair, her chin only a few inches above his thigh. His dark eyes trapped hers, and she froze.

No, she told herself. She would not let this man know what a coward she was. She bobbed up in a single nervous jerk, pretending the move was deliberate by reaching back to wind her unruly hair into a bun.

"Don't," Javier said. He brushed a curl from her eye. "It's pretty like this."

She completed the impromptu knot. Once her hair and mind were better tamed, she reached again for the drawer that he was still blocking. She could not tell if he was teasing her or just being obtuse.

"Excuse me," she demanded. Slowly, reluctantly, Javier rotated his body to the side, allowing Georgie to reach into the desk.

She grabbed a small bag of silver coins and held it out for him. "Here's the rest of December's rent—twenty Mex—along with what I owe you from the store. I'm not paying for the desk, though," she said with a stubborn grin. "That belongs to the school now."

Javier made no effort to take the money. "Where did this come from?" He did not sound happy, which made him the strangest creditor she had ever met.

"Manila finally came through—they sent my last few months' back pay, plus a small capital budget for the school. If I'd been more patient, I could have paid Tina all by myself."

The *hacendero* was scowling at the bag like it was a sack of fish guano. "I didn't come for that. And as for the rent, your fiancé—"

"Archie's not my fiancé." She paused. "Not anymore."

A couple of questions flickered across Javier's face, but he did not ask them. Since this man rarely seemed to mind his own business, Georgie was impressed.

"Your, ah, colleague, then," he finally continued. "He's already asked for more time."

"He has?"

"Actually, he told my overseer that I wasn't going to get my 'goo-goo' money anytime soon—or something to that effect."

"He said that?" But she knew he had. After all, this was Archibald Blaxton of the Beacon Hill Blaxtons. "Your man must have been—"

"—a little cross. But not surprised."

"I'm so sorry."

"Why?" This time Javier sought her hand without hesitation. "Blaxton's no longer your responsibility, right? This is certain…you'll not go back to him?"

"No!" She flinched a little at her own forcefulness. "I mean we're finished."

Javier's fingers eased off hers and drifted up her arm. No words were spoken, but with that one gesture he asked a question, and, despite herself, she answered with a shiver.

Georgie broke his light touch by pushing the bag of coins back at him, shaking it twice.

"Why are you so eager to hand over all your money?" he asked. "What are you planning?"

Georgie wanted to tell him that it was not what she was planning, but when. God-and-Bureau-of-Education-willing, she could save up enough by the end of March to get out of here. School would be over for the summer, giving her time to continue her search for Benji. She hated to part with the cash, but paying off Javier was the first step in separating herself from the obligations of this town, this school, and her former fiancé.

"Just take it," she said.

"Georgina—"

"You're the landlord," she said, over-enunciating as if she were speaking to an unruly schoolboy. "I'm the tenant. I pay you something called rent. Here you go: rent." She shook the sack again. When he still did not take it, she dropped it squarely on his lap.

"Ow," he groaned, removing the offending weight from his groin. "Careful there." He tucked the money behind him, and her heart did not know whether to leap or sink. She was freer now—but poorer.

Their business was done—at least as far as Georgie was concerned—but Javier did not leave. Uncertain of what to do or say next, she waited. She reached back to scratch an itch below her shoulder blades, but when the motion pulled her blouse tight across her chest, she dropped her arm, hoping he had not noticed.

"I actually came here today on my mother's behalf," Javier said, rising to his feet. "She would like to invite you to our house tomorrow night for dinner."

Georgie had never met Lourdes de Altarejos, so it seemed unlikely that the woman would single her out. "Why me?"

"Because this is your first *Sinulog*."

He had to know how weak that excuse sounded. "What a considerate woman. And you say she raised you?"

"Her lessons didn't all take."

"How big of you to admit the flaws in your nature."

"An inherited nature, which still leaves you insulting my mother." Javier took a step closer. "She will be ready to hear your apology personally at six."

Georgie knew she should refuse but could not find the will to do so. She wanted to meet his mother; she wondered what Javier's home life would say about him. And it was not like she had to dodge Archie anymore. She was free to act as stupidly as she chose.

"I'll send a *calesa* for you," he said, leaning in. "*¿Está bien?*"

The buttons of his jacket were almost flush against her chest, but she did not back away. Against her better judgment, she actually nodded.

"Good."

Georgie tried to look anywhere but his eyes. She noticed a scorched strip of sugar cane that had settled on the edge of his lapel, ruining the beauty of the black silk seam. Debris like this engulfed the whole town when the fields burned, and even indoors she needed to shake out her own clothes every night. Without thinking, she started to pick off the char, but Javier caught her hand and held it there, right against his heart. He framed the side of her face with his hand—thumb against cheekbone, fingers woven in the hair behind her ear.

"Georgina?"

"Yes?" She looked up.

"Breathe."

She exhaled, but it did not slow her pulse any.

Javier tilted her face higher and held it there, appraising it like a collector. She tried to back away from the scrutiny, but his grip was sure. "What are you afraid of?" he asked softly.

That he would steal her soul? That she would be too easily tempted? He would kiss her; that she knew. If she even hinted at inviting him upstairs, he would bed her this very afternoon. That prospect had made her nauseous with Archie. Now she just felt dizzy.

"You're not answering my question," Javier whispered.

It almost seemed like he did not want it answered, the way he bent down and brushed his lips against her hairline. Then his lips grazed her freckles. The tickle along her spine spread to her tailbone. This man manipulated her so easily she should have been ashamed—but shame required focus, and she could not think at all.

His whisper was light and warm: "I'm going to kiss you now."

"I've been kissed before," she said, meaning it as both warning and permission.

He laughed against her temple. "Oh, have you? Did you like it?"

She breathed out a word. "No."

And then she kissed him.

CHAPTER THIRTY-THREE

The Kiss

Javier let himself be kissed. It was both more difficult and more enjoyable than he could have imagined.

He opened his lips just enough to let her in, and he followed the slow rhythm she set. He only allowed his tongue to dance a bit in her mouth, not take control of it. When he tasted the tart sweetness of *calamansi* juice on her tongue, the intimacy almost broke his restraint—almost. But this was her moment. If he could not check his desire, he would end up taking her maidenhead against the silly math problem on the blackboard. Today would not be the day.

"Ina." He murmured the nickname he had only used in his head. "My beautiful."

"I'm not."

He pulled back and smiled. True to form, she could not let even a compliment pass without argument. "I'm the beholder, and I say you're a beauty. Try not to be contrary." But he liked her contrariness, even now. It reminded him that an intelligent, strong woman was sharing a part of herself with him.

Georgina wrapped her arms around his neck, pulling him closer once more. She was tentative but learned quickly, moving her mouth harder against his. When she shifted, rubbing her hips against him, Javier groaned.

"This is not the best place for this," he admitted between kisses. But he could not stop. He had waited so long, and he did not care if they were caught.

He moved to her ear and nibbled it lightly, earning him a delicious quiver. Her response—a little bit of the virgin's alarm mixed with just enough of the vixen's desire—was so intriguing that his mind strayed to places it should not go. He thought about how these two roles would play out over her face as she came. Could he lead her upstairs and let her coax his clothes off?

No, he warned himself. All he had started out wanting was a simple kiss, and now his greed was taking over. Her hunger had infected him, but she was not ready for more. Not yet.

He let go and stepped away.

Reluctantly, Javier watched as Georgina—dazed at first—slowly regained her wits. She turned, and it was all he could do to not reach out for her again. Instead he watched as she scurried to the other side of the desk, interposing the huge chunk of hardwood between them. He would respect the barrier for now.

"I beg your pardon," he said, apologizing for both of them. The bulge in his trousers belied any real regret, though. He could not pretend to be unaffected.

"I think you should go," she said softly.

He liked to think there was more than a little reluctance in her voice, but he did not trust himself to be objective.

"The *calesa* will be here at half-five tomorrow," he said. "My mother and I will await you at the house."

"A chaperone sounds like a good idea."

Javier smiled. He nodded, adjusted his jacket and pants, and turned to leave. As he walked out the door, he remembered the bag of coins on her desk.

Let her try to return them again, he thought. Next time she would get what she paid for.

CHAPTER THIRTY-FOUR

El Baile

It was dusk by the time Georgie's carriage traveled up the sloping brick drive of Hacienda Altarejos. White lanterns lit the path, dotting the big violet sky like freshly minted stars. Georgie had been poised to leave the house wearing her chalk-dusted cotton frock until Julieta shared what everyone else in town already seemed to know: this "dinner" was really a full-blown *baile*. Georgie had almost shown up dressed as the wrong Cinderella—the stepchild, not the princess.

Fortunately, she still had one nice dress that was not torn, mildewed, or stolen: a pale gold gown in silk with gentle ruffles along the low neckline. She had copied the pattern from Miss Delavenue's shop on Hamilton Place but had not yet worked up the nerve to wear it. What had been fashionable décolletage in Boston might be scandalous in Bais, and she usually tried to avoid attention—a laughable goal for a lanky copper-nob in Asia.

Now she lingered in the *calesa*, inspecting the square manor house for the first time. A wooden top floor overhung the gray stone foundation by a few feet on all sides, an elegant-yet-clumsy layer cake decorated in white and green frosting. The upstairs screens were pulled open, releasing sounds of music, laughter, and clinking glass into the night air. Georgie was reluctant to leave the familiar security of the carriage but, at the awkward insistence of Javier's driver, she finally dismounted and walked through the large arched door of the house.

It always surprised her that the entrance to the noblest homes in the Philippines went through the stables. The furnishings were bare on this floor: a few pew benches against the walls for waiting laborers, an assortment of old furniture and tools, and a large desk in the well between the double staircase.

At that desk sat Geno, the property manager Georgie had met when first renting the schoolhouse. He was working hard despite the upstairs festivities. A small crowd of men waited for him to call each in turn to get paid. Well, "paid" seemed the wrong word, Georgie thought, since no actual coin changed hands. As each man approached, Mr. Canda scratched out lines of numbers by the worker's name in the ledger. She had sympathy for the men, knowing what it felt like to be a debtor in someone else's books.

When she approached the grand staircase, Geno smiled at her. *"Maestra, buenas noches."*

Georgie greeted him shyly. *"Buenas noches, señor."*

He leaned one elbow on the desk and pointed up. *"Don Javier está arriba."*

For the hundredth time, she considered turning around and fleeing, but the same wicked curiosity from the afternoon kept her here. She took a fortifying breath and began climbing. The stairs were shallow and short, and though the tomboy inside of her would have loved to take them a few at a time, she was not dressed for such gymnastics.

No servant announced her—how could they in the middle of such a racket? The band played on a slightly raised platform, out of the way of the throng. They were in the middle of a rousing version of "Hot Time," a song Georgie was now convinced that Filipinos played just to drive her crazy. The song's desperate verses did nothing to ease her anxiety: "You're all mine and I love you best of all, and you must be my man, or I'll have no man at all. There'll be a hot time in the old town tonight, my baby."

Georgie tried to shut out the music and focus instead on the vision in front of her. The room was painted a pale teal that she found particularly striking against the dark wooden floor. Carved moldings—the design as fine as lace—divided the large space into separate salons. Imported crystal chandeliers lined the ceiling, their glass prisms dribbling tiny rainbows of light like butterflies.

The house was full of people whose undergarments probably cost more than Georgie's entire wardrobe. Some men wore Hong Kong bespoke suits and cravats. Others donned the native *barong tagalog*: a loose, sheer piña shirt that hung outside the pants. To an outsider used to the European tucked-in, buttoned-up mode, it may have seemed like a sloppy substitute for formal dress; but the barong's fine weaving and intricate stitching lent a particular elegance to the costume. The women wore fluffy, elegant piña blouses with tulip-like sleeves that narrowed at the wrists. No one seemed to lack a fortune in jewels; Señora de Teves even wore a regal tiara on her carefully coifed head.

Georgie pulled at the ringlets along her hairline, futilely trying to straighten them without upsetting her only heirloom piece, a filigree comb with pearls. Julieta had helped her tie her long hair into a fashionable style copied from a Harper's illustration, but it was just too much red on top of too much woman, and now she had the stares to prove it.

To her left she spied an escape into the empty dining room. There she pretended to inspect a banquet table prepared for the dinner service. She walked its length, appreciating the bounty: plates of cold vegetables, cucumbers in vinegar, pigeon with mushrooms, carved beef rounds, and a ham in the center of sausages laid out in a sunburst pattern. This was the food of Europe, and Georgie could not say she was disappointed. She liked Philippine cuisine well enough, but she would never understand the appeal of a few popular dishes, like *balut*—hardboiled duck embryo—or *bagoong*—fish sauce left to rot in earthen jars until its taste was as ripe as its smell. Fortunately, they did not seem to be the favorites of the Filipino elite either—at least, not tonight.

She felt the heat of another body behind her. She turned slowly, knowing full well whom she was going to find. Sure enough, Javier drew her to his side, and for some reason she let him. He tucked her palm into the bend of his elbow and held it there. "I'm glad you finally made it, Maestra. Your ride here was smooth?"

"I wasn't quite ready when your driver showed." The truth was that she had stalled as long as she could before Julieta had finally pushed her out the door as insistently as a servant could without getting fired.

"A women's toilette is never done, I suppose." Javier smiled at his own spin on the old proverb.

"You're allowed to compliment me on how I look, not complain about the process."

He looked down at her bosom. "You do look nice."

"Señor," she quietly scolded.

He raised his eyes to hers, and she saw that her weak chastisement had amused him. "You haul out etiquette when you can't think of another way to push someone away," he said.

"Still, you shouldn't take the liberties you do."

"Liberties? Name one."

She could respond with a long list of his indiscretions, but she did not have the courage to describe them out loud—especially the intimacy of his kiss. Instead, she approached the issue obliquely.

"You called me 'Ina' when…"

Georgie felt herself flushing with embarrassment at the memory of his embrace. She could almost feel his lips again as they explored her neck.

Javier was not at all fazed by her unfinished protest. "Do you recall what you said in Manila about that nickname?" he asked.

Of course she did, but she would not admit it.

"You said it sounded confident and exotic," he said.

"And it's just as bad a fit now as it was then." How could he not see that? Her confidence was a sham, and being mannishly tall with a face full of freckles was about as unexotic as she could imagine.

A waiter arrived with a glass of champagne. Georgie did not need the drink; she already felt unsteady on her feet. Nevertheless, she sipped her sweet, bubbly drink, not wanting to like it.

"I bet this was expensive."

Javier took this as a compliment, not the judgment she had meant it to be. "My mother bought several cases in Europe."

"Oh? How often does she travel there?"

"When I was quite young, we used to go abroad with my father every other year. Now, though, we may be sipping the last of the stock," he said, winking at her. "Enjoy it."

"No plans to return?" Her tone, more than her words, carried an implied barb. She did not find false poverty amusing, especially amidst such an ostentatious display of wealth.

"We have our good years and our bad years," he said, a little wary.

"And this is which?"

He seemed to struggle with how to answer. "Not one of our best. You needn't worry, though: we pay our bills and treat our workers fairly, no matter what."

"Really, Don Javier? How many workers' opinions have you surveyed?"

He took one of her hands into his and spoke to her as if giving an oath. "Georgina, I'm a man of my word. If I make an agreement, I do exactly as I pledge. My employees understand that. My creditors understand it. I wish you would too."

Georgie wanted to believe him, but there were lingering questions that she could not let pass. "What about Rosa?" she asked, despite the irony of choosing this particular woman to champion. "She doesn't have many nice things to say about you."

"You mean Rosa Ramos, the woman who lives with your—"

"Mr. Blaxton's nurse," Georgie said.

Javier did not challenge her characterization, which was a kindness. "I'm curious to hear what she has said against me," he said.

Georgie didn't really know the details, so she kept it vague. "It's what you've done to her family."

"If I've mistreated them so badly, Maestra, then why is Rosa's mother here this evening?"

"What?"

"Over there." Javier moved Georgie to the door and nodded his head at a distinguished woman in a jade-colored dress, no doubt Doña Altarejos. The doña addressed two servants, one of whom strongly resembled Rosa. "If the Ramos family is so upset with us, why would Vicenta still be working in our house?"

"I don't know," Georgie admitted. "The handsome boss?"

She had meant it facetiously, but—judging by his toothy grin—he had taken her at her word.

"I'm handsome, am I?"

She paused, trying to think of a way out of the compliment. "I meant insufferable."

A small hand gripped Javier's elbow, interrupting his gentle laughter. He looked down and smiled even wider. *"Hola, Mamá."*

The woman in the jade dress had snuck up on them. The doña shared her son's angular nose, resolute chin, and square shoulders—powerful features, to be sure, but on the doña they were tempered by the elegance of a small, slim frame. Her eyes were darker than Javier's, almost black, obscuring the emotion behind them.

"Mother," Javier said, "This is Georgina Potter, the *maestra Americana*. Ina, this is my mother, Lourdes de Altarejos."

"Doña Lourdes, it's an honor to meet you," Georgie said brightly, hoping it would make up for calling Javier "insufferable" within her earshot.

Lourdes curled her thin lips into a dry smile—and in that gesture Georgie saw the true resemblance between mother and son. "I like that you are keeping my Javito on his toes. That is the expression, yes?"

"I told you that you'd like her, Mamá." The crazy man actually seemed to be pleased. "Ina was concerned about *tsismis* from Rosa."

"Do not worry," the doña said in excellent English. "It is easier that she blames others than admit the truth of her father. Peping is a...difficult man with drink."

Georgie understood that.

"He's also a troublemaker," Javier added. "A ladrone."

That was quite a censure. These days calling someone a ladrone could be a death sentence.

Lourdes drew Georgie close in an unexpected gesture of familiarity. "A few months ago Peping began more trouble," she explained. "He shot his own cousin and ran away. If he comes back, we will arrest and hang him." She spoke with the gentle but firm authority of a lifetime landowner.

"Rosa tells it differently," Georgie said, not sure why she was pressing the point.

"Maybe Rosa misses her father." Lourdes's eyes softened. "Her life was not easy, you know, even if she is very beautiful—maybe because she is beautiful."

"Everyone knows why she says what she says," Javier said, nodding his head. "They don't take her seriously."

"Archie does," Georgie said. "Which means other Americans do too."

Javier flicked his hand toward the crowded room. "Do you think we suffer from a lack of society?"

"Who is Archie?" Lourdes asked.

"Maestro Blaxton," Javier said.

"*Ah, sí,*" she said. "I worry for Rosa. She has hopes for that man, I think."

Javier shifted uncomfortably but spared Georgie by explaining for her. "Mamá, Mr. Blaxton was once engaged to Miss Potter, remember?"

The doña's eyes popped open wide. "Oh, yes, I am sorry, Maestra."

The woman seemed sincere, and after all she had only repeated what everyone else had been saying for weeks—and she had done it more tactfully to boot. "That's all right," Georgie said. "I'm starting to think that Rosa may be too good for him."

Lourdes's laugh was surprisingly deep for such a compact woman. "You will learn that some men are disloyal from the start, others by chance. I prefer the second, but always it is painful. Few are born steadfast, who wait for their match until thirty and one years of age—"

"Mamá," Javier tried to interrupt.

"Thirty, I apologize. Your birthday is June, so not yet."

It took a few seconds for Georgie to realize that the doña was suggesting that Javier had chosen his match: her. Though she could not help being flattered, what the woman suggested was impossible. She could not stay here in Bais—this posting was a means to an end, not the end in itself. She had to leave before she ran out of either money or will. Toying with Javier could jeopardize everything, so she had to be more careful. The problem was that she had never been any good at careful.

CHAPTER THIRTY-FIVE

Russian Service

J avier could see the change in Georgina the instant his mother
hinted at marriage. The *maestra* looked around like a cornered
animal seeking the best route of flight.

He knew Mamá meant well, but for all her sophistication she was
still a Negrense at heart. Her faith was in God, family, and sugar. She
believed that any young woman should be eager to take her place in
the line of *hacenderos*, a link between distinguished past and future
glory. On the other hand, Americans viewed life by weekly subscrip-
tion. Georgina seemed to already be planning her next serial adventure, though she would not tell him where or when. He had thought
Blaxton to be his only obstacle, but clearly the man was small beer.

"Come, Ina," he said. "It's time to eat."

Javier needed to distract her. He took a seat next to her at the ladies' table, a choice that earned him some whispers. Javier knew that
if he left her alone, though, she would run right down the stairs and
out the door.

A line of servants made the rounds, offering delicacies from the
sideboard. They added food to the plates faster than the guests could
eat it. Between labor, food, and alcohol, the cost of this *baile* would
wipe Javier out for the next few months. Still, it was a necessary part of

the shell game. Negrense elites respected a casual-but-tasteful display of wealth: to spend either too much or too little was to invite talk of impending financial doom. Javier hoped that he and his mother had gotten the balance right.

Georgina had not been sitting for very long before she jerked in surprise and jumped away from the table. She bent down to peek underneath the table. "There are people under there," she said quietly to Javier, though everyone could hear her since all conversation near them had stopped.

"Just a few children."

"They...touched my legs."

He shrugged. "Slapped them, probably."

"Yes!"

"They're killing the mosquitoes."

Her eyes narrowed. "You hire children to slap mosquitoes for you?"

"We give them treats and leftovers to take back home when they're done."

"You don't even pay them?"

"They love being here: the music, the fancy clothes—they would work for free, but the sweets and leftovers are an added bonus. Ask them yourself, Maestra."

He knew the children went to her school, but she did not seem eager to duck back under the table to talk to them. She let out a deep breath and shook her head. "I don't understand you," she said.

"What do you mean?"

"They should be out playing."

"They are playing. If I told them to leave, they'd stand outside and stare up at our silhouettes through the *capiz*, listen to the music and laughter, and wish they were here. So, we give them a job, one that keeps them out from underfoot—"

"But they are underfoot!"

He laughed as if she had meant it as a joke, but he appreciated her concern. Her passionate protection of children was a good quality in a teacher, and an even better one in a mother.

The noise of a half-dozen restarted conversations signaled the return of their limited privacy. "My mother likes you," he told Georgina as she settled back in her seat. "She approved of you teasing me, which is not something girls around here are raised to do."

"She seems like an unusual woman. Not exactly what I expected."

"Depending on one's perspective, Lourdes de Altarejos is either a pious traditionalist or a reckless eccentric."

"Which is it?" Georgina asked.

He shrugged. "The truth varies day by day. When I was young, she had a phase where she dressed in men's clothes around the house."

"Why?"

"She claimed they were cheaper—it had been a lean harvest the year before. She was also reading a lot of Georges Sand at the time."

"What did your father say?"

"I think he was amused. He said that Mamá managed to make trousers look like the height of Paris fashion."

Georgina laughed. "That sounds sweet. Sometimes I'm surprised my parents got along well enough to even have two children."

"You mentioned your brother when we met in Manila."

She looked at him with something new in her eyes. Wariness? Fear?

"He was a soldier?" Javier asked. No other American had any business writing from Basey, Samar—either then or now.

She nodded.

He could not just come out and ask the obvious question, so he waited awkwardly for her to speak again.

"I've not heard from him in a year," she finally said.

Maybe he was just a bad correspondent. Javier clung to that silly hope for a minute. "He could be busy fighting the war," he offered.

"There's no more war. Taft declared peace last July."

"Well, as long as the Governor says so." The words were out of his mouth before he could stop them.

She sighed. "You have to admit things have calmed down."

"Calm?" He thrust his thumb toward the open eastern window. "The mountains right behind us aren't even calm—and Negros has been a stronghold of pro-American sentiment since before the Spanish left. If this is calm, you can just imagine what conditions are like in Samar or Jolo—"

Hay sus, what was he doing? Could he not put away politics for one night, even to spare Georgina?

"—But maybe that's good for your search," he added hopefully. "It could mean your brother's still in uniform."

She shook her head—a small, weary motion. "Not according to the Army."

Javier did not know how to respond. There were so many places in the islands where a man could lose himself if he wanted. "Tell me more about him."

Georgina's face softened. "Benji is...impulsive, but gentle. Old-fashioned. Once war broke out, he rushed off to the Hanover Street recruiting station, eager to win a girl's hand with feats of valor in Cuba. He has all sorts of notions like that."

"Did it work?"

The *maestra* took a sip of her champagne. "Of course not. Clara was just an empty-headed flirt, but Benji always believes the best in people. It's gotten him in more trouble than I can recount."

Javier thought it sounded like a family trait. After all, half of Chinatown had been clothed by Georgina's gullibility. "So then what happened?"

"Instead of fighting the Spanish, his unit was shipped to China, where he barely survived the Boxer riots. He wrote to me about the brutality there, and I...I don't know. It's strange, really. When he was Stateside, he hated the drilling and the boredom of Army life; in China, all he wanted was to go back to the easy days of marching, when people didn't spit on him as he walked past. He wasn't meant to be a soldier, I think."

"It sounds like you were very close," Javier said. Most young men did not bare their souls like that to anyone. It was hard enough to admit the pain to themselves. "He was your younger brother?"

"No, older." Georgina cocked her head. "Why? You seem surprised."

"It's just the way you talk about him. You're very protective, as if you raised him."

"Oh no, he took care of me, no matter what." She locked eyes with Javier, emphatic on this point. "After China, he was sent here. He even served in Taft's honor guard in 1901."

Lucky him, Javier thought. But how did a man go from parades in Manila to exile in Samar? The latter might as well be across the River Styx. "And then?"

"He was sent to Balangiga, and the letters he wrote from there were...awful. I don't know how else to describe them."

Javier thought that "awful" might be an understatement. He read the papers, like everyone else, and could only imagine the conditions in Balangiga leading up to the gruesome attack. The entire town had run amok, killing almost fifty Americans with bolos, axes, picks, and shovels. That kind of close personal violence did not erupt out of nowhere.

"After that, Benji stopped writing at all. No one knows what's happened to him."

"Would the Army tell you if he were lost?" Of course, Javier thought, maybe they did not know for sure. The townspeople had mutilated the abandoned corpses of the soldiers, hacking them beyond recognition and leaving the scraps for the hogs. He set down his fork and knife, no longer interested in eating.

Georgina copied him and pushed her plate away. "They only telegraph the officers' families, I've learned—though I had to travel all the way to Manila to find that out."

"So you came to the Philippines to find him." The pieces were falling into place. Georgina had not really come here to convert the Little Brown Brother; she had come to rescue her own.

"I've written two men in his unit, both who say he survived, but the trail dies out after Benji switched regiments. The Army says he was discharged sometime last year, but their records are in such disarray..."

Javier was loath to add to her gloom, but he felt it was important to speak the truth: her brother may have survived, but his innocence probably had not. "Samar was—is—a big mess, not something that your brother would want you to get involved in. Maybe he wants to handle his troubles on his own."

He could see her struggle with his suggestion before rejecting it. "No, Benji's still a silly, happy young man underneath it all—no matter what he's been through."

"I'm sure that's the Benji you knew, Ina, but—"

"No, everyone loves him," she said. "He's darned near perfect."

"Okay, okay," he said, hands up. He had not heard Georgina curse before—nor had he ever seen her so stubborn, without a lick of humor to temper the bite. "I'm sure you'll find him. He's probably just taking the long way home, seeing Europe or India before he has to find a job."

"You think so?" Small tears formed at the edges of her eyes.

Had they not been sitting in the middle of so many nosy onlookers, Javier would have enfolded her in his arms. This woman of steely faith now seemed fragile, and he would not disappoint her.

"Yes," he lied.

Javier was not sure of anything, but he would find out. He had enough friends from school to canvas all the islands of the Visayas. The Cuayzon family network had hundreds more. If the news was good, he would share it with Georgina. Until then, he would have to distract her. "Tell you what, come dance with me."

"The music hasn't started yet."

He almost laughed. "This is my house, my *baile*. I'll make it start."

She looked around, still hesitant. "What if people aren't finished eating?"

"Who cares?" he said, trying to lift her mood with a devilish grin. "Besides, the mosquitoes at this table are killing me." Javier was rewarded with only the shadow of a smile, but it was a start.

CHAPTER THIRTY-SIX

Rigodon

Georgie was determined not to dance, but Doña Lourdes made it a difficult resolution to keep.

"Javier," the woman said, "Do not hide Maestra Potter in the *comedor* all night. They start the *rigodon* soon."

Mother and son seemed to be of one mind, their goal to keep Georgie at the hacienda as long as possible. But talking about her brother had only made her feel more rushed to leave.

"Thank you, but I don't dance," she said. It was true, and by repeating it she hoped to avert embarrassment on everyone's part.

"You will with me," Javier stated. He attached her hand to his arm and led her to the large living room where space was being cleared.

Fighting with the man no longer held much appeal. She knew Javier well enough to read the skepticism in his eyes—he did not really think that she would find her brother. Nor did he think Benji was circling the globe on a Grand Tour. His gentle lies had lifted her spirits a bit, but she still did not feel very talkative.

Pressed against Javier's arm as they waited for the band to begin, Georgie studied his *barong tagalog*. It was simple ivory with a plain collar—elegant and traditional—not dyed or striped or ruffled. He had also chosen geometric embroidery over floral. Still, it was not exactly a modest garment. Though the piña felt sturdy and substantial where it brushed her skin, it was so sheer it displayed his snug undershirt with remarkable definition.

"Why wear a shirt so thin that you need a second layer?" she asked, eyes fixed where his short sleeve revealed some bicep. "Isn't that hot?"

One eyebrow shot up. "It depends with whom I'm dancing with."

She sighed, more at her own failure to avoid innuendo than his ability to seize upon it. "Can you please be serious?"

He flicked the loose tail of his shirt. "I've always been told that the Spanish required the *indios* to wear these so we couldn't hide our daggers underneath."

Georgie wondered if these islands had ever known peace. "Is that true?"

"It's certainly the kind of thing the Crown would have done, but there's no specific law anyone can point to." Javier paused, his brown eyes studying her. "It makes a good story—and at Spanish expense, too, which makes it even better—but in truth the barong is probably all Filipino. Do you like it?"

Georgie looked up the shirt line and across his chest. "I do."

He leaned down and whispered in her ear. "I would wear anything to catch your attention, Ina. Or nothing."

Georgie had no idea how to respond. "Please," was all she could spit out.

She looked away, her face a flaming red mess. The band had moved to the great room and was ready to start playing. Javier guided her toward the cleared floor.

"Wait!" she insisted, but he ignored her and kept walking. She had gotten into enough trouble just by commenting on his eveningwear. What would happen when they danced? "You know, you really should find a partner who knows what she's doing."

"I'll only dance with you, Ina, so don't bother trying to pass me off like rotten fish."

"People eat rotten fish here," she said helpfully.

"I'm going to have to insist," Javier said. "But don't worry—the *rigodon* is simple and I know you're a quick study."

She tugged at him hard enough that he stopped and turned to her. "You're entirely too confident in my abilities," she said.

"You play all those crazy games with the children, so you're obviously agile, and you've got enough coordination to hit some crack shots off a pretty good bowler. I've seen you."

"Bowler? You mean pitcher? You've seen me play baseball?"

He nodded. "If you've enough coordination to whack the ball past the tree line, you can walk to music, Maestra. Now, stop stalling and come learn something new."

Georgie let go of his arm. "The only way I'm getting on that dance floor is if you drag me," she said.

So drag her Javier did—or as close to dragging as he could in the middle of a crowded room. He seemed to find the situation funny, too, and even Georgie couldn't keep from smiling, mostly at herself. By now all eyes were on them, so she could not back out without making even more of a scene.

They stood arm-in-arm with another couple, the four of them forming one side of a large square of dancers.

"Just pay attention to Mrs. Flores next to me"—Javier nodded to his left—"or her daughter Julia across from you. Nothing in this dance goes too quickly. Trust me."

"Oh yes, trust you."

In reply, Javier held her hand even more firmly than before. She was at least encouraged by the fact that most of the other women in the dance wore thoroughly impractical clothes, including some very long dress trains attached to finger hooks. Moreover, their shoes were scant slippers affixed to their feet by narrow strips of leather. If they could manage to dance in those get-ups, Georgie figured that she would be okay.

The music began. She and Javier walked forward to greet the couple across from them, bowed and curtsied, and turned to walk back.

The other two sides of the square repeated the action. The second time they approached the couple no one stopped. Instead, they walked past each other and exchanged sides of the square.

"This is easy," she whispered.

"I told you," Javier said.

"Does it get harder?"

"Barely. That's why it's my favorite dance. That, and the hand-holding," he said, looking down at where they were joined.

Soon they were walking again, another simple shift to the other side. She had a view of the whole room and became aware of some unfriendly looks coming from the maidens in the corner. "Why are those other girls staring at us?" she asked.

"I don't know."

Sure he didn't. "Liar."

Javier chuckled. "Probably because you're talking. You're not supposed to talk while dancing."

That was no doubt true, but the looks directed her way were more malicious than disapproving. "Who's the beautiful one in the middle? She looks like she's about to pull out a dagger."

"Apparently my tales of brigandage have frightened you too much, Maestra. You're imagining things."

It was an obvious deflection. "I know you know her," Georgie said. "You know everyone."

The dance's complexity kicked up a step. Javier walked in front of her and back, then across the circle to do the same in front of the woman there. It was like watching him trace out a narrow "Z." When he returned, he nudged her forward to draw out her own "Z."

The action did not disrupt her interrogation. "So?" she asked when she returned to his side.

He shook his head. She could not see him straight on, but she thought he was grinning.

"Javier…"

"Her name is Maribel Mariano."

"And…?"

He paused a beat. "She's the woman most people in Bais expect me to marry."

"Does 'most people' include Maribel?" she asked, sizing up the lass, who resembled a more poised version of Allegra.

Javier glanced at Maribel before facing his partner again. "Probably."

"Why her?"

He shrugged. "Right families, bordering land, appropriate match. That's generally the way things are done."

"Your mother wants you to marry her?"

Javier looked at her like she was crazy. "Good heavens, no. My mother expects me to make my own choices. But since I returned from Europe, people have been waiting for me to find a wife—or at least a mistress."

"A what?"

They were moving again before she could make him answer. All the couples exchanged partners, and the older woman who was now on the *hacendero*'s arm cooed at him, practically plastering herself against his side. A mistress, indeed. Javier had the gall to look smug. On their way back to their original positions, he dropped his head a bit and whispered to Georgie: "Green is your color."

She ignored him, but that did not stop him. "I like you jealous," he added.

"This is fun for you, isn't it?"

"Oh, absolutely," he said, laughing. "It's the only reason I would let that hussy near me."

"I'm glad I can provide you with such entertainment."

His grin just grew bigger. "Me too."

"Are you going to explain the mistress comment now?" she asked.

"Not a chance."

"Of course not."

They exchanged partners again; and though Georgie was not about to affix herself to the young man beside her, she could still engage in some flirtation for turnabout's sake. Though four inches shorter than she, the man carried himself with considerable pride. Moreover, his face was friendly. Quite friendly.

By the time Javier returned to her side, he looked a bit less amused. Before she could enjoy her revenge, though, the dancers wove around each other in the fastest movement of the dance, and the crowd applauded the quickening pace. Mercifully, it was all over in a few minutes, and her host led her off the floor.

"Well, what did you think?" he asked.

"A pleasant dance, actually. I met a nice young man, the mayor's brother, I think."

"I don't get jealous, Ina."

"Are you sure?" she asked, tauntingly.

He looked down at her, and something in his eyes changed. His ease was gone, as well as his restraint. He leaned down and spoke into her ear. "They can look at you, talk with you, even dream about you—as long as I get to have you."

Well, she thought, she had only herself to blame for asking.

CHAPTER THIRTY-SEVEN

Innocent Ride

Javier knew that, for a man who rarely attended *bailes*, he was making quite a spectacle of himself at this one. But now that the party had served its purpose, he wanted a little privacy with Georgina. "Come with me to see the festival in town," he suggested.

She looked up at him. "Leave? Now?"

For him, now was not soon enough. "*Sí*, why not?"

The *maestra* looked around the room and nodded toward Lourdes. "Won't she mind?"

Javier knew that he had been an abysmal host all night, doing nothing but follow Georgina around, and that that would not change, even if he stuck it out until the last carriage left. "Mamá can manage. She always has."

Georgina was silent for a moment, most likely paging through all her possible excuses. "I can find my own way home," she suggested.

He shook his head.

"Fine," Georgina said with a sigh. "I want to see the fiesta anyway. But then you'll take me straight to my house."

"You mean my house." He had no idea what possessed him to say that.

"Right now, it's my house. I paid you the rent. I can't help it if you're too daft to take the money."

The *maestra*'s protest pleased him—further proof that he was losing his mind. He placed a hand lightly on her back and guided her to the top of the stairs. Before he could escape with his prize, though, his mother appeared. Though she whispered quietly in Cebuano, her discretion did not conceal her alarm.

"Should I be letting you take this woman home alone?"

"One might think you don't trust your own son." Javier knew that his protestation of innocence did not match the feral look in his eyes.

The doña was diplomatic. "I think that if her mother were here, she'd prefer a chaperone to accompany you both."

"But as my mother—and one whom, I might remind you, wishes to someday be a grandmother—you might let us have some time alone. Besides, Leo will be there."

"Your *cochero* has very selective hearing when he wants to."

"Which is why he's still my driver." After all, discretion was the highest virtue in any decent domestic servant. "Mamá, don't worry. It's an open *calesa*, and we'll be riding right through town." Javier knew the arrangement was proper enough—even if barely so.

"I suppose…"

"Do you like her?"

"I do." His mother poked him in the chest with a small, strong finger. "And you'd best remember that, Javito."

The *hacendero* took his mother's hand in his and squeezed it. He had a plan, after all—and now that he knew about Georgina's brother, he felt even more confident that he could make it work. Once he found Benjamín for her, the *Americana* could rethink her long-term future. And he would search as long as it took.

"Be careful," Lourdes warned. "Don't overwhelm her."

"I can be patient."

The doña cackled in response. "You have many, many wonderful qualities that a mother can be proud of," she said. "Integrity, honesty, and good sense to name a few. Patience, however, has never made the list."

Javier wanted to argue, but he was not sure that she was wrong. "Don't worry, I'll be perfectly behaved. Very proper, very boring, very careful."

His mother stepped aside, and Javier led Georgina downstairs. He had no choice now but to act the gentleman, if only because the small *calesa* was as public as he had said. Its best feature was the cramped seat that forced Georgina to sit knee-to-knee and thigh-to-thigh with him, like they had in Manila months ago. Next time he would have Leo rig up the brougham, which was not only snug but also enclosed.

The first few minutes passed in silence, the only noises the rhythmic clipping of horse hooves and the creaking of the carriage wheels. A single lantern lit the way, illuminating the leaves of the banana trees along their path. The reflected light faded to a beautiful glow against Georgina's pale skin.

It was cool out, and typical of foreigners in their first year in the islands, Georgina had not brought a jacket with her. She would learn that the true sign of a seasoned expatriate was a temperate wardrobe. Despite the complaints of the Americans and the Spanish before them, it was not always hot in the tropics. When she began to shiver, he reached around her and rubbed his hand along her bare arm. She registered a split second of shock at his touch, but her need for comfort won out over decorum. It was a minor breach of his promise to his mother, but he assumed that Lourdes would not want the *maestra* to be chilly.

Georgina was the first to speak. "So tell me what I'll see tonight at the festival."

"Mostly dancing. That's what the word *sinulog* means."

Her eyes met his. "You seem to like dancing."

Actually, it depended on his partner. Stepping out on the floor with a beautiful woman made dancing's merits obvious. In fact, the more repressed formal society was, the more Javier treasured the sexual play dancing allowed.

"We'll just watch," he assured her. "The *sinulog* is a far cry from a quadrille. This one's an energetic frenzy, a form of prayer to please the Santo Niño, the wooden image of the child Jesus."

"It's too bad my mother didn't join me on this trip," she said, leaning back on his arm. "I think she would have loved meeting people even more superstitious than she."

"What about your father?"

"He would have hated the Philippines, for pretty much the same reason."

"You don't talk about him much."

Georgina watched the passing foliage, occasionally swatting a banana leaf out of the way.

"He's dead now," she said.

"I'm sorry."

She shrugged. "I miss him more than I thought I would. You know, when he smiled, he had this dimple high on his right cheek, above the stubble of his beard, and it was so hard not to be charmed by that. It's probably what my mother fell for in the first place."

"You make it sound like a tragedy."

"An Irish Catholic stepping out with a 'bloody Prod?' Where I come from, that's as tragic as it gets. Though, in fairness, Papa's true church was the pub. Had he spent half as much time in St. Francis's as he did in Carlin's, he would have been the most devout man in Boston—and maybe the richest on Washington Street. He could have left something for his widow other than a beer tab."

Javier knew this maudlin turn in conversation was his fault, but he wanted to know more about her family. "What have you told your mother about your life out here?"

"The essentials: the weather, the insects, the snakes—"

"Ah, yes," he said, chuckling. "I did hear something about your reptilian adventure."

Georgina smiled and shook her head. "I've also written to her about my total lack of privacy."

"That's all the easy stuff, though, isn't it?"

She sighed. "I don't even know where to look next for Benji, but how can I tell her that? If I return empty-handed, she'll be devastated. And then I'll have to take care of her on my own. I don't mind doing it, of course..."

More pieces fell into place. "Blaxton was your ticket," Javier said with new clarity. "If you'd married him, you would have been able to provide for your mother indefinitely."

She blushed. "It was...an inducement, but I also thought Archie was a better person than he is."

Javier did not hold it against her. Her sacrifice was honorable. "What will you do now?" he asked.

"I don't know. I can't stay out here looking forever, especially if I don't have a job. I'm not sure I will after this term ends." She seemed to think a moment. "Mother Randall at Sacred Heart said I could always come back and teach with the nuns."

Clearly that was not her first choice, and it was no wonder: she was not meant for spinsterhood. Javier's mind raced. He had less time than he originally thought—maybe only a few months. What had he said to his mother—that he would be proper, boring, and careful? That might not be possible.

They approached the outskirt of town, and the *calesa* could not press into the crowds without risking injury to the revelers.

"Maybe we should start this grand adventure on foot," he said. Javier stepped down and offered his hand to Georgina. Even after she was safely down from the carriage, he did not let her go.

CHAPTER THIRTY-EIGHT

Gambling

The fiesta was everything Georgina hoped it would be: loud, colorful, and joyous. Women danced in outrageous costumes, boys wrestled bare-chested—and, of course, men crowded the cockpit. Javier tried to keep Georgie out of this avian temple of Filipino masculinity, but she insisted on entering. As temples went, it was dirty and smelled of coconut wine, but she still loved it. Men carried their cherished gladiators in their arms, massaging flesh under feathers like corner-men soothing champion boxers. A local wag once said that in case of fire a Filipino would rescue his rooster before his wife and children—and hadn't Georgie witnessed that with her own eyes in Manila?

Georgie expected a stoic, dignified battle. Instead, the two owners smashed their roosters into each other, inciting them to madness. The birds flared their hackles, and their tiny heads grew as large as baseballs. When released, they attacked in a flurry of feathers, pecking at any vulnerability. Each cock had one foot equipped with a tiny Moorish sword, which it used to strike a deadly blow from the air. The best fighter of the two knew to wait on the ground until the moment when his opponent touched down his feet. In that split second, the landing prey was defenseless. The end often came quickly, the winner sitting on his opponent to mark his conquest.

The birds were not the only ones in a frenzy. Fists pumped in the air as men hollered encouragement to their champion. One energetic man managed the crowd—a barefoot Filipino with arms outstretched like Christ on the cross. "What's that man doing?" Georgie asked, pointing.

"The *kristo*?"

"They actually call him that? Isn't that sacrilegious?"

"This is God's service, at least around here." Growing into his role of tour guide, Javier placed a hand on her back and leaned in to explain. "The *kristo* runs the show: he keeps track of the wagers, the odds, and who owes what to whom. It's all in his head."

"Really?"

"Right now, he has just brokered a bet between the two men he's pointing at."

Georgie watched the *kristo* make quick signals to his right while his left hand searched the crowd for a matching wager. "How does he remember it all?"

"It's his job."

"But if he's that intelligent, surely he could have found a job that paid for shoes."

Javier laughed. "Likely he can afford shoes, but that doesn't mean he wants them."

Georgie stared at him.

"Okay, maybe not," Javier admitted.

She looked back at the *kristo*, wondering if he had children at her school. He probably did. "Just imagine if we had been here early enough to give him the education he deserves."

"He might see it the other way, Maestra. Had you not ruined your students' memories by making them dependent on the written word, they too could have had bright futures in the cockpit."

"Ah, yes, pesky literacy. Shall I remind you who provided the slates and blackboard?"

Javier feigned contrition, but it was hardly convincing. Meanwhile, a new set of adversaries was brought into the circle, and one of the birds caught her fancy. Though all the gamecocks tonight were beautiful—glorious mixes of brown, green, red, blue, and black feathers—this one was pure white. Father Ávila, the curate of Bais, carried it into the ring. No doubt the Stinnetts would count the priest's presence here as proof of Catholic degeneracy. To them this sport was the physical embodiment of everything evil in the islands, yet here was the spiritual and moral guide of the town not only condoning it, but actively participating. Father Ávila stroked the bird's feathers gently while people placed their bets.

Priest or not, Georgie liked the bird. "Bet on the white one for me," she said to Javier.

He stiffened. "What?"

She repeated herself. "The padre's white bird. I want to bet on him."

"Ina," he began, sighing her name more than speaking it. "You know I have the barest respect for convention, but you're pushing even my boundaries. The crowd seems to have finally forgotten about you at this point, and I'd like to keep it that way."

Georgie knew that she was being reckless, but there was something about the incongruity of this moment that thrilled her. No one in her life could have anticipated the events that brought her here, to a dirty cockpit in the boondocks of some inconsequential Pacific island, accompanied by a half-barbarian/half-gentleman who was trying to seduce her. She had walked straight into the devil's lair with her eyes open. She had never felt so daring or free.

Georgie turned to the *kristo*. "I guess I'll have to place the wager myself."

"Stop," Javier warned. He swallowed once, then again. "You know, the white isn't favored."

"The priest is not a good trainer?"

"No, generally clergy are some of the best amateurs around. What people object to is the color. It means he's not a true game breed. He's tame, like a hen."

"That's unfair," she said, now considering increasing her bet. She was a sucker for the underdog.

"It's not just a Filipino thing. The British think the same. You've heard of 'the white feather' of cowardice?"

She ignored him. "How much can we bet?"

"The Americans have set the limit at fifty dollars—but if you want to get out of here with your pearls, you'd better stick to one dollar."

Javier was probably exaggerating the dangers, but she did want to keep what little jewelry she had. "Two then. I've got it." She started to pull out her coin purse.

He grabbed her hand and held it against her bag, his face pale. "Please keep your money hidden. I'd prefer you remain the silent partner in this transaction. And I mean silent. *¿Me explico?*"

She put a free finger to her lips and pressed them closed. Javier shook his head, seemingly bewildered by his own forbearance. Still, he did it: he raised his hand and made a quick gesture. In no time at all, the bet was taken.

"Not only must the white survive," Javier explained, "but he has to pin the other to the ground and peck him twice. Otherwise, it's a draw."

Like the previous contests, this one was over in a blink.

Georgie practically giggled as they left the cockpit ten dollars richer.

"Remind me to invite you to play cards with my mother's friends," Javier said. "We could make a fortune."

"Then why are we leaving? If I put this ten on the next fight, maybe—"

"No."

"But—"

"No."

Georgie laughed. She did not need to bet any more, but she enjoyed teasing Javier.

As they turned the corner, though, her mood soured. She saw the loser leave the pit with his dying rooster in his arms. "His precious pet..."

Javier looked down at her, surprised. "Do you feel bad for every opponent you crush?"

"No one has ever collapsed dead on the floor after I've beaten him." This was a contest, maybe even sport to some, but it was not a game to the bird.

"Come here," Javier said, taking her hand and guiding her behind the cockpit to what could only be described as an avian hospital. None of the men looked like real doctors, but they had as many needles, threads, and salves as a surgeon. Javier nodded to the injured red. "That bird gets treated better than most people around here."

"But what will happen to him?"

He squeezed her hand. "Dinner will happen. There's a special dish for it, *talunan*, that keeps the meat tender. It is delicious."

Indulging in grief over a dead rooster suddenly felt a little bourgeois. People were hungry, after all, and they honored the bird's sacrifice in their own way. She nodded that she understood, and Javier guided her out.

Fortunately, the revelry from the *sinulog* around her was contagious, and it soothed her melancholy. She and Javier made their way back toward her building in a slow, comfortable amble.

"Why aren't more of the people from your party here this evening?"

Javier turned to her, his eyes so dilated in the torchlight that the dark coffee edges had almost disappeared. He would have looked menacing had he not been smiling. "And which activities can you imagine those guests participating in? The parade? The wrestling?"

"Oh, definitely, the cockfighting."

"That's quite an image, actually."

Georgie shrugged. "I suppose they would feel as out of place here as I did dancing the *rigodon*, surrounded by all those young girls searching for husbands. That Maribel girl couldn't have been more than…what, sixteen, seventeen? Twenty-two has never felt quite so old."

Javier shifted his arm behind her back and ran his fingertips slowly down her neck and spine. She felt his light touch everywhere—even the places it wasn't, like the backs of her knees. "I happen to like a woman with a little bit of experience," he whispered.

Though it was cool outside, the strength of Georgie's blush made her sweat. "I haven't, uh…I mean, I'm not experienced."

"No?" Javier squeezed her closer. She felt her equilibrium slip, as if the champagne from the party had finally hit her bloodstream. "Naughty you," he said. "What I meant was, a woman who's educated in something other than needlepoint or preparing consommé."

Ah, the man was full of surprises. "Why do I think that you know all about consommés?"

"Well, they are tricky, which is why I mentioned it."

She could not help but laugh. "Tricky how?"

"You have to serve them quickly, you know, before the fat gels."

Georgie felt herself relaxing into the crook of his arm. "I can see you'd make a proper wife."

Javier was not at all chastened. "Only for the right woman," he said.

She nudged him, pretending his words had been a joke, not a declaration. "So where did you learn to cook? It seems an unlikely skill for a planter."

"I used to hide from my Latin tutor in the kitchen. No one thought to look there, and the cooks were nice to me."

Javier made his childhood sound both playful and piteous at the same time. It was hard to hate him for his money—after all, she had eaten with his silver, drunk from his crystal, and been waited on by servants at his mansion. Moreover, she had enjoyed it all, in sharp contrast to her luncheon at the Blaxton household. Both Archie and Javier had grown up lousy with money; and though Archie may have actually been the more disciplined child of the two, the men they became could not be more different.

"Did you take anything seriously as a child?" she asked as he escorted her inside the classroom.

He closed the door and leaned back on it, shutting them in together. Light from outside illuminated the edges of the room, but only just. "Fidelity. I've always taken that very seriously."

He stepped closer.

"Fidelity?"

She retreated as he advanced.

"When I make an oath, I keep it," he said. He stood right in front of her. "If I pledge myself to my family, my retainers, my land, my wife..."

Wife?

"...then I live up to it."

Georgie could not concentrate with him this close. It was too stuffy in here. Javier backed her against the foot of the staircase. He might have led her right upstairs had she not stopped him with a hand to his chest.

"Thank you," she said, attempting to paint limits with her voice. "I had a lovely time."

"It's still early."

"It's almost two in the morning."

"The dancing will probably go on at least until dawn, and it will only get louder as everyone gets more drunk. You're not going to sleep anyway."

Anyway?

"Time to go," Georgie said. "The more people on the street, the more witnesses to see you walking away from my house. Feel free to look a bit disappointed—yes, just like that."

"May I at least kiss you?" he asked, leaning in.

After six hours of this man's undivided attention, her defenses had worn thin. "Just one kiss?"

"If you want," he said, pointedly leaving her the opportunity to change her mind. He must have seen her fragile restraint crumbling. He hovered over her, waiting for an answer. He looked taut, expectant, and ready. The second she nodded, he moved.

Javier was deliberate, but not gentle. His lips firmly led hers, opening her mouth just enough to tease out her tongue. She tasted the coconut wine, a drink that he bought for her at the fiesta but that she had not liked. This more intimate taste was far better.

He reached up the back of her neck, loosened her bouffant, and released the curls into a cascade down her back.

"*Qué bonita*," he murmured.

He guided her to the wall at their side and pinned her there. Georgie knew that at some point she must draw the line. She was discovering that they had different definitions of what one kiss entailed. Javier seemed to think that every part of their bodies should touch, so he pulled her tightly against him.

She squirmed a bit to loosen his grip, but the movement only encouraged him.

"*Ina, querida mía,*" he whispered. "Don't tempt me."

A part of her wanted to do exactly that. Every time his hardness pushed against her, it tempted her in return. Soon she was moving against him without his help and guidance, trying to get closer to the bliss. Javier pulled his head back to look at her. She closed her eyes, embarrassed by the scrutiny.

"Open them, *cielito*. I want to see you." When she did, the hunger in his dark gaze scared her a little. The warm glow of the lamps outside did not soften his face.

"What do you want from me?" she whispered.

"Everything you can give." Keeping her gaze, he reached down and gently caressed the dress over her breast. "I've not been able to keep my mind off what's under this silk." His fingertips found her nipple, and it rose obediently to his touch. He pinched the soft fabric around the tip and then smoothed it with his palm. The two sensations—hard, then gentle—warmed her all the way to her groin. Her body felt new to her, untested, as if Javier understood its secrets better than she.

She wanted to learn his. As they kissed again, she reached for the front of his trousers. When she felt the solid bulge, he bit out a moan. She ran her hand down his length, trying to get its measure. Javier moved under her hand, now her prisoner. Georgie had never felt so powerful, nor so undone.

She took a step to the side and drew him with her. Her foot some-how found the first stair up to her empty apartment. Julieta was at the festival tonight, and tomorrow was Sunday. Who would even know?

But then an angry American voice spoke from the darkness. "So I was right about you, you fucking whore."

CHAPTER THIRTY-NINE

Pride of Race

"How long have you been skulking around here, Archie?" Georgie tried to keep her voice even, telling herself that if anyone ought to feel ashamed, it should be the intruder.

Blaxton made his way out from behind the room divider and moved into the dim light. "Long enough," he said.

His gait was uneven and he struggled with his consonants. Georgie guessed that he had been drinking for a few hours. He probably couldn't find a hole in a ladder, yet he had somehow managed to catch her in Javier's arms.

"It's disgusting: you two, walking round like lovers, making a spec"—he hiccupped—"spectacle of yourself."

Javier started to step forward, but Georgina stopped him with a hand on his chest.

"A spectacle?" she asked. "Like you with Rosa?"

"You don't understand anything," Archie sniffed. "I'm saving you from your worst mistake, Georgie. I can help you fight this...weakness."

"Why don't you stay out of my personal affairs?"

"Affairs, plural?" He looked ghostly in the lamplight, a yellow bile of hate radiating from every pore. "How many pickaninnies have you got?"

Georgie flinched but said nothing. Archie's insult begged for a fight, but she refused to pour kerosene on the fire. Let him get it all out of his system, she thought. Let him say his ugly piece and go away.

"Everyone just loves the *maestra*," Archie singsonged in a nasal falsetto. "Special favors did the trick, didn't they? You're running a regular little chippie house."

"Listen here, Blaxton—" Javier said, moving toward Archie again. Georgina blocked him, this time with her whole body. She knew that Javier was furious—and he had every right to be—but if he hurt the American, no matter what the provocation, it would be hard to keep him out of prison, or worse.

"Please Archie," she said, "Just go."

"One letter from me will ruin your rep-reputation in Boston forever. Just imagine what your papist mother will think. I should have expected it to run in the family—first your brother..."

Georgie froze.

"...searching for his pigmy slut. Shoulda let them all die in the jungle. Good riddance."

"What are you talking about?" Her voice wobbled with the beginnings of hope. "Have you heard from Benji? You know where he is?"

She watched as Archie's expression transformed from disgust to amusement. But he said nothing.

Questions raced through her head faster than she could ask them. "Benji is with a woman? Is he married? He should have told me that he got married, but that doesn't matter, because he's safe, right?"

Archie looked at her like she was a dim-witted child, but still he said nothing.

"Where is he?" she asked, her voice rising with each word. "How can I find him?" She felt a sudden panic over time lost. Why was she going to cockfights and kissing *hacenderos* when she could be on her way to see her brother? "Archie, tell me—"

Javier placed a hand on Georgie's shoulder, but it was the weight of her despair that rooted her to the floor.

"Blaxton," Javier said without emotion. "Where did you get this information?"

Archie could not hold his silence any longer. He was too happy to let the hammer fall. "He told me himself."

"What?" Georgie screamed.

"Confessed everything in writing like I was a fucking correspondence priest. Goddamned craw-thumper."

"You never told me any of this."

When Georgie arrived in the Philippines, Archie had told her that his letters to the Army camps had been returned unopened, and she never thought to doubt him. Georgie knew that her fiancé was selfish and self-absorbed, but why would he lie about something so important while they were still engaged?

"What else do you know?" Javier asked. "Where is Benji now?"

"Who cares? I bet he'd rather rot in the jungle than watch his sister whore for the natives. Let him drink himself to death in peace."

Javier's hands were flexing in and out of tight fists, but his voice remained calm. "I asked you a simple question: where is Benjamín Potter now?"

"I don't answer to your kind." Archie crossed his arms and smiled a smug, crooked smile.

"You bastard!" Georgie shrieked, and then pounced on Archie before Javier could stop her. She threw her fists into any part of him she could reach. With her size, athleticism, and sobriety, Georgie's fury was a force to be reckoned with.

She pummeled away at Archie, backing him into the wall. The American was too drunk to effectively shield himself, but the alcohol dulled the pain from her blows, and he started to laugh. Georgie lunged for his throat to squeeze it hard enough so he wouldn't ever laugh again, but Javier pulled her away.

Despite her attempts to regain control, full-blown sobs of frustration and heartbreak broke through. "Make him tell us something!"

Archie snickered. "Dumb bitch."

Javier grabbed Archie's lapels and held him tightly against the wall. "I suggest you tell her what you know. Better yet, give her the letters."

"I didn't keep them—"

Javier slammed Archie harder against the wall. "Where are they now?"

"Burned," Blaxton said, drawing the word out to savor it.

"When were you going to tell me about this?" Georgie cried.

"Ha!"

Javier tightened his grip. "If you don't want life in this town to get very difficult for you, Maestro, you'd better tell us everything."

"I don't talk to monkeys, even if they do wear pajamas," Archie said.

"Blaxton—"

"You've no power over me."

"What I have," Javier explained calmly, "is a tremendous amount of influence over everyone in this town, including the people that cook your food, guard your house, pump your water, and even share your bed. You rely upon them for everything. The insurrection is not over, sir, and an unpopular *Americano* could be a tempting target to the ladrones."

Archie's face flushed with renewed outrage. "Are you threatening me?"

"I am making an observation."

"My friends in the Sixth will hang your black ass for this!"

"And what will you tell them—that you withheld information about a missing American soldier from his family? An American hero of Balangiga, no less? You might find your Army friends less sympathetic than you think."

"No one will care about that lousy traitor," Archie said, but he did not sound very sure.

"Tell us everything," Javier warned. "Now."

Archie seemed to have used up his last reserves of defiance, and it only took one more shove to get him talking.

"Your brother didn't have enough stomach for the fight," he moaned. "Resigned in Manila and sailed back to Samar to find his whore. Last I heard he was in Catbalogan." He said that like it was a death sentence. "Forget about him. He's gone."

Javier let go, and Archie fell into a crumpled heap at his feet. "Get out of here."

Archie obeyed, stumbling as he weaved through the rows of desks.

"There's got to be more," Georgie cried after him, but Archie did not look back. She turned to Javier. "Why did you let him go?" she whined, unable to help herself.

"Any longer with that dog and I would have killed him." He drew a hand down his face, the strain of the evening starting to show. "We've got what we need, and now I know where to find out more."

Georgie had no other choice but to trust him. At least she knew Benji was alive and out there somewhere. Now she could make a real plan.

"How big is Catbalogan?" she asked, wondering when the next boat would be leaving. She would knock on every door there if necessary.

Javier shook his head in warning. "You can quit thinking what you're thinking. It's absolutely too dangerous for you to go to Samar, full stop. There's hardly any government worth the name out there."

Georgie didn't care. She had very little to lose at this point.

Javier opened his arms wide. "Come here, Ina."

When she did, he engulfed her and kissed the top of her head.

Georgie looked up at him. "You heard him, the words he used." She was embarrassed that she had let Archie's vulgar insults go unchallenged.

His dark eyes met hers squarely. "It's all right."

She knew it was not all right. The longer Javier stood by her, the more ugliness he would face. So would she.

Still, she nestled in closer, letting Javier hug her tight. He held her for several more minutes, whispering many reassuring words, but none meant as much as his last promise before he left: "If Benjamín's out there, Ina, we'll find him. Trust me."

CHAPTER FORTY

Promises

Georgie could not sleep. Benji could still be in the country, maybe even a few islands away. It took tremendous willpower to keep from throwing a bag together and hopping on a steamer at first light. She could walk the twenty-five miles to the port in Dumaguete if she had to, and she could wait there as long as it took to find passage to Samar. Her heart and soul were already making the journey, and her body was itching to catch up.

She had one problem, though, and it was a big one: money. If she left her job in the middle of the term, the Bureau would fire her, leaving her penniless. No more salary, no passage home, and no family to fall back upon. How long could her search last without money?

She would have to wait for the break at *tiempo muerto*, the vacation months between the last planting and the first harvesting of cane. It would give her a few more months to save for the trip, but could Benji survive the delay? What if he was in danger?

No, she could not think like that. She prayed that he was safe in Catbalogan, maybe living with some Filipina beauty. She imagined an idyllic scene of provincial domesticity, complete with nipa hut and dark-haired baby. Georgie would get there to find that her happy-go-lucky, irresponsible brother simply had not given a thought to the worry he was causing his family. She would hug the stuffing out of him…and then she would kill him.

When morning finally came, she fought against every desperate impulse in her body and stayed put. The whole day passed, and the next. Still she stayed. Classes began again, and she sleepwalked through them. Her students were just as tired from the festival as she was, so no one cared.

Javier did not show up at the school until the third day. He rode his horse right up to the doorway and dismounted gracefully. The children were already filing out and took little notice of his presence.

"Hello," Georgie said, smiling weakly.

He stepped warily into the schoolroom.

"Don't worry, Archie left for the day already. He tends to keep to himself."

And thank the heavens for that, she thought. Pretending everything was normal in front of the children had been an additional strain. "I'm glad you're here, Javier."

He smiled, but before he could say anything, she forced out the rest: "I need to ask you a favor."

He spread his hands in front of him. "Anything."

Georgie took a deep breath. Pride might ordinarily have stopped her, but she had more important problems today. "I need a loan. Just a little one…"

Javier did not look surprised. Actually, he looked annoyed. He crossed his arms in front of himself.

"I can't imagine the fare is terribly much," she mustered on. "At least not to Catbalogan, and then—"

"No."

"But wait, I haven't finished. I'll pay you back."

"Georgina, you are not going to Samar. I told you that already."

Now she was the one who was angry. "Who the hell are you to tell me where I can and can't go?"

"Right now, I'm the one who cares about you and your safety. If your brother were standing here right now, he'd agree with me."

Georgie snorted. "If Benji were standing here, I wouldn't need to go to Samar!" She sighed, knowing that she was being petty but not able to help it. Desperation did not inspire good manners. "Please, Javier."

He grimaced. "I would give everything I have to help you—I am trying to help you as we speak. I have business contacts with agents all over Samar and Leyte: in Catbalogan, Calbayog, Tacloban, Baybay, Borongan—"

"Now you're just making names up. Baybaygangan, Catgotyourtongue…"

Javier smiled. "Those are the biggest towns, Ina, and you haven't even heard of them. Imagine what the small ones are like. And what would you do once you got there? Catbalogan is not like Bais, where the local children hold your hand as you walk down the street and the mayor's brother flirts with you at a ball. There's hardly a street to walk down—only five miles of real road exist on the whole island."

"Oh, come on." She wondered if he would invent anything to prevent her from going.

"I'm serious. The island is one big jungle, and most Filipinos are just as afraid of it as the Americans."

"It can't be that bad."

Javier shook his head. "How can I get through to you?" he asked, a weak smile failing to mask his frustration. He rested on the edge of her desk, and then settled in to explain. "Okay, let's say that you manage to steer clear of the *insurrectos*—which is not as easy as it sounds—even the peaceful Samareños won't help you find an American soldier. Do you know how many people there have died at the hands of the *Yankis*?"

The newspapers had made that clear enough. General "Hell Roaring Jake" Smith had told his men to make the island a "howling wilderness" and kill every male capable of carrying a bolo, which he defined as anyone over the age of ten. Georgie did not believe the Marines had actually been that cruel—at least that was what the men had said at their courts-martial—but no doubt the casualties were still in the thousands.

Javier lifted her chin with his fingertip. "Why won't you trust me to handle it for you?"

She considered his offer. "You'll tell me the instant you hear from your friends?"

"So you can run off without me? Hell, no! But just because I refuse to endanger your life doesn't mean I'm going to betray you like Blaxton." He took a hold of her hand. "Even if I have to kidnap Benjamín, you'll have him back."

"If you go, I'm going with you."

"Ina…"

"Promise you'll take me."

Javier took a deep breath and looked her in the eye. "I need you to be patient, okay? Neither of us can go anywhere, not for a while. I spent the last few days cabling anyone I have any influence with, getting the names of everyone who might be of help. I sent regular post too. Now you need to give it some time. Once I get answers, I'll let you know. Then we'll talk."

"We'll make a plan together?"

He hesitated, pinching together the inside corners of his eyes with his thumb and forefinger. It looked painful. When he raised his head, the words he said seemed to cause him even more pain. "We'll make a plan together. I promise."

Part VI: February 1903

Manila, Luzon, Philippines
July 2, 1901

To my dear sister Georgie,

...Some call it moral degeneration, of course, but most of the men keep sweethearts. While twenty-five dollars a month would hardly get a man's boots through the front door of a reputable family home in Boston, here it is a high recommendation. Few marry, but that does not seem to be an impediment, despite the ubiquity of priests. Tommy Baird told me a similar tale of handfasting in the "ould counthry"—couples lived together as man and wife in a trial union, and the bastards produced were thought no discredit to the mother. Sometimes I wish that Mom and Pop had been allowed to part as peaceably, but then I would not have gotten you as a sister. I suppose there is something to be said for the tyranny of marriage, even if I do not plan to trade in the shackles of the Army for those of a woman....

Your loving brother,
Benji

CHAPTER FORTY-ONE

Ambushed

J avier wasn't sure that he trusted Georgina to not get the money somewhere else and run off to Catbalogan. He needed to keep her here in Bais, which meant he needed time—and help. Two weeks later his chosen accomplice arrived from Manila, and he marched her straight to the school. Allegra was thrilled to be home and even happier to pay a visit to her American friend.

"Allegra, you're here!" the *maestra* called, unfolding her tall frame from the chair and rushing to meet the young woman in the doorway. They hugged in the American fashion before kissing on both cheeks like Spaniards.

"I feel we never say goodbye, *querida*. Your letters are good company to me in Manila."

"Why didn't you tell me you were coming back?" Georgina asked. "I'd have gone out to Dumaguete to welcome you off the steamer."

Allegra skewered Javier with a look before making up an answer. "I wanted to surprise you."

"What about your studies?"

The young woman waved her hand. "The sisters tell me to finish classes on dressmaking and drawing—not my best marks."

"That's putting it mildly," Javier muttered. His ward was unwilling to be fully domesticated, much to the chagrin of the Daughters of Charity. "The report you brought home had some particularly scathing remarks from Sister Elenteria."

Allegra looked up to the heavens, as if only they could set Javier straight. "My teacher for artificial flowers? She thinks the gospels themselves tell her how to sew roses of silk."

Javier tried not to encourage his cousin with a smile, but she had a flair for insults. "Nevertheless, Allegra, those were the only classes left in your degree."

"Did I say I failed, Javi?"

Now he smiled. "No, not exactly."

Allegra stood tall—her full five feet and two inches—looking very pleased with herself. She was being unnecessarily and predictably dramatic. "This is why I like you Americans, Georgina. You only do the important things, but you do them double as hard. Santa Rosa closes for a month at holiday, but the Americans open a whole new institute, just for teacher training. They gave so many tests, but last week they published all who qualify. Look!"

Allegra popped a folded newspaper out of her bag and showed Georgina, who promptly hugged and congratulated her. Javier was slow to understand what they were celebrating, so he took the paper. "Qualify for what?" he asked, opening the pages.

"For *maestra*," his cousin said, pointing at her name in the list: Allegra Romero Alazas. The clerk had even Americanized her two Spanish last names—a small thing, really, but he noticed.

"What about Santa Rosa?" he asked.

Allegra shook her head. "These are the American Philippines now, Javito. What use is a Spanish degree? It is obsolete!"

Indeed, he thought. He had to admit that Allegra had learned more English in one month with the *Yankis* than she had in two and a half years with the nuns—and the Americans probably did not make her thread a single needle.

"Forget I asked," Javier said, leaning down to kiss his cousin on the cheek. "I suppose we have even more to celebrate than I thought."

"¡Qué bueno!" Allegra always loved a party. She had not forgotten her purpose here today, though, the one he had drilled into her the whole way back from Dumaguete. She turned to her friend. "You must come to the *casa* for dinner tonight."

"That's kind of you," Georgina hedged, "but don't you think your first meal home should be alone with family?"

"We are like sisters and it is my special night. Of course you must come." It was a command—and even if delivered by a small thing like Allegra, it was impossible to ignore.

The *calesa* ride through town was monopolized by the women's discussion of potential suitors for Allegra, although she had not yet met any of the men because most were unattached brothers and uncles of friends. Suspicious of their qualifications, Georgina kept asking about each man's age, looks, and the strength of his heart. Javier would have laughed, but the reality of the dilemma hit him: a respectable husband, not to mention a lively one, would be hard to find without a significant dowry.

Javier pushed his troubles out of his mind to better enjoy the evening. Allegra's homecoming was as joyous as he imagined. Lourdes held her niece close for a whole minute and was generous with her tears. His mother gave Georgina a hug, too, and then marched both women up the stairs, an arm around each of their waists. No one seemed to stop talking long enough to breathe, not even during the meal, and it was a wonder that anyone had a chance to chew. The *Americana* was a good sport too. Even though she turned green at the sight of fish heads in the vinegary *inun-unan* stew, she stubbornly forced it all down, skin included.

When it was time for coffee, Javier retrieved a bowl filled with dark brown nuggets, each about the size of pea.

"Chocolate?" Georgina asked.

He shook his head. "Better."

She picked one up and inspected it, rubbing her fingertips over its tacky surface. She brought it to her mouth tentatively, and he laughed, remembering her caution with the *bodbod*. Once she decided that it was safe, she sucked the morsel until her lips puckered. "It's sweet," she finally declared.

"It should be. It's sugar. When I boil the cane water off, some of the muscovado beads up like this. We keep some for ourselves because it has good flavor."

"A little bitter, too," Georgina said, her concentration as focused as a sommelier's. "Very rich."

Allegra grabbed a couple drops for her coffee, crushing them in the bottom of her cup. "Our sugar is known for its quality."

Javier smiled at the pride his family took in the hacienda. "*Gracias, primita.* I'm sure that's why you drown yours."

His cousin laughed and grabbed two more.

After dessert, Javier suggested a walk outside. There were only a few more weeks of cool, bug-free evenings left, and they should enjoy them, he explained. His mother sent Allegra to chaperone, though one would have thought Lourdes knew her niece better than that. Javier had already agreed to pay the girl a Mex to disappear. Allegra was a better extortionist than chaperone, and as they walked down the stairs, she whispered in Cebuano: "Two."

"What?"

She smiled innocently, but behind Georgina's back she held up two fingers. Javier nodded briskly. Courtship had all sorts of hidden costs.

The three of them walked away from the house, Javier guiding Georgina on his arm. Once they passed the tree line, Allegra kept on walking and winked at him before slipping away.

Casa Altarejos sat on a small hill overlooking Javier's cane. From here there was a clear view of the entire hacienda, right up to the mountain ridge. His furthest fields had recently been harvested and burned, leaving a brown boundary ring. The cane closest to them would be the last of the harvest. The tops of the plants still waved green against the dark pink horizon. This land was all he had in the world, and in his mind he offered it to her.

"It's beautiful," Georgina said.

"It is." And so was she. Javier wondered how the sunset could soften her freckles but make her eyes glow even brighter and greener.

"I can see why you love it."

"That's not all," he said, taking her hand and slowly guiding her along the open path. They did not talk as they walked; the touch of their hands said enough.

They rounded the eastern ridge, and she stopped abruptly. "Oh!"

Javier followed her gaze down to the brilliant blue sea in the distance.

"I didn't know you could see the water from your house!" she said.

"Only from this spot. My father cleared the trees on this side so my mother could see her childhood home." He used his free hand to point across the strait. "That's the island of Cebu over there, though I wouldn't recommend trying to swim to it. It's about ten miles away."

She peered up. "So your mother could see her home but she couldn't get there."

"What can I say? My father was a romantic."

He got the laugh he was looking for, and it made his smile even bigger. He hugged Georgina hard. When he released her, she meandered to a stone bench and sat down. He sat too, and once again their hands joined, resting together on her knee. When she looked at him, he read no hesitation in her eyes. Right now she was neither Bais's *maestra* nor Benjamín's sister. Tonight Georgina Potter was just Ina.

"I'm glad you like it here," he said. "It's my favorite place on the whole hacienda. It's where I go when I need to remember what's important."

"It makes me wish I could paint. I could take a little piece of this"—she waved her arms at the scene—"home with me." She looked up at him, her eyes shining. "You know, sometimes we all need that reminder."

Javier pulled her into his chest and kissed the top of her head. He knew that she was torn. But sitting here on this bench, he felt closer to her than anyone else in his life—even closer than during their encounter in the schoolroom. If she could love this land, she could love him too.

CHAPTER FORTY-TWO

Carried Away

Javier's carriage—a fully-enclosed brougham this time—was waiting for him when he returned Georgina to the house. Allegra had not quite caught up, but he could hear her laugh ring out behind him as she and her friend Adelita made their way up the path. Georgina stopped beside the carriage, and Leo swung the door open for her.

"We can wait for my cousin to join us," Javier offered.

Georgina watched Allegra amble toward the house with her friend. It would obviously be a grand production to pry his cousin from Adelita just to keep up a heretofore inconsistent standard of propriety. "No," she said. "It's okay. Let's go."

Javier was not about to argue. He helped her into the enclosed carriage and shut the door behind them. He had barely leaned back on the seat when Georgina was in his arms. He held her head with one hand as he kissed her, and used his other hand to pull down the shades.

Her daring little tongue tasted like sweet coffee. *"Corazón,"* he whispered. He only needed to breathe the words to be heard, even with the clatter of horse hooves outside.

Despite her height, she was slim and maneuverable. He pulled her onto his lap and kissed the curve of her neck. At first she jerked away from the tickle but then relaxed under his lips.

"My Ina," he murmured as he reached for her breast. Georgina exhaled hard and arched her back, pushing into his hand like a spoiled horse. With each caress her body twitched, a lovely response. It did not take long before they were back where they had left off on her staircase weeks ago.

His hands roamed lower, greeted the whole way with beautiful whimpers. She squirmed a little as he rubbed between her thighs.

"Oh," she moaned, a little surprised.

"Do you like that?" he whispered. Javier reached for the hem of her skirt, pulling it and her petticoat into her lap, exposing split cotton drawers that hugged each thigh. He searched by feel for the open placket.

"Please, Ina, let me touch you, let me show you how it can feel."

"I want to, but—"

"We can stop," he said, even though his body was screaming with the need to continue. With a few quick motions he could open their clothes, spin her around, and be inside her. Instead, he moved his hand down to her knee, telling himself that doing this right was worth the sacrifice.

"I don't want to stop."

"You want this?"

She looked at him, her eyes wide and black in the night. "Please," she whispered. "Yes."

As he kissed her again, Javier's hand found its way through her open drawers into a soft thatch of curly hair. He found his target and gently pressed his finger against it.

"Oh," she sighed against his lips

He circled slowly. When his finger slipped to the side, she maneuvered her hips back under the pressure. Each time, his thumb restarted its teasing dance, never quite giving her what that she wanted.

Reaching deeper, he swiped her opening and began pushing inside. Georgina's breath caught, and she retreated.

He paused, letting her set the pace. As their mouths reconnected, she tilted her hips up, urging him to continue his exploration once more. His finger slipped forward and back, growing slick and warm, moving in time with his thumb.

"Ah...ah...Javi," she cried softly.

"Does it feel good?" He knew that it did; she had a look of total concentration on her face. He turned his ear to listen to her small sounds as a second finger joined the first. Her body eased around him, making room. Javier's pace quickened to match her unconscious thrusts. Georgina's reactions were so open, so earthy, that she was easy to please.

Her lips parted as she rose toward a small peak. He stilled his hand, delaying her reward. She gave a short, unhappy whine, and he hid his smile against her cheek. She went higher the next time, only to be denied once again. By the last peak, Georgina was visibly frustrated. Javier felt her crescendo approach even before she did, and this time he did not slow down.

"Come for me, Ina." The wave overtook her, and she gasped in shock. Javier lightened his grip but made sure to wring every last bit of ecstasy out of her. Each time he thought she had finished, another tremor jolted her. Patiently, he eased her through them all.

Afterward, Georgina lay so still that he worried she had passed out. Her only movement was her soft breath against his temple. Javier's fingers were still inside her body when the carriage drew to a stop.

They had arrived at her house. His house.

He kissed her forehead lightly. "Marry me, Ina."

CHAPTER FORTY-THREE

Doubling Down

Georgie grabbed Javier's wrist and pulled his hand away from—out of—her body, and he reluctantly complied.

She flushed in shame. Although she was not much of a Catholic, she could still vividly picture the devil waiting for her, gleeful at yet another fallen woman destined for eternal damnation. The problem was it was so easy to fall, especially around this man.

She pulled herself up off Javier's lap.

"PleasethankyourmotherforawonderfulmealIhavetogo." The words spilled out like a ritual absolution.

"Wait," Javier said, taking hold of her arm. "Don't go. We need to talk."

Here? Now? "No, I'm sorry—"

"Ina, please don't do this."

Her arms and cheeks still tingled when he called her "Ina." Nevertheless, she unfastened the latch and moved the door a few inches before the waiting *cochero* swung it open the rest of the way. Holy Mother of God, she had forgotten that the driver was up front, barely four feet away the whole time. Covered carriage or not, the man must have heard something. She had not been quiet.

Georgie almost fell off the narrow metal step in her rush to escape. She felt like both the court harlot and court jester in one. She dashed inside her classroom, knocked into a bench, cursed, and quickly shut the door behind her. She leaned back against the hard wood, took a deep breath, and reflected upon her own stupidity.

She had never imagined the things Javier had done to her. The fact that she enjoyed them so much did not help. She banged her head against the door in meek self-flagellation, and then pushed away. She carefully threaded her way through the rest of the benches and went upstairs. Once in her bedroom, she curled into a ball in the middle of the thin mattress. Guilt was tiring.

She woke from a light doze when she heard the boards of the stairs creak. Was Julieta checking up on her? Until this moment, she had not been afraid of intruders in Bais. She drew in a big breath, ready to scream loud enough to waken a town hung-over from two months of holidays.

"Ina?" a voice whispered from the living room. "Are you awake?"

"Javier—what…what are you doing here?"

"It's so dark. Where are you?"

He sounded closer now, probably just beyond the doorframe. No doubt he could see her outline on the bed.

"You shouldn't be here."

"I know," he answered softly, taking a step closer. "We're going to talk, *querida*, whether you want to or not."

"Is your carriage out front?" she asked, worrying about all the wrong things. "People here expect their *maestra* to have some morals."

"Leo dropped me off down the street. No one saw."

"You hope."

Javier sat down beside her on the bed. "You never answered my question."

Her chest tightened at the slightly agonized tone of his voice, and she knew that he must hate being trapped like this. It was humiliating for them both. "Don't worry. You don't need to offer for my hand just because of…before. It was my fault too."

"That's what you think—that I felt honor-bound to propose?"

She nodded.

"And you're telling me not to worry."

She nodded again. This time her head moved like it was made of lead.

"Okay," he answered softly. "So I'm off the hook."

It hurt to hear him put it that way. Would this be the sum total of her life: two offers of marriage, both made out of desperation?

"Yes, you are free to go." She said it flatly and finally, hoping it would be the end of this humiliation. She could better bear Archie ruining her reputation with strangers in Boston than face this man's relief to be rid of her.

Javier surprised her by taking her hands in his. "Can we get back to my original question now?"

"What?"

"Ina, I want to be with you. You're beautiful—"

"No, I'm not."

"Not to mention argumentative," he continued. "Stubborn, critical, and clever too."

"And you like these qualities?"

"They're the best of all." He raised her hand to his lips and kissed it. "They make you unique."

"Clearly you don't know many New Englanders," she said.

"One is all I need, forever."

Who had forever? She did not plan to be in this country six more months, let alone a lifetime. But even so, a part of her was thrilled. To belong to this place, to this man—no, she pushed the possibility out of her mind. It did not make sense to pine over what could not be.

"You know I can't stay," she said. There was more to her mission here than just getting her brother out of Catbalogan; she also had to see him home. Javier's roots in the Philippines were deeper than the sugar cane he planted, and he would never follow her to the States.

"Benjamín can live with us in Bais for as long as you want." He folded a loose curl behind her ear. Since they could barely see each other in the moonlit room, it seemed more of an excuse to touch her than anything else.

"I don't want Benji to come out here. I want him in Boston."

The air was so still that she could hear Javier swallow in frustration. "Why?"

"My mother—"

"We'll bring her here. We'll hire people to take care of her for once," he promised. "And I think she'll manage to find an acceptable Catholic mass somewhere in town."

Georgie did not laugh. "You don't understand."

"*Cariño*, I understand more than you know. For example, I understand that taking Benji home won't magically restore the brother you remember."

"Aren't you the one counting the days until the Americans leave?"

"There's nothing I want more for my country than independence, but there is some benefit to the American presence." His hand cupped her whole head now, his thumb brushing her cheekbone. Like before, the touch made every nerve in her body jangle.

"What do you expect from me?" she asked. "To be the mistress of a sugar plantation? I know nothing about your life."

"As if you couldn't rise to any challenge, Georgina Potter. I will keep you busy, though, no doubt about that. We can be partners, sharing the burden, passing it on to our children—"

"Our children?" Her imagination drew a picture before she could stop it. She saw them: brown-eyed, maybe a glint of red in their hair. They would swim on the beach below the fields. The littlest would cry and raise his arms to be carried out of the way of the rising tide. A proud little girl would ride on a caramel-colored horse in front of her father. It was a possible future, a far better one than any open to her in Boston. Georgie had never wanted anything so much in her life.

Javier nodded as if he could see her vision and approved. "I promise to be very diligent in my efforts," he whispered as he leaned in to kiss her neck. "Is there anything else you will need?"

"Snow?"

He burst into laughter. "We'll have to travel for that, I suppose, but Boston has nothing on the Spanish Pyrenees. Once the sugar market recovers, I promise we'll go."

He was offering her a fairy tale, which by definition was too good to be true. She could not believe in Javier's magic until she spoke with the one person who could advise her best. "I need to see Benji first," she said. "I need to know that he's okay. Then I can think about...us." Whether Javier understood it or not, this was a concession.

"Fair enough," he said with a sigh. His rough chinbone nuzzled her cheek. "What shall we do until then, *querida*?" His tone made clear what he wanted.

She wanted it too. Every time he touched her, he chipped away at what little will power she had. He seduced her with dreams she had already given up on. But even if this dream came to nothing, she had little to lose anymore. Archie had seen enough to believe her virtue already gone. If she was already a ruined woman, at least she should earn the title.

"Stay," she said. The word was halfway between a command and a question.

He pressed a kiss against her temple. "Okay."

"Though if you tell anyone here—"

"I'll guard your secrets with my life."

Georgie believed that. "What if I get pregnant?"

She could feel Javier smile against her skin.

"That's what you want, isn't it!"

"Ina, if allowed into your bed, I'm going to try my hardest to get you pregnant. There will be no task to which I will apply myself more enthusiastically."

She felt an immediate response. Her body seemed in cahoots with this devil. "Certainly you learned things in Europe to avoid...that outcome?"

"There are some relatively effective methods," he admitted.

"Yes?"

"All of which I've forgotten."

"Liar!" she said, punching his arm playfully.

Javier held her face so close that she could now see his eyes in the dim moonlight. "We can do what is expected of us, allow ourselves to be watched ruthlessly while I steal a few kisses whenever possible—I could accept that until we find your brother." He shifted his arm behind her and leaned in to whisper in her ear. "Or, we can be lovers. Bigger risk, bigger reward. But if you carry my child, you're mine. Forever."

Oh God, she thought. "And if not?"

"I'm not a pirate. I won't stash you away in Bais against your will. But don't expect me to let you go easily."

She was willing to face that problem when the time came. "You're really going to try to get in my bed?" she asked, daring him with her tone. She was surprised by her own boldness.

He understood the game. "Yes," he said.

"Tonight?"

"Yes."

"And try to get me pregnant?"

"Oh, yes."

"Prove it."

CHAPTER FORTY-FOUR

The Ante

Javier felt for the candle and match on the bedside table. "We need a little light," he said.

"Why? Might you get confused?"

Javier laughed. *Hay sus*, he loved this woman. She was less brave than she pretended, but still curious. "Sometime we will try this all by touch," he explained. "Right now, though, I want to see you."

He stood and pulled her up, her back to him. He drew each pin out of her hair until her rich auburn locks tumbled down to her shoulders. He ran his hands through them, massaging her scalp with his fingertips. "Relaxed?"

She nodded, still shy, and in no way relaxed. Javier turned her around so that she faced him. He kissed the line of red hair that framed her face, then her eye, then her nose, and then finally her mouth. She responded openly, meeting his tongue with hers. She coiled her arms around his neck and pulled his body closer. She moved against him, and he wondered if she knew the power she had over him.

"I love you, Ina."

That earned him a blush and the smile he was waiting for. "I love you too."

"Now," he said, "let's help you out of this." He looked at her frock, a little disappointed by the number of buttons down the front. He undid the one below her collar and then worked his way down the rest. "Do you always go to bed fully clothed?"

"No...I, uh, I do have a few nightdresses."

Javier gently kissed her exposed collarbone. "When you're my wife, you won't need those any more."

He unfastened her cotton skirt and let it fall to the floor. Georgina stood before him in her corset, chemise, petticoat, and drawers—still far too many layers. Undeterred, Javier stripped her of garment after garment until she wore nothing. Then he admired his Venus. Her breasts were modest but pert, with light pink areolae, each the size of a silver crown. Self-conscious, she hid her brownish-red triangle of pubic hair behind her hands. Javier pulled them away, not hiding his interest in what he uncovered. He placed his palm flat against her curls, reminding her that he had been there before. He did not want her to be afraid.

She interrupted him before he could continue. "Now you."

Javier complied enthusiastically. Although he had taken care with her garments—neatly folding each item across the back of a chair—he hurriedly threw his own barong, undershirt, and trousers on the floor. He faced Georgina in his silk underwear.

"Lie down, *querida*," he said, guiding her back to the bed.

The only other beings awake at this hour were mosquitos and the happy crickets whose song blew in with the cool tropical breeze. Javier untangled the mosquito net from above the bed and hung it down the sides of the mattress. He spread out the weighted rings so that it enclosed the two of them in a white cloud.

He stretched out by her side, not exactly sure how to slow things enough to satisfy her. He had never been anyone's first. Georgina's body was both dangerously arousing and a little daunting. He knew from his explorations in the carriage that he did not need to worry about a barrier, but he still had to make sure tonight was perfect. It was his audition for the role of a lifetime.

He reached out and cupped her breast, thumbing the hard nipple. Encouraged by the change in her breathing, he dipped his head and sucked on the point. When he bit lightly with his teeth, Georgina let out a clear moan. He rubbed his rough cheek across her sensitive skin and glanced up. "Do you like that?"

She nodded, her eyes firmly shut.

He returned to her breast and gave it another gentle suck. Like in the carriage, she arched up her back, pushing into him. "Why does that feel so good?" she asked.

If she was still talking, Javier knew that he could do better. There was no sense in being hampered by Puritan morals. He smiled against Georgina's abdomen as he kissed lower. He paused to admire her freckled thighs before settling in between them.

CHAPTER FORTY-FIVE

Square-Toes

Georgina sat curled in a ball at the head of the bed, her back against the wall. Javier had tried to put his mouth...well, she couldn't think about that. Right now, she wished she had a sheet or blanket to cover herself.

"Ina?" Javier sat beside her and massaged her ankle. His touch there felt both safe and intimate at the same time.

"That was so...it's not—"

His black eyes managed to look warm. "My little square-toes. Okay, maybe I got carried away."

"Easy words for a man who still has his underwear on."

"Is that the problem?" He rose to his knees and set his hands on the drawstring of his drawers. He slowly untied the knot and let the silk fall away. No longer constricted, his cock sprang up tall. Fascinated, Georgie did not avert her eyes.

"Good," he said, smiling. "Curiosity is good." Javier crawled forward into the gap between her legs. He did not touch her, just presented himself for inspection. "You can touch me too."

His shaft pointed high, the smooth pink head peeking at her through the foreskin. She reached out and fumbled a little, only grazing him lightly with her hand, but Javier shuddered nonetheless. He looked as vulnerable as she felt—and her fear slipped away.

Javier watched her hands longingly. "Here," he said. "Let me help you."

He wrapped his larger hand around hers and pulled them both down the whole base. Together they moved up and down, up and down. He looked her in the eye. "I won't last long if we keep doing this. Is that what you want?"

She did not know what she wanted, but she was curious enough to want to see what happened if she kept going. "Does this feel as good to you as being inside a woman?"

"Nothing will feel as good as being inside you."

"Are you sure?" She watched their hands move. "This seems to be working."

He closed his eyes for a moment of concentration before answering. "If you want to keep your virginity," he offered, "we can find ways to do so."

"Ways?"

Javier smiled. "I have to warn you that some of the better ways involve my mouth."

"Oh." The idea no longer seemed as shocking as it had five minutes earlier.

"And maybe your mouth, too," he added.

"Oh." She blushed because that sounded...interesting.

Suddenly, Javier pulled out of her grasp and bent over to kiss her on the lips. It was a quick and surprisingly chaste move.

"Either way, let's lie down."

She nodded. They disentangled and sprawled out next to one another. Javier propped himself up on his elbow and gazed down at her torso. He used his free hand to cup each breast in turn, as if to remind himself that he could do so at his leisure. His touch felt like the best and worst of tickles.

"Now, where did I leave off?" Javier asked with a smile. "Down here?" He let his hand wander below her waist. His fingers pressed in, and she eagerly accepted the intrusion. "Yes, your lovely quim."

The obscenity was doubly exciting because he said it with admiration. Georgie's body quickly gave up all pretense of propriety and began moving with his hand. When he withdrew it, her hips chased it into the air, only to retreat with the next thrust. Just as she felt the rise of the wave, she was tossed back into the trough.

"Javi, please."

"What do you want?"

She wanted it all, but she could not say so. "Please..."

Fortunately, he understood. "I need you on the edge of losing control before I enter you."

"I am," she begged.

He may have uttered a response, but she was not really listening. When he withdrew his hand entirely, she whimpered a little too loudly.

"Don't worry, Ina, I won't leave you empty for long."

As he raised himself above her, she felt his hardness rub against her thigh. She reached down to guide him, but he gently pushed her hand away. "Slower is better, *querida*, at least at first. Relax."

He drew himself shallowly along her wet folds.

"Open up for me," he whispered. He tugged at her buttocks, and she lifted her hips up into his grip. Javier looked back up into her eyes, his expression soft and compassionate, even though she could sense the strain in his body. "I've got you." She felt him place the head against her opening.

His forehead rested against hers as he entered slowly. The pressure burned a little, but by rocking back and forth, little by little, he worked his way in. It surprised her that nothing happened easily—that her body did not just obey and accommodate him. Afraid that she was not doing it right, she tried to tilt her hips to capture more of him. "I...I can't take any more."

He kissed her ear. "*Dios mio*, I'm sorry. I don't want to hurt you."

She was about to tell him that was not what she meant, that she did not want him to stop, when he reached down to rub that magic spot right above her opening. Georgie forgot everything. She closed her eyes and moaned, pushing onto him, getting more. She squeezed her walls so she could feel how much.

"*Ay*, no, don't do that."

"Why not?" she asked, confused. "Doesn't it feel good? It does to me."

He was all the way inside her now, and she clenched again to emphasize the fullness.

"*Mierda*," he said, just before losing all restraint.

He drove into her. She felt his warm breath against her ear, heard every slap and suck of their bodies, and even smelled their coupling. Every sense was linked to this man. Her inner walls pulsed and pushed against him. She built to a crisis and then slipped away, along with half her wits.

Javier continued to thrust: shorter, harder, grittier. He grunted with each stroke, almost as if it hurt. Head back now, eyes closed, he pumped six or seven more times until he froze inside her. He held himself tight against the end of her channel until, finally, he sighed and collapsed.

He slid to one side to free her torso but did not pull out. Georgie felt wetness leak out of her body onto the sheets, but she held her man tighter, reveling in the connection. Unlike in the carriage, she did not feel ashamed. How could she? Before had been only about gratification; this was about belonging. She felt that he could talk her into just about anything right now.

Javier kissed her fiercely on the lips. "I meant to go slower to make it better for you."

"It gets better?" she asked.

He nodded, pleased with her answer. "Marry me."

She shook her head. Javier could talk her into almost anything—but not that. Not yet.

CHAPTER FORTY-SIX

Tina's Warning

Javier rushed through his daytime responsibilities, marking the hours until he could sneak over to Georgina's place and make love to her again. It had been that way for three glorious weeks, and his appetite for her was not fading. Lately, he had started waking her up in the middle of the night too. It was a hell of a way to live his life during milling season.

No matter how busy he was, though, Javier had not neglected his promise to find Georgina's brother. No doubt Benji would barely resemble the man who had left Boston full of naive patriotism. Blaxton had called him a drunkard. Well, that was fine: Javier would let the man drink away the rest of his days on the hacienda if that meant Georgina would stay too. What better place to nurture a rum habit than a sugar plantation?

Javier had sent a personal note to Guillermo Cuayzon's lieutenant in Catbalogan, and he prepared for a long, drawn-out search. Within the month, though, he was summoned to the de facto public post office of Chinese correspondence, Tina Yuco's shop.

It did not matter that it was a busy Friday in the fields; he got there as soon as he could. When he walked in, Tina was nice enough to get right down to business.

"Don Javier, you must be careful of Lope Cuayzon," she said in Cebuano. "He's not a good man."

Though her own family had been in the Philippines for generations, Tina's loyalties lay with her *sangley* compatriots. It was unprecedented to hear her speak of a Chinese trader like this, especially one who carried the Cuayzon name.

She handed Javier a letter. He slid his finger under the seal and opened it, but it was written in Chinese. He gave it back to Tina. "What does it say?"

She read quickly but, much to Javier's frustration, did not translate it aloud. Instead, she asked a question of her own. "This Potter man—is he related to the *maestra*?"

"Yes. He is her brother."

Tina looked down at the book she had been writing in, made one or two characters on the ledger, and closed it. This was not a good sign—since this merchant could carry on three conversations while performing advanced mathematics in her head, if she needed her full attention to talk to Javier, she probably had bad news.

"Potter is in Catbalogan, apparently a good customer of a Cuayzon *amo*."

An *amo* ran a Chinese brothel, often out of the back of an opium house—big business. So far the report matched Blaxton's characterization of Benji as a debauched veteran. "How much does he owe?"

Tina shook her head. "Lope won't say until he finds out how much you want this man. I would wait many months to respond. That will drive down the price."

Sound advice if Javier was negotiating for a carabao, but not for a brother-in-law. "I can't leave him there. I have to go as soon as possible. A week, maybe."

"No, you play into Lope's hands that way. And the fields are not closed yet—you shouldn't even think about going until April."

Tina stood to lose money if Javier's harvest failed, but he still bristled at her reminder of his duty to his land. His workers would continue to cut, pile, and haul the cane to the mill; clear the waste; soak the cane tops; and plant a new crop—all whether he was there or not. Men had been dancing these same steps for a hundred years in Negros. They were not about to forget them now just because the *hacendero* left town. And, in any case, Javier trusted his overseer without reservation. The fields would close on time, and he would still have an hacienda when he returned home.

Besides, what would Georgina do if he did not deliver Benji? Next month she would be on vacation herself—God forbid she take off for Catbalogan without him. Javier had to retrieve her brother, dry the man out from his addictions, and bring him home to his sister as fresh-faced as possible—before she could start snooping around on her own.

"What else do you know about Lope?" he asked Tina.

"He's Guillermo's cousin's son."

Half of the Cuayzon agents in the islands were Guillermo's cousins or nephews, but this was a significant relation, nevertheless. "I'll get him to help me. He could cable Lope—"

"Then you might as well bury Potter in the ground yourself."

"What?"

Tina motioned for Javier to come behind the counter and sit at a table set for tea. He really did not like the direction this meeting was taking; it felt too much like a condolence visit.

She poured the tea herself. "The last thing you need is to get caught in between them. Ever since the British firms were forced out of Samar, Lope's been trying to absorb the whole abaca market. He's done well, and he has his eye on moving to Manila."

Javier considered this for a moment while he sipped his tea. Abaca, or manila hemp, was the premier material for rope-making, something that every navy needed, merchant or military. The *Yankis* planned to make abaca the biggest industry in the Philippines, larger even than sugar. As a result, hemp was the one product traded freely with the United States. It was taxed leaving port in Iloilo and Manila, but the duties were refunded upon arrival in San Francisco. This set-up allowed savvy agents like Lope to dominate the trade simply by understanding how to file the right paperwork. Lope had his eye on a fortune, and if Guillermo Cuayzon did not watch out, his cousin would control the entire family syndicate within a few years. Javier was not thrilled to find himself in the middle of a *sangley* civil war. "I had no idea."

Tina nodded. "The closer you tie yourself to Guillermo, the harder Lope will squeeze. Your best bet is to send an agent in your stead. Eventually. If you rush there, he'll know he has you."

She was probably right, but Javier had to risk it. "Did Guillermo ask you to warn me?"

"Even as close as you are, he would never tell you any of this. I thought you should know."

Clearly, the hard-boiled Chinese shopkeeper had a soft spot for the clever American *maestra*. Javier felt a twinge of possessive pride, but it was fleeting: Georgina was not yet his. Before he could win her, Javier would have to travel to Catbalogan and bring back Benji.

Part VII: March 1903

Las Piñas, Luzon, Philippines
August 6, 1901

Dearest Georgie,

...We head out to goo-goo land tomorrow. We have orders to board up the whole southern coast of Samar, denying the villain Lukban his access to guns and supplies. I do not care much for the dirty war these insurrectos fight: the only difference between an amigo and a boloman is how many teeth show in his smile. Never mind! My lieutenant tells us that the only privilege we soldiers have is to growl and do our duty....

From now on, you may address your letters to "C Co. 9th U.S. Regular Infantry, Basey, Samar." Of course, it is anyone's guess where and when they will be delivered.

Your loving brother,
Benji

CHAPTER FORTY-SEVEN

Secrets

Allegra stood at the top of the steps leading down into the schoolroom, threatening Georgie with her imminent departure if the American did not hurry up. She had been doing so for half an hour already. "This is not a *baile*, Ina," she called out. "Wear anything you want."

Was every Altarejos calling her Ina now?

Georgie had to admit that the nickname was growing on her, and after a month in Javier's arms, it somehow fit. While she hardly thought herself transformed into a siren, she did feel more sensual, more alluring. No matter what happened now, she would always have this confidence, the most important gift given to her by her first lover.

Georgie stuck her head out of the bedroom. "Really…anything? You said it was a special family occasion."

"*Sí*, but it is casual." The Filipina put a finger to her lips in thought. "Intimate is a good word."

Georgie turned away and ran a hand over her rumpled linens. Intimate was a little too close to the truth. Javier had sworn to keep their affair secret, but had his cousin rooted it out? Until Georgie knew otherwise, her best bet was to play the prim schoolteacher to the hilt. She put on her standard shirtwaist and did not bother to wipe off the chalk dust.

"Okay," she announced, emerging from the bedroom for Allegra's appraisal, only to find the Filipina halfway down the stairs.

"*Finalmente!*" came the cry from the schoolroom below.

Georgie laughed and followed her friend. As soon as the two climbed into the waiting *calesa*, Allegra started to argue with the *cochero*.

"Along the river?" Georgie interjected. "Why do you want to go that way?"

"You understand me!" Allegra looked pleased—and suspicious. "Javito teaches you Cebuano, maybe?"

The man had taught Georgie a lot, but not his language. "I was just interpreting your hand motions," she explained.

The Filipina smiled and gave Georgie an affectionate hug. "As you want, *prima.*"

Prima. My cousin. Georgie told herself it was a normal endearment among friends, nothing more. She hoped to discourage Allegra's domestic notions before they caught the attention of any of the gossips in town.

At least right now people had something real to talk about, which was the only good thing that could be said about the latest tragic incident: Mr. Montgomery, the incoming Division Superintendent of Schools of Oriental Negros, had been murdered by ladrones on his way south to take up his post. Georgie wanted to know which idiot had advised the man to trek the central roads alone, laden with cash for the February payroll. The killing had thrown the whole district into chaos.

The only silver lining was that no one had taken the time to check up on her little schoolhouse in Bais. Once someone did, Archie would make sure that Georgie was sent off without a penny in severance. Every single day he reminded her of this fact. It was bad enough she had to talk to Archie at all, after he had deliberately let her brother slip through his fingers. In her weaker moments, she hoped that some of his supplies of tinned meat would turn rancid—not enough to kill him, but just enough to make him very, very ill.

A sharp jolt took Georgie's mind off her toxic thoughts. She gripped the edge of the carriage tightly as they bounced along the riverbank road. "Tell me again why we're going this way?"

Allegra pulled her hair back and fixed it with a pin. "The fields burn today," she grumbled. "There is much smoke on the main road."

Smoke was the mark of harvest, a reality that Georgie thought everyone accepted. Just last week, Javier had explained the convenience of fire: it stripped dry leaves from the cane and exposed the watery stalk for cutting. The flames also cleared the ground, killed insects, and created fertilizer for the next year's crop. Knowing all this made Georgie more tolerant of the acrid smoke, even though it left a thick black film on everything in the house.

Allegra was not as accommodating. She motioned to the clouds on the horizon, a pinch of worry creasing her brow. "It is bad everywhere, but imagine you live next door. One year Casa Jordana almost burned down. Tiyo Lázaro said it was a mistake, but sometimes the men try to make fires too close to the house on purpose."

"Would they really do that?"

"The ladrones are getting stronger. They put the torch to an hacienda out west." Allegra frowned. "I wish Javier stayed closer to home."

Georgie knew exactly why Javier had spent most of his evenings away from the hacienda. True, he never came to her until after supper, but that was only because Georgie demanded discretion, not because she was being considerate of his family's needs. She felt a little guilty about that. She would loan him back, but how could she explain borrowing him in the first place?

"Maybe he is just busy," she suggested.

"He is always busy," Allegra agreed. "You know, Ina, I worry about you, too, alone in town."

"Oh, no, I'm fine, really." She did not admit that she had six feet of protection in her bed most nights.

"You can stay with us," Allegra offered. "It would be such fun!"

Georgie could just imagine the cousins competing for her attention in that pajama party. Filipino manor houses were not known for their privacy: all the rooms, even the bedrooms, had carved wooden vents across the tops of the walls to allow air to circulate. Neither she nor Javier could be quiet enough for such a layout.

"Thank you, Allegra, but I'm fine."

The young woman opened her mouth to argue, but then seemed to think better of it.

A few minutes later the *calesa* pulled up the brick drive to the house and stopped next to a cheerful Doña Lourdes. Even Georgie knew that this welcome was unusual: high-bred Filipinos were friendly, but they usually awaited guests in the second-floor living room.

Lourdes led them upstairs, where Georgie discovered just how much the woman favored her. Stacks of gold and silver coins covered a large table, maybe several thousand dollars worth. Allegra explained that the money came from the recent harvest, and that the women of the family—Georgie notably included—would spend the next few hours counting it. How did the table not collapse under the weight of so much metal?

"Usually we need many days to count," Allegra explained, "but not this year."

"Why's that?"

"Javito said I could tell you." Allegra motioned to the table and whispered seriously. "This is not enough."

Georgie almost choked on her own words. "Not enough for whom? Croesus?"

The Filipina counted off on her fingers. "After we pay all the slashers and migrant workers, the overseer will take his share. Geno is paid well, of course. It is a good job. I could do that job, and cheaper too. Better than making flowers or playing piano," Allegra muttered. Her eyes flicked back up to Georgie's, and she smiled an apology. "Then we pay to take the sugar to Manila, pay our bills in town, and pay the cooks, maids, and *muchachos*." She gestured at the coins. "This is not enough."

Georgie did not know whether to believe that. Everything about Javier screamed wealth; it was what she liked least about him.

"We are the patrons, you see," Allegra continued. "Hundreds of people count on us. We must be true as steel, or make them believe so."

Georgie looked again at all that money. She had to ask. "The burning of the fields, the ladrones, and now this. Are...are we...safe?"

The slight princess seemed to transform into a stone warrior. "We are never safe until all is paid out."

That was not the answer Georgie wanted to hear. With a tilt of her head, the doña directed them all to take their places, and then motioned a reluctant Allegra to the piano to entertain them with a light waltz. The instrument was painfully out of tune, but Lourdes swayed with the music anyway. Georgie sat and counted silver coins from every mint in Asia, but her mind could not concentrate fully on the task. Instead, it raced through the same questions again and again. Javier worked so hard, so how could he be in trouble? At night he often told her about his day: the new laborers he recruited (a tenth of whom promptly disappeared after a small advance had been paid), the mill that seized up every other week but that he had learned to fix, the side deals that he did with fishermen to supply food to his laborers. He did all this, and he was still losing money?

After a few hours, the doña took Georgie's figures, finished her own tabulations, and sighed. "It is what we expected. No more."

"Is it enough?" Georgina asked.

Lourdes tapped the metal nib of her pen against the inkwell in a nervous rhythm. "Maybe, if we are careful. But maybe not. Without Javier here, I cannot be sure of anything."

"When's he coming in?" Georgie knew that Javier could spend all day and night in the fields, but his workers would have to stop sometime. She was neatening up her rows of silver coins, waiting for an answer, when she looked up to find both women staring at her. "What?"

Allegra spoke cautiously. "He had a letter from Tina Yuco."

That was not so unusual. Everyone did business with Tina. "And?"

Lourdes took over. "Javier left."

"To go where?"

"He does this for you," Lourdes said. "We will keep you safe—"

"Where?" Georgie gave the woman her hardest look. "Tell me."

Lourdes's sigh sounded especially patronizing, but at least she did not beat about the bush. "Samar."

Georgie's first reaction was elation. "He found my brother?"

"Well...not exactly."

Georgie might as well have swallowed all the coins in front of her, given how far her stomach dropped. "What does that mean?"

"There is some news, but nothing is for certain. Javier has gone to meet with some men there, and if your brother can be found, he will do it."

"Men? Which men?" Georgie stood and pushed away her chair. "I have to go too. I should be talking to these people, not Javier."

"Of course you cannot go to Samar," Allegra said. She reached up and took Georgie's hand. "Do not be silly."

The American jerked away. "What gives him the right to go without me? Benji is my brother, my responsibility!"

Georgie realized that Javier must have been planning his escape for days, maybe weeks. She had spent night after night in his arms, and the whole time he had been keeping this from her. Even worse, he knew that Georgie had not forgiven Blaxton for his secrets; he knew that, yet he had done the exact same thing.

The doña spoke quietly, but firmly. "Georgina, please. He is doing this for you, don't you see? Really, Samar is the last place he should be traveling right now, but this is what a man does for his bride."

Whoa, Georgie thought. What had Javier told them? This was not their deal. She did not appreciate him dangling her brother as some sort of matrimonial blackmail.

"I am not marrying your son, Lourdes, I'm sorry. Certainly not if I can't trust him."

The older woman frowned, but she did so with remarkable dignity. "But I thought—"

"I don't care what you thought. Javier does not get to butt into my family business just because we are sharing a bed!"

Unruffled, Lourdes looked past the open threshold into the neighboring dining room where two young girls were setting the table. When there was no telltale tittering, the doña turned back to the American standing in front of her. "Keep your voice down."

"Why bother?" Georgie no longer cared about her reputation in Bais. So much had just changed. "When I find Benji, I'm taking him home with me to Boston."

"You cannot find him, not by yourself," Lourdes said. "No one goes to Samar right now. Not even Filipinos, if we can help it."

Georgie grasped the edge of the table in a vain effort to stop shaking. "Do you really think that Javier can do this by himself? He doesn't even know what Benji looks like, for God's sake! And, even if by some blessed miracle Javier does find my brother, why would Benji leave Samar with a stranger? He doesn't know that I'm here in the Islands in the first place."

"Javier can be persuasive," Lourdes said with a typical mother's pride. "You will see. Then you will want to marry him."

"I've never had any intention of marrying Javier," Georgie said flatly. She put Javier's wager out of her mind.

"He loves you." The doña's voice wavered a little. "He has never loved any woman before."

"I'm trying to save my brother's life! Would you be wasting your time matchmaking if it was Allegra dying in Samar?"

The woman in question rose and placed a hand on Georgie's shoulder. "But Javier will return soon enough, you will see."

"You of all people should help me," Georgie said, shaking her shoulder loose. "I thought we were friends."

"This is why you must not go, Ina. Please."

"I will go, and you will help me."

Both women shook their heads emphatically.

"Oh, yes, you will." Georgie turned to Lourdes. "Otherwise, you will see what betrayal feels like. Let me ask you: what will happen if the local merchants—the ones whose children come to my school—find out that Javier Altarejos skipped town before pay day?"

Allegra took a step back. "But he will be back soon."

"How do they know that? What *hacendero* in his right mind would leave before the fields are closed? And then, when everyone starts to look at how much he owes…"

"You couldn't." Lourdes brow lowered in anger. "If the laborers believed this, they would burn this house down around our ears."

Georgie shoved handfuls of coins into the center of the table. "This should be enough to buy both your lives."

Both women drew in a sharp breath. Nobody spoke, but the Filipinas' faces showed an unmistakable combination of anger and fear. Georgie did not want her friends hurt. She would never do what she was threatening, but she had to make them believe that she would. They would hate her, but Benji's life was worth the price.

Finally, Allegra spoke. "What do you want?"

"I need to catch up with Javier. Where is he?"

"I don't think you can—"

"Allegra," Georgie said, glaring at her. "No excuses."

The Filipina looked at her aunt, who nodded. She faced Georgie, still wary of the crazy Yankee. "He is in Cebu by now, but his steamer to Catbalogan will not leave for a week. He sent a telegram."

Allegra went to a small table that opened on a hinge to reveal a neat writing desk. She picked up a slip of paper stamped with "The Eastern Extension Australasia & China Telegraph Co." It said:

```
STEAMER TO SAMAR DELAYED ONE WEEK STOP TRAVEL ON
AEOLUS FIFTEENTH MARCH JAVIER
```

"The *Aeolus*," Georgie repeated out loud. "Good. I can catch a steamer to Cebu this weekend. Who is he meeting in Catbalogan?"

Again, there was silence. But then Allegra's eyes briefly shot left, a dead giveaway. There had to be more telegrams. "Get them," Georgie ordered.

After a flurry of Spanish between the two Filipinas, Allegra retrieved two more slips from the writing desk and handed them to Georgie. The first was addressed to Javier and read:

```
SEND DETAILS YOUR ARRIVAL STOP PROCEED THIRTY
EIGHT CALLE SAN BARTOLOME
```

The second was a receipt of a message Javier had sent:

```
NEED POTTER IN PERSON STOP WILL DISCUSS TERMS
```

Georgie looked at the name at the top and read it aloud: "Lope."

"Lope Cuayzon," Allegra explained. "He is a Chinese merchant in Samar. We know the family."

Georgie nodded but did not speak. She stared at the trader's name. Lope. Wolf. This was the man who could find her brother?

She tucked the pages into her bag. "Thank you," she said.

"Do not thank us," Lourdes said. "We have not done you any favors. You have not met Lope Cuayzon yet."

Georgie was long past caring. Even if this Chinese fellow was dangerous—and even if Samar was Satan's armpit—what choice did she have? Sit here for the next month and wait? To hell with that, she thought.

She pointed to Allegra. "Now, there's one more thing—"

Allegra said something in Spanish that sounded quite nasty, but Georgie ignored it.

"—You say you want to teach, Allegra? Starting Monday, the girls are all yours." She paused and then added, "Just don't talk to Maestro Blaxton if you can help it."

Ignoring Allegra's distress, Georgie fled the room, ran out of the house, and commandeered the Altarejos *calesa* for the ride home. She had packing to do.

CHAPTER FORTY-EIGHT

Surprises

After more than a week's wait in Cebu, Javier boarded the steamer bound for Catbalogan. From the deck, he watched the afternoon sun baptize the whitewashed Customs House. It was Sunday, but back on the hacienda his men would be working anyway, as per his instructions. The drought dictated as early a harvest as possible, before the heat desiccated the final fields of cane. He would lose in the yield, but it was better to harvest something rather than risk ending up with nothing. Javier hated the fact that he could not be present to supervise the harvest. He wanted to oversee the soaking of the *puntas* before they were replanted, a particularly important step when the summer looked to be even hotter and drier than last year.

Still, none of this is what worried him the most. He repeatedly told himself that he had done the right thing, but the refrain felt hollow, especially when he imagined Georgina's reaction when she discovered he was gone. He needed enough of a head start that he could return with her brother before she stewed too long, but the steamer delay had already put him behind schedule. And if Benjamín could not be found? In that case, he was especially glad he had not let her barge into the middle of the war for nothing. He reminded himself of this wisdom one more time before turning from the railing.

"Hello, Javier."

"Ina, *qué demonios!*"

His woman approached him, arms crossed and shoulders squared. She looked severe in her high-collared shirt and prim skirt.

"How did you know where I was?"

Georgina reached into her bag and pulled out two thin, torn pages. Their cream color with bold red print gave them away as Eastern telegrams. He could not imagine how she had gotten Allegra to turn those over.

His face must have betrayed him. "Don't worry," Georgina said. "Allegra didn't give me these willingly. She can be rather fierce, you know."

That much was true. No doubt the first man his cousin targeted would either marry her or flee the hemisphere. "*Querida*, I'm sorry, but I couldn't tell you I was leaving until I was gone."

"Why ever not?" Georgina asked in a falsely sweet voice. Her American sarcasm drove him mad, and she knew it.

"Because I knew you would insist on coming!"

"And yet here I am," she said, leaning casually against the railing, her hip cocked to the side.

He had underestimated her. He thought she would accept a fait accompli, and now he would pay for his mistake.

The sea breeze rustled a few curls out of her high bun, but the loose strands did not soften her expression. He had heard Englishmen joke about the temper of the Irish, but he had never before witnessed it in person.

Javier wanted to be reasonable, but he did not have the time. "You need to get off this ship before it leaves port, Ina. You can stay here in Cebu until I get back—"

Georgina cut him off. "You and I are going to Samar together."

"You stupid woman!" He hit the rail with his hand, sounding a ping as flesh slammed the metal. "You think you can do whatever you want, and damn the consequences!"

She did not respond, which he took as confirmation.

"What about school?" he asked.

"Yes, that would have been a problem, but fortunately you brought Allegra home, along with her newly minted certification. If there's anyone who can whip Inday Benitez into shape, it's her."

Javier's leaned down and rested his elbows on the rail, head in hands. "How did I end up here?" he whispered.

All he wanted was a helpmate, someone to stand with him as he tried to save the hacienda—and a few children to give the place some joy, to make it worth saving.

Though he had whispered the question to himself, Georgina answered it. "You made the same mistake as Archie—you lied to me." She spun and strode across the deck.

Javier hated being compared to Blaxton. He hated it especially because it was a little bit true. He chased after her. "I'm not keeping you from your brother, you mule-headed fool! I'm fetching him for you!"

"Oh, goodness, thank you," she said, bitterness at full blast. "Thank you for not bothering me with any of the details about how Benji had been found, if he was in good health, or whether he was even alive. All that vital information may have proven too taxing."

"That's exactly the point! I don't have any information. I barely have a ghost sighting, and even that's three weeks old." He knew as soon as he said it that he had made another mistake. He wanted to throttle himself.

"Three weeks? I see. You said lots of pretty words to me in those three weeks, Javier, but none of them mentioned my brother. You really screwed me, didn't you?"

On her face, Javier saw the hard look of someone who had nothing to lose: reckless, intractable, and numb. "Georgina," he warned, "there are some things that cannot be unsaid."

"There are some things that cannot be undone either."

He took a deep breath and tried to speak more gently: "Please, at least give me a chance to explain."

She did not say anything, but she did not walk away.

"I didn't tell you, because...well, I didn't want you here. I still don't want you here."

"That's your explanation? Holy smoke, you're bad at this."

He stayed the course. "I can't reasonably predict what I'm going to find in Samar—other than cholera, of course. The place is Bedlam. It's taken the Americans two full years to set up a civil government in Catbalogan, but a half-hour's ride out of town and you're right back in blazes."

"I'm not planning to leave town—"

"Not until you hear some trumped up rumor from the town drunk that your brother is one *barangay* over. Then, next thing I know, you'll have hired a horse and be on your merry way," he said.

She did not dispute it. "If my brother is out there, then I'll be safe with him."

Again, he felt an overwhelming urge to grab Georgina's shoulders and shake a little cussed sanity into her. "You don't understand," he ground out. "Your brother may not be safe! Far from it. The Army captured the *insurrectos*, but in the process they've caused such abject misery on the island that the people have turned to religious zealots— brutal 'popes' who promise to deliver an independent kingdom of Samar."

Georgina waved away his concerns. She probably believed her search was wholly personal, immune from politics, race, and rule. She refused to think of herself as a colonial official. He did not like to think of her as one either. He had almost suckered himself into believing her a servant of the people: all of the benevolence, none of the assimilation. But even if she were not a paid representative of the Insular Government, she was still an American. To the Samareños, it was the same thing.

"Javier, I don't care if the people worship magic beans," she was saying. "That's not why I'm here."

"This isn't a fairy tale, Maestra. No matter how silly you find their faith, given enough motivated men, bolos can beat rifles. Even the Army rarely leaves the bosom of their garrison. They give that job to the Filipino constables."

"I'm not going to plant a flag there. I just want to ask some questions around the city—a city where you admit that Americans have restored law and order."

"But for how long? Samar has been on this merry-go-round for hundreds of years, you know. The Americans may not understand what they have set in motion, but everyone else does. No one has any interest in helping the Americans because the minute they do, the population of the entire town will be marked as collaborators." Javier could tell that his innocent *maestra* did not understand the implication. He had to make it very, very clear for her. "Then one quiet night, without warning, hundreds of *Pulahanes* will stream in from the forest. They can twirl bolos in both hands, did you know that? They will kidnap the women and children—well, the lucky women and children—behead the men, steal the food, and set a torch to whatever they cannot carry."

Georgina's face registered a bit of concern—not enough, but it was a start. "How does this make the *Pulahanes* any better than their oppressors?" she asked.

"Who said they were better? Righteousness does not require third-party approval. This is fast becoming a civil war. Don't try to make sense of it." But Javier could see her trying to do exactly that.

Georgina looked up at him with big green eyes, and it took all he had not to smile and reassure her that everything would be okay. He could not make that guarantee.

"Don't you see," she said. "You're just making me more worried about Benji, which I had not thought possible. I have to rescue him—at least, I have to be close by."

"Cebu is close enough."

"No," she whispered. "I have to be there, in Catbalogan, when you find him."

When Javier found him. Was that a concession? *Hay sus*, please let it be a concession, he thought.

"If I let you come to Catbalogan," he warned with a wag of his finger, "then you'll follow my rules, my plan. Most importantly, you cannot leave town. You will not even leave your room without my permission."

"What? No way. You can have the rest of the island, but I'm perfectly capable of running my search in town."

"Are you serious, *querida*? Your search? You can't even find a Chinese laundry in the middle of bloody Chinatown!"

He could not hear Georgina's reply over the roar of the boat's engines firing up, but he doubted any of it could be found in a Thomasite primer. The boat pulled away from the shore, and Georgina sat down on a deck chair. She stared straight out to sea, deliberately avoiding his gaze. She was as angry as he had ever seen her, but Javier could endure her anger as long as it kept her alive.

CHAPTER FORTY-NINE

S.S. *Aeolus*

Georgie wanted to pitch Javier overboard. She might have tried it, too, had she not felt a creeping seasickness coming on. What she needed now was to sit in the fresh air and calm down. She could not afford to show any further weakness. She had already conceded one key point—that she would allow herself to be cloistered in town—and she would not yield any more than that.

Javier sat quietly next to her for the first hour of the journey. Though Georgie would have liked a break from his frowning face, she did not move when the supper bell rang. Her stomach had started to settle, but she would never be well enough to eat food from the galley. Instead, she pulled out her own small kit: Spanish-style bread rolls, carabao cheese, and a few pomelos.

Javier looked at her. "Eating native these days?"

"Being a prig won't get you dinner."

"I'm fine." But his rumbling stomach said otherwise.

She wished he would just go get his own food and leave her alone, but if he insisted on keeping watch over her, there was nothing she could do about it.

Unfortunately for him, his gut was as stubborn as he was. It growled louder the second time. She held out a small roll. "Just eat it."

"Really, I'm—"

"Lying. Shut up and eat." Georgie did not want much anyway. Before she had taken her first bite, she had not thought it possible to fill her empty belly. Now, though, she could not imagine finishing. She hated boat travel. "If you don't take this *pandesal* in the next five seconds, it's going to be fish food. Five, four, three, two…"

The *hacendero* waited almost the full count, and then grabbed the proffered roll just before she whipped it past the starboard gunwale. Too bad. Georgie had wanted to see if she could make the throw into the wind. Giving in to his hunger, Javier motioned for the pomelo. He peeled its thick rind, always a chore, and gave most of the sweet grapefruit back. She ate a little and wrapped the rest in a handkerchief for breakfast.

For the next hour they barely spoke. Georgie pulled her shawl close and hunched over, rubbing her arms with her hands. Javier also kept to himself, but he watched her carefully.

"You don't have to stay out here," he said. "I'm not going to get off this boat tomorrow without you, believe me. Go ahead and find your stateroom."

Stateroom: that was a grand word for a vermin-infested closet. "I'm sleeping on this chair, actually."

"On deck?"

"Yep."

"All night?"

She rolled her eyes and replied in Spanish for perfect clarity. "*Sí.*"

Given the look on his face, she may as well have said that she was going to bathe in the boiler. "You have a first-class ticket, right? That entitles you to a room, Ina."

"'First-class' on a filthy smoker like this just means you don't sleep with the fighting cocks."

"I thought that you said you could travel rough."

"I'm not the one whining for a stateroom!"

Javier said no more, but Georgie knew that she had not really won the argument. All she had proven was that she was easily ruffled.

Javier moved his chair closer to hers, clearly planning to remain by her side the whole night. She tried to look at the bright side: his presence would at least ward off any over-solicitous cabin boys. Despite the wind, she dozed off almost as soon as her head hit her makeshift pillow, a cork-filled life jacket.

Georgie woke up shivering several times, but she eventually managed to sleep soundly. When she sat up, she realized why. At some point during the night, Javier had covered her in his coat, tucking it tightly around her body like a mummy. Now that the sun had risen, she was sweating. She pulled the sleeves out from under herself and handed back the impossibly wrinkled garment. "I'm sorry."

He smiled—a nice one, with none of the anger from the night before. "Don't apologize, *querida*. I placed it there."

"You could have kept it for yourself. You look like you didn't sleep at all."

Javier rubbed his face with both hands, as if that would erase the dark circles under his eyes. "I wouldn't have been able to rest anyway."

Georgie didn't believe him, but she did not want to argue about it, either, so they sat in silence for a few more minutes. Her attention drifted to the distant shore, eyes panning the tropical green-scape.

"I'm sorry, Ina," he finally whispered.

"For what?" She was not implying that Javier had nothing to apologize for, just that she wanted to know which transgressions he was specifically referring to.

"I understand why you're angry, but please know that I have your best interests at heart."

"You think so, at least."

He shook his head gently. "I still do. If I had to do it over again, I would still leave you in Bais."

More proof that he was one of the worst penitents in the history of relationships, she thought. She did not need him to don a hair shirt, but she had expected some sort of pledge to mend his ways. "You would change nothing?"

"Well," he began, smiling slyly. "I might tie you to my mother's grand piano before I left. But, you know, lesson learned."

Georgie wanted to give him a good whack, and the heavens must have agreed because a rumble of thunder broke open the sky. The initial drip of rain quickly became a torrent, and everyone fled indoors. At first she and Javier followed the crowd, but as they entered the open galley, she caught a whiff of fermented fish paste mixed with the stale stench of human perspiration. No doubt this room was where the third-class passengers had camped for the night.

Georgie's stomach turned. She put a hand over her mouth and nose, hoping she could prevent a full-scale revolt of her digestive system. "There's no way I'm staying in here."

"Ina, don't be a fool. Come inside."

She reversed out the door and plastered herself against the chart house wall, taking shelter under a small overhang that should have been enough to protect her against a normal storm, one where the rain fell straight down. Unfortunately, precipitation in the tropics tended to move sideways. "You go. I'm staying here."

He remained by her side. Javier was not perfect, but he generally let her be as imperfect as she wanted in return. In fact, he claimed to like her headstrong nature, right up until the moment when he did not. Had he really expected to smooth her out with a good bedding, or even a month of them? What kind of person would she be if she simply handed off her quest to the first man she slept with? Her brother deserved more loyalty than that.

The ship slowed, waiting for the storm to pass before attempting a landing. It was a maddening delay. Twenty minutes later, Georgie and Javier were soaked but no closer to their destination. Then the rain stopped.

The *maestra* walked to the side of the ship, seeking what sun she could find to dry her clothes right on her body. From here, she could see a cozy batch of homes nestled under a panorama of mountains. Catbalogan was smaller than she thought it would be, but it was pretty in its own remote way. The natural barriers of hill and bay concentrated the population into clusters of bamboo. There was a road—a rickety boardwalk, really—that wrapped around a patch of mangrove trees to reach the pier. The surrounding wilds had to be the densest jungle she had ever set eyes on.

Javier joined her at the port side bulwark. "You'll be happy to know that you've managed to survive one of the most pirate-infested shipping lanes in the East Indies. Crews used to lie in wait here, preying on the Manila galleons as they emerged from the strait up ahead." He pointed to a narrow passage, hardly big enough to be an outlet to the Pacific. "Practically the whole city is descended from these outlaws—not a cooperative bunch."

Realizing this was yet another of his lectures on why she should not be here, Georgie sighed. She did not want to argue anymore.

He sensed her irritation and changed the subject. Motioning to land, he said, "That's strange."

She did not like strange, not right now. "What?"

Javier shielded his eyes with his hand and scanned the coastline. "We should see hemp—raw rope—drying in the sun all along the shore here."

"Maybe they took it in because of the rain?"

He looked at her briefly. "I doubt it. They would have to move it back and forth all day."

"So what does an empty beach mean?"

"I don't know, cariño." He shook his head. "But it can't be good."

"Why not?"

Javier rested his hand on hers and squeezed. "Sometimes even grass doesn't grow in the middle of a war."

Georgie swallowed hard. She looked at the picturesque town in front of her. It seemed so peaceful. How bad could it be?

CHAPTER FIFTY

Hemp Baron

I t looked to Georgie like the whole town had turned out to welcome the S.S. *Aeolus'* arrival in Catbalogan. It was probably the most exciting event in weeks.

Javier had managed to make his jacket appear fresh, and even the lines under his eyes had lightened. Had he been a soldier, he could not have looked more ready to do battle. He grasped Georgie's arm just below the shoulder socket. "Let's get in line," he said.

"Would you please not hold on so tightly?"

He nodded, but did not loosen his grip. He led her to the ramp, where they waited their turn to disembark. Once they set foot on the dock, a man approached. His and Javier's finely tailored suits must have recognized each other, even if the men themselves did not. They shook hands and made small talk in Cebuano before Javier introduced Georgie in English. "Lope Cuayzon, may I present you to my fiancée, Maestra Georgina Potter."

Before she could react to this public announcement, Javier gave her a look of silent warning: she was not to correct him.

"Pleased to meet you," she stammered out, realizing that it would do no good to quarrel in front of the stranger. "Thank you for offering to help us find my brother, Mr. Cuayzon."

The Chinaman was a few inches shorter than Georgie and at least two decades older. His face had the waxy paleness that she knew was highly prized in the islands. He nodded his head in greeting. "You are teacher, yes?"

She was not sure if that was a question or an accusation. The man's English was clear enough, but his tone was distrustful. "Yes, I was assigned to Bais in October."

"Hmmm...yes, I know of American teachers. There are two in Calbayog. Not yet for Catbalogan. Maybe you make school here? Teach my children."

Though finding work in town could pay the bills until she found Benji, the thought of this particular man's patronage seemed strangely uninviting. "I can help, of course, but I do hope to be reunited with my brother rather quickly—"

"Yes, yes," Lope said, brushing his hand through the air. The motion was more dismissive than encouraging. "You stay with family, Maestra. My wife sees honor with American guest."

Georgie tried to refuse politely. "I don't wish to trouble her. I'm sure she wasn't expecting company."

"Stay. Don Javier too." It was a command.

She was stuck. Had the *hacendero* intentionally orchestrated this arrangement, he could not have done a better job trapping her. Now she would be expected to spend her days with Mrs. Cuayzon and the children, far away from the search itself. Lope took her silence as assent.

As they walked to the trader's house, Georgie observed the town that would be her prison. She could not help comparing it to Bais, unfavorably so. If this was the center of a profitable hemp industry, she wondered where the grand plantation houses were. She quietly asked Javier.

"Hemp's a different kind of business," he whispered. "Thousands of small farmers sell their product to brokers like him. He effectively runs this town, but his goal isn't to set down roots. It's to make enough money to be promoted back to Manila."

The truth of these words became clear when the hemp baron led them to his modest but well-appointed home over a storefront. In the corner of the *sala* someone had stacked a dozen bolts of Chinese silk against the wall. Next to the silk were a pile of carefully folded screens, more than could possibly be used in a room as simple as this. The family seemed to be storing their treasures for the day when they could display them all, maybe in a grand villa in Manila.

Once in her designated bedroom, Georgie laid out a few of her things. Javier snuck in behind her and placed a hand on her shoulder. She tried unsuccessfully to duck from his touch, but he nudged her around to face him. "I'll find him for you, I promise," he said.

"If we were staying on our own, I could help you look. Maybe these bar owners would talk to me."

Javier's eyes grew wide in disbelief. He shook his head. "Cuayzon can help us. That's why I contacted him. He owns several of the establishments that Benjamín may frequent. Without his approval, people won't talk to an outsider. Besides, *querida*, where else do you think we'd stay? There are no inns. If I were alone, I could stay at the parish house or rent my own rooms—"

"Let's rent, then."

"We can't rent a house together. Not unless we are married. Of course, we could take care of that today." He looked down at her, smiling but serious.

She knew he liked the idea. "No, and that reminds me—why did you say that we're engaged?"

"It's not a lie, *amor*."

She looked into his eyes and did not argue. But she did not know the truth of anything anymore.

CHAPTER FIFTY-ONE

Finding Paca

Lope Cuayzon was nothing like his Manila cousin, Guillermo. Javier knew this from their first evening together. The Samar agent personified every American prejudice of John Chinaman, right down to his business hocking opium. Of course, the Americans had helped Lope live down to their expectations—not only had they kept opium legal, they introduced a forty-five percent tariff that hooked the American taxman just as much as any addict, and they allowed its use beyond the Chinese community, doubling the demand for imports. Lope was a savvy businessman and was not content to profit only from opium's wholesale trade, so he built up a network of dens, bars, and brothels where he could sell directly to his customers without a middleman.

There was no way Javier was going to allow Georgina to accompany such a man anywhere, let alone on his tour of vice in southern Samar. After an uncomfortably long tea with the Cuayzon family, the men made their excuses and left. Javier alternated between anxiety and amusement at the thought of leaving Georgina behind in a house where no one spoke English, but he had no choice. He had to keep her as far away from Lope as possible. Frankly, Javier did not want to spend much time with the man either.

Lope owned several saloons at the port that catered to Americans, each marked with the Stars and Stripes hanging in a window. Javier's inquiries about Ben at these bars proved fruitless. By the time he spoke with the last three Americans drinking at the Red Star, Javier wondered if Ben Potter had ever been to the town—no one had heard of him. Javier did learn that the Americans had constructed a small prison at Calbiga, down the coast from Catbalogan. Could Ben be there?

Lope seemed happy enough to hire a boat for the journey, but he insisted that they interrupt their search—not yet in its third hour—for refreshments. Lope commanded the boatmen to stop along the way at Hiabong, a sleepy bayside village known for its green mussels. Javier hinted that he would prefer to keep moving, but good manners kept him from being more insistent. Lope led Javier to a well-laid table and ate his fill of shellfish. Passing street vendors satisfied every other gustatory whim, too, from noodles to coffee to coconut wine. The dinner felt endless.

Lope's stomach now satisfied, they resumed the search. Hiabong's saloons and *casas* were a bust. Javier saw nothing except robust games of roulette, blank-faced opium smokers, and raucous women. At Lope's insistence, he put a few coins on *jueteng* and suspiciously won the lot, fifty Mex. The more the *sangley* crowed over his guest's good fortune, the more Javier was convinced the game was rigged. So far the trip felt like an overture to a con.

By midnight they were only halfway to Calbiga. Javier was not thrilled to be out on the water at such a late hour, even if the moon was bright and the rowers competent. Had this been a pleasure tour, the *hacendero* would have had no complaint, but tonight he wanted to get on with it or go home.

As if they could read Javier's mind, the rowers abruptly beached the *banca*, hopped out onto shore, and dragged the vessels away from the water line.

"Are they tired?" Javier asked his host. "Maybe we could hire more men?"

The *sangley* studied him carefully. "No, the ones we have are fine."

"I don't understand."

"Don Javier," Lope said, using his formal title with enough impatience that it bordered on impolite. "I understood that you wished for my help."

"Of course, and I'm glad to have it." It was true, even if Javier was suspicious of the man's priorities.

"Then I am helping you," Lope said, leading Javier away from the boat and toward a town he identified as Paranas. "You see, men are men. A red fur devil like your friend Potter has only one thought in his head, much like you and me."

Javier did not appreciate being lumped into any category together with Lope Cuayzon, nor did he enjoy the man's arm around his shoulders, but he deliberately chose not to shake off the embrace. Lope had successfully illustrated his dominion over this dark corner of the world, and Javier needed him.

"What thought is that?" he asked.

"Power. Well, not just that. Power, money, influence—all have the same source."

Lope stopped walking when they reached an overgrown dirty shack. In Javier's gut, he knew that this had been the *sangley*'s intended destination from the beginning. Javier had never seen this particular place before, but he had seen a handful like it throughout the world. It sat on the far edge of town, was dimly lit, and had *capiz* windows shut tight to keep any noise—or occupants—from escaping. The last detail set it apart from the other lively *casas* they had seen tonight. Had Lope shown him a pit like this in Catbalogan, Javier would have raised his chin and walked out. Unfortunately, he was trapped in the company of his companion—there was no road back to the capital from here.

Javier looked over at his host again. "You think sex is the source of a man's power?"

"You confuse a flower's stem with its nectar. Potency, Don Javier, is the key to it all." Lope opened the door and stepped inside. "Come in. I have something special for you."

Javier had no choice, so he reluctantly stepped through the door. The small hall was empty except for an older woman who disappeared upstairs after a nod from her boss. The whole thing seemed rehearsed, with Javier the only actor who did not know his lines.

The *ama* reappeared with a young girl wearing only a burlap skirt that hid little of her barely pubescent body. "You'll like her," Lope promised. "This little cherry will be a nice distraction for a few days, eh?"

The *hacendero* kept his face expressionless, but his insides roiled. He had never been a connoisseur of this type of tragedy. He wanted to shove a few coins in the girl's hand and tell her to run for it. Where would she go, though? Her parents had likely sold her to the *ama*, and if she disappeared they would have to pay back the *gratis*. No doubt they would return her themselves rather than do that. The girl would get nothing for her trouble except angry wardens.

"I appreciate your generosity, Lope." Javier felt anything but appreciative. To be brought to this hellhole was an affront, and they both knew it. If he took the child upstairs, Javier would be accepting Lope's patronage at the cost of his own soul. On the other hand, if he walked out and rejected this "hospitality," Lope would take offense, and Javier would never get Ben Potter back. It was a pernicious and unwinnable test.

Lope waited for the *hacendero* to make his choice. The girl stood mute, too, her eyes downcast and her arms folded weakly across her chest. Javier stepped forward and took the girl's hand. He tried to ignore the thin trembling of her fingers in his. "Thank you."

Lope's face split in a satisfied smile. "My pleasure."

No doubt Lope would take his pleasure afterward, Javier thought. The only person Javier hated more at this moment was himself for not giving this ogre the beating he deserved.

Still holding the girl's hand, Javier looked at Lope and asked, "Shall we be off then?"

"What?" For the first time the grinning pimp seemed confused.

"It's late and I'm ready to return to town. We can begin our search again tomorrow."

"You…you cannot mean to take this girl home with you?"

"Why not?" It was not Javier's home, after all, but Lope's. It was the home where the merchant's wife and daughters slept, the family that he kept insulated from his real appetites. And, of course, that was his point.

"This is the way of the world," the *sangley* lectured, not amused by the challenge.

"Are you taking her back then?" Javier held out the girl's hand but did not let it go. This had to be slim reassurance to her.

Lope blinked. "No, she's a gift."

"You are sure you want to give her to me?"

"Well, for as long as you are my guest, but—"

"To use as I wish?"

"Of course," Lope said, smiling once again at the word "use."

"Well, this is quite a happy coincidence, thank you. I had hoped to find a lady's maid to help my fiancée during our visit. This girl seems eager."

Before Lope could renege, Javier removed his barong and bundled the girl into it. It left the *hacendero* stripped to his undershirt while the child prostitute in his arms now wore a piña drape worth three month's food. This small amount of justice made him feel a little better.

Javier led the girl out of the *casa*. Once they cleared the threshold, he saw a wild look flare in the child's eyes, and he knew that she might bolt at any moment. But if she were to be caught—and she would be—he could not save her again. They had only one shot at this, and Javier squeezed her hand hard in the hope that she would heed the warning.

Because he did not speak the girl's dialect, and because he could not have spoken freely in front of Lope anyway, he said nothing to go with the squeeze. He would have liked to tell her that her best chance at a future lay in the hands of a stranger, a woman, even if that woman did not know it yet. He had no idea how he would explain any of this to Georgina, but when she learned the truth, she would never let this girl return to the brothel. Maybe this new responsibility would keep his beloved in Bais. Maybe this child could succeed in taming Georgina where Javier alone had failed.

The girl obediently followed the men into the *banca*. It was a long, awkward trip back. They slipped into Catbalogan just as the sun began to rise over the mountain. Javier led his "gift" into the house as quietly as possible and laid out a sleeping mat on the floor of Georgina's room. The girl's eyes grew wide when she saw a white woman asleep in the nearby bed, but she visibly relaxed when it became clear that she would be left alone for the night. She curled up to sleep, hugging the oversized shirt closed around her middle. Javier did not want to give the wrong impression by removing his pants in her presence, so he climbed into Georgina's bed fully clothed, careful not to wake his lover, even as he pulled her into his arms. Unable to bear another minute of consciousness, he dropped off to sleep instantly.

CHAPTER FIFTY-TWO

Dressing Paca

Georgie awoke alone, but she could have sworn that she had not slept that way. If Javier had been with her, though, he had not left a trace. At least, that was what she thought before she noticed the note on her bedside table.

> *Ina, I am leaving a girl named Paca in your care. Treat her as you would your own sibling, which is the best protection I can imagine.*

But Georgie saw no girl. The living room was empty—no surprise since Señora Cuayzon probably slept as late as every other bourgeois matron in the Philippines. Georgie was sure to find more activity in the kitchen, but it would be presumptuous for a guest to barge in there.

> *The Cuayzons know that the girl is our responsibility, but they are not happy about it. I cannot stress this enough: she must be by your side from morning to night. This is not for your safety, but hers.*

Javier was rarely so insistent, which meant she needed to find this child now.

The *maestra* searched the house, noting along the way that the dining room was spotless, almost as if the night before, she and her hostess had not spent a silent eternity there. Every dish was clean, dry, and placed neatly back in the cupboard. The maids in this house worked hard at all hours.

Her other search options exhausted, Georgie crept up to the kitchen door and slowly opened it. She stood there for a moment before either cook noticed her.

"*Susmaryosep!*" The younger one dropped her pan, and scalding oil splashed up in a noxious geyser.

The larger woman jerked back as some sprayed over her ankle. She did not seem to be badly burned, but one would not have known it by her yelling. She swatted her apprentice with the back of her hand, but even that did not pull the girl's attention off from the gigantic white woman standing in the doorway.

"Have you seen Paca?" Georgie asked, interrupting the chaos. Of course, no one understood English, so she tried again.

"*¿Ves a Paca?*" Spanish was also a miss. All she had left was Cebuano, if that.

"*Hain si Paca?*" She tried to remember the word for girl. "*Babaye. Batang babaye.*"

These few words ignited a flurry of conversation that, had it been less one-sided, might have been called an argument. The older cook had the last word, scolding her assistant for a whole minute. Then the woman pointedly went back to her cooking, as if rudeness alone would make the pesky foreigner leave. More than anything, Georgie was amused by the dismissal. Who did they think they were dealing with?

The younger cook got down on all fours and began to clean up the floor. She glanced up at the tall American as one might eye an oncoming storm, her discomfort a critical weakness. Georgie gaped at the girl with as little shame as most Filipinos showed her. She even crossed her arms and leaned against the doorframe, to emphasize that she would not be easily dismissed.

Eventually, the girl made a slight nod to the floor, barely a sign. Had anyone else seen it, they might have assumed she was simply scrubbing vigorously. It was enough for Georgie, though, and she flashed a brief smile of thanks.

Georgie took the stairs two at a time. The family store was a respectable establishment as far as she could tell, but something did not sit right. How much trouble could Paca have gotten into in just one morning?

Georgie heard people in the back office, but the store was empty. She walked to the doorway and peered in. Several Chinese men were drinking tea and crowing at each other over some numbered slips of paper. For a moment Georgie considered turning around before they noticed her, but instead, she cleared her throat. The men already stopped talking and stared. The sight of the red-haired *Americana* rendered them speechless.

Speechless was as good as she was going to get. She tried *"batang babaye"* a few times, but she could have just as easily been speaking Gaelic. These Chinese knew less of the native languages than she did. Out of ideas, she walked into the storeroom and poked around. The men were too stunned to stop her, so she opened and closed doors as if she had that right.

She heard water sloshing behind one door. Georgie opened it to find a girl scrubbing the floor. She could have been just another of the family's servants except for one crucial difference: the women upstairs wore tailored uniforms, but this girl wore a rice sack with holes cut for her head and arms.

"Paca?" Georgie asked quietly. When the child looked up, the *maestra* knew that she had found her mark.

"Paca, come here now." Georgie pointed to the spot of floor right next to her. The girl did not need to understand English to obey the command. She came right over, sliding to safety behind the American's back as Georgie turned to the men.

It was not surprising that a wealthy family like the Cuayzons would put every country mouse they found to work. Eight-year old Georgie had worked her own share of hours in the O'Shea family tailor shop, age no barrier to industry in either America or the Philippines. But Paca was under Javier's protection, and the Cuayzons should have respected this. These were the people she was counting on to find and care for her brother.

Though she did not need any more bile running through her soul, she allowed herself to vent every ounce of frustration from the last six months: every time she had been made the fool, every time she had been cheated, and every time she had been lied to. And because this past week had been particularly stressful, she dug up some colorful vocabulary learned on streets of Lower Roxbury. She may have even made a few things up. Spite had never felt so cathartic.

"And if you come within twenty feet of this girl again, I'll grab the nearest bolo and cut off your pricks. Understand?"

The men stared at her. Eyes wide and mouths open, they seemed to understand nothing, least of all why this stranger was yelling at them.

Georgie reached down, grabbed the girl's hand, and yanked it a little too hard. She had probably overdone it. It had felt good, but now she wanted nothing more than to get out of here.

She dragged the child into the store, over to the shelf of ready-made clothes—a luxury in this nowhere town—and rummaged through the stack. She tossed aside the larger *camisas* as if they were dirty rags. Let those idiots in the other room clean up her mess. She was taking the clothing too.

She used her seamstress's intuition to estimate Paca's size. The girl was the same height as many of Georgie's students in Bais, but thinner, if that was possible. She found a shirt that Paca would not drown in and handed it to her.

Instead of immediately pulling it over her head as Georgie would have done, Paca first rubbed the cloth between her thin little fingers, treasuring the soft Indian cotton. Georgie ransacked another pile and handed over a wide drape that could be wound into a native *saya* to replace the girl's burlap "skirt."

Paca stood, mouth open, staring at her American rescuer. Georgie realized that in her agitated state she was not providing Paca much reassurance, so she approached the girl slowly, cooing soft words. She held another *saya* as a screen to give Paca some privacy as she changed.

Georgie nodded toward the new clothes, and then to Paca. "You wear, okay? Put these on."

The girl had tears in her eyes. Georgie cursed herself for scaring the poor thing.

"*Imo,*" the *maestra* said quietly. She pointed to Paca again. "They're yours." Georgie had commandeered them, not bought them, but she dared anyone to point that out. She was feeling fierce.

The girl dressed quickly. They would deal with the need for underwear later; Paca had probably never owned any, so for now there was no rush. Paca watched quietly while Georgie picked the burlap skirt and rice sack off the floor and tossed them in a trash basket.

The girl reached over, took the *maestra's* fist, and threaded her own fingers inside. They left the store together, walking hand in hand.

Javier was going to have a lot to explain tonight, Georgie thought.

CHAPTER FIFTY-THREE

Zumárraga

The morning start had been tense. It could hardly have been otherwise, after the crass power play Lope had attempted in the whorehouse. Though Javier successfully defused that situation without openly confronting Lope in front of his people, he was offended that Lope had thought Javier might debase himself in that way. Of course, Javier could do nothing to help all the too-young girls under Lope's control, but he had done what he could for Paca, and that felt right.

He had had enough of Lope's games. If Ben was within Lope's reach, the *sangley* would have determined his precise location within days of Javier's initial inquiry. This extended tour had been a show for Javier or Georgina's benefit, and it was time to pull the curtain. That morning Javier told Lope the sightseeing was over. "Tell me you have news," he had said. "Real news. No more *putas*. No more *casas*."

Lope nodded, and though Lope seemed resigned to the new reality, Javier could read the anger in his eyes.

Javier and Lope approached Buad Island in the *sangley*'s boat. They had braved some rough water in Maqueda Bay and were now heading to Zumárraga, a tiny outpost on the southwestern corner of Buad. He thought that he might as well have reached the end of the known world—there were more people living on Hacienda Altarejos than on the whole of this island. This place looked dangerous for anyone, whether an American veteran or a Filipino sugar planter.

The rowers pulled the *barota* onto the beach. The dark gray sand was not inviting.

Javier followed Lope into a large ramshackle building on the outskirts of the Godforsaken town. Inside, the *amo* seemed both relieved and anxious to see them. The subordinate nervously relayed his latest news to the boss in the native Waray dialect.

Lope turned to Javier and explained: "You are very lucky. The American was almost stolen away by the ladrones."

To Javier, this claim sounded suspiciously like an attempt by Lope to reassert his authority. If the man needed to puff himself up again before Javier could get to Ben, fine, he would go along. "How close is almost?"

"There was an argument between the leader and another member of the group, a woman, and they changed their minds—not before doing extensive damage to my property."

No doubt if this American really was Benjamín, Lope would bill Javier for the damage—as well as for all of Lope's other "help."

"Show him to me."

Lope chirped some orders to the *amo*, who nodded and tilted his head in the direction of a dark flight of stairs. Javier hung back a bit as they ascended. The sweet smell of opium hung thick in the air—he had learned to hate that smell these past few days. Upstairs, they tunneled through the fog of hop. Addicts reclined on threadbare rugs, their eyes open but unfocused, drifting in their own aether.

They entered a room with a fully dressed man whose noxious smell had apparently earned him a private suite. Lope and the *amo* waited outside the doorway, signaling for the *hacendero* to make the identification himself.

Even prone, the man's gangly form gave away his foreign origins. He had long stringy hair, and his overgrown beard was matted with dirt. It was impossible to determine the man's age from a distance—and Javier was loath to get any closer—but the man seemed to be at least in his forties, too old to be Ben. Either Lope was poorly informed of the goings-on in his sordid little empire, or he was still playing games with Javier. Nevertheless, Javier had to confirm for Georgina's sake that this was not her brother.

The wood floor groaned loudly as Javier took a tentative step into the room. He edged closer, his footfalls reverberating in his own head like thunder. He hoped the laced smoke would not affect his own judgment. The last thing he wanted to do was to break Georgina's heart by mistaking some wretched stranger for her flesh and blood.

The man's eyes were open and unblinking, their unnatural blue glowing in the dim room. He was still enough to be dead.

"Excuse me, señor," Javier said.

The addict started at the sound, alive after all. He shifted his gaze toward Javier—or past him, it seemed—and his eyes grew wider, probably in fear of some recurring hallucination. A stain spread on the man's trousers as he wet himself.

Javier turned away revolted, unable to handle any more. This had to be a perverted joke on Lope's part: dragging Javier out to this horrid little piece of nowhere and parading him in front of such useless human filth. As he turned to leave, the man called out behind him: "Hugo? Hugo, is that you? Row harder. Harder, Hugo…"

Javier did not know what the man was talking about, but he was very familiar with his accent. Part of him wanted to pretend that he did not recognize Georgina's broad Boston "ahs" in the man's voice, so that he could walk away. It might be better to return with a corpse than to bring home this mess.

He forced himself to return to the whimpering man's side.

"Save her…We can't leave…."

Javier crouched in place, a few feet from the putrid American, and tried again. "*Oye!* You there! Listen to me. Are you Benjamín Potter?"

"I meant to save her. Please…"

"Save whom?"

"You shouldn't have come. Why…?"

Javier did not have the patience or the olfactory endurance for this nonsense. "Hey, pay attention. Are you Potter?"

The reprobate rolled his head on the floor and sobbed.

"Can you hear me?" Javier asked. It did not seem so, but it was hard to tell whether the problem was physical or mental.

After a minute or two more, the American had cried himself into a dark and spiritless sleep. Javier studied him, paying special attention to the face beneath the muck. His eyes had squint lines from the sun, but otherwise they were smooth. And though his hair and beard were tangled and dull, they were pure sandy brown, without a hint of gray. Forty had been a bad guess.

There was something hanging around his neck. The *hacendero* took a deep breath, lunged forward, and grabbed the silver disc. He yanked the necklace off the man's neck and retreated to the hall where he could examine it more closely. The front had a simple Greek cross with the word "Red" written in the middle. The back was more informative: "Co. C, 9th US Infantry, U.S. Vol."—the same unit involved in Balangiga.

Javier returned to the man. His eyes watered from the stench. He used his mouth to breathe instead of his nose, but the air around the man even tasted bad. He tried to unbutton the man's fetid hemp garment, but it had so many layers of debris that the fastenings had hardened into place. Javier looked back at Lope and the *amo*, but neither indicated any willingness to help.

Javier grabbed both sides of the shirt and ripped them apart. The *hacendero* shifted the man's weight forward and wrestled one emaciated limb out of the fabric. It was like trying to undress a carabao lying on its haunches. A mite infestation had peppered the addict's skin with red blotches. How contagious were mites?

Oh well, Javier thought. In for a penny, in for a pound. He wrenched the upper arm free. There, he found what he was looking for: a tattoo of an eagle, its wings spread, coming in for a landing. Under that, a name: "Clara."

Javier had found Benjamín. *Hay sus.*

CHAPTER FIFTY-FOUR

Waking Ben

Georgie woke up to a thud. The wood floor out in the living room creaked, and then there was some shuffling followed by another thud. She reached for Javier, but once again he was not there. It was unsettling how easily she had become accustomed to him in her bed, but now, in the darkest of night in an unfamiliar town, she had to make do alone.

It took Georgie a minute to find her robe and light a lamp, but after that she wandered into the living room to see what was going on. She got a few steps into the room and froze. A very tall, very thin man was strewn out on a wooden recliner, his feet propped on the elongated armrests. In another setting he could have been mistaken for a planter napping in the shade, but his body resisted the graceful lines of the wicker backrest, slumping in all the wrong places. And despite wearing freshly washed (and not yet dry) underclothes, the stranger smelled revolting.

Still, there was something about him. She placed the lamp down on the table beside his head. Under the shaggy, overgrown beard, she could make out the shape of Benji's nose, the almost feminine curve of his eyebrows, and the full eyelashes that had entranced so many young girls in Boston. Georgie collapsed onto her knees and sobbed.

What occurred next happened so fast that she did not realize she was in trouble until it was too late. Benji pinned her to the hardwood floor, his arm pushing down across her neck. His bright blue eyes were open wide, glaring without a hint of recognition.

"B—"

He cut off her windpipe and she could not finish his name. Even though her brother was little more than skin and bones, he gave no quarter. He sat squarely on her chest, what weight there was left of him set firmly on her throat. She pounded desperately with her fists and feet.

"Why?" died in the back of her throat.

The black came.

When Georgie woke up, she wondered why she was not in her bed in Bais. Why on earth was she on the floor? Where was Javier?

Loud grunts drew her attention, but she could not see well enough to make out what was going on. Her limbs were so heavy. She struggled to lift her head, but the room dimmed when she did that. She lay back on the floor and took a deep breath. It took all her strength to resist the tempting call of sleep.

Slowly, she mustered the energy to raise her head. This time she kept breathing, and oxygen alone was enough to ward off the darkness. She used one hand to push her torso off the floor, but she could not support the weight for long. Her next attempt, she was able to prop herself up on one elbow, but she still could not see clearly. Where was she?

She heard a man retch. Then the corner was silent.

"Ina?"

"Javier!" She tried to reach out, but her arms responded awkwardly, like the marionette of a drunken puppeteer.

Her lover surrounded her. He pulled her into his lap, kissed her forehead, and hugged her tightly to his chest. When he drew back, she saw that he had a split lip and a fresh bruise on his cheek. Who could have done that?

And then she remembered.

Georgie pulled herself out of Javier's grip and sat up unsteadily. "Benji!" she called.

"Ina, stay away from him."

She shook her head. She couldn't stay away. Not from Benji. Not ever.

She scooted toward her brother, moving slowly so she would not startle him. "I'm so sorry. I never should have woken you like that."

"Valentina...my Valentine...is that you?"

His voice was so full of pain that Georgie's eyes stung with tears. "No, it's me, Georgie. I'm here to take you home."

"Georgie's far away...Boston...so far."

"No, I'm right here."

Benji lifted his head from the shadows. She could see his strangely unfocused pupils, constricted to the size of pinheads. It made him look unearthly, unnatural. Had he been blinded at Balangiga?

"It's me, Benji! Mama and I miss you so much. I'm going to take you back—"

Her brother pressed his fist into the floor and said, "No, I can't. I...just can't."

"Hush, it will be okay," she reassured him in the same tone that she would use with a small child. "I promise."

She continued to crawl to him, repeating the same soothing words, when a hand gripped her shoulder. "Ina, don't."

"What are you doing?" She shook Javier off so violently that it caused a stab of pain in her head. "Leave me alone."

"Please, don't get near him."

"What are you talking about? He's my brother!"

"He's been stewing in his own filth for months."

She ignored Javier. Who cared about dirt? Dirt was just dirt. Benji was alive!

When she reached her brother, she pulled his head into her lap and let him blubber into her robe. He wept now, all fight in him gone. Georgie ran her fingers through his rough, ragged hair, trying to convince herself that this was real. Benji was really here with her, finally.

She noticed a small line of blood coming from his nose and looked up at Javier. "How could you have hit him?"

"How could I...?" Javier's hand pulled at the back of his neck. "Ina, he almost killed you!"

She kept stroking her brother's head. "He was confused. If he had known who I was, he wouldn't have hurt me."

She felt the force of Javier's incredulity before she even saw his wide brown eyes. "He did hurt you. Do you know how long you were out?"

"Shhh...," she soothed to Benji. "I know you didn't mean it."

"*Hay sus*, that is disgusting." Javier stood in front of them both, his arms crossed, the picture of scorn. "I have no idea how you can let him do that"—he waved his hand at her wet lap—"all over you."

No doubt all he could see was tears and snot, not love and relief. "Well, you don't have to touch him."

"Who do you think washed him in the sea? Carried him here? For all the good that did us—I should have left him outside to bleach in the sun for a week." He paused. "We wouldn't even been able to wash him at all if he hadn't been so high. Thank God we have enough hop to keep him knocked out through next year, if necessary."

Georgie gasped. "You drugged him? How could you do that?"

"You really think he's a stranger to it? Take a good look at your brother, Ina."

Benji's sweaty skin was stretched tight across high cheekbones, his eyes sunken. The lines crisscrossing his face made him look decades older than his twenty-five years. He had passed out in her arms, eyes rolled back into his head. It was too much to bear.

"What happened to him?"

Javier shook his head as if she could answer her own question well enough. "It's hard to believe you two are related. You must have gotten all the temperance in the family."

Had Georgie been standing, she would have slapped Javier across the cheek. Hard. "I didn't tell you about my father so you could throw it back in my face. I'm surprised you even brought him back to me, if that's the way you feel."

"I said I would find your brother, and I did. He may not be the gallant hero you hoped for, but I am a farmer, not a sorcerer."

Georgie looked down at the limp, fragile man in her arms. Benji needed her protection more than ever. She did not know how to help him, but their mother would. She had to get him back to Boston. "When can I take him home?" she asked.

"Ina, if you think I'm letting you go anywhere—"

"You have no choice. He is my family. You are not."

Javier's jaw twitched, and his lips pressed into a flat line. "There are complications," he said carefully.

"We can talk about us later."

"I'm not talking about us. Whatever you're planning, you cannot just walk out of here with this man."

"Why ever not?"

Javier sighed. "Because you can't afford him."

"What?"

"Your brother belongs to Lope."

CHAPTER FIFTY-FIVE

The Truth

Javier watched as Lope's *muchachos* cleaned up Benjamín, washing him better this time and trimming his beard so that he no longer looked like an Old Testament prophet. Most impressive, though, was the change of clothing that they procured for the lanky American. Javier did not ask where the clothes came from, but he suspected that some tall Insular official found his clothesline a little lighter this morning. Potter was more easily dressed when he was dopey, so the *muchachos* kept him that way for a while. The time would soon come to wean him off the stuff, but Javier figured that withdrawal would do little to improve the man's personality.

He already regretted finding Ben. It would have been better for Georgina to remember her brother as a jaunty young man rather than this pathetic sod—a judgment Javier stood behind but regretted expressing aloud. With Javier not able to stomach an insincere apology and Georgina still angry, it left them not talking—and, unfortunately, they had a lot to talk about. Javier stayed close in the hope that he might find the right moment or the right thing to say.

Paca hovered, too. She never went farther than 20 feet from Georgina

"How long will the child be staying here?" Georgina asked.

"That's difficult to explain. I'm sort of...borrowing her."

The *Americana* stared at him.

"Maybe we could throw her in our luggage when we leave," he suggested. Javier knew that flippancy would not help his cause in the long run, but he was tired.

"We can't 'afford' Benji. You 'borrowed' this girl?" Georgina glared at him. "What the hell is going on?"

He motioned to the sofa, grateful that she was speaking to him at all. "Where do you want to start?"

"Let's start simple: the girl."

That was not starting simple. He still had not figured out how much to tell Georgina about his first night in Paranas, especially the *casa* where he had found Paca. He had to tell her enough that she would see the need to take the girl off the island, but if he implicated Lope directly, she might do something crazy like torch the man's house. Javier could not foot the bill for all of this woman's crusades. "She was in danger, Ina. I rescued her from a brothel."

"She's barely more than a child!"

"Yes, I know it's ugly, but nevertheless—"

"Did any of those men—"

"Not yet, *querida*. But I couldn't walk away knowing it would happen, so I found a way to bring her here to you."

"What happens now? How do we get her back to her family?"

Javier sighed. "Her parents are the ones who sold her. If we return her to them they will do it all over again."

"They wouldn't do that!"

"Unfortunately, they would. Even if they wanted to keep her, they couldn't repay the advance they were given, probably all in rice. They've eaten it all, no doubt." He looked into Georgina's eyes to show how serious he was. "Lope told me that she was one of eleven children. What kind of life do you suppose she had, even before soldiers burned down her village and shot her family's carabao? People all over Samar are scavenging wild *camote* to survive. Her family found a way to feed ten children by sacrificing one."

"But—"

"They probably convinced themselves that their daughter was being taken to the big city to become a maid or cook."

"But—"

"I told you before how bad things are here. The Army said they were going to make this island a 'howling wilderness,' and they succeeded. Some people have nothing left to sell but their children."

Georgina shook her head. "We could tell her family the truth. This time they might fight for her."

Javier was not about to pay for another search party, nor would he round up Paca's family to torture them with their choice all over again. "Ina, I would rather believe the worst of her parents if that gives her the most protection."

Georgina folded her arms across her chest. "So we leave her here with the Cuayzons? This girl should be free to choose her own future."

"Paca!" Javier called.

The child crossed the room in about half a second. "*Sí.*"

Javier spoke in clear, slow Cebuano, which he hoped was close enough to the local Waray language to be half understood. "Where are your mother and father?"

The girl pointed to him and Georgina. "No, not us," he gently explained. "Mother of Paca, father of Paca. Where?"

She would not answer.

"Where is your village?" he tried again, sure that she grasped more than she was letting on.

Still nothing.

"Where do we take you?"

Paca pointed at them again. "With you I go. Can work—work very hard for lady."

Javier shook his head. He tried to explain that he and the lady had to leave, but that they would help her find her family first. He tried to be as reassuring as possible, but the girl broke into sobs before he could finish. She begged them to take her. She fell to the floor, grabbed Georgina's ankles, and pleaded.

"You know she should be in school," Javier said, trying to ignore Paca's agony so that he could keep himself from tearing up. "I know a good teacher."

The *maestra* ignored him and gently petted Paca's hair. "It will be all right, Paca, don't worry. You don't have to stay here. We'll keep you safe." She turned to Javier. "She could go back to the hacienda with you."

"Just me?"

"Well, Allegra will look out for her, of course. She's the *maestra* now."

Javier did not like that Georgina was writing herself out of this possible future, but neither did he want to start the same argument all over again. He added a reassuring hand to Paca's shoulder, and she settled down to sniffles and hiccups. He would find a way to protect her, but this was not his biggest problem right now.

"Before we can do anything about this girl," he said to Georgina, "we have to free Benjamín to leave Catbalogan."

"No one can keep my brother here against his will. He's an American!"

She spoke of Ben like he was the guest of honor at Governor Taft's dinner party, not a man who was so drug-addled that he had attacked his own sister.

"Your brother has accumulated massive debts to Cuayzon. If he were not American, he would already be dead."

Georgina drew back, shocked. "How?"

"Gambling, opium, and... other vices."

"How could he have spent so much money?"

"According to Lope, Ben was trying to find someone, a woman, and he borrowed money to hire search parties, but nothing turned up. Then he gambled against his debt in the hopes of winning a big purse. But even if the games were fair—which they probably weren't—he didn't stand a chance. Of course, the greater his debt, the less sober he stayed."

"How could Benji borrow money if he was intoxicated all the time?"

Javier raised his eyebrows. "The opium was probably cheap compared to the gambling debt, and—as you pointed out—Ben is an American. Lope hoped that someone rich would show up to claim him." He spread out his hands. "Here we are."

He watched her think about that for a minute. "How much does he owe?" she asked.

Javier had not seen the numbers yet, but he had no doubt that Lope's usurious terms would make repayment nearly impossible. "A lot. I'm working on finding that out."

Georgina was trying to be brave, but failing. She wiped the corners of her glassy green eyes. The sight of her distress rendered his own resistance useless. He had come this far, and one more little lie was not going to hurt.

He leaned forward, touching his forehead to hers. "We'll find a way out of this, *amor*."

CHAPTER FIFTY-SIX

Withdrawal

Javier decided that it was time to cure Benjamín—if there was anything left worth curing. Lope—no doubt happy to put some distance between his household and the unkempt addict—provided the visitors with a small house, which Javier was sure he would pay for when all was settled. Two of Lope's guards were posted outside, leaving no doubt as to the actual status of his "guests."

Javier stopped dosing Ben Saturday night. By Sunday the man paced restlessly, his legs kicking out awkwardly underneath him. Soon he collapsed into bed, racked with chills. Georgina piled blankets high on top of him, but he still shivered, oblivious to the sticky heat outside. Raised bumps covered his sallow skin like a plucked chicken. It seemed like every half hour he threw up in the *lavadera* bowl. His body tried to purge every last drop of bile from his empty belly, and Javier hoped that the addiction would go along with it.

Unfortunately, Ben's nausea was not confined to one end of his body. He soiled the sheets and mat so many times that no one could do the wash fast enough to replace them. Once he could crawl out of bed, he barricaded himself in the *banyo*—which, as in all local houses, was located on the patio next to the kitchen. The sounds and smells emanating from it kept anyone from trying to cook. The only person who dared enter that part of the house was Georgina, but half the time the stench had her doubling over too.

These horrors could not compare to the sound of Ben's nerve-shattering screams every night. The opium had held his demons at bay, but without it they were slowly eating him alive. Javier thought it was as much as he deserved, but Georgina was unwavering in her mission to save him, which she thought she could do through love…and a lot of chicken broth. Ben, of course, had no patience for his sister's attention. He snapped at her, batted her hands away, and repeatedly ordered her to leave him alone.

Every time Javier was in danger of growing sympathetic toward Ben, he took a quick peek at the bruises on Georgina's neck. No, Benjamín Potter was not easy to like. Still, Javier offered up a half dozen palliatives, including alcohol, quinine, bromide, cannabis, betel quid, and laudanum. Georgina rejected them all because she did not want to replace one addiction with another. Javier tried to convince her that total withdrawal was inhumane, but she wanted Benji sober as quickly as possible, and chicken soup was all she had on offer.

"Just drink the soup," Georgina ordered, holding a spoon up to Ben's lips.

"The last thing I want to do is eat," he replied, biting off each word through gritted teeth. "I can tell you where it's going to end up in ten minutes. You might as well pour it in the chamber pot and save me the trouble."

"That's why you need this. You're losing all sorts of fluids, and that only makes you feel worse."

"It isn't possible to feel worse. You could chop me into pieces with a bolo and it would be an improvement."

Javier perked up at the thought, figuring that if the American repeated that loudly enough, someone might take him up on it. Ben was not a popular fellow with the two servants "borrowed" from Lope.

"Come on, it's just soup," she cajoled.

"What's the point?"

And on it went, neither sibling giving in. Javier felt the most pity for Mrs. Margaret Potter—how she survived the rearing of these two mules he could not imagine. Maybe if the two siblings kept fighting—and if Ben kept vomiting (and worse) on the fine Narra floors—Lope would cut his losses and cast them out. Wishful thinking.

"Drink this water then," Georgina said.

"No."

"Benji—"

"Leave me alone, and stop calling me that. My name is 'Ben.'"

She ignored him. "Listen, Benji, you can't die on me. What would Mom say?"

"I can't go back to her like this."

"We'll get you cleaned up and—"

Ben interrupted her. "I can't go back home at all. You might be able to lug me as far as Manila, but that's it. Once I'm on my own two feet, I'm gone."

Georgina smiled at him as if indulging a foolish child. "Gone where? To another opium den? I think not."

Her brother never had a chance to respond. Instead, he retched in the bowl Paca faithfully held beside him. The little girl was the strongest of them all. She had even cleaned the *banyo* twice, which was the fiercest test of loyalty that Javier could imagine.

Javier pulled Georgina into the other room to let Ben to suffer privately. "*Querida*, how will you hold him in Manila without any help? Lock him up in your hotel room? What about when you need to sleep?"

"What are you suggesting I do?"

He knew better than to answer that question truthfully. "Consider what he's asking. Let him go. If he wants to return to Boston, fine. If he doesn't..."

Georgina looked at Javier as if he were suggesting euthanasia. "Would you leave Allegra to die in her own excrement?" she asked.

"You're already doing everything you can to heal him."

She put a hand on her hip and glared. "You just don't like him."

"After the way he hurt you—"

"It was the drugs that caused him to do that," she insisted.

"There's a lot more than opium that's wrong with Ben Potter. If you can't see that, nothing you do will help."

Georgina looked out the open *capiz* windows. The pink sunset gave her tired face some sorely needed color. Javier wanted to reach out to her, but knew she would not be receptive to his touch. Instead, he followed her gaze to the islands on the other side of the bay.

"It's this place," she eventually whispered. "That's why I need to take him home."

"I promise that if we get him to Bais—"

"No," she said quickly. "I mean my home: Boston."

"Bais is your home now, Ina. With me."

Georgina looked at him. She could not hide the longing in her eyes, and for the first time in these past few days he thought he might have a chance. "I want that, Javier. Really, I do."

He could hear the "but" in her voice, and sure enough it followed: "But I can't abandon Benji for your sake, or anybody's. And as good as this country has been to me, look what it has done to him. I owe him."

Javier knew that Ben had protected his little sister from their father's temper, but that was a long time ago, and the besotted mess in the next room was not really the same person. "You said your brother signed up for the Army when some silly chit refused his hand. That seems rather self-serving of him: to leave you behind simply because he was broken-hearted."

"Our father was already dead by then. He would have never left Mama and me vulnerable. Never. I know you're not seeing him at his best—"

"I should say."

"But," she said, her jaw hard, "I've got to help him now. Can't you understand that?"

Javier tried. He thought about Allegra: when he had asked her to, his cousin had returned to Bais without hesitation. If Allegra believed that Javier needed to be dragged halfway around the world to save his life, she would do it, too, and God help anyone who got in her way. So maybe he did understand, but he did not have to like it. "Make me a deal, Ina."

"What?" she asked, wiping tears off her cheeks. Javier resented each drop.

"We'll wait here until Benjamín is ready to travel. Once he's ready to go with you—voluntarily, mind—then we'll talk about us. Our marriage. Our children. I meant what I said earlier. Our engagement is not a joke."

"You'll let me take Ben home?"

"Only if he wants to go—and only if you're not pregnant," he said in a low voice. "If those two conditions hold, I'll let you deliver him to your mother in Boston. You can see that they're both settled well, and then you'll return to Bais to marry me."

She bristled. "I'll not abandon my sick brother when he needs me most, just so I can run off and roger my way through the Far East."

"Is that all I am to you?" he asked, furious. "Just a fuck?"

Georgina's eyes widened and her chin fell, but whatever she was about to say was interrupted by her brother's call. "Georgie? Are you there?"

In a flash, she was back at Benjamín's side, and after some gentle cajoling, she convinced him to drink the blasted cup of soup.

Javier stood where he had been left, now forgotten.

He thought about what Ben had asked for that morning, when the two men were alone.

"You know what it would take," Ben had said. "You have that much left."

An overdose. Yes, he knew how much. He had it.

"Give it to me. No one would know."

God forgive him, Javier had considered it. But he had not done it. Now he wondered if he had made a mistake.

CHAPTER FIFTY-SEVEN

Help

A day later Georgie sat alone with her brother. She could hardly blame the last two servants for quitting. If the smell didn't do it, the patient's attitude was enough to drive anyone away.

"So who's the goo"—Ben caught himself—"guy helping you?"

Georgie wondered if this place had made Ben both an addict and a small-hearted bigot. "Don Javier? He's a sugar farmer, an *hacendero*."

"How'd you get mixed up with someone like him?"

She gritted her teeth and swabbed her brother's forehead with a damp cloth.

"Did you hear me, Georgie? Or do you only respond to 'Ina' nowadays?"

Georgie tossed the cloth back into the bowl, splashing water all over the floor. "You know I've been working as a schoolteacher in Negros. One of my friends there, a rich mestiza named Allegra Alazas, started calling me 'Ina.'" It was better than admitting that Javier had given her the pet name. "You know how Filipinos like to use nicknames. It caught on." Actually, it had only caught on in one house, but Ben did not need to know that—just like he did not need to know that Allegra and Javier were cousins.

Her brother huffed quietly. "I can't think of you as anything other than Georgie," he said.

"And you'll always be 'Benji' to me."

Ben smiled weakly, maybe for the first time since their reunion. "So, tell me more about 'Don Javier.'"

She heard the sarcasm in his use of the title, but chose to ignore it. "What do you want to know?"

"This guy brings you to the boondocks of Samar without a chaperone? And the way he looks at you…"

Georgie was not sure how to defend Javier exactly. He had made countless offers of marriage, but since so many of them had been delivered in bed, they probably would not count in his favor. "He's a good man, trust me."

"I'm watching him. If he so much as—"

"What? What could you possibly do? You're barely able to sit up on your own. Besides, don't you think it's a little late to rediscover chivalry? Where have you been these past few years?" If Ben was trying to protect her chastity, he was too late—and he probably knew it.

"I've seen all kinds of operators out here. It's a classic con: he makes sure that you feel indebted and then—"

"Then what? He seduces me? Don't you think trekking all the way to Samar is a long way to go for sex? Why can't you believe that maybe someone likes me for who I am?"

Ben squirmed a little, probably more due to his bone ache than to her rebuke. "I've learned to judge a man by his friends," he pronounced.

"You mean Lope? You think he's Javier's friend?" She threw up her hands. "You idiot! None of us would even be in this man's house in the first place if not for you."

Georgie turned away, unable to look at her brother without wanting to smack him. She stared out the open window, seeking calmness from the rhythm of the waves rolling in and out.

"What does it matter, anyway?" she wondered out loud. "You and I will be leaving for Manila soon. After I wheedle some money out of the Bureau, we'll take the first steamer to Boston."

"I wish you'd listen to me," Ben said, shifting his head on the pillow. "I'm not going anywhere."

She thought that once he was healthier—a decent weight, freshly trimmed and shaved, and maybe even a pressed suit—he would change his mind. "You will feel better soon," she said. "Besides, your family needs you at home."

He looked away. "People here need me more."

"Who could possibly be more important than your mother? And Aunt Kate and Uncle Robbie..."

Ben paled and looked like he might be sick again. She brought over the bedpan.

"How is Mama?" he asked in between gasps of air.

"Worried about you, but she's okay. Still doing lots of parish work...the usual."

Georgie wondered if she should fess up about the family losing the shop. Maybe if he knew how hard things really were back in Roxbury, he would change his mind about staying here.

"I've been meaning to tell you..."

But she trailed off, unsure of her timing. She and Mama had kept this secret from Ben for so long—really since he had joined the Army—that it was hard to finally admit.

"Tell me what?"

Georgie allowed the approaching footsteps to distract her. "Who's that?"

"Another of your suitors perhaps?"

She strained to listen. One voice was unmistakable. Its low cadence hummed through her body before she could make out the words.

Javier knocked politely on the doorframe. And with him was a pleasant surprise: Father Andrés. The two brothers looked alike, right down to their harried expressions.

She stood to give Andrés a big American hug, and he accepted her enthusiasm with a chuckle. "It's good to see you, too, Maestra. You look lovely, as always."

Javier made introductions, but Benji would not meet the priest's eyes. Instead, he turned away like he would be sick again. She could not tell whether he was being deliberately rude.

"Ben is not feeling well," Georgie offered.

Father Andrés nodded. "Which is why Javier called me—he believes that I'm the only one at the hacienda who does not work, so he thinks I am free to answer his every cable."

"It's not Holy Week yet," Javier said. "What else were you doing?"

"Just because holidays are the only services you attend, *hermano*, doesn't mean they are the only ones I offer." Andrés turned to her. "I came as soon as I could, Maestra, and I brought two nurses from the San Luis Gonzaga convent infirmary in Cebu. We traveled a little roughly from Tacloban, which is why we weren't here sooner. But they are resilient women and ready to work right away. Let me get them—"

"No," Georgie interrupted him before she knew what she was objecting to. All she knew was that she could not turn over her brother's care to Catholic nuns. What would they say when they recognized the cause of Ben's illness? Their pious condescension could be worse than her own lack of medical expertise. "I appreciate all you've done, Father, but I only need a little help with the cleaning and cooking, that's all."

"You're tired, Maestra. The circles under your eyes do not lie; you need rest."

"It's my duty to take care of my brother."

The priest looked at Georgie with compassion that was dangerously close to pity, but she would not be moved...until Ben's scratchy voice spoke up from behind her.

"Bring the nuns," he said. "It's a good idea."

Her face flushed with humiliation, and she felt the sting of new tears. "I can do this," she insisted.

"You're not a nurse, Georgie."

"What haven't I done for you, Ben? Given you?"

"That's not the point."

"Then tell me," she pleaded. But her brother sighed and turned away, his weak arms crossed in defiance. After six days and nights of enduring Ben's vomit, feces, and bile—the latter both physical and verbal—he had fired her.

She brushed past both Javier and Andrés and fled the room. Ben called out to her, but she kept going. Let him try to catch her. That would be quite a resurrection.

Down the stairs, out the door, and down the street—she did not stop until she reached the water. She plopped down on the rattletrap dock and watched the fishermen as they put away their nets. From this distance, their lives looked enticingly straightforward. She looked at one after another, wondering about each man's problems, thinking that they could not be half as complicated as hers. Then she caught herself, ashamed of her own arrogance: she knew well that poverty was the worst complication of all.

The priest was right about one thing: Georgie was exhausted. It should have been easy for her to let the nurses take over, but it felt like one more disappointment in a long line of them. Why was she so maudlin? She should be happy. She had found her brother. So what if he was a little prickly?

She heard the boards behind her creak, and like a sentimental goose she recognized the footsteps as Javier's.

"*Querida*, don't take it personally," he said. "A nurse will be better for him."

He crouched close enough to speak quietly, but not so close as to risk upsetting her any further. She thought that no one else tamed her temper so well. Then again, he could set it off rather spectacularly too.

She sniffed. "Paca and I have been taking good care of him."

"We all know that, even Ben."

"Clearly, he doesn't," she said curtly, turning to face Javier. "But has he lacked for anything? No."

"It's not a matter of your attentiveness, Ina. It's more about a man holding onto his dignity."

"But that's what I was trying to help him do! What do you think those nuns are going to think of him when they learn the truth?"

"He'll never have to see them again. That's the point. He wants a little privacy."

"How can it be better to let a sour-faced nun see your tallywag?"

Javier smiled at that. "Two nuns and one child prostitute: they balance each other out somehow."

Georgie did not want to laugh, nor give in, but her reluctance was beginning to feel a little ridiculous. She looked past Javier to see Father Andrés standing nearby, waiting to be admitted into their conversation. She beckoned the padre over.

"I apologize for my tantrum, Father." In all honesty, she could not think of what else to call it. "After the threats I made to Doña Lourdes and Allegra, you must hate me. I'm surprised you came."

The priest reached out and touched her shoulder. "I was able to convince the women that you were bluffing. You were bluffing, right?"

"Of course! I just hope they forgive me."

"If you ask their forgiveness personally, I think they will grant it."

Georgie shifted uncomfortably. She wanted to make it up to her friends, of course, but her brother was her most important concern right now. That meant that she had no intention of returning to Bais. "Ben will recover, won't he, Father?"

The priest considered the question carefully before answering, and she liked that. Hollow reassurances did her no good. "How many days since his last dose?" he asked.

"Almost seven," Javier answered.

"Recovering from such an addiction is a terrible experience, but not usually a fatal one. I imagine he's had the worst of it by now, though the symptoms may still flare up for months. Some recommend the use of morphine to ease off the opium."

Javier shook his head. "Ina won't allow any of that. I've tried."

"It is a controversial method," Andrés conceded. "Healing the physical dependency is only one part of the battle. The underlying causes of drug use need to be addressed too, or else he may relapse."

Georgie honed in on Javier. "See, that's what I mean! All those 'underlying causes' will cease to exist in Boston," she said. "It's the only way he can get back to his old self."

Javier's mouth flattened into a scowl. "He'll be quite the silver-tail, I'm sure."

"Maestra, pardon me," cut in Father Andrés. "A change of physical environment may only affect the method of use, not the addiction itself. There is no shortage of heroin pastilles or opium tincture in America."

She shook her head. "Ben was an athlete, a shortstop for the Roxbury Bull Dogs—not the type to tipple paregoric or cologne. He barely even drank lager. It's this place that has corrupted him."

Javier looked out at the water and said nothing.

"A tonic might be more attractive in the future now that he's had a taste," Andrés said. "Opium is a sinister drug, drawing the user in with feelings of such euphoria that some even call it a religious experience."

Georgie thought that a rather blasphemous description from a priest. "Not my brother," she insisted. "Not Ben."

Andrés raised his brow, looking at Georgie as if she had just pronounced her brother the King of Siam. She told herself that she didn't care what a backyard padre from the boondocks thought. The Philippines were toxic to her brother, so they were going home. This had to work.

Part VIII: April 1903

Hacienda Altarejos
Bais, Oriental Negros
el 7 de abril de 1900

Querido Javier:

Although I may not say it enough, the day you returned home from Europe was one of the happiest of my life. If anyone can guide the business through these strange American times, it will be you, the so-called "hacendero inglés." I hope you do not resent this sobriquet from your men, as a nickname of this sort is almost always an indication of affection.

When my time finally arrives, you will find everything in order. The estate is left to you. I trust you to take good care of your mother and Allegra. In deference to your mother, I have left one small impropriety out of my will: please see that Emiliana's Cebu property goes to Andrés. It is enough to excuse the lack of any other inheritance, yet it will be nothing that you miss. Remember that you alone carry my name and my legacy.

I know relations between you and your brother are strained, and undoubtedly this is my fault. I pushed too hard in the beginning. I hope that you and Andrés may come to terms one day. Wherever I am headed, such a reconciliation would lighten my soul.

Con todo mi cariño,
Papá

CHAPTER FIFTY-EIGHT

Choices

Javier could not help but think what a strange ensemble they made: two squabbling Americans, a grumpy Filipina nun, a near-sex-slave, an opium kingpin, and himself, an on-the-rocks sugar baron. Paca was the only happy one of the bunch—as long as she stayed close to Georgina and far away from Lope.

They had just seen Andrés off on the steamer back to Bais, but not before the padre made one last delivery. Several days before, when everyone else was sleeping, the brothers had met in the privacy of the dimly lit kitchen. There, Andrés had reached deep inside his robe and pulled out two hidden bags of silver coins. A cassock had to be the answer to a smuggler's prayers, Javier thought.

Andrés had not been able to hold back a grumble as he handed over the money: "I hope you know that this could have cost me my life, bobbing around these pirate-ridden backwaters with a fortune in silver."

"As if anyone would rob a padre," Javier answered, with less concern than he felt.

"The Church is not always popular out here, you know that. Not with this *Pulahanes* madness flaring up again. I'm lucky I wasn't beheaded."

"Drés, I appreciate everything you've done. So does Ina."

"I don't think she has any idea, actually." The priest hesitated before continuing. "I admire the *maestra*'s pluck, but—"

"Thank you, anyway," Javier said, cutting off his brother's warning. "Did Geno have a hard time putting this together?"

"He didn't put it together. He couldn't have—you left nothing for him to sell."

Nothing but the land itself, but neither man would dare say that out loud. "Then where did you get it?"

The normally expressive priest mumbled: "My inheritance."

It was not really an inheritance. It was guilt money, the cash settlement Javier had set up when their father was forced to exclude his bastard from his will.

"Drés," Javier began, saying the name like it was a plea. "You can't—"

"I will live off the chapel benefice, and if I need to I can sell the Cebu property. I've been thinking it's silly to hold onto that, anyway— I'm never there—and the Americans are paying an awful ransom for anything on Calle Magallanes."

Javier pinched the bridge of his nose between his thumb and forefinger. He should never have let matters get this out of control.

Andrés put a hand on Javier's shoulder and waited for the *hacendero* to meet his eyes. "Listen…it's your business if you lose this money—it was yours to begin with, and you never had to give it to me. But we're even now."

"I'll pay you back. I promise."

"Don't worry about me," Andrés said. But then he shifted uncomfortably, undermining his own reassurance. "You should know, Lourdes may have sold some chinaware—"

"Mamá is involved? Drés, I appreciate your help—more than I can say—but are you bloody insane?"

"I'm the crazy one? Me?" The padre's short temper, especially around Javier, was his most obvious inheritance from their father.

"Your mother needs to know. You're out here risking our birthright, and your timing couldn't be worse."

"Our birthright now, is it? I had to twist your arm to come to Bais in the first place."

"Well, it is home to me now, even if I'm the curate, not the heir. I don't plan to let you gamble away everything Lázaro built."

Javier sighed. "I'm hardly gambling."

"It's not a card table, but it amounts to much the same." Andrés looked at the money. "I just hope it's enough to free that rakehell and get all six of you home."

"Six?" Javier counted four: himself, Georgina, Ben, and—if he could manage it—Paca.

"You're responsible for getting the nuns back to Cebu, *genio*."

"You know, those two are pretty hardy. I sort of thought they might swim."

Andrés laughed despite himself. "Don't you dare. I'm in enough ecclesiastical trouble as it is."

"I'll see them home, even if we all have to bunk with the game-cocks." The deck of the steamer was Georgina's preferred place to sleep, anyway—if only she would make the trip with him. As fear squeezed his heart, Javier almost asked his brother to stay. He had never been one to depend heavily on others for solace, but he had never been this afraid before. He could not bear to vocalize his greatest fear: that he would lose it all.

Apparently, Andrés could read the terror in his face because he took a deep breath and spoke more kindly than Javier deserved: "Don't worry. Even if you fail in this, all is not lost. You're a smart man. You'll find work somewhere...maybe America?"

Javier snorted. "Thanks."

"I wasn't kidding," Andrés said and then grinned. "You'll need to run that far just to get away from me."

"If it comes to that, I won't be able to afford to run anywhere." Nor would he run from the one person in the world who might still love him, no matter how strained their relationship. He pulled his brother into a tight hug, and Andrés returned it with a firm clap on the back.

"Fight hard." Those were the priest's final instructions.

Now his brother was gone, leaving Javier to finish this battle alone. The *hacendero* just wanted to get on with it—it had been over two weeks, and one way or another he had to return to Bais.

Lope had already shown him an accounting of expenses incurred, along with Ben's scrawled initials on several promissory notes. The American verified his mark readily enough, but he offered no suggestion on how he planned to pay the debt. Clearly, Ben had expected to starve to death in the hop joint where he was found, and he openly resented everyone, even Georgina, for ruining his foggy exit from this world. Javier thought they all should have been more obliging.

Despite Javier's impatience, when the summons finally came to join Lope in his office, he suddenly wished that he had another night or two to stall. The Chinaman handed Javier a brandy neat. Lope lifted his glass, made a polite noise, and nodded his head. Had Javier not known what the *sangley* did for a living, he might have mistaken him for a gentleman: he carried himself as if he were the emperor of China, not a back-alley warlord.

"My man has finished the tally." Lope handed Javier a piece of paper, on which was written a single number: 2692. An odd number—it was either an authentic sum or contrived to look like one.

"Mexican?"

Javier immediately regretted asking. He would have been better off just assuming it to be Mexican silver and letting Lope correct him if it was otherwise. If Mex, he could probably clear the debt in a few years. If not...

"Gold," Lope said.

With great effort Javier hid his reaction behind an impassive mask, but his stomach pitched and turned in the same revolted fashion as it had at the *casa* of virgins, only this time it was his own arse on the auction block. Javier calculated that at the current exchange rate, Benjamín's debt amounted to over 7100 Mexican silver dollars. That was over half what Javier had borrowed from Guillermo earlier in the year—cash Javier had used to pay off the installation of a sugar mill. He could run his entire hacienda for several months on this much money. How could one man chalk up such a ludicrous debt?

Javier bluffed. "Lope, you'll be lucky to recover anything at all from this American. Give me a real number." He passed back the paper as if it were not worth considering.

The *sangley* laughed. "Ah, I think I will recover the debt, señor. I've seen the way you look at the woman, and I have seen the way she tends to her brother."

Javier remembered the two Potters walking on the beach back from the dock. Georgina had held Ben's elbow with a cozy familiarity that made Javier jealous. She had done her best to interest her brother in conversation, too, and the more she tried to lift the tone and spirit in her voice, the more animated her hands had become. It was endearing, and Javier had strained to listen to every word; Ben, on the other hand, had hardly bothered.

Now Javier felt his hand tightening around his glass. How could he risk putting his mother out of her home for such a wastrel? He reminded himself that he did it for Georgina and not Ben.

He looked directly at Lope and said: "One thousand Mex."

That number earned him a laugh, one without a drop of humor. "You are amusing," Lope said.

In fact, Javier was not feeling very droll at all. He held up the tally slip. "No man could possibly consume this much opium." Seven thousand Mex would buy half a ton of the stuff.

"Don't forget the gambling. Mr. Potter has no luck at all, no matter what the game."

"I'm hardly going to pay for his losses at *fan-tan* or *jueteng*—only a swindler would encourage a white man to play those for money."

"He entered of his own free will."

"He was drugged! Was anything that he did really his choice?"

Lope rubbed his chin as if deep in thought. "Since you are very special to my cousin Guillermo, I could accept a little less. You want Mexican dollars? Let's make it six thousand and be done with it."

That was hardly a concession. "I can pay you fifteen hundred, that's all."

"An insult. I have kept your friend safe when many wanted to harm him. Some of my men risked their lives, and it is only heaven's will that they weren't killed."

Javier thought the story of the *Pulahanes* attack was a fiction—but even if true, a rebel attack was the cost of doing business in Samar these days, especially if you were the primary hemp merchant on the island. It had nothing to do with Ben. "My offer is a good one," Javier insisted. "And it's cash. Today."

He had hidden Andrés's silver under Ben's stained bed mat—a place that no one, not even the industrious nuns, would look.

Lope waved his hand. "My friend, do not worry. You have time to pay me in full. I trust you."

Trust? Javier half expected the man to choke on the word. Someone like Lope spared his trust only for a price, one in gold and silver. At least Javier did not have to wait long to find out exactly how much silver.

"Five thousand," the *sangley* offered.

That was still an impossible amount, and Javier said as much. He offered eighteen hundred. Lope acted as if forty-five hundred was the height of generosity. And so it went. After several more minutes back and forth, they narrowed in on thirty-six hundred Mexican, along with a guarantee of Paca's freedom. It was closer to the middle of the range than Javier had dared hope when the haggling had begun, but still twice as much as he had with him.

"You've offered your land to Guillermo," Lope said. "I want the same consideration."

"My hacienda is not for sale."

"Isn't it? Just this past September you put up four hundred acres in exchange for 12,500 Mexican."

"That was a mortgage, not a sale. And since I will pay my debt, I'll keep my land—all of it."

"Then that's what we'll call this, *amigo*: a loan. Let's see, you gave Guillermo over thirty-one dollars Mexican per acre. Of course, my cousin is a poor negotiator, and that was also before you had these other liabilities."

Other liabilities that Lope was making up as he went. "The land is worth double that and you know it."

The problem was that it suited Lope to deliberately undervalue the land so that he could claim more acreage. If Javier got thirty-one an acre, he would only have to put up about one hundred acres in order to guarantee the debt.

Wait a second, Javier thought. Was he really considering this? He was torn between fighting the very idea of a mortgage and trying to negotiate the best one possible.

"Now, Don Javier, be realistic. Land around here is overpriced at ten dollars an acre. And that is if the owner has the creditworthiness to justify such a price."

Javier had no intention of tying his hacienda to the vagaries of the Samar markets. He said so.

"I'm sorry, my friend," Lope said, sounding remarkably genuine. Javier supposed all good thieves sounded genuine. "Even if I take fifteen from you, my local partners will want the same. The highest I can go is twelve."

Twelve dollars per acre would give this shark three hundred acres of Hacienda Altarejos on default. Javier could not let that happen.

"Twenty-four dollars," Javier said, with a finality that he hoped could not be misunderstood.

Lope shook his head. "On the contract, I will be listed alone for two hundred acres at eighteen dollars in a straight mortgage—"

"What?"

"—and if you cannot pay me by the end of harvest, you forfeit the land."

Javier had seen enough fish being cleaned to recognize an old-fashioned gutting. If he signed this, he might very well be done for. A straight mortgage meant that if Javier could not pay, he lost his land forever—with no chance to lease it back through a *pacto de retro* re-purchase. This was not the way most people in the Islands—Cuayzon family included—did business.

Lope smiled at him, as conciliatory as the wolf he was named for. "I am sure this is all unnecessary, though, because you will pay your debts."

Javier studied the reddish brown brandy in his glass and considered his choices. His boldest move would be to sign the agreement and default immediately, giving up the two hundred acres without a fight. That loss alone might be survivable. But then his other creditors, suppliers, technicians, and intermediaries might lose faith and demand repayment—and one of those creditors was Guillermo Cuayzon, who held notes on four hundred more acres. Very quickly, over half of Javier's land could be lost.

And that was not even the worst of it: when word spread to Bais, his cane slashers might smell weakness and revolt. In some ways, he could not blame them. They would not want to work for Lope in any case.

Of course, if all that happened, the Altarejos family would be forced to abandon their house—the one piece of property on which Javier would still have clear title—for their own safety. Agriculture in the post-war Philippines was a confidence game, and he was losing confidence fast.

Was any of it worth saving, though? Javier wanted to go home and sit on his father's bench on the hill high above the water, the same place he had taken Georgina only two months before. Back then Javier had told her that the lookout was where he went when he needed to remember what was really important. Then he had held her, and she had relaxed into his arms. He had imagined them sitting there thirty years down the road, surrounded by a cluster of playing grandchildren. But without her, he would look out on the turquoise waters of the Tañon Strait, and he would be totally, unmistakably alone. So, really, what was the point?

The land by itself had once been enough to fill his heart, but it was not anymore. He made the deal.

CHAPTER FIFTY-NINE

Possession

Later that night, Javier lay back on his pallet and stared at the ceiling. He could not sleep. He tried to damp down his vibrating nerves, but the more he focused on not thinking, the faster the unbidden thoughts arose. Soon the agitation spread throughout his body, and he rolled over at least a dozen times before he finally gave up and took a walk through the house. It was no surprise that he eventually found himself in Georgina's room. Only one thing was going to help him sleep well tonight.

He quietly woke Paca and instructed her to move her floor mat into the *sala* with the nurses. She left without asking any questions. Among other virtues, the girl was discreet.

Javier closed the wooden door behind him, wincing as it squeaked. It was dark out, not even a quarter moon, but his eyes adjusted quickly enough to keep him from crashing into the *lavadera*. He stood and stared at Georgina's peaceful face. The dim light washed out her dark red hair and freckled cheeks. One day he hoped to make love to her in full daylight: such were his dreams.

Unfortunately, he seemed destined to remain the nocturnal interloper. Worse yet, he was running out of time. The steamer *Mauban* left for Manila the next day, and Georgina planned to be on it. She would not delay even one week for another boat. Javier was not sure which emotion he felt most strongly: anger that she would leave him, fear that she would not come back, or self-pity that it mattered so much.

He pulled the light sheet back and slipped into her bed, careful not to wake her. He wrapped his body around her and let her measured breathing soothe him to sleep.

Much later, in the awkward early dawn when only the outline of the world was visible, his eyes blinked open again. He found himself on his back in the middle of the bed. Georgina's leg was thrown over his body and her pelvis rested snugly on his hip. She was a dangerous temptation, but more urgent than his physical desire was the responsibility he felt to shelter this woman—to care for her, nurture her, and love her. Tending to Ben had taken its toll, despite the help of the "serenity sisters." Javier tried to keep his lover's exhaustion in mind, hoping his nobler thoughts would ease his more base frustrations. Besides, as long as she was asleep, he could still pretend that tomorrow would not come.

But soon Georgina woke up without his help. Her breathing grew shorter and her limbs restless. When her eyes finally opened, she saw her man-sized pillow and rose onto her elbow.

He was relieved to see her smile. "I forgot how nice it is to have you next to me while I sleep," she whispered.

"I remembered."

She clucked at him. "That's not what I meant."

"Ina, I'm hurt," he teased. "I meant that in the most innocent way possible."

Georgina reached down and rested her palm on his pajamas. "This doesn't feel so innocent to me."

No, it really was not, he acknowledged silently. "I'll give you five seconds to remove your hand, *querida*, before I take it as an invitation."

She smiled. Instead of withdrawing, she fumbled with the front placket of his pajamas. "It's been a few weeks," she explained as she awkwardly worked the buttons.

Once upon a time, Javier might have done the gentlemanly thing and helped her, but he had learned a few things about Georgina in their time together. First, she did not take help well. Second, she was worth the wait.

Before long, he was lying on the bed completely naked, arms behind his head, while she tugged him gently. He was surprisingly desperate for her touch after only a month's celibacy; he could take her slow tease for only so long.

When that moment came, he rolled her to her side and took over. He suckled a breast through the fabric of her nightgown, the cotton creating a pleasant friction under his tongue. Soon enough Georgina lost focus on what her hand was doing. Javier was grateful for the interruption; without it he could not last.

He eased her gown over her head and gently moved her onto her belly. Georgina turned her head to him in question, and the flutter in her voice matched the anxiety on her face. "If I'm lying like this, how will you—"

He interrupted with kisses, which silenced—but did not relax—her. That was okay for now. He wanted her to feel a little of his fear as well as his anticipation. He placed a small pillow beneath her abdomen and then traced his hands the rest of the way down her sleek curves.

"Trust me," he whispered.

He nudged her thighs apart and slipped two fingers into her. She uttered a gritty little moan, and he thrust in and out a few times just to hear her repeat the noise.

He felt her growing excitement and withdrew his hand. "Leave your shoulders on the bed, sweetheart, and rise up on your knees for me."

Javier helped shape her body, bending her legs and fitting them underneath her hips before drawing himself into position behind her. He angled his cock down a little and nudged it against her opening. That simple touch—his glans to her labia—gave them both a little shock. It had been so long that it felt new all over again. Georgina twisted away at first, but then bobbed backwards, searching for him.

He would not let her set the pace. He kept his penetration slow and easy until he was fully seated, but did not stay there long. Instead, he pulled most of the way out until she let out a disappointed sigh. He took a breath, held her firmly, and heaved forward again. She whimpered in pleasure as he repeated the movement.

From his knees he watched her splendid bottom, round, firm, and brilliantly white. There was no sound but the slow draw of flesh on flesh. He felt decadent. Powerful. "Push against me, Ina. Take me as deeply as you can." She owned his soul; he needed to occupy her body.

He stretched forward until he was leaning over her, holding himself in place with one hand on the mattress. He brought his other hand around her front and teased her clitoris—gently at first but harder and faster as her hips responded. He felt her muscles grasp him as she came quickly. The sensation was almost enough to send him off, too, but he used all his self-control to hold back. He was not ready to end this yet.

When she sank back into the bed, he followed, still buried in her. He kissed the back of her neck, then her ear, and then down her shoulder. He continued to move in and out of her, counting slow beats. When she regained her breath, he reached under her and softly stroked her once again. He did not let her dance away from his touch, no matter how sensitive she was.

"Again," he commanded.

When he felt her arousal return, he pressed harder. She moaned, and her passage grew sloppy around him. As he thrust, his body covered hers from hips to shoulders. Georgina's noises grew louder and louder until he finally covered her mouth with his free hand. She bit down on the flesh of his palm as she came, and he responded by grinding down on her. She pushed back into him, accepting his dominion. He seized in orgasm and spent with one long grunt.

When it was over, both of them were panting hard enough to be heard in the next room, but Javier no longer cared who knew. He wanted to tell every last man on the street that she was his woman.

He moved to roll off her, but she reached back to hold him. "Stay."

"Of course." Forever, if he could. He kissed her temple repeatedly and listened to her breathing slow to a peaceful cadence. Only after he was sure that she was asleep did he slip out of her body and off the bed. He found his underwear in the tangled sheets and dressed. He was so intent on his silent escape from the room that he never saw the first punch land.

CHAPTER SIXTY

Fight

The nose-ender rocked Javier off balance, sending him to his knees.

Javier was not sorry that it had come to this. All thoughts of taking it easy on Ben pretty much ended with the sight of his own blood on the *sala* floor. Javier rose to his feet and flexed his fingers before tightening them into fists. A hard skull could outlast any of the twenty-seven bones in the hand, but it was not for his own comfort that Javier wished he had a good set of gloves. He wanted them so he could give Ben a true thrashing. It no longer mattered to him that he had come to Samar to save this man.

The American had a distinct height and reach advantage, but Javier had at least a stone of extra muscle weight. Since Ben had barely been able to walk a half-mile the day before, the fact that he could fight at all was a miracle—or just evidence of the steel will that was characteristic of the Potters. Ben circled Javier, but his movements were jerky, as if he strained to move each muscle separately. Job's turkey would have a better chance of surviving this fight, Javier thought. It was as much as Ben deserved.

Then, out of the corner of his eye, Javier spied a disheveled Georgina in the doorway. In all the chaos, she had put on her gown inside out and backwards. "Javier! Ben!" she cried. "Don't do this!"

Ben paid no heed to his sister's plea. He struck again.

Javier dodged the wild jab and spun around so that his back was to the bedroom. Even though he could no longer see Georgina, he could still hear the panic in her voice.

"Both of you, stop!"

Javier could not afford any distraction, so he ignored her, just like her brother had. He then punished that brother, lunging forward to deliver a cross-hook-cross combination. He heard Georgina gasp as he bloodied Ben's nose and landed two in the man's left eye.

The American weaved out of the way, jabbing furiously to keep Javier at a distance. It was a good defensive move, but brawls are not won on defense. Javier was ready for the obvious cross that followed, and he juked right. The slow attack left Ben's chest wide open, allowing Javier to land a few rapid blows to the bellows before the American could pull back again.

It was almost too easy. Ben's eye was already swelling, and it would be a blinker by morning. The American swayed a little on his feet; one more punch would send him to the floor.

"No more," Georgina called out in a rough voice. "Please!"

Javier made the mistake of looking over at her. A true mess, she was. Tears streamed down her face, making her eyes nearly as puffy as her brother's. Seeing Georgina like that drained the fight right out of him.

With a sigh, Javier turned his attention back to Ben and lowered his hands in resignation. He spoke slowly in the hope that the deliberate effort would help him temper his fury. "Potter, face it, you've had enough. Let's call this thing."

Ben actually spat on the floor. "Yellow son of a bitch," he bit out before charging Javier again, a quick frontal attack that was impossible to dodge.

"No!" Georgina screamed fruitlessly.

Together, the two men crashed into an end table, which collapsed under their combined weight. Ben's claws, elbows, and knees were everywhere. It was like no scrap Javier had ever been in, and it was all he could do to keep the man from gouging his eyes out.

For some reason, Georgina screamed at him, not Ben. "Javier, stop it!"

He turned his head toward her in disbelief. "I tried!" he yelled, but that brief moment of distraction was all Ben needed to maneuver both bony knees on top of Javier's arms, pinning him to the floor.

Ben now took advantage of Javier's immobility to deliver several blows to the head. "Don't you ever touch my sister again!"

For a dope fiend, the man's fists had a lot of power, especially when unopposed. Javier felt a quick twinge of panic. If he did not work his arms free, he might not have much of a face left at the end of this. He jerked and pulled, but he could not overcome the rage of this crack-brained bedlamite.

With all the blood splattering around, Javier could not even see his attacker, let alone Georgina. After a few more punches, Javier felt something inside himself give—and it wasn't just his nose. He had never been one to quit, but he now realized that there was no way to win. In either victory or defeat, he still lost his prize. "*Hay sus…*please," he whispered hoarsely to anyone who would listen.

"Ben, don't do this!" Georgina cried. She sounded closer, but Javier could not see her. When he felt the weight on top of him pull back a bit, he knew that she was trying to intervene.

"Ina, stay out of it," Javier called out.

"What are you doing, Ben? Let him go!"

Georgina kept pulling on her brother. Javier felt more than saw Ben throw her off, and she landed on the floor with a loud thump.

"Ina!" Javier cried. He tore his limbs loose in one quick move and rolled out from under his assailant. His right arm was numb and useless from loss of circulation, so he used his slightly more mobile left arm to swab the blood from his face. Javier was not happy with the scene before him: Georgina lay on the floor, holding her own reddening cheek.

Javier started toward her, but Ben cut him off. "Get away!" the American warned.

"You hit her, you son of a bitch!"

Georgina's frantic gaze followed both men. "I'm fine," she insisted. She kept her hands away from her face as if her eye did not sting like hell. The broken blood vessel told Javier a different story.

Furious, Javier would have liked nothing better than to launch himself at Ben again, but he held back for Georgina's sake. He covered his bloody nose with his sleeve.

"Fucking savage," Ben said, glaring at him. "Goo-goo filth."

"You punched your own sister. Your father would be proud." Javier tipped his head up and pinched his nose, but the nasally sound of his voice did not mask his resentment. "I should have left you in Zumárraga, *cabrón*. Better yet, you should have done the decent thing and died in Balangiga like a man."

"Javier!" Georgina looked at him, her face a mixture of disbelief and outrage—a combination that looked an awful lot like hate.

"You would be better off without him," he explained.

"That's not your decision to make!"

Actually, it had been. Without him, Ben would not be free of Lope. But he could not tell her that.

A part of Javier wanted to fall to his knees and beg, apologize, plead—anything to get her to love him again. But that part of him had lost the battle. All of the bloodletting that he had done for Ben and Georgina—it ended now. He had hemorrhaged money and land, all for naught. He had to chuck up the sponge before he also lost his self-respect.

Javier walked over to a letter desk that was tucked so far in the corner that it had been spared the fate of the rest of the room. He pulled out an ink jar and tried to open it, but his fingers were both too sore and too bloody to do the job. So he threw it against the far wall, and it blew apart in a satisfying crash.

"What are you doing?"

He ignored Georgina and walked over to examine the broken glass. He stepped on a small shard, but he ignored that too. He crouched and picked up what he was looking for: a blue-black ball of opium tar that had he had hidden inside the jar.

He smiled grimly when he saw Ben's eyes grow as wide as their swelling would allow. Javier stalked toward Ben. He did not fear another attack. He had Ben's full attention now.

"This is how much I had left before your sister decided to 'heal' you." He looked at the uneven blob—only slightly smaller than a baseball—and then back at Ben. "How long would this last you, Ben? A week? Two?"

The American swallowed his drool.

"Maybe it would only last you a day," Javier continued. "Your last day on this earth, if you did it right."

Georgie gasped. "He would never do such a thing!"

"Tell her the truth," Javier said, holding out the opium. "Tell her you'll always want it. Even if you live, you'll spend the rest of your useless life wanting this bloody hop, from the moment you wake to the minute you fall asleep. It won't end there, though, because you'll even dream about it. It will never let you go, not until it kills you."

Ben did not respond. He did not have to.

Only one person in this room did not know the truth. Javier reached for Georgina's hand and set the ball—now slick with Javier's blood—into her palm. "Here. Take this with you to Boston, Maestra. See how long it lasts."

Eyes wide, she stared at the mess. "But things will be different there—"

"Why don't you go and find out for yourself? Take this"—he crushed her fingers around the sticky ball—"and that"—he nodded at Ben—"and leave."

He turned from the two Potters and walked away from the wreck he had made of his life.

CHAPTER SIXTY-ONE

Leaving

What a mess, Georgie thought. A couple of very reluctant nurses patched together the two purpled men. Javier had gone out and retrieved the sisters from their early morning prayers, and now they paid him back by sighing their disapproval every few minutes. One nun placed wads of rolled cotton into Javier's nostrils and washed the dried blood from his face and chin. The swelling around the Filipino's eyes had abated a bit, but there was not much anyone could do for a broken nose—not that Georgie spared any sympathy for him. She could not believe how he had taken advantage of Ben's poor condition, laying into her brother like a prizefighter paid by the punch.

Ben was lucky he had escaped as well as he had. No matter how alarmingly bruised his eye looked right now, Georgie knew from experience that the flesh would eventually heal. Roxbury was a rough neighborhood to grow up in and the Potter home had presented its own hazards, which meant that she had learned firsthand the resilience of the human body. The worst blow of the night had really been to Ben's spirit, not his complexion. Her brother walked with one foot in the grave already—how dare Javier suggest that he fall in the rest of the way? How could Javier claim to care for her and then say something so callous?

Georgie piled the broken furniture on the patio. Then she finished packing her own things and sat down in the living room to rest. Ben was no help at all, but at least he was getting cleaned up by the nurses and, afterward, receiving the attention of a barber. By the time he reappeared in the living room, his hair was cut short and his beard trimmed to a civilized length.

"I can't believe it," she said. Her brother would hardly be mistaken for the Ghost of Benjamin Potter Past, but it was still a marked improvement.

Ben came to Georgie's side and bent down to kiss her cheek. His overall pallor had improved this past week, and his bright blue eyes stood out clear and true—at least the eye that could be seen beneath the swelling. Those irises were the single feature of their father's worth inheriting, and were distractingly pretty for a man.

"Do I look okay?" he asked.

On closer inspection, he had not lost his haunted look. He still fidgeted uncomfortably, suggesting that his body had not fully healed from the withdrawal. Nonetheless, the young man that stood in front of her was a closer approximation of the one that she remembered from home. "You look wonderful," she said. "Who found you the barber?"

"Lope's man. He threw it in as a bit of a bonus."

"A bonus for what?" she asked, but Ben was already directing the servants to pick up their luggage.

"You ready to go?" he asked, holding out his hand to escort her downstairs.

There was one last thing she had to attend to, and she preferred to do it in private. "Give me a minute, Ben."

Her brother dropped his hand and looked at her with a hard expression that she did not recognize. "That man doesn't deserve another word from you. He got what he paid for."

"Listen to me," she snapped. "It's my business, and I'll not apologize to you for it. Besides, you don't really know him—"

"Spare me," Ben said, his words clipped. "Your pickaninny friend is hardly the victim here."

"And you are? Were you brought here against your will, hop forced down your throat, and…God knows what else? I've not been enlightened with all the details."

Her brother clenched his jaw shut and glared at her, but Georgie gave no ground. Somehow he had goaded her into taking Javier's side. The silence between the siblings was uncomfortably long.

Finally, he motioned toward the door. "Your Mowgli is out there on the balcony. Don't be long. We have a boat to catch."

Georgie shook her head in frustration. If there was anything that could make Ben enthusiastic about leaving for Manila, it was the prospect of leaving Javier behind. The two brought out the worst in each other. At least they would never meet again.

She walked out to the patio and found Javier standing against the railing by the bay. She knew that he could hear her steps, but he did not move.

"Javier," she said, but he still did not turn. "Javi?"

His head rotated a few degrees, giving her a shallow view of his discolored face and nose. She still wanted to be mad at him, but she could not help but feel the void left behind by his missing *tendre*. Normally he would have swallowed her in his arms by now. Javier had always been an affectionate lover: even when reading or talking, he had always held on to a part of her, even something as simple as running this thumb over the inside of her wrist.

No matter what, he had never, ever kept his back to her—not until now. The proud line of his turned back told her that Javier did not think she deserved the consideration of any kind of ending, even a tearful one. He would not comfort her as she walked out on him— even if she ached for it.

"I'm sorry about some of what I said," she said. "You're a good man, Javier, and that's why I fell in love with you—"

"Not enough."

"There is no 'enough,'" she pleaded. "There's just reality—"

"Will you come back?"

She sighed, knowing that his interruptions were a way of keeping his distance. Her warrior had stood tall against war, prejudice, disease, and bad fortune—but she alone had brought him low. All she could respectfully offer was her honesty.

"I don't know, Javi. I have to get Ben home. His recovery has only begun—who else can see him through it? You would do the same."

He folded his arms across his chest and stared back out to sea.

"You would!" she exclaimed. "You would put the needs of Allegra and your mother above your own: you would travel to the edge of the earth to find them, live among strangers, humiliate yourself on a daily basis because you did not fit in no matter how much you tried. You would do all that for family, and you would not stop until you succeeded. You wouldn't rest until they were safe."

"Please stop," he said, his voice chilly. "I can't listen to any of this rot anymore."

"What's 'rot'—my duty to my brother? How could I live with myself, knowing my happiness was built on his pain?"

He did not answer her right away, and Georgina hoped that he was considering what she said. She knew what family meant to this proud *hacendero*. He had to understand.

"I think it's best that you go now," he said.

He would not even look her in the eye. "That's it?" she asked with disbelief.

He did not answer.

Georgie stood quietly behind Javier, hoping that he would turn and say something that would ease her pain. But he did not, and Ben's not-so-subtle rustling in the living room awkwardly beckoned for her.

Quiet tears dripped down her cheeks, but Javier could not see them. She turned and walked out of his life.

CHAPTER SIXTY-TWO

Manila Again

On the way to Manila aboard the S.S. *Mauban*, Georgie and Ben passed by a volcano so perfectly conical that she thought it deserved a whole page in a new Thomasite primer. Given her current mood, though, any text she wrote would end up sounding a little macabre:

> Mount Mayon is a volcano.
> It erupted six years ago.
> How many people did it kill?
> How many churches did it burn?

Georgie sighed. She had been cross the entire trip. The lush scenery should have put her in a better mood, but she spent most of the time seasick, closely guarding a tin pail she had cajoled off a deck hand. The sea was especially choppy because of an approaching southern storm. The seamen expected the typhoon to turn to the west and head toward Indo-China, but not for a few days yet. Javier's path back to Bais would send him right through the wake of the tempest, a fitting tribute to the end of their affair.

Georgie retched in the pail again but got nothing but bile. This did not surprise her since she had barely eaten today. Nothing would settle her stomach—nothing except, to her great surprise, the galley's guava jelly, the same substance she had once found so vile. No matter how many dirty spoons had gotten there first, the preserves were the only thing she could keep down her gullet.

The trip took only two days—and, fortunately, since cholera seemed to be under control in Manila, their ship was waived through quarantine without a hitch. Georgie could not have handled another hour, let alone week, on the listing deck.

On land, Georgie felt none of the same enthusiasm, purpose, and hope that she had felt on her first arrival six months ago. Back then, the city had charmed her with its Spanish tile roofs, moss-covered walls, quaint moat, and surrounding ring of lush mountains. Now, when she should have been in high spirits after successfully finding and retrieving Ben, her mood had grown so sour that she could not help but notice Manila's every flaw. As their *calesa* circled Intramuros—one of the last true examples of a medieval fortress town—she realized that the moat she had once admired was really a putrid swamp.

"Ben, can you smell that?"

"I don't think there's a thing in this city I can't smell," he said. His attitude had not improved since Samar; and despite the allowances she made for his illness, he was getting on her nerves.

"That pest-ridden water is one of the worst sanitation hazards in this city," he continued, pointing to the dike to their left. "It's no wonder cholera killed thousands. When I was in the Army, they talked about draining and filling that thing. The officers even wanted to turn it into a golf course. I'm surprised the swells haven't gotten their way."

The *calesa* wound along and over the Pasig River, passing from one neighborhood of expatriates to another. Georgie listened to the sounds of the city change from the rolling Spanish of Intramuros to the musical Fukien of Chinatown. She traversed Manila's most recent linguistic border—marked by the clipped impatience of American English—when the driver pulled up to the front door of the Oriente.

As uniformed boys helped her out of the carriage, Georgie was again struck by the size of the hotel. The entryway was grand, the dining room cavernous, and the stables almost as large as the Army's. By any city's standards, it was fine lodgings; but after living in Negros and Samar for five months, Georgie thought it a veritable Metropole.

The spacious room assigned to her and Ben had a neatly appointed four-poster bed and, of course, rich hardwood floors. She smiled at the slick shine of the Narra boards and wondered when they had last been polished. If the staff brought her a pair of burlap socks, she would be happy to pitch in—though right now all she could do was look at the bed longingly, despite the fact that it was still the middle of the day. The bamboo matting, scratchy sheets, and rock hard pillows that had made her so miserable last September looked quite inviting to her now.

Before she could plop down on the clean sheets, Ben grabbed most of the bedding and threw it to the floor.

"Hey—"

"I'll sleep down here." He punched an overstuffed pillow flat to match the others. "We could both have beds, you know, if you trusted me in my own room."

Georgie exhaled, seeking some reserve of inner calm. "We can't afford two rooms. If I don't manage to collect my back pay from the Bureau, we're not going to have enough cash to get home, even on steerage."

"Then why are we staying at this stuffy old palace? There are cheaper joints around."

No doubt Ben was an expert on doss-houses throughout the islands. Georgie, however, had earned a little comfort, and she did not want Ben anywhere near those places. "The water is clean here and I feel safe. Besides, they said they would send up a cot."

"Stop treating me like a disobedient child, one that you have to chain to the bedpost when you leave the room."

"Don't be silly," she said without conviction. In truth she wondered where he would go if left unsupervised. How many blocks was it to the nearest opium den? This was a wonderful hotel, but it was still in the middle of Chinatown.

She raised her voice to a new, brighter key and spoke half-playfully, hoping it would smooth the edges of her words. "I'd like a sober dinner companion, okay?"

"What?"

Georgie sighed. Did she really need to spell it out?

Ben held up his hands and gave her what she asked. "I'll be a regular teetotaler, I swear."

"Whisky, too?"

As soon as she said it, she wondered if she was taking things too far. Where would she draw the line? Ale? Tobacco? Would a single beer or cigarette really lead him back to the hop-pipe? She was not trying to insult him, nor hurt his feelings. But it was hard to have a sensible conversation with him when he was doing his best imitation of a granite statue.

A wave of nausea overtook her. The guava jelly would have its revenge, after all. She covered her mouth, picked up the room key, and disappeared out of the room without explanation. Even sick, she had the presence of mind to lock the door behind her. As she ran to the washroom she could hear Ben test the knob and curse. His ruckus could be heard down the hallway—and no doubt throughout the hotel—disturbing the quiet siesta hour. It was going to be a long trip home.

CHAPTER SIXTY-THREE

Money

Manila during Holy Week was dead quiet. Georgie would not have believed that a capital city could empty so completely and still manage to function, though how much work was getting done was debatable. Even the Bureau of Education only opened for half days—when it bothered to open at all. Unfortunately, anyone unlucky enough to be working in the summer heat was hardly going to lend Georgie a sympathetic ear. It did not take her long to realize how grossly she had underestimated Uncle Sam's parsimony in her plan to cash out and go home.

Nevertheless, like a bureaucratic Sisyphus, Georgie went every day to retell her story from the beginning to yet another administrator. Everyone she spoke with was clear on one point: if she did not complete her contract, the Bureau would not give her a dime for her last two months of work. Though they sympathized with her brother's situation, they did not think that a grown man needed a chaperone to take him home. Since she forced Ben to accompany her on these trips to the Bureau, they had said as much to his face.

If they thought they could out-dog a Potter, though, they had underestimated both her will and her financial desperation. After nine days of relentless effort, she finally succeeded in arranging a morning meeting with General Superintendent Elmer Bryan. Actually, it was Ben who arranged the meeting. During one of her fruitless pleading sessions with an intransigent gatekeeper, Ben scrawled a note on the back of the secretary's cigarette card, threw it at the woman, and barked at her to take it to the super. Barely a minute later, Mr. Bryan emerged from his supposedly inviolate meeting.

He spoke directly to Ben without any pleasantries. "You were there?"

Ben seemed to nod, but the motion was so slight that Georgie was not sure.

Bryan registered it. "How? Was it, did he—"

"Joe was shot in the chest. It was quick."

The superintendent removed his round wire-rimmed glasses, making his eyes shrink even further into his broad, grim face. "At least that's a blessing. How did you know to find me?"

"The kid never shut up about the high reach of his principal from the little town of Kokomo. He planned to work for you after his enlistment was up. Said a soldier's life wasn't what he thought it'd be."

Bryan gave a small, wry smile. "He'd always wanted to get out of Indiana—though I doubt he meant to go all the way to Samar."

Ben shrugged. "Few of us did, but it was our duty. I'd do it again."

Wide-eyed, Georgie listened to her brother talk, stunned that this proud man was the same surly pup whom she had been dragging around the city.

Bryan extended his hand to Ben. "Thank you, sergeant. I appreciate you sharing this with me. It will help me rest a little easier tonight."

The men spoke for a few more minutes. Ben cajoled the superintendent into issuing Georgie her back pay—including a bonus for the night classes that she had never gotten around to teaching. Georgie was shocked by her reversal of fortune, and she was even more shocked that she had her hitherto uncooperative brother to thank for it. Winning concessions by abusing the superintendent's grief was questionable, but she took the signed endorsement, thanked the man, and left his office without dwelling on the details. Altogether she had barely enough to get the two of them home, but it would do the job. She wasted no time getting to the transport agent's office on Escolta, where she booked third-class berths on the S.S. *Korea* for the next morning. Fast was more important than comfortable.

In the *calesa* en route to the Oriente, Georgie finally asked about poor dead Joe. Ben looked away from her, past the horizon, and said: "The idiot didn't have a chance. The townsfolk got most of the company tanked at the fiesta the night before. Joe couldn't have fought off a swarm of mosquitoes."

"That's why he got shot?"

Ben laughed bitterly. "He wasn't shot. The *insurrectos* could never figure out how to fire our guns. Joe was *bolo*-ed like the others, his throat cut ear to ear."

"But you said—"

"I said what that man needed to hear. What good is the truth? That's not how Bryan wants to remember his student. Hell, I didn't much care for Joe, but it's not how I want to remember him either. I'd forget it all if I could."

"Is this what wakes you up at night?" Sharing a room had not been restful. "You're usually screaming—"

"I don't want to talk about it."

"Maybe if you—"

"Ever." Ben looked away again, ending the conversation.

They disembarked from the *calesa* in silence and entered the hotel's dining room. Georgie would not spare an additional dollar to have the meal delivered to their room, so they sat awkwardly across from each other at a vast table. Ben turned his menu over and examined every word of the wine, beer, and spirits list, but in the end he did not order a drink.

Georgie ordered rice croquettes with jelly, while Ben chose the roast beef. At first, Georgie was pretty sure she had the right of it: Ben's cold beef had a silvery-green cast to it, and she could not watch him eat it without becoming a little nauseous. However, as palatable as the rice croquettes were going down, she should have known better than to think that they would stay there. The fried food and tropical heat did not mix well, and she spent the rest of the evening emptying her stomach in the bathroom.

Georgie finally fell asleep well after midnight, and she was still groggy when she woke in the morning. She turned to ask Ben if his stomach felt any better, but he was not there. His balled-up sheet had been tossed on top of the empty cot. Georgie told herself it was okay; she knew Ben's habits well enough to know that he did not sleep long, nor did he sleep well. He paced the halls at night, listening for strange noises.

She got up and peeked out the door, but saw no one there. After she finished her toilette a half hour later, Ben still had not returned, so she headed downstairs and looked in the empty breakfast room. She then checked the front desk, but he had left no note. Nothing.

Georgie dragged her feet out the front door of the hotel in the vain hope that he was taking a walk around the square. She watched the morning flurry of *calesas* on the plaza, and felt the same sinking mix of shame, rage, and helplessness that she had experienced when her clothes were stolen by the phantom laundryman. She had been just as much a fool this time around, but this time the villain was her own kin.

She took a deep breath. Ben could not be that far away, and he was surely coming back—she needed to believe that. One thing was certain: their departure would have to be delayed. Muttering under her breath about how she would re-shine Ben's eye when she found him, she walked east toward Plaza Moraga.

Georgie arrived at the steamship agent's office just as it opened for business. Cleaning women were wiping the morning dust off the *capiz* shades, and a man was on the roof straightening the long sign that read, "Castle Bros Wolf & Sons—Manila and Iloilo." The huge firm sold everything from fresh produce to ship engines. Georgie noticed wistfully that one of their main trades was in sugar, and that gave her pause. She did not appreciate the reminder of the life she had passed on for her miserable rogue of a brother.

She walked up the stone stairs to the second story, where the firm's retail business was housed. Fortunately, the agent who sold them the ticket yesterday was already at his desk. "Mister, ah…Mister—"

The heavyset man turned. "Freeman."

"Of course, Mr. Freeman," she said convincingly, as if she had been anywhere close to coming up with the name. "Nice to see you again."

"You as well, Miss Potter." He had obviously remembered her name.

"I need to change our departure date, if possible."

"Change your date?"

"On the steamer out," she explained while searching for her tickets. She raked the inside of her handbag with her fingers and inspected each smaller compartment twice, but they were not there.

"The tickets you just redeemed?"

The truth was slow in settling on her. She searched the bag once more, but the tickets were still missing. "What do you mean redeemed?" she asked, looking up at Mr. Freeman.

He confirmed her worst fears. "Your brother just left here ten minutes ago."

"Ben was here?" she asked weakly.

Mr. Freeman nodded. "He probably meant to save you the trouble."

"He changed our departure?"

"Well, no," the agent clarified. "As I said, he returned the tickets."

"What did he get for them?" She asked the question out of stubbornness, but she knew the answer.

"A refund, Miss Potter. Cash."

Cash. The word twisted Georgie's stomach. "Oh my God," she whispered, holding her hand to her mouth. Almost every cent she had in the world had just walked out the door in the hands of an opium addict.

She was right back where she had started. No, worse than that, she realized. This time she had no fiancé, no job, and no way home. Her brother could have taken one ticket and lived off the money for months. Instead, he took both and left her stranded and alone. Not even their father had ever been that heartless.

CHAPTER SIXTY-FOUR

Stranded

Georgie barely made it back to her room before vomiting the *pandesal* she had eaten for breakfast. The plain, dry roll was supposed to soak up the riling acid in her belly, but right now nothing helped. She moved her smelly washbowl to the window ledge so that the stench would not trigger another heave. She had been sick so often recently that she could not remember being well. That was when she acknowledged what she should have known weeks before: she was pregnant. Unemployed, abandoned, and pregnant.

Georgie sprawled out on her bed and tried to shut her eyes tight against reality. When were her last monthly courses—maybe back in February? Time ran together. She did not remember bleeding in Samar, but she had been too anxious to even eat, let alone consult a calendar.

She opened her eyes, not quite ready to give up hope. There had to be another explanation, she thought. Malnutrition could explain her missed menses—her clothes did fit looser than ever. Women were supposed to gain weight when expecting, not lose it, right? Or did they lose it first, then gain? They were said to be "increasing," but when did that increase actually begin? Georgie did not know, and her own ignorance horrified her. Wellesley had taught her Caesar and Virgil, not the useful bits of biology.

She had to face reality. There was one symptom of pregnancy that she did recognize, and it was all over the hotel's white porcelain washbowl. It made sense. She had not been ill a single time during the month-long crossing of the Pacific, but now she was regularly seasick, land-sick, and every other kind of sick, all day long. Javier had probably won their little wager even before leaving Bais. She never should have doubted his determination.

"Javier," she said aloud, unsure whether she spoke the name to curse, conjure, or exorcise. She wanted him here, but he would never forgive her for letting herself get duped by the very brother who caused this whole mess, a brother she was still unwilling to let go. The truth was, she would never give up looking for Ben. God help her, she was a sucker.

No, she was worse: she was a coward. Even if she could find her way home, how would she raise a mestizo bastard in Boston, a city that barely tolerated white-skinned Irish children born in Church-sanctioned wedlock? Was unconditional love from her family enough to make up for the anonymous hatred of strangers?

Could she stay in Manila instead? The tropics offered more ethical latitude, despite—or even, she thought, because of—Catholicism. Devout Filipinos like Lourdes de Altarejos accepted the inconvenient consequences of sin while excoriating the act itself: her adoption of Allegra and her kindness toward Andrés was solid enough proof. But even if Filipino society accepted the child, the ruling American clique would not tolerate the child's unwed mother.

These were questions for another time. Right now Georgie needed to focus on where she would sleep tonight. One thing was for sure: she could no longer afford to stay at the Hotel de Oriente. She had paid up through this morning in anticipation of her departure on the *Korea*, but now she had to clear her room before the staff insisted that she pay for today. She packed in record time and accompanied her belongings downstairs.

She hoped that she could check out without being asked about her puffy, pink eyes and runny nose. Those hopes were dashed when she saw the brass nameplate of the one person at the hotel who knew her: "Moses J. North, Manager, on duty."

North turned to her, and Georgie forced out her best imitation of a smile.

"Miss Potter," he said. "Are you quite all right? Please, there's no need to worry. My porter told me that you missed your steamer—and of course you are welcome to stay with us as long as you need."

"If you knew what I could pay, you would say differently."

"We do have discounts for long-term residents..."

She could not afford that either. "I think I need to find a whole different class of hotel."

"I see," he said. The hotelier scrutinized her a moment and then let the matter drop. Georgie appreciated his discretion, even if it was reluctant. "May I have a forwarding address for your correspondence?" he asked.

It was a polite way of finding out if she knew where the hell she was going. She had no idea. "If you have any suggestions..."

North helpfully drew up a list of his competitors, ranking them from solidly second class to barely respectable. "These top two usually have their guest lists published in the papers, as do we," he said. "These others down here are more, ah, private."

Georgie did not want the man to think she was trying to hide. Not yet, at least. She needed value more than anything, and she said so. She also said that she would send word where her trunk should be delivered, which seemed to reassure the man a little.

"If there is anything more I can do for you, Miss Potter, please do ask."

He started to say more but then thought better of it, and she was thankful for that.

"I"—the quiver in her voice betrayed her—"I'll be just fine."

Within the hour, she was climbing up the dark stairs to her new room at the Kentucky Hotel and Saloon. She was not sure at all if she would be fine. The hallway of the hotel—and calling it a hotel was generous—was almost too narrow for her trunk. She had had to walk through a crowded saloon to get to the front desk, and soldiers had actually whistled at her as she ran the gauntlet. The place would get even noisier after the men migrated upstairs with their temporary companions.

She took a deep breath and told herself that she could do this. Really, she had no choice. The Kentucky had little to recommend it other than price, but she could stay here for almost a month for what a single day had cost her at the Oriente. And while there were a dozen other places like it in Binondo, this was the cleanest she had seen in the price-range.

Once settled in, Georgie spent a miserable and sleepless weekend holed up in her room. On Monday morning, she took a hack to the Bureau of Education, planning to beg for any job available. She walked through the lower entrance of the Ayuntamiento Building and headed upstairs to the Marble Hall. She dreaded explaining to these bureaucrats why she was back. Still wringing her hands, she steered around the statue of Spanish explorer Sebastián del Cano and walked right into an equally stunned Allegra.

She backed up a step, and the two looked at each other in silence. Five minutes earlier, had Georgie been pressed to name the one person she would be most ashamed to see, it would have been this woman. Fate was adding insult to injury.

"Maestra?" Allegra finally squeaked, as if she could not believe who she saw, either. The Filipina hastily tried to put on a neutral face, but her use of the title gave away her discomfort. Allegra had never, ever called Georgie anything as formal as *"maestra"* before. She was dressed for business and well made-up, but her face looked haggard.

"Allegra, nice to see you." It was terrifying, of course, but also nice. "Maybe now I should call you maestra, too?"

Allegra tilted her head and looked pointedly at Georgie. "I do not know."

"You did take over my classes, didn't you?"

"The Bureau called me here so I can apply for the job."

"Apply? But I thought—"

"—they would just give an American job to a native? And I have no recommendation, now that Señor Blaxton left."

"Where did he go?" Georgie did not care about Archie one way or the other, but for some reason she had thought of Bais and everyone in it as frozen in time. She should have known better.

"He went home." Allegra shrugged. "Rosa's baby is too far along for him to do anything but marry her or run."

Georgie frowned, though this news only confirmed what she had already guessed. Archie's choice was predictable, but she could hardly judge him too harshly, given her own predicament. "I'm so sorry for Rosa."

"She is heartsick but maybe better off, I think. And I finished school on my own."

"You managed all the children? Boys and girls?"

"It was not so hard." The young Filipina could not hide the note of pride in her voice.

There was probably much more to the story, and the old Allegra would have drawn out every detail, but instead she clamped her jaw shut.

"Well, I'm glad you stayed on," Georgie offered, struggling to keep the conversation going.

"I will be paid one quarter as much," Allegra finally continued, frustration punctuating every word. "But I have no choice. After the auction we need money more than ever."

Georgie felt her stomach pitch, and she reflexively held her hand to her mouth, just in case.

"Javier just gave it all up," Allegra continued bitterly. "He called it…"

"Oh my God…"

"A fire sale."

Georgie swallowed a little bile. "No."

"*Sí*. He had a choice: make payroll or pay the interest on the loans." She looked right at Georgie. Not a bit of Allegra's mischievous joy poked through her otherwise familiar visage. This was a different woman. "This way there is no revolution. No angry workers. We live and the house still stands."

"Thank God for that," Georgie whispered.

"You are happy for us, then?" Allegra said with uncharacteristic sarcasm.

Shame stung her eyes. "Allegra, I never meant any of what I said…"

The young woman began to turn away, but Georgie grabbed her shoulder. "I swear. You have to believe me." The last few words she choked out over tears.

Allegra shrugged. "Maybe, maybe not. Javier had to sell all the land anyway, to pay off the debt. He could not let a man like Lope loose in Bais."

"Lope? What does he have to do with it?"

Allegra laughed once—a perfunctory, brittle sound. "Please."

"Really, I don't understand."

Georgie's denial sounded forced, even to her own ears, but she had no idea what else to say. At the same time, a strange tickle in the back of her mind told her that she might not want to hear what was coming next.

"Do not play stupid, Georgina. Not with me."

She looked into Allegra's cold eyes. "I wouldn't dare."

"Javier had debt before—we always have debt—but the difference between the rock you can carry and the boulder that will crush you is often very small. In this case, the weight of one person: your brother."

Georgie felt her chest draw tight enough to choke the air out of her lungs. What a naive ninny she had been! She had been so relieved to get Ben out of Samar that she had not questioned why he had been suddenly free to go. How much had Javier paid for his release? If he had to sell his hacienda, it must have been a fortune. Why not tell her? He could have hurt her with the truth so easily.

"We have to stop this—"

"You are like Mr. Wells with his time machine? You cannot stop it. It is done. The land is gone. Last night I watched it sold to a stranger, an American. He paid more than any of our neighbors could, so the Americans conquer us twice."

Georgie did not know what to say. The truth was too awful to face: she had brought down two families, not just one.

Allegra cocked her head, squinting at Georgie suspiciously. "You really did not know?"

Georgie was too tired to continue protesting. She shook her head and half-swooned onto a wooden bench in the hall. "I can't believe it," she said, dropping her head into her hands to cry. "I just can't. Everything I've done is wrong. How could I have been so wrong?"

"*Hay sus,*" Allegra said with disgust.

Through her tears, Georgie could see the Filipina's small feet pointing at her, waiting for something. But all Georgie could do was bawl. Allegra shifted awkwardly from foot to foot, uncomfortable with the display of emotion from her former friend. Eventually, she sat down on the bench too. After several minutes of Georgie's messy sobbing, Allegra offered to let Georgie use the large *pañuelo* she wore around her shoulders as a handkerchief. At first Georgie tried to wipe only her eyes with it, but the long trail of snot running down her nose was unavoidable. She could not even cry right.

"I'll wash it for you," Georgie offered. But Allegra sighed and shook her head—she did not seem to care about the scarf.

Georgie had a desperate realization: more than anything, she wanted Javier here. She loved him and did not want to keep his child from him. In a small corner of her mind, she had held on to the image of Javier as a proud and doting father. That image brought a new onslaught of weeping. She should have gone to him right away when she realized she was pregnant, before she had learned about the auction. Then, at least, she could have naively begged for his forgiveness. Now, knowing all that he had lost because of her, she could not face him. She was the worst kind of coward.

When Allegra spoke, she sounded agitated, but her voice had lost its edge of unkindness. "I wish he was done with you."

"He is. He wouldn't say goodbye. He couldn't even look at me, and now—"

"*Idiota!*" Allegra shouted. "He did it for you the whole time—chasing your brother, taking the debt, adopting that little girl."

"Paca?" She looked up through wet eyes.

"The *puta*, yes. She is safe."

"Thank God." Georgie looked up through bloodshot eyes. "But I've lost Ben. Again. He ran off. There's nothing to show for Javier's sacrifice."

"He will not be missed, your brother." Allegra wrinkled her nose as if the smell of the city had finally caught up to her. "I am quite sure Javito would rather not have him around. But you are another matter."

"How could he forgive me?" Georgie looked into the Filipina's unyielding eyes, sure that Javier's would look the same.

"I wonder," Allegra said and shrugged. "But he is not me."

Georgie took in a deep breath and held it. She never thought she could be afraid of this diminutive Filipina, but she was. She exhaled. "I'm pregnant," she said.

Allegra's look of disdain melted into pure shock. "How long?"

"I don't know. I just found out"—Georgie caught herself—"I just realized it."

"And you would take his child away from him?"

"No." It was not the most convincing denial.

"If you think I will let you run away like this," Allegra said, "you are mistaken."

Strangely, Georgie felt relief at the threat. She was so tired of making the wrong decisions. She wanted someone else to make the right ones for her.

Allegra was not finished. "Do you think Javier would not do everything to protect his own child? He has not proven to you the kind of man he is? You would give up on this man?"

Georgie thought she had been believing the worst about herself, but she realized that she had been believing the worst about Javier. "I don't want to."

Allegra sat back, and spoke with authority. "You must wait until I finish my audition here at the Bureau."

"You mean interview."

"Mmm, I think audition is the better word. I need a few days. Then we will go to Bais together."

Georgie nodded. She smiled as bravely as she could, even though the idea of waiting felt impossible. She wanted to depart this very minute.

"You may not leave Manila," Allegra commanded, waving a finger.

"Of course not," Georgie agreed.

"You may look for your brother," Allegra decided. "That will keep you busy. Busy is good. You will not have time to make up silly stories in your head."

Silly stories like ones where Javier did not want her anymore? Would it matter if he took her back for duty's sake instead of love? Georgie figured she was better off not thinking, just as Allegra commanded. "Okay."

"You have one week only, and then we take the steamer home, with or without him."

Georgie nodded obediently.

"You must be at the dock Saturday morning early," the Filipina continued. "The *Bélgica* leaves at ten. Well, of course, it will not really;

it will leave in the afternoon. But we must be there by eight, in any case."

"I will be there by six." She would sleep on the dock all week if she had to, if it might result in Javier's forgiveness.

"If you are not there, I will find you."

Georgie wanted more than anything to hug this fierce woman, but she knew Allegra's anger was not an act. It would take time to earn the woman's trust again. For now, it was enough to be by her side. "I can stay with you, if you'd rather."

"*Hay sus*, no."

Georgie smiled. "I'll be there Saturday. I promise."

CHAPTER SIXTY-FIVE

Instant Messages

17 APRIL 1903 09:32
TO: JAVIER ALTAREJOS, BAIS
BENJAMIN POTTER QUIT MANILA SISTER DESTITUTE HAS
DECAMPED HOTEL PLEASE ADVISE
MOSS NORTH

* * *

17 APRIL 1903 13:11
TO: MOSS NORTH, HOTEL ORIENTE MANILA
ENSURE SAFETY GEORGINA PERSONALLY DISCREETLY STOP
WILL COVER EXPENSES
JAVIER

* * *

19 APRIL 1903 21:02
TO: JAVIER ALTAREJOS, BAIS
HACIENDA AUCTION CONCLUDED WINNER LIONEL HARGIS
TAKES POSSESSION FIRST MAY
GUILLERMO

* * *

20 APRIL 1903 11:49
TO: JAVIER ALTAREJOS, BAIS
FOUND LOST SHEEP WITH UNBORN LAMB STOP BRINGING
HOME SATURDAY STOP TRY NOT TO LOSE HER AGAIN
ALLEGRA

CHAPTER SIXTY-SIX

Noise

It was not even dawn on the morning of her scheduled departure, but Georgie was already fully dressed and anxious to get started. She ventured downstairs and found the hotel clerk still sprawled out on the floor behind the front desk, either fast asleep or passed out. When he did not respond to her calls, she splashed a little water on his face to rouse him. When he finally came around, she asked him to rustle up some porters and send them to her room as soon as possible.

It had been a frustrating week. Her search for Ben had been a half-hearted distraction, only helpful in keeping her thoughts off what she really wanted to do: get back to Javier. No doubt she would pace the deck of the steamer the whole way to Bais.

Now the day had finally come. As she was packing up the last of her belongings, there was a knock on the door. She was surprised that the desk manager had managed to wrangle the *muchachos* so quickly. "Just a minute," she called out. She pulled the thin strap taut across the top tray of her steamer trunk, shut the lid, pushed the latch in, and turned the key. Done.

Her hands free, she yanked the door open and pointed to her trunk before she realized who stood in front of her.

"Javier!" Without thinking, she jumped into his arms. Had this man been the only life buoy in the middle of the Pacific, she could not have held on any tighter.

He held her just as tightly. "*Cariño*," he whispered, easing the pressure of his hug just enough to run his hands along her back. He nudged her away from the door and maneuvered her into the room, keeping her face nestled into the curve of his neck the whole time.

She released him and closed the door. It would not do to start the most important conversation of her life in full view of the other "residents" of this doss-house. She shut all but one of the *capiz* windows, too, leaving enough light to see Javier clearly as they sat down together on the edge of the bed.

"How did you find me?" she asked. "I didn't even tell Allegra where I was staying." She had been too embarrassed.

"I have my sources." Javier looked around the tiny room and shook his head with disdain. "I had hoped Mr. North was exaggerating."

"It's not that bad," she said, not sure at all why she was defending the grim hotel or her place in it. "They have a back entrance through the kitchens, and the cooks are real nice."

"So they told me."

"Who?"

Javier laughed, a welcome sound, even if it was at her expense. "Good thing you're a teacher and not a spy, Ina. Mr. North has been keeping an eye on you; he arranged for a guard to watch this hallway at night."

"That was totally"—she was about to say unnecessary—"thoughtful."

He smiled. "You're welcome."

"You told him to do it?"

Javier lifted a hand and gently cupped her cheek. "When North's cable came, it wasn't even a question."

"But," she asked quietly, "after everything that happened—everything you and I said in Samar—why would you do that?"

"No matter what you chose to do, I needed to know that you were safe."

Her original euphoria twisted into worry. "Is that why you came here now? To see me off safely?" Just because he came to Manila did not necessarily mean that he wanted her back.

"Then another cable arrived," Javier said. He let his hand fall to her stomach and pressed his palm against her womb.

"From Allegra," she whispered.

He nodded and did not move his hand. "Why not you?" he finally asked. "Why wasn't it you who told me?"

"I wanted to." When he had refused to say goodbye in Samar, she assumed that he had given up on her—as he probably should have. "I was ashamed."

"Of our baby?"

"No! Of myself. I was so wrapped up in my search for Ben that I lost sight of everything else, especially what I want for us."

"What is it that you want for us?"

She gripped his hand—for strength or understanding, she was not sure which. Probably both. "I want our family, yours and mine."

When he did not respond immediately, she panicked a little. She had hoped to refine her apology on the boat to Bais, but she was being forced to improvise. "I didn't cable you because I thought I was too late—that I had lost my last chance. You probably don't believe me now but—"

"Ina—"

"I wanted to come to you. This"—she tapped the trunk with her fingers—"is supposed to be loaded on the *Bélgica* at nine. Allegra has my ticket. If it had been up to me, we would already be there. I've almost left without her several times this week."

"But you didn't."

She could not tell if he was playing with her now, but her confidence was sinking. She dropped her hands into her lap. "Well, Allegra paid for my ticket."

"Good."

Georgie looked down at her fingers twisting in his, afraid to admit the full truth but aware that she had no choice. "Ben ran off with my money. I know I shouldn't have trusted him, and I know—"

"Ina, stop. It doesn't matter."

"But you don't know everything—"

"I know enough."

"It's my fault that you lost everything—"

"Ina—"

"—and I'm sorry. You have to let me say it, okay?"

"Okay," he said.

The happy crinkles around his eyes encouraged her to press on. "You are my family," she said it again, more solemnly this time, as if it were an oath. "And I will never forget that again. I know that it seems like you gave up your land for nothing, but I will make it up to you somehow."

Javier rolled his eyes, a habit that he had copied from her. He was becoming more American than he knew. "*Querida*, you don't need to."

"But—"

"But," he said, "if you insist, maybe I know a way." He pulled his hand out of hers so he could tug her shirtwaist loose and bare her belly.

"Javi, the porters are coming—"

"No, they aren't. I told the clerk not to disturb us for at least an hour." He pressed gently below her navel. "Are you sure about the baby?"

She looked a little plump, that was all.

His caress reminded her of the other places that had gone untouched for weeks. "If you saw my washbasin every morning, you wouldn't need to ask."

He looked up at her. "I should probably feel bad about that." His actions said otherwise, though, as she was stripped of her chemise. He reached behind her and undid her skirt. "I could tell you how much I love you, Ina, but I think it would be better to show you."

"Here?"

"Are you afraid they will hear us?" Leaning in to nuzzle her below the ear, he whispered, "These walls may be thin, but I know you can be quiet when you need to be."

"No."

He paused. "No?"

"Yes to making love. No to being quiet."

She could feel Javier smile against her neck. Not much later, they checked out of the Kentucky Hotel and Saloon, leaving behind a small dent in the wall behind the dresser and many wide-awake neighbors.

CHAPTER SIXTY-SEVEN

New *Hacendero*

It took only four days to get home to Bais, but Javier knew that for his pregnant soon-to-be-bride, even a half-week on a rocking boat had to feel like a year. Georgina did not sleep or eat well for most of the trip. Javier hated every minute of her misery, even if he was as proud as a gamecock to be the cause. Once they reached home, his mother made some candied ginger to calm Georgina's belly and then put the young woman right to bed—alone.

Javier was now an *hacendero* without an hacienda. For the first time in his life, he had plenty of time to waste, and he was not sure what to do with it. He sat in the heavy wooden chair in his office and examined a painted miniature of his grandfather, the first Altarejos *hacendero*—though Altarejos was not even the Spaniard's true name. When *Capitán* Hilario Vélez y Perales resigned his Army commission in Manila, he had balked at the idea of returning to his sowish wife and homely children in rural Altarejos, Spain, so he reinvented himself as an eligible feudal lord on the new frontier of sugar. Hilario "de Altarejos" eventually dropped the preposition from his nickname, won himself a thousand acres of virgin soil for saving the life of the *alcalde-mayor*, "married" a lovely mestiza who never knew that she was only a mistress, and planted himself a legacy.

Now, sixty years later, Hilario's grandson had lost all of that legacy but an old house, a few tiny fields, and an expensive-yet-outdated sugar mill. Javier took grim satisfaction in having denied Lope his land by letting Guillermo liquidate it. Javier had included a few parcels that he owned free and clear in order to raise enough cash to satisfy all his other creditors too.

But Javier did not second-guess the decision, especially now. He knew that the little bit of money left over would buy safety for his expanding family. His dependents had doubled in less than a year. His mother, cousin, wife, unborn child, foster daughter, and probably—before too long—mother-in-law would all rely on him as head of the family. Javier had to make some hard choices. Despite his brave words to Georgina, he did not know what to do next, nor could he keep putting off the difficult decisions. He had no more time: the baby already had enough of a head start on their wedding.

Their baby. The fourth generation of Altarejos. Compared to that, his financial humbling did not signify. So what if some city dandy showed up in the coming weeks and made a mockery of his sugar business?

Andrés knocked on the frame of the open door and walked in. "*Hermano*," he said, and gave Javier a quick hug. "It's good that you're back. We should talk over your plans for the wedding."

"What is there to talk about? You say a little mumbo-jumbo in Latin and the thing is done. From your lips to God's ears, or something like that."

Javier liked teasing Andrés. Maybe now that Javier was no longer the *hacendero*, and therefore no longer Andrés's employer, they could concentrate on just being friends again.

"It's a little more complicated than that," the priest said. "There are a few choices of prayers and hymns, but I imagine it would be better to talk to Ina about those details. She might have heard one or two before, since she actually attends mass."

"Just wait until she's feeling better, eh?"

Andrés gave him a skeptical look. "If I wait for her to get well, I'll be planning the baptism before the wedding."

Javier shrugged. "Some of my favorite people are bastards."

"How nice for them," Andrés said with a smile, "but my mother was married."

He was correct, but it was a technicality in Javier's opinion. Andrés had always known who his real father was, even before Javier had told him.

Javier looked at the painted miniature of Hilario, whom both brothers resembled, and the Spaniard's proud face steeled him to do what needed doing. "Drés, I'm grateful that you're performing the ceremony. And I wish that I could give you some guarantees for the future—but the benefice belongs to the land, of course, since it's the workers who attend mass. I don't know this Lionel Hargis, nor do I know whom he'll want as curate. He is American, so maybe he won't care so much about the position. I'll put in a good word for you and so will Padre Ávila—"

"Javier, don't worry about it."

"How can I not? I begged every priest from Jaro to Rome to get you here, and now, because of my actions, you could be cast out after only three years. What if Bishop Ferrero decides to look up the old complaint again?"

The priest rested a hand on his brother's shoulder. "Don't worry about me. I shall still have my curate next month. In fact, I'll be busier than ever."

"How can you be so sure?"

Andrés pulled a sheaf of papers from inside his capacious cassock and set it on the desk.

"You have more pockets than I thought," Javier said, gently poking Andrés's loose black uniform. "You don't have a *lechon* tucked away in there, do you?"

"Yes, I carry roast suckling pig on my person." Andrés sat on the corner of the desk and pointed at the papers. "Of course, I am more resourceful than you give me credit for. Read them. They arrived yesterday."

The packet had a stamp of assurance on the front: "Lionel D. Hargis, Attorney-at-Law." The seal was already broken. Javier unfolded the pages and started to read the official document:

> *Court of Land Registration. [Registration of Title. Case No. 266.] To the Attorney General of the Philippine Islands and the Director of Lands, both in Manila P.I., and the municipal council of Bais, Emilio Teves and Antonio Siguenza, these two in Bais, Oriental Negros, P.I., and to all whom it may concern...*

Javier read through almost two pages of surveyors marks, just to be sure this was what he thought it was: 830 acres, all in one title.

"I don't know this Hargis…"

"That's why I chose him—that, and he's not been in Manila long enough to figure out how to cheat me. Not beyond his rates, at least. He thinks he's still in San Francisco with what he charges."

"He's…"

"My solicitor, Javier."

Javier returned to the document and resumed reading:

> *Whereas an application has been presented to said court by Andrés Gabiana y Mendoza, represented by his attorney Lionel D. Hargis, No. 18, Plaza Cervantes, district of Binondo, city of Manila, P.I. to register and confirm his title in the following described land: A piece of land known as Hacienda Altarejos, situated in the municipality of Bais, Province of Oriental Negros, P.I.*

Javier turned to Andrés, annoyed for a reason that he could not quite understand. "Is this spite?"

"What?"

"Revenge against me or Lázaro or—"

"Are you so opposed to your bastard brother having the land?"

"Not at all. An hacienda founded by a bigamist should be inherited by a whole line of bastards. It might even be written in the title somewhere."

"*Amigo*," Andrés said with a sigh. "Don't be an ass."

Javier's eyebrows lifted in surprise. For his pious brother, "ass" counted as quite a strong curse. "And you're not a bastard, as you pointed out. Are you no longer going to be a priest, either?"

Andrés shook his head. "I took no vow of poverty. I've always thought this *hacendero* thing looked pretty easy, especially the way you do it, so I'll try my hand at it part-time."

Javier sat back in his chair. "Are you trying to humiliate me?"

"No, *hermano*, you do a fine enough job of that by yourself."

"*Hay sus...*"

Andrés lifted a hand to his brother's shoulder, a steadying gesture probably meant to remind them both that they did not want to let this slip into a real fight. "Someone has to look to the future. Would you really rather see this place in the hands of a stranger than trust it with me?"

Javier had to take a breath so that he would not answer peevishly. "No," he said, "I would not."

"I am doing this for you, for your family, for my family."

"But how?"

"The Cebu house. I sold it. The city is swarming with Americans, and my lawyer suggested that I subdivide the property and sell off the back parcels as slots of raw land. You wouldn't believe what these *Insulares* are paying—they grabbed it up. I guess Hargis knew what he was doing. The man may be worth his outrageous fees, even if he is a Protestant."

Javier leaned forward again, trying to digest it all. "Maybe this is the right thing. I know I'll like working with you—"

"With me?" Andrés gave a dramatic grunt. "You'll work for me, older brother. My new overseer—if you pass the interview."

Javier was dumbstruck. He looked up at Andrés and finally understood why the Spanish friars had been so threatened by the idea of native priests. Javier had made the same mistake as the Recollects: he had assumed that the man would be so satisfied with the leftover scraps of hacienda living that he would never ask for the filet. But Andrés had protected the land, even from its own *hacendero*. Moreover, since Andrés would have no heirs, the land would pass on to Javier's own sons and daughters, a result far better than he could have ever hoped.

He laughed. What else could he do? He laughed and laughed and laughed. It was perfect. He picked up the title, folded it, and handed it back to the priest.

"Thank you," Andrés said. "So far there doesn't seem like much to do. And to think of all those late hours you spend in this office, pretending to work."

Javier had never pretended anything, but he knew Andrés was playing him. "It's *tiempo muerto*, Padre. Just wait until the summer's over. And by the way, you can't have my office."

"Goodness, no, this is still your house, after all."

"Will you build your own?"

Andrés gave a quick shake of his head. "What do I need that I don't have in my rectory?"

Rectory seemed too grandiose a word; the priest's residence behind the tiny chapel was hardly more than a room.

"We could add another desk downstairs for you," he offered.

Andrés smiled. "The *hacendero* and the *encargado* side by side? I like it. But don't get any ideas and start acting above your station."

"Will the Church allow you to keep this, Andrés?"

"It's no more than I owned before."

"I think I didn't understand how much you owned before. I suppose it is rather convenient to employ oneself."

"True—though, as the boss around here, I need to clarify some of my expectations."

"I know what you can afford for my salary, Drés, and it's not much, not if you want to stay out of debt. And what about Geno—"

"He's already setting up his own homestead in Tanjay." Andrés waived his hand. "We can talk about all these earthly matters later. I meant spiritual expectations."

Javier paused. "What are we talking about?"

"Mass. Every day."

The priest said it like it was a done deal. Although Javier was not about to give in, he thought the bluff boded well for Andrés's negotiating skills as *hacendero*.

"Every month should be more than enough," Javier countered. "I have a day job, you know."

"Every week then. Sunday mass. You must set an example on the Sabbath."

Javier scolded himself for being so easily managed in the very first test of their new roles, but he had no choice but to agree. He leaned back in his chair. "*Hay sus.*"

"Exactly."

Andrés stuck out his hand. Javier ignored it and stood to hug his brother. When they broke their embrace, they nodded to each other in mutual respect.

Javier left his office and snuck upstairs to peek in on his sleeping wife. Careful not to wake her, he gently eased onto the bed and pulled her back against his chest. As he held her tight, she nestled into him. Last year he would not have believed how good it felt to be "benevolently assimilated." This cozy life may not have been what President McKinley had meant by the "blessings of good and stable government," but Javier thought it was blessed nonetheless.

Epilogue: 1904

Dearest Georgina,

It is impossible to compose an adequate apology, though I have chewed through two pencils trying. I could write that I am sorry a thousand times, and it is truer than you know, but it would not make this letter any easier for you to read, so I will spare you that. I do not expect forgiveness. I think your husband was right—everyone would have been better off had I died in Balangiga. However, since I did not, I must keep muddling along. All I can promise you is that I will not muddle my way back to Samar; I will not repay your love by dying there a third time.

Each day sober is a step back into life. I have found a job carving a road through a cliff-face aptly named the Devil's Slide, and the task has given me something I have missed for years. Not the cool air—though it is refreshingly brisk here, which is why our pampered civil government has given itself this summer capital in the first place. The steady purpose of the work is really what draws me: the mesmerizing arc of the pick axe as I strike it into volcanic rock, the visible result of each day's labor, and the silent exhaustion afterward. It feels like how I would pray if God did not speak my language. Many days it seems that He does not.

I may never be able to get rid of the war in my head. My physical wounds healed in three weeks, but everything else may need three lifetimes—the bolo is a far duller blade than the hate that swings it. The unfinished revolution has followed me here into the mountains, as the native press has been happy to report. Not only have some of our laborers gone on strike, but a timekeeper was attacked by bolomen. A bridge was set to the torch. Horses have been cruelly mutilated. A suspicious dynamite charge killed four Americans. I do not care what you may say; these were not accidents. Are you sure this is the country for you?

Are you happy, Georgina? Are you happy with him? Is he a good father? If he is not, you can be assured that I stand ready to protect you and Pilar. Are you surprised that I know about my niece? I am, as well. I made the fortunate mistake of writing to Mama in Boston, only to learn that she lives with you in Bais now. Aunt Kate's response was informative on other matters, too, if one could read past the well-deserved scolding. She left me with no doubt that the pen is mightier than the spanking.

Though I may never be able to sufficiently explain myself, Georgie, I will make you proud once again to be my sister. This time I will find you.

With love,
Ben

Acknowledgements

*M*uchas gracias, *merci beaucoup*, and thank you to my outstanding group of beta readers: Andy, Laura, Priscilla, Regine, Sarah, and the other Stephen.

Maraming salamat to all my friends in the Philippines who shared with me their country, culture, and history over copious amounts of San Miguel.

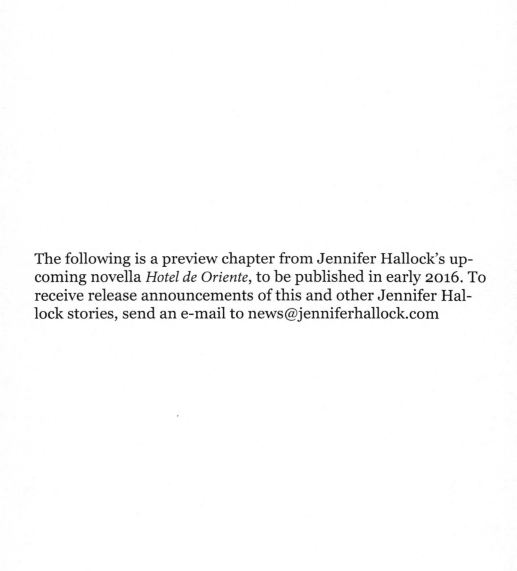

The following is a preview chapter from Jennifer Hallock's upcoming novella *Hotel de Oriente*, to be published in early 2016. To receive release announcements of this and other Jennifer Hallock stories, send an e-mail to news@jenniferhallock.com

CHAPTER ONE

Pawn

Della Berget lashed her steamer chair to the bow rail and wrapped herself snugly in a rubber poncho. Wave after wave of sea spray beat against her face as the *Kilpatrick* tumbled through the mouth of Manila Bay. She laughed as the ship bucked the waves— laughed or squealed or shrieked or whooped, she did not know. It hardly mattered since her grandfather, Hughes Holt, Representative of the Second District of West Virginia, was not there to be embarrassed by the sound. He had shut himself away in the first-class lavatory to keep his seasickness a state secret. Great men did not like to be brought low by their stomachs.

Too bad for him, Della thought. He could not see their approach to Manila, a city of red Spanish-tiled roofs set against distant green mountains. He could not see the charming mismatch of Intramuros, an old Spanish walled enclave in the style of Gibraltar, plunked down in the middle of the tropics. He could not see how close both he and Della were to their individual-but-intertwined destinies.

In the calmer waters close to the city, a steam launch approached from starboard. It carried men with tanned, rested, and salubrious faces. These were men confident in the working order of their digestive systems, Della noticed. They were the men who would inspect the *Kilpatrick* to determine if the smallpox outbreak in Singapore had made it aboard ship.

How the Bureau of Health distinguished between the early stages of smallpox and ordinary seasickness was a mystery, especially when the decks were so crowded with soldiers that those who could not force their way to the railing had to vomit in buckets, in their shoes, or on the deck. These boys had enlisted to prove their manliness through the forge of battle, but instead they spent their last day of peace in white-knuckled unmanly terror. Of course, had they possessed any sort of readiness for ocean travel, they would have joined the Navy instead of the Army. Sadly, a number of them would not live to prove themselves more seaworthy on a transport home. The guerrilla insurrection of the Filipinos was proving a costly one.

Fortunately, the transport passed inspection, thanks to the timely appearance on deck of Congressman Holt. A progressive in favor of new American markets in the East, her grandfather had been a loyal friend to every Philippine appropriations bill that came his way, and local officials would do nothing to impede his disembarkation.

New boats clustered around the *Kilpatrick*: clumsy native craft about seven feet wide and fifty feet long, each with an arched hood of dried grass. The pilots maneuvered their floating houses against the white hull of the enormous transport. If one miscalculated, his boat would either be sucked under the *Kilpatrick* or tossed up against its side. The Filipinos jockeyed to get the best position in front of the line, where escape was easiest if the water got rough; and the American crew tried in vain to direct the chaos from the steps above the water. All the seamen gestured frenetically, trying to make themselves understood in different languages above a furious wind.

Della smiled. She felt right at home.

Once the lighters were stacked three or four deep along the length of the *Kilpatrick*, she and her grandfather scrambled over the inner boats to get to one at the head of the line. Holt dragged Della into the darkness under the musty hood, sat her down, and turned back to look after their luggage.

She smelled her new neighbor before she saw him. The rooster was tucked under a bench in a nifty bamboo cage, and—if his flared neck feathers were any indication—he did not appreciate sharing accommodations. Piled on top of the cage was a thick, scratchy hemp cover, but Della would not yank it down. Doing so would engulf the bird in darkness, and losing a sense against one's will was never calming, she thought.

Their boat got under way. Holt, still the biggest cock on board, dealt with stress in his usual way: self-important tirades. At first, Della paid attention to his tantrum because it amused her. Her grandfather could work himself up over anything—he even blamed the swelling around his eyes on the climate instead of on the time he had spent bent over the toilet in his stateroom. Della tired of his complaints, so she shut her eyes.

But she soon realized her mistake—there was much to see outside—and poked her head around the edge of the matted roof to watch their approach into the bowels of the city. They pulled past a large fort flying an American flag and headed into the mouth of the Pasig, a river as wide as the Potomac but ten times as crowded. Bossy American steamers, lighters heavy with food and livestock, outrigger fishing boats, and single-man canoes fought upstream for a space at the north-side dock. Her boat won a place and tied up in front of a huge warehouse marked *Produce Depot*.

The place swarmed with natives, all eager to sell trinkets to the new arrivals. Della was the first to be hauled to shore, and since she was used to being a curiosity, the open stares did not bother her. People pawed her arms to get her attention, but that was okay too. She was starved for touch. And no one here assumed she could understand their strange words—a freeing lack of expectations.

Her grandfather did not know what to make of all the chattering brown people hawking everything from pineapple sticks to jasmine flower necklaces. It was not the welcome he had been expecting.

Della closed her eyes again and let her feet feel the activity of the city surrounding them: the quick strike of horse hooves, the plodding thud of huge horned carabao, and the irregular beat of cart wheels moving across uneven stones. The air was spiced with sweat, humidity, and a dash of excrement.

She opened her eyes just in time to see an escort approach. This man, indistinguishable from the other Americans in his white pants and white jacket, introduced himself to her grandfather. His eyes darted past Della as he gave a quick, awkward smile. Obviously he had been told about her in advance.

He extricated his charges from the disappointed crowd and led the guests to a line of two-wheeled carriages. Della carefully watched the driver's hands secure the horses before she climbed in.

The entourage rode in a line through the beautiful, crowded streets. There was a strange jumble to the buildings, as if all the architects had been given instructions in a foreign tongue and each had interpreted the plan a little differently. One thing they all had in common were the large, colorful signs that advertised the wares kept inside:

Adolfo Richter, Fabrica de Sombreros.

The Central Studio, Photographers.

Singer, Máquinas para Coser.

Above the merchants' shingles were rows and rows of windows, each a checkerboard of wood and ivory shell. All were slid shut against the heat of the day. The crowds, the colors, the textures—it was a silent symphony.

The line of carriages pulled into a traffic circle—or, rather, a traffic oval—and passed an ornately appointed cigar factory. It was a three-story building with balustrades, carved arches, and five-ball lamps on the balcony. The carriage stopped next door, in front of a building just as grand. Also three stories, it was a little less Morocco and a little more Madrid. Three large arches decorated both sides of the grand entrance. This was the Hotel de Oriente, the Waldorf Astoria of Manila.

Della watched her grandfather disembark into the small crowd gathered near the door of the hotel. Waiting there were a few obsequious bureaucrats eager to keep their funding; one or two local elites seeking favor; and a few reporters whom Holt himself had summoned with cable updates from each major port of call: Malta, Port Said, and Colombo. The newsmen were unconcerned about their shabbily-tied bows, non-existent jackets, and soiled armpits. Their words would be dressed up just fine under the mastheads of the important papers of Washington and New York. It was her grandfather's job to woo them, not the other way around.

Holt turned to Della, his wrinkled face aping concern for his precious ward. It was an act, one that she was prepared to play out with him. She walked obediently to his side.

There were too many people talking at once. She wanted to ask them to take turns, but this was his show, not hers.

"Congressman," one of the reporters said, pushing forward impatiently. Della concentrated on the man's mouth as he spoke. "You must have heard by now of the proclamation of martial law, but you still felt it safe to come to the Philippines. Do you disagree with the general's order?"

Della turned to watch her grandfather. She knew he had expected this question, practiced for it. "The Army's final blow must be the hardest. It is because of General Arthur MacArthur's order that we are closer to civil government in the Philippines."

The reporter asked the inevitable follow-up: "You think the guerrillas are finished? The war is won?"

Her grandfather smiled, ready for his moment. Della carefully watched his words.

"I ask you," he said, "if I had any less faith in the future of peace, would I have brought my granddaughter here with me? Surely, if these islands are safe enough for a vulnerable woman like my Della here, they are safe for any American. Not only is she young and naive—the girl is deaf."

Della glanced back at the reporter, anxious to see what he would make of this. He looked to be struck as dumb as he probably assumed she was. The bureaucrats and hangers-on nodded their heads but looked bewildered. The other reporters gave her piteous looks, as if she were blind to their condescension, not deaf to it.

Della shaped her features to show timidity, fear, and just the right touch of vacancy. The guise was a small price to pay for her passage. The next step would be harder.